WASTED

BOOK TWO

Also by the author:

GUIDED
MIDNIGHT SHERBET
DEAD FINE

This book may contain mature scenes,
including bullying, peer pressure, suicide,
and references to sex.

Suitable for older readers.

WASTED

WASTED

Copyright © 2023 by Emma J. Smith

The following novel is a work of fiction. Any resemblance to persons, living or dead, is a coincidence; all characters and settings are the product of the author's imagination.

ISBN – 9798864295618

All rights reserved. No part of these works can be reproduced, scanned, rewritten or translated in any form, digital or traditional, without the permission of the author.

emmasmithbooks.com

for everyone who enjoyed
Guided, and helped make my
author dreams come true

PART ONE

Dear diary,

I'm so terrified that someone will find this book and read it, so I'll keep things short and sweet. But I couldn't not write down how I'm feeling right now. I need to get it out, somehow. I'm scared that if I don't, it'll build up and up inside me...

Until I can't help but tell <u>someone</u>.

The guilt is the worst. It's thick and strong and won't go away, and haunts me every night as I'm trying to sleep. I've suppressed the events of that weekend so much that it now comes to me in the form of Lexie, first, as I start remembering all that happened with her... and how we betrayed her in the worst possible way. We were supposed to be her friends, the four of us. We were supposed to <u>look after</u> her.

I honestly thought it couldn't get any worse than her death. I thought... thought things were getting better, at least in some way. That the four of us were invincible, would last forever.

But now another one of us is dead. Four has turned to three, and I can't talk about it, daren't say her name out loud or write it down. In so many ways, we betrayed her too, and that's not okay. She trusted us. Ever since Lexie died, the four of us have had each other's backs. We were there for each other, and promised we always would be.

Not anymore.

I hope she's out there somewhere, reading this, knowing how sorry I am. Because I am sorry. I've never been sorrier. I'd give anything to do that night differently, but I can't. What's done is done.

Another one of my best friends is dead, and I'll never reverse that. I'll never talk to her about boys again, put my arms around her in a windswept tent, laugh as she crashes through the river on a kayak with her hair in the wind and her smile lighting up the entire countryside, like it always did.

I can't write any more of this, I'm sorry.

Not now.

1

A box, concrete walls and floor, a window to one end. They've painted the surface cream in an attempt to be inviting, but it's bare, cold, spiderwebs hanging in each corner. The table feels like ice against my knees, tip-tip-tapping, over and over, unable to stop my legs moving.

"Hello, Lucy."

I try for a smile, but my mouth is glued shut, eyes unable to stay in one position. I look up, only to look down immediately. Officer Joy is watching me. She looks friendly enough – she *is* friendly enough – all light brown skin and chocolaty curls and perfect eyebrows, but I know better than to trust her.

I know better than to trust *anyone*.

"How are you doing?"

I'd laugh at the irony of the question, if it was funny. But Officer Joy is deadly serious, peering at me with a face of concern, trying to read me, get inside my head. My knee is still tapping against the table, trainers hitting the floor over and over and over, over and over –

"It's been a long time since we last spoke, hasn't it?"

I glance up to meet her eyes then, frowning. Is she taking the piss? It's been five years – we both know that. Five years, almost to the dot. Five years since one of my best friends died, tumbling into the water from the tyre swing high above, drowning in the fast-flowing river. Five fucking years.

There was a service held for Lexie almost exactly two months ago, to celebrate her life and memory, commemorating half a decade since the accident that killed her. We dressed up in pink, her favourite colour, the kids of Vibbington prancing about in unicorn headbands and onesies. We ate biscuits and chocolate, and Mrs McCoy sold postcards printed with some of Lexie's old paintings. She was raising money for a bullying prevention charity, apparently.

Chloe bought ten.

There was no remembrance service for Macey. A few people left flowers on the bridge she jumped from that night, but they wilted and died within days, leaving a mangled mess of petals and pulp for the council to clear up. A few of her old friends posted on Instagram about it, including Rosie Abara, who still lives in the area, but the rest have moved onto uni now, even graduated, found new friends, new lives. After all…

It's been *five years*.

Five years. Five years of grief, of guilt and regret and torment, of wishing we'd all done something different, done things *right*. Five years of feeling like there was a hole in each of our lives, of drifting apart, becoming new people, transforming ourselves so that we were no longer just *the ones who got away.*

Five years.

I was interviewed in this very room, after Lexie died, all those years ago. They called us in one by one to talk with Officer Pudrow, to tell him our experience of being friends with Lexie, show him photos and gifts and cards, talk him through the night she died, step by step. I did well, he said. Well enough that I received a lollipop, one of those Chupa Chups ones you get in petrol stations. It was apple, I think.

Maybe orange.

It seemed traumatic to us all, back then. Our friend had *died*. We were twelve years old, tiny and frightened and supposedly innocent, and we'd already experienced one of the most difficult parts of the "real world".

Death. Death was traumatic.

But we barely knew the meaning of the word.

"Lucy?" Officer Joy drags me back to the present. She's still gazing at me intently, trying to figure out what I'm thinking, where my mind is wandering. I stare back at her, eyes snagged on hers, unmoving this time. "It'll make this process a lot easier if you talk to me, Lucy. We want to get to the bottom of what happened, okay? We can't do that unless you cooperate."

My mouth is set in a firm line, arms crossed. Cooperate? What good is cooperation going to do, now? What's done is done. The past can't be unfolded, recovered, turned back by *talking*, telling her the truth.

The past is the past. Nothing I say will ever change what happened, will bring those people back.

That's exactly how I felt all those years ago, too, when Lexie died. Like it was done, over with. Like talking about it, trying to uncover the truth, going over her death in all its gory details, would only ever make things worse.

"Lucy." Officer Joy is firmer now, harder. She places both hands on the table, flat, as if that's going to help. "Lucy, you need to tell me what happened that weekend. Another one of your friends is dead, and so are two more people. You were there. You saw what went on. Come on, Lucy – start from the beginning. What are you hiding?"

I shake my head, curling my lips inward. It seems to be growing colder in the room, but that may just be me. I'm shaking, hands trembling and cheeks goosebumped, skin tight above my skull. I'm developing brain freeze, icy tendrils unfolding and wrapping themselves around me, squeezing, stretching. Silence falls, the corridor outside just as quiet, the only sound coming from Officer Joy's shallow, unstopped breathing.

"Lucy?" she continues, reaching out to try and grasp my hand. I pull both away, under the table, knitting them together on my lap. "I like to think I'm a safe space, Lucy. I know this is hard, but... I'm here to help. I only want to know the truth, so that we can bring people to justice, if we can."

Justice.

Justice was served that very weekend, two weeks ago, when *he* died. He, who shall not be named. He, who stole the lives of those who didn't deserve to die, who *never* deserved to die. He, who still haunts my dreams each night, who won't leave me alone, leave *us* alone –

There are tears leaking out from beneath my eyelids now, dripping down my cheeks and nose, landing on the table with a gentle *plop, plop, plop*. My heart is pounding and there's a lump in my throat the size of a pebble as I try to focus on the table, on my breathing, fingers scrabbling –

"Lucy, I didn't mean to upset you," Officer Joy cuts in, roughly pressing stop on the recording device attached the edge of the table. She stands, rushing round to my side of the table, and attempts to hug me from the side, rubbing my shoulders. I don't know if the police are supposed to touch us, but Vibbington's a small town, and Joy doesn't care for rules. "I'm sorry, Lucy. Would you like a drink?"

I shake my head, shoulders surging up and down. I don't know what a drink would do, right now. Officer Joy is helpless, unsure of what to say or do, flapping beside me.

"I'm really sorry for your loss, Lucy," she adds, voice more sympathetic now, softer, quieter. "First Lexie, now this. Take some time out, then we'll continue this interview tomorrow, okay?"

Tomorrow. Tomorrow's no different from today, as far as I'm concerned. I'll still have to relive it, relive that horrendous weekend, tell her exactly what happened, in all its gory details.

Wind, whipping round our tents in the middle of the night... Shouts and cries and a horrible, thumping stab... Blood dripping down my hands, my neck, my ankles...

And a seventeen-year-old's screams erupting into the night as she –

"I'm sorry," I say at last, voice wobbling, gagging like I'm going to be sick. "I – I need some fresh air –"

I push away from the table, rushing from the room and into the long corridor, stretching on and on and on either side of me, no end, no way out, no escape from the truth –

There's a bin to my left, and I only just have time to stick my head inside it before I'm sick, sick everywhere, like I can't stop, like my insides are spurting out of me. I throw up until there's nothing left inside me, no emotion, nothing, simply painful, hollow emptiness, jabbing at my gut.

First Lexie, now this.

When will it ever *end*?

2

Mum is in the waiting room, reading a Colleen Hoover paperback and nibbling a granola bar. She glances up upon hearing my footsteps, face breaking into a strained smile and feet moving to greet me.

When we were first asked to come to the station, I said I didn't want her in the interview room with me, luckily being eighteen by just two months, no longer required to have an adult present. She stresses too much about the tiniest, most ridiculous things, and has already been through enough these last five years, enough trauma and confusion.

She was in pieces after Lexie died, all those years ago. She booked me into counselling sessions, made me go once a week after school, didn't want me to continue with Guides after it was revealed that Macey caused the accident and it was all a big, dangerous web of lies. Both my parents were concerned I'd lose interest in school, stop caring about friends, hobbies, the future, if I had to relive that trauma over and over, every Tuesday night.

I didn't, of course. I'm still a straight-A student, five years later, an avid hockey player, into fashion and boys and sport like any other teenage girl my age. Until two weeks ago, I was seemingly unaffected by the accident... as far as everybody else was concerned, anyway.

But now this. If losing one friend wasn't bad enough, someone up there wanted me to lose another, watch more people die, attend more funerals, more remembrance services. Another three deaths had to happen, right in front of my eyes. Fresh trauma. Fresh memories, fresh nightmares, waking up screaming in the middle of the night to find my concerned parents patting my back, holding me close, insisting I drink some water, trying to calm me down…

And fresh blood, of course. Fresh blood, everywhere, dripping down my hands and breast and onto my feet, my new white trainers, ones bought specially for the camp.

Mum doesn't know about the blood, of course.

"Hello, love," she says, folding me into a hug as I reach her. She's warm, all fuzzy brown hair and big green eyes and woolly jumper, and envelops me in her concern. I'm stiff, face still wet with tears and lips pushed closed. "Did everything go okay in there?"

I pause, unsure of what to say.

Did everything go okay in there?

It didn't, not really. Three people are dead, and I'm the key to unlocking it all, to revealing to the police what really went down that weekend, who really caused those deaths, all that destruction. All I needed to say was what happened, who the instigator was, pinpoint the moment everything started to go wrong.

But I couldn't. I was so pathetic that I couldn't even speak, couldn't tell Officer Joy whose fault it was, that it was nothing to do with me, that me and the other girls are innocent and that *she never deserved to die*.

"It…" I pause, as Mum pulls back to search my expression with her eyes. Seeing me cry usually sets her off, but I can tell she's trying to hold herself together now, stay strong. "I didn't feel ready to talk about it yet. I need to come back tomorrow, discuss it with Joy again. She still has a lot of questions."

I can't help but feel guilty when Mum's face breaks, mouth downturned with sympathy. Even more than me, she just wants this to be over with, for things to go back to normal. As much as she needs to find out what happened that weekend, for my sake as much as hers, she won't push me, doesn't want to put me through more than I've already had to deal with.

"Really? Does she not understand that this is a lot for you to deal with? Your mocks are in a few weeks, Lucy – you need to be in the right headspace, you know?"

I nod. I do know. Of *course* I do.

"Yeah. Let's… let's go home, Mum."

It's a five minute drive or so from the station to our house on the outskirts of Vibbington, across town from where Lexie's family still live, in their falling-to-pieces semi. Mum is silent, pressing play on her Westlife CD as we drive, fingers gripping the wheel. It's November now, all cold and frosty, only a couple of weeks till December. The town is alive with autumnal colours… browns and reds and fiery orange, interspersed with the last dregs of green.

Brown, red, orange, green.

Brown, red, orange, green.

Westlife plays on, Mum turning up the volume just a tad, as we continue down Vibbington's streets, sunlight fading, horizon faintly pink in my eyeline.

Brown, red, orange, green…

We pull up the drive, living room light on, TV playing through the window. Dad must be in; the house looks lived in, alive, despite everything around us entering a stage of decay. It takes everything I have to pull myself out of the car and open the front door, Mum on my heels, heart heavy and feet like rocks, dragging, immoveable.

Dad is stood in the kitchen, cheeks pink and apron tied round his waist. I can tell he's been in here cooking since he finished work. The kitchen smells of frying mince and onions, of Bisto gravy granules and boiled potatoes. His face breaks into a beam the minute we walk through the door, and he lets out an excited whimper and opens his arms to wrap us in one of his infamous group hugs.

"My girls!" Swaddled in my parents' arms, I feel him plant a wet kiss on my forehead before they pull away, all eyes on me. "How did it go at the station?"

That question, again.

"I'm going back tomorrow." I watch Dad's expression change from kind to concerned, warm to worried. "I didn't feel ready to talk, so… Officer Joy wants to ask a few more questions."

"More questions?" Both parents exchange glances then, the unspoken passing between them. "But… does she not realise you have mocks coming up, and this is *clearly* a traumatic time for you?"

"It's just protocol, I guess. It's a murder investigation. It's not like when… when Lexie died. They need to find out what happened to… *her*. They know it wasn't an accident." I shudder, trying not to meet their eyes as I add, "I… do you two mind if I go and get on with some homework? I need to get it done for… tomorrow, I think. And I want to make a start on my history flashcards, what with mocks and all."

"Fine, fine." Dad tries to smile, forever playing the role of the supportive parent. It's obvious he wants to continue the talk, ask more questions. "Make sure you come back down for cottage pie, eh, Luce? It'll be ready in an hour or so, we'll come and knock –"

"Okay."

I leave them staring after me as I disappear down the corridor and begin to make my way upstairs.

My bedroom door is ajar, like I left it when Mum called up to me just two hours previous, ready to set off for the station. The light's still on, phone thrown across the bed, face downturned. I take off my shoes, leaving them neatly lined up by the door. The whole room is neat, organised, everything in its place.

It infuriates me now. I cross the carpet to my bed, flopping onto it on my back, head hitting the pillow, hand reaching for my phone.

It's been spammed with notifications since I last went on it, and the battery is down to 23%. Most are from Snapchat, from my hockey team, discussing the match on Saturday, the match I still haven't decided whether I'll attend. Mum insisted I took a few weeks off school after that weekend, understandably, until the funeral was over and people had stopped talking, asking questions. The funeral was on Monday, sooner than expected. I still haven't taken a step into the sixth form block.

The next notification comes from the group chat I share with my best friends, Nora and Alicia. They're discussing something which happened in history today – someone revealed they'd shagged someone else, and Nora took it as a personal insult, considering she had a crush on that boy a few months ago. They both go wild when my Bitmoji pops up, but I leave a simple "hey" before disappearing again, back into the list of chats.

The third is from Ethan. Ethan, who's checked in three times today to check I'm okay, worried that I'm not responding to his messages, concerned about my mental health, reassuring me that he's here if I need to chat, if I want to discuss any of my problems with him.

> **I'm okay – just got back from the station, had to answer a few questions. Thank you for checking up on me, it really means a lot.**

His Bitmoji pops up right away, all big brown eyes and chubby cheeks and fluffy coat hood, grinning at me through the screen.

> **No problem :) what else are friends for?**

And then:

> **Just drop me a text later if you want to play Minecraft and crack open the sour cream Pringles :D I'm in all evening x**

My heart stops fluttering in my mouth, suspended on my tongue as I try to figure out how to respond. Ethan Morgan is one of the sweetest boys to ever exist, and the loveliest to attend Vibbington Sixth Form by a landslide.

If he hadn't come into my life at such an inconvenient time, I'd probably even... *like* him.

Because I don't like him – I've told myself that, over and over. I can't like him, not now. It wouldn't be fair on anyone.

I click off the chat, deciding to leave it and reply once I've gotten all my revision done, written tomorrow's Shakespeare essay, made my flashcards on Elizabeth the first's religious policies. My mocks are only a few weeks away now, and I'm nowhere near prepared, for once in my life. Besides... work is the only thing that can distract me from my mind, from all that's going on around me, from all the blood, dripping down my neck –

The fourth notification. I swallow, all the blood running from my face.

It's from the camp group chat.

The camp group chat, the one which, five years ago, included Lexie, Orla, Chloe, Kayleigh and I. I click onto it, palms slick with sweat and heart thudding, eyes wide as they sweep across the screen. Two Bitmojis are visible at the bottom of the screen, out of the four other girls in the chat. Lexie, Orla, Chloe, Kayleigh.

Lexie's account has been inactive for five years, as long as her ashes have been resting in the air around Vibbington, tossed over the hills and far away.

There are now two inactive accounts in the group chat, almost as clear as if we'd drawn stark crosses across their names.

Two girls dead, three girls living. It's almost as though someone's counting down, slaying us one at a time.

Had to go into the station this morning, answer a load of questions.

One of the living girls put this in the chat just half an hour ago, full stop and all. The other replied, a simple "same". They're watching now, waiting for me to reply, for me to say something, anything.

My hands are slow, working their way across the screen, trying to type something legible.

Same. I couldn't say anything. Still can't talk about it. It seems so pointless. He's already dead, he can't hurt anybody else. I don't know what telling the truth would do now.

I hesitate before pressing send, holding my breath as I watch them read it, then both Bitmojis begin to type, those three dots dancing over and over on the screen before me.

It's not just that. You know what we did. We could get into big trouble, too. They might not see it as self-defence.

My heart's still pounding, throat dry, eyes straining to read the words on the screen before me. *You know what we did.*

The second girl stops typing, disappearing off the chat without saying anything. I do the same. I don't know how to respond, how to talk to them, whether I want to agree to that. These girls aren't my friends anymore. They haven't been for almost five years, drifting apart just months after Lexie's death, splitting into four directions, only brought together by the Guides group we all felt obliged to attend.

They're not my friends. They're not even people I'd choose to associate with, if we hadn't been forced into attending that camp together, just the four of us and Sharon.

They're not my friends, and yet somehow fate has found a way to intertwine our lives again, twisting us together in a knot of secrets and lies and betrayal, three deaths splayed on the ground before us.

They're not my friends. They're something much, much deeper.

Something I'll never escape from, now.

3

I met Orla when I was four or five, starting primary school as a nervous infant, all big green eyes and snotty noses, pigtails and wavy hair. The teachers always thought we were twins, since we looked so alike and were practically joined at the hip, doing everything together. Knitting club, gardening club, dance and hockey and netball, a different sport every night. There was nothing Orla and I didn't share, no distinguishing factor, no *real* way to tell us apart.

We stayed closer than close throughout primary school, never wavering. Orla only lived a few streets away from me and so we quickly learnt the way to each other's houses, spending alternating weekends baking and drawing and doing crafts in our bedrooms, starting podcasts and YouTube channels and so-called creative writing masterpieces in notebooks bought from the pound shop. We came from the same sort of families, lived in detached properties on respectable streets. My mum's a social worker and Dad is high up in the bank, and Orla's are both doctors, of course. It's where she gets her brains from.

We were always *those girls*, growing up. Never the most popular, the prettiest, the coolest... but the nicest, the smartest, the ones the other kids respected. We were in the top groups for each subject, excelling at maths and English alike, though Orla was always cleverer, more dedicated to her studies. We scored highest in the class in our year six SATs, moving up to secondary school only to be placed in top set for everything, together, once again.

We'd always been part of the Guide community, since we were five years old and our mums signed us up for Rainbows. We made dinky cross stitch purses in the school hall, moving up to Brownies a few years later, spending our time there being made sixers, enrolling new brownies and organising activities, leading game nights.

Then we joined Vibbington Girl Guides.

I still remember the first evening. We knew Kayleigh and Chloe from Brownies and school; we only moved up to the secondary a year later, where they were in most of our classes. I wouldn't say we were close, then. But we were certainly close enough to be considered a "group".

The Guides' sessions were held at the church instead of the local junior school, like Rainbows and Brownies. We were new and sticky and terrified, dressed in our red and blue uniforms, trembling, when Macey approached us, asked our names, told me I should leave my phone at home in the future, before pushing a paling Lexie McCoy towards us.

"This is Lexie," she explained, placing a hand on her back and shoving her forwards. "She's new."

Lexie was new, all right, but she hadn't joined one of the primary schools in Vibbington. She'd instead started year six at a nearby village school, so we'd never seen her before, had no idea who she was, where she'd emerged from. We took her in cautiously, the wary uncertainty of kids pondering whether to make friends with the new girl, deciding whether she looked cool enough, a worthy addition to her group. It was Chloe who made the first move, wrinkling her nose and tuning in on the bedraggled unicorn hanging from Lexie's hand.

"I like your teddy," she said, smiling at Lexie, expression like plastic. Even at ten-years-old, Chloe was fake, not to be trusted, never to be taken seriously. "It's really cute."

There was no way on earth Lexie's dirty, one-eyed unicorn could be considered "cute", but her eyes lit up and a smile burst onto her face. I felt awful, in that moment – already aware that we were leading her on, drawing her closer. Aware that this would end in disaster.

"Thanks! His name's Mr Sparkles – I've had him since I was a baby."

Chloe, clearly trying to suppress a smirk, grinned again and eyed it in distaste. "Mr Sparkles." Exchanging a look with Kayleigh, her lips twitched as she added, "What an original name."

And that was the start of everything.

We started hanging out as a five, after that, every day at school, every night after. Lexie transferred to our juniors for year six, needing the added support – and friendship – and although she was in a different class, she'd sit with us at lunch and break, meet us outside the gates when the bell rang. We all lived in Vibbington, just a few minutes' walk from one another, with the exception of Lexie, who had to get dropped off and picked up, severely poorer and residing on the other side of town. We were in most of the same classes once we started at Vibbington Secondary School and Sixth Form, though Lexie and Kayleigh weren't always in top set, lacking the motivation necessary, instead settling for second or third.

We did everything together, those two years before the accident. Everything. The same clubs, the same hobbies... ate in the same canteens, went to the toilet together, had sleepovers, attended parties and discos, got our hair done together, our nails, as a five. We were almost twelve years old, and fitting in was the only thing that really *mattered*, made a difference in our lives. Lexie was always behind us, picked on by Kayleigh and flat-out bullied by Chloe, but we never cared enough for us to say something, to try and stop it. We were simply happy to have friends, to fit in… to not be the one who was constantly picked on, abused.

We continued like that for two years, right up until the camp – the first camp, the camp which took Lexie's life.

That was when everything changed.

It was inevitable, of course; things never could have stayed that good, when there were so many secrets between us, so many lies, regrets, all those secrets.

We felt responsible, in a way.

Responsible, and drowning in guilt.

Drowning in that river, a river filled with mistakes, points we fixated on, points which could've changed everything –

In the weeks after Lexie died, we were united, tied together in our knowledge that we were the survivors, the ones who got away. We were interviewed by the police, both individually, parents present, and as a group; we spoke to the headteacher, and to our subject teachers, about the trauma, how much we were struggling. We spoke at her commemoration event, too, told the church what an amazing person she was, how much we'd loved her, how much we missed her. I made a PowerPoint. Orla helped, though it was half-hearted, uncertain. We played it to the rest of the church as they cried.

At school, we were treated like we were special, untouchable, surrounded by wonder. One of our friends had *died*, drowned, fallen to her death from a tyre swing in the dead of night. People acted like we were artefacts in a museum, spectacles nobody wanted to talk to, but simply watched from afar, in shock.

It was Chloe who drifted first. She'd always been too cool for us, the prettiest in the group, the ones with the money, the clothes, the expensive parties, the makeup and hair and boys. By Christmas, she'd started hanging round with the most popular girls in our year, bought herself a Burberry handbag and a whole head of blonde highlights. By the Easter holidays, she'd slept with Ben Margate in year ten, months after her thirteenth birthday party… which none of us had been invited to.

Kayleigh was next. She tried trailing after Chloe at first, trying to impress her, to join her gaggle of new friends. It didn't work. Kayleigh was a little dumpy, with too-big eyebrows which joined in the middle and little to no fashion sense. Chloe did everything she could to cut her off, to stop hanging round with her, until she finally took the hint and came crawling back to us.

Which also didn't work. Orla and I had always been different to the others, into sport and our studies and being generally *good*. We had nothing in common with Kayleigh, who was too busy searching for popularity to take anything seriously. Everything changed when Kayleigh started talking to Ben Margate, weeks after he'd ended with Chloe. It was obvious that he was leading her on, but she was stupid, young, naïve.

He sent her nudes to Chloe, who leaked them to our entire year using an anonymous Instagram account.

I don't think there was any one in the school who didn't see them.

She stopped attending Vibbington Secondary School and Sixth Form, travelling a good forty minutes a day to get to Throwsley High.

Orla and I only stayed as a two for a few months longer, until the end of year eight. It wasn't as though we didn't have things in common anymore, or weren't good friends. We were still closer than close, still spent all our time together, talking about *everything*.

Except Lexie.

We never talked about Lexie.

But there's only so long you can avoid something like that, pretend it doesn't exist, move cautiously round the elephant in the corner of the room without disturbing it.

When Orla met Aaron, it changed everything. He was her first boyfriend, a speccy, smart guy with zero personality and a pale, spindly complexion. They've been together ever since, as far as I'm aware. He started eating lunch with us, hanging round at Orla's at the weekend, asking to come along when we organised cinema dates or trips into Hull.

He wasn't just her boyfriend, but her new best friend. The dynamic now felt… uncomfortable. Like I was the tagalong, not Aaron.

I started seeing her less and less over summer, pretending not to get her messages, telling them I was busy whenever they tried to arrange anything as a group.

They probably appreciated it.

We started school again in September, now miserable year nines faced with picking our options and finding our first boyfriends and cementing our social status. Orla had achieved two of the three, so our friendship was already, in effect, broken. I stopped walking to and from classes with her and Aaron, stopped messaging her each night to ask about homework, stopped eating lunch with them.

I found new friends without much difficulty, friends I'd known for years, friends who'd never had the chance to become my *besties*. Nora, Alicia and I were all on the school hockey team. I'd known them since we joined the C team in year seven, and we'd now been promoted to the B team together, were in some of the same classes, into the same tacky pop groups, fans of the ice cream parlour in town and Harry Potter obsessed. Eating lunch with them occasionally turned to most days, then every day, then weekends and holidays…

We've been best friends ever since.

Nora's like me, in most ways. She's sensible – we all are – but not so sensible that she doesn't have a strong sense of what's wrong and what's right, what you should and shouldn't do. She's half Italian, half British, ridiculously pretty and slender and smart, fluent in both languages, tanned from spending every summer on a beach in Sicily. We have the same humour… short, sharp and witty, completely random at times.

Alicia's just Alicia.

We're all in sixth form now, a few months into year thirteen, on the school's A team for hockey. Nora is captain, though Alicia and I do just as much fundraising and organise training sessions when Nora is too busy. We all do history and English lit at A-level, though Nora also does geography and sociology, I take politics, and Alicia occasionally turns up to photography (apparently).

The only thing the others don't do is girl guiding.

I'm a ranger, now, one up from Guides. Until two weeks ago, it was the only day a week I'd see Orla, Chloe and Kayleigh, even after we drifted apart. We all felt obliged to continue going, for Lexie's sake, for Macey's sake… and for Sharon's sake. She runs the local Ranger group, though us four are the only members. It became necessary that we didn't give up.

None of the other girls go to sixth form in Vibbington. Orla went to do A-levels with Aaron at a nearby college with a reputation for getting students into Oxbridge, and Kayleigh started a hair and beauty course at another. Chloe left school to take over her mum's cosmetic company around the same time, doing one day of training a week at a nail salon.

We kept the group chat, though we never really use it, and I still have framed photos of the group hung around my room. We get on fairly well when we attend Ranger sessions each Wednesday, not mentioning Lexie's death, Kayleigh's leaked nudes, how close we all were, once upon a time.

But now one of us is dead. Another girl; another young life, wasted. First Lexie... now this.

It somehow feels like our fault all over again.

4

Nora and Alicia meet me at the bottom of the drive on Saturday morning, at ten on the dot. I'm not seeing Officer Joy until three or four.

Mum's taking me, again. She's almost finished with her Colleen Hoover novel so she's going to borrow one of my A-level texts. I'll probably be in there a while.

It's freezing for November, properly biting, and my best friends are parked up with the heating on and hats and scarves and gloves wrapped around them. Nora toots the horn as I make my way towards them, pulling open the door and scrambling onto the back seat.

"Hey, bestie," she says, giving the horn another toot, just for luck. "We've missed you!"

"It's only been five days," I reply, but I can't help but smile as Alicia stretches to give me a hug from where she's sat in the passenger seat, decked out in a fur-trimmed pink coat and white accessories, all dark blue jeans and straightened hair. She smells of strawberry lip gloss and cigarettes, and her false nails dig into my bag as she squeezes me.

"Five days too long," she huffs, pulling back to look at me properly. "We've been worried about you, Luce. You've barely even answered our messages…"

It's true. I'm not the best at responding to snaps, even when I'm not emotionally traumatised.

"Sorry, sorry." I hold my hands up in surrender as Nora

turns the key and pulls away from the curb. She's curled her long black hair and has brought out her leather jacket especially, corduroy jeans and angular boots a staple of any Nora Baio outfit. "I've just... you know. I've been with the police, or... just... existing."

My best friends exchange a glance, before Alicia jerks her head, indicating for Nora to keep her eyes on the road.

I haven't told them what happened that weekend, of course. I'm not crazy. I haven't told anyone, not even my parents, much as they're curious and think they can help. Like the others said... *You know what we did. We could get into big trouble, too. They might not see it as self-defence*. I don't want to risk my closest friendships by telling the truth, letting them know exactly what happened two weeks ago... What I did, what I saw.

There's no doubt Nora and Alicia would have a lot to say about that weekend if they knew what *really* happened.

They know as much as the news, the local newspapers, the internet. That three people died, that weekend: two grown men, and one girl, a girl we all went to school with, knew quite well, once upon a time. They know that one of the men had a record for GBH, that the other runs a charity making sculptures from old, forgotten toys. They know the facts, not the gritty details. They know colours and brands and dates and times, not the volume of the blood, the weapon of choice, the rain beating down as I –

They might have suspicions, their own speculations, imaginings. But if they want to know more about what happened, they know not to ask me.

"Have you heard any more about Sharon?" That's Nora, bringing me back to reality. She's watching me in the rear-view mirror, until Alicia jabs her arm and gestures, once again, for her to focus on the road ahead.

I shake my head, remembering too late that they're facing forward and can't see me. Sharon. "No. No, I don't think her condition's changed at all. She's still in the coma, and nobody's allowed to go in and see her."

Because not only do me and the other surviving girls know what happened that weekend, know how those people died… Sharon knows, too.

Only she's been in hospital for the last few weeks, lying flat on her back, deep in a coma.

After the police turned up that weekend, they exploded onto the campsite to find Sharon on her back in the tent, wrapped up warm, the way we'd left her. We thought she was dead, but the paramedics felt a light pulse, and carted her into the ambulance on a stretcher through the rain. They're still trying to keep her conscious, I can only imagine. Feeding her through a tube, and keeping her alive on a machine that bleeps its communication with the world.

God knows what we'll do when – *if* – Sharon wakes up any time soon. God knows what she'll say, or what she'll want to keep a secret, conserving her image as well as our own.

God knows what she even *remembers*.

"Shit." Alicia inhales sharply, turning to lock eyes with me again. "This, Luce, is why we're taking you out today. To take your mind off things, yeah?"

"I need to be back by three," I say, pulling a face. "They want to ask me more questions down at the station…"

The drive into Vibbington's centre only takes five minutes or so, but the roads are icy, and Nora is forced to focus on not spinning out of control. Her electric purple nails tap the wheel as she spins it, disappearing down Exchange Street and towards the car park behind the supermarket, early Christmas traffic mulling all around us. I feel almost trampy in the back behind them, a shadow of my usual self, makeup-less and bedraggled in an old hoodie and baggy jeans.

Unlike my old friendship group, Nora, Alicia and I effectively are equals, despite our differences. We're always well-dressed, posting the perfect photos on Instagram, getting good grades, taking part in the sixth form's student council each week. When It-Couple Owen Sharpley and Lilz Dart got caught up in a horrid murder case over the summer, we watched from the sidelines, hands over mouths, declaring that could *never* be us. We fit together, socially speaking. We match.

But not today.

We park at the back, pulling to a stop and locking the doors as we clamber out. I instantly regret not bringing a coat, shivering as we walk in a line towards the centre of Vibbington. There's a wind whipping up now, dancing round us as my best friends natter and I walk, as though gliding, the world around me just a foggy haze, nothing real.

It's the first time I'm properly going out since... since that weekend. Last time we parked here, walking through this very cut-through, dressed up in weekend outfits to disappear into Vibbington together, I was an ordinary teen, the kind of teen who lives an ordinary, fun life, ordinary, ordinary, ordinary. She hadn't watched a girl die, seen the dead bodies of two more men, felt the blood drip from her hands, her neck, drip, drip, dripping –

Act normal. Don't let them see you're thinking about it, stop thinking about the blood, *all that blood* –

"The others are in the café," Nora says, grinning at me as Alicia scoots round my back and we link arms, as a three. "And you know who else will be there, Luce..."

I mock rolling my eyes as they chortle, but my heart is beating fast and my tread is just a little bit firmer as her words toss over and over in my mind.

Ethan.

I haven't seen Ethan since before I went on that camp, when we had our last ever date. It had become a weekly routine of ours, choosing my house or his to go and play Minecraft and make tea together, resorting to voice calls every other night and video games I could play on my crappy Xbox. We'd usually choose his, as his parents worked late, and would take over the kitchen making meals which almost always went wrong.

It started off innocently enough, with me helping Ethan with his politics revision and him testing me on my English lit quotes. We do the exact same A-levels, so he sits next to me in almost all of our classes. He only kissed me the fourth time, taking me completely by surprise. We never discussed where things would go, however, and I'm thankful for that now. I don't want to be with Ethan. Not now… now that I know what I'm capable of.

"Have you seen him since…?" Alicia asks, before flushing, the typical response after bringing up that weekend. "I mean, I know that's not your priority right now, but…"

I shake my head, squeezing her arm to say that it's okay, I understand. "We called for a bit last night and played Minecraft, but… I think we're just friends after all. We only really discussed the game, and he was there for comfort more than anything."

It was before I went to bed, and Mum and Dad were asleep in the next room, so I had to be quiet. He updated me on the gossip from our politics class, how two girls had scrapped over the colour of the new textbooks, and tried to engage me in a debate about the scare factor of creepers over endermen, before I told him I needed some rest and hung up. We messaged a little after, him telling me how nice it had been to hear my voice, and I felt sick to my stomach as I placed my phone down, turning over onto my side and squeezing my eyes shut, tight.

"I don't even know if I like him," I continue, shrugging. We're turning onto the high street now, shoppers gathering around us, Christmas lights all aglow. "We literally just play Minecraft and revise, Nora. It's not like… it's not like it's anything serious."

"But that's so *cute*." Nora rolls her eyes at me, doing a little skip in her boots and landing on the heel with a *crack*. "Luce, he clearly wants to be more than friends, and he's literally the nicest guy to ever exist. He called you so you had someone to talk to, to take your mind of things, and you freakin' play *Minecraft* together. If you don't want him, I'll have him!"

She doesn't really mean that, though. Ethan Morgan is a nice boy, the soft, tubby kind, the kind you can joke with and who shares his fries with you, the kind most girls would only ever see as a friend. He's someone I only saw as a friend until a few months ago. It's probably best he stays that way, for everybody's sake.

The café looms above us, the epicentre of our teenage lives, buzzing with life as we peer through the window. There are some year twelve girls sat by the window, a group of boys engrossed in a game of D&D, some kids and their grandparents snaffling brownies and milkshakes. And Ethan Morgan, sat with a group of year thirteens on a table at the back of the café, supping his signature coconut smoothie and tipping back his head as he laughs out loud.

I barely have time to process my racing heart and hot

cheeks, as the bell jingles overhead and Alicia pushes me into the café.

"Lucy!" The cry comes from the far end of the café almost immediately, followed by a waving as three boys stand up, beaming and gesturing for me to go over. My eyes go to Ethan and lock on, unable to refocus, hit by a sudden burst of nausea. Brown eyes, like melted chocolate, peering into mine, and pale, just freckled skin; a grey hoodie, one I know smells of sour cream Pringles and Daisy, his dog; all that soft, brown hair, fluffy, like clouds, hair I want to run my fingers through –

Oli is to his side, one of Ethan's best friends. He's a tall boy, one my dad would call a proper geezer, with a round belly and a kind of "proper" dress sense, all shirts and straight-legged trousers and jumpers. He's popular in sixth form for being class clown and current president of the student council. Oli only just lost out on being head boy last year to a certain Kevin Jones.

He stands up now, smiling. Kev, their quiet counterpart, all skinny seriousness and polite handshakes, instantly forgiven by Oli when the results came out because you just *can't* be mad at Kev. He's too sweet and genuine; he has an obvious crush on Nora, one he only exercises when he's not busy studying. Nobody else dares do five A-levels, but Kev's a different breed. It's that exact combination which makes the three boys so iconic. The brightside Skittles to our darkside, the peanut butter to our Marmite, the red Quality Streets to our Purple Ones.

Alicia and Nora lead the way, weaving through the tables as I follow. Heads turn, of course, as they always do when I'm with my best friends. Nobody's looking at me though.

Nobody but Ethan.

He's staring at me as we reach the table, brown eyes concentrated and lips slightly parted. He's staring in a way that makes me shiver, causes my hands to shrivel into balls and my heart to thud, thud, thud, scarcely aware of what's going on around me as Nora and Alicia greet the boys, kissing their cheeks and doling out hugs. He's staring as though he wants to walk round the table and take me in his arms, throw me onto the table, kiss me as though what happened that weekend was just a horrible dream and this is my real life, Ethan and my friends and the café and coconut smoothies…

That part is just wishful thinking.

Ethan smiles at me, understanding passing between us. He gets it. He gets why I'm dressed like this, like I don't own a single nice item of clothing, gets why I haven't done my hair or makeup, haven't been acting the same as usual, replying less, smiling less, struggling with conversation. He gets it. He gets that, although I won't talk about it, I'm traumatised from that weekend, from the deaths, from –

"It's nice to see you, Lucy."

It's really nice to see him, too.

5

"Coconut smoothies for the three of us, please," Nora orders, passing the menus to the waitress, who takes them with a nod. "And… quesadillas, yeah? Just plain cheese, no chicken?"

I nod to confirm, as does Alicia. The waitress is a girl called Nima, who was in Macey's year back when she died. We don't really know each other, but she must've seen my picture in last week's paper, which brought up the Lexie case as part of its story. The four girls involved in her accident now embroiled in another case, this time possibly a murder… or several.

Her eyes linger on me a moment too long before she turns and disappears into the kitchen to prepare our quesadillas, candy-pink bob swaying.

"Wasn't she…?" Nora doesn't need to finish her sentence as I nod, eyes down, indicating that I don't want to talk about it, that she doesn't need to state the obvious. She picks up her phone instead, holding it in front of us all and calling, "Selfie!"

We smile, all six of us, glossy and perfect, beaming into the camera. We know the drill. Nora taps away as she uploads it to her story, covering us in hearts and smiles and stars.

Glossy and perfect, beaming into the camera. I'm paler than the rest, skin dull, hair straggly. It's not a real smile, and I'm not my real self, not the Lucy everyone knows and loves. I look like I've seen a murder. I look like I've… contributed to a murder. I don't fit in with the others in the photo, don't look the same as them, with their perfectly made-up faces and expressions which aren't hiding anything, eyes not overshadowed by death. I stick out like a sore thumb. Anyone viewing this photo would pick that out in an instant.

While I'm on Instagram, the others chatting and sipping from Ethan's existing smoothie, I flick through my stories, the ones from people I know, thumb tapping. And there it is. A photo from one of the girls, the girls from the camp, a selfie posted just minutes ago. A false smile, rosy cheeks, the perfect filter.

How can you do that – how can you act so false – when one of us is *dead*?

How can you even hold a smile?

I flick off it at once, switching off my phone and placing it down on the table with a thud. Kev flinches but goes back to his history flashcards with the slightest of glances, and Alicia and Oli are too busy flirting to notice the clatter. Nora is tip-tapping on her phone still, taking photos of the table, the smoothie, the brownies Kev has ordered but barely touched.

Only Ethan catches my eye, holding steady, brown against green, smushed together, unbreakable.

"You okay?" he mouths, expression soft, hands reaching under the table to meet mine. I feel my heart shudder as our fingers meet, melting together, one huge, sticky mess beneath us.

Just friends.

I nod as I pull away.

Nima brings our food in just five minutes, presenting three plates of steaming quesadillas and salad. She pushes mine a little closer than the rest, smiling, that same understanding passing between us, even giving me my coconut smoothie first, with extra sugar sprinkled round the rim. I flush, mumbling my thanks as she pats my shoulder.

I don't want any special treatment, and I don't deserve sympathy, not like that.

The food is great, of course. Steaming wraps filled with cheese and something which vaguely resembles tomato ketchup, but the posh kind, all rich and creamy and melt-in-your-mouth. The smoothies here are iconic, but I can barely stomach mine, the sweet liquid sticking to my throat, struggling to go down.

Ethan is still staring at me.

Does he have to keep staring at me?

Alicia and Nora are talking. Oli is replying. They're discussing mocks, and the Christmas party Oli's planning on hosting before we break up. A party isn't what I want, not right now. And two weeks... two weeks feels so, so far away. Who knows where I'll be then.

I'm not stupid. Realistically, the police are going to find out the truth. Whether one of the other girls spills something, or Sharon wakes up and tells the whole story, or they find more evidence on the campsite, somehow, something which hasn't yet been uncovered, wasn't destroyed by us or the rain. Realistically, I don't think I have two weeks left. Realistically, I don't know how I've even going to get through the next few hours and cope with the next interview, the one with both Pudrow and Joy, the one which could change everything for all of us.

If the three of us were charged, for whatever reason the police saw valid, would Alicia and Nora still want to be friends with me? We all know what happened when Owen Sharpley was arrested, and his supposed best mate invited everyone round for a pizza party and good old gossip. Would

Ethan still like me, for that fact? He likes the Lucy who plays Minecraft and eats Pringles and snuggles up with him and his dog on his bedroom floor, the Lucy who helps him cook homemade pizzas and kisses him under the glare of his LED strip lights. He likes the Lucy he thinks I am – they all do. Who wouldn't?

"Lucy?"

I glance up, hearing my name ring clear from someone's mouth. Lucy. Even my name speaks volumes. It's so vanilla, so nicey-nicey, so… fake.

They think I'm a Lucy.

I don't *feel* much like a Lucy. Not anymore.

Did I ever?

"Lucy?" Oli repeats my name, a playful smile on his face, waving a hand to get my attention. "You up for a Christmas party, Luce?"

"Sure." I smile back, nodding, as Alicia squeezes my knee beneath the table. "Sounds great."

"Thought it might help take your mind off things, yeah?" His cheeks have coloured a little now, as they always do when people talk about what happened, acknowledging the fact I'm still caught up in one of the biggest murder cases East Yorkshire has ever seen. "And you could invite those two other girls, the ones who went to the camp with you, who we all used to go to school with. Might do you all some good, do you think?"

You could invite those two other girls. I try to imagine messaging that hollow group chat, waiting for the two alive girls to reply to my party invitation while the dead stay dead, unable to activate their old Snapchat accounts, but I just can't. I don't even want to invite them to a party, for them to infiltrate my life all over again, as selfish as that sounds.

In a way, I just want to forget.

"Sure," I repeat. "Sounds great."

Ethan raises an eyebrow as though he sees straight through me, but says nothing. Alicia and Nora both grin at me, taking simultaneous sips of their smoothies as Oli adds, "Epic! It'll be a right laugh, yeah?"

A right laugh, I'm sure.

"What are we doing tonight, anyway? Anyone up for a Maguires, or...?"

"Lucy needs to get home for three," Nora interjects. "She has another interview with the police, so we're gonna drop her back once we're done here. Though... I suppose we could pick you up later if you're feeling up for it, Luce? You could all come round to mine?"

"I don't think so." My answer is immediate, shooting straight out of my mouth. I'm shaking my head vigorously, cheeks pink. "I'll probably feel a bit... you know, after the interview. I'd rather just have a quiet night in, but thanks for the offer."

"Understood." Nora smiles at me, but I can tell she's disappointed. Me saying no to hanging out isn't part of her great masterplan to get things back to normal. "You'll be back at school on Monday, yeah? We can do something in our frees, if you want..."

"I still need to do my UCAS stuff." The others pull a face, so I copy their disgusted expressions without thinking. "I haven't even written my personal statement, so I need to do that sooner rather than later, and start revising for my mocks, and properly choose a course... and a uni..."

There are only two months left, technically, until we have to have applied, be awaiting offers. I've only really looked at Durham and York, being close and with a seemingly good reputation, but now, after everything that's happened, I can't help wondering whether I want to go further afield.

Escaping Vibbington no longer looks so unappealing.

Nora and Alicia are already dead set, of course. Nora spotted a geography course which offers a term abroad in Italy, near to where her family live, and Alicia found a fashion history course down in London which ticks her boxes. Ethan is hoping to do an apprenticeship in Hull with a journalism company, but it's a competitive role, and they only offer two or three spots across the whole of Yorkshire.

There's still that niggling doubt in the back of my mind which ponders whether I'll even get to go to uni, or whether my impending criminal record will ruin any chance I have of living a respectable, normal life. I certainly won't get into a Russell Group if they find out what I did, or even that I was an accomplice in... *that*. That thing, the monster in the back of my mind, in all of our minds, threatening to show itself –

There's a lump in my throat, tears in my eyes, a painful block in my chest. The others have gone back to chatting, but Ethan gestures for me to stand, leading me away from the table and through the café, unresponsive to the queries of our friends, the calls from behind us. Unspeaking, he leads me outside and we stand, backs against the wall, staring at Vibbington's main street as it buzzes all around.

It's cold, a wind whipping all around us, even more ferocious than it was on our way here this morning. Autumnal weather has taken its hold and I can't help but shiver, eyes watering, both because of the cold and because the lump in my throat won't stop growing, getting bigger and bigger, till my whole mouth feels swollen and sore.

Without saying a word, Ethan wraps his coat around my shoulders, zipping it up without me even putting my arms through the sleeves. He doesn't try to touch me, just stands there, protecting me from the confused glances of passers-by and nosy old people who've either seen my picture in the paper and want a good gawp, or who just don't understand why the random teen in the middle of Vibbington is crying, big, splashing tears which don't seem to stop as I lift a hand to wipe them.

It should be embarrassing, crying in front of Ethan like this, without a reason, any kind of trigger.

But it isn't.

It isn't at all.

Ethan remains silent, moving forward so that he's facing me, shielding my entire body from the rest of the town, the rest of the world. I can't meet his eyes, don't want him to get any closer, give me a hug, even stare straight at me.

It's enough just knowing he's there.

6

"Are you sure you're ready for this?" Mum watches me out of the corner of her eye, frowning. We're in the car park of Vibbington's police station, still in the car, my phone clutched between my fingers. It's buzzing with good lucks, so I switch it to silent, turning it over in my hands. "You didn't cope well with the interview yesterday, and I don't mind sitting in on it with you, if you think it'll be too much..."

"It's fine, Mum." I can't catch her eye, terrified she'll see how much I'm shitting myself, how much I *really* don't want to do this interview. "It's just Pudrow and Joy – I've spoken to them both heaps."

Officer Pudrow and Officer Joy are technically officers from Throwsley, North Yorkshire, a good forty minutes or so away, but they were drafted in for this case seeing as they've dealt with us before, when Lexie died. Just like time has stopped in my own life, time feels frozen in Vibbington Station, where the investigation is slow, stunted, unprofessional. Five years ago, they were some of the first officers on the scene when we awoke to find Lexie's tent empty, Macey writhing guiltily as she claimed not to have seen her, not to know anything. They were there when Lexie's body was found, down the river somewhere, drowned, puffy and blue and lifeless.

Pudrow held interviews for Orla, Chloe, Kayleigh and I, parents sat one step behind on hard-backed chairs. A week later, Joy visited each of our homes to find out more about our relationships with the deceased.

Talking to the police has always made me uncomfortable, whether I'm twelve or eighteen, a kid or something much greater. Even when they're not accusing you... the way they pose their questions makes you feel like you know more than you're letting on, like you're hiding something and they're going to find out *exactly* what.

"Were you good friends with Lexie, Lucy?" they'd ask, making sure to maintain eye contact, scarcely blinking. "There were never any problems, were there?"

Even though I was good friends with Lexie, much closer to her than the other girls were... I felt like I was lying to them. That's their greatest talent, you see. They can make the innocent guilty, the guilty even guiltier, hiding something no matter what.

"Well, I'll wait in the car this week, with a book." Mum frowns now, staring forward at the station and shaking her head. *The Kite Runner* was on her lap, and just looking at it made me want to travel back to a time when my A-level texts were the most important thing to me since... since forever. "There's something about that place, Lucy. Police stations put me on edge. I don't know how you do it."

"I don't really have much choice, do I?"

"You always have a choice, Luce." She's quiet for a moment, then leans forward to plant a kiss on my cheek. "Good luck. Just tell the truth and you'll be absolutely fine."

It's still cold out, but I'm wrapped up warm now, all fluffy gloves and thick scarf and bobble hat. The door to the station is automatic, and slides open as I approach it, blasting warm air my way.

The reception area is empty, nobody behind the desk,

toilet door unlocked. I know what Mum means about police stations putting her on edge. The whole room is too bright, too clinical, a bit like a hospital, posters and adverts smothering the notice board and Perspex surround. Even the carpet is spotless, scratching the bottoms of my trainers and making a horrid sound as I cross the room.

I ring the bell, of course, hoping someone will come running so that I don't have to wander the station myself, searching for Officer Joy or Pudrow. There are a few other officers stationed here, officers who are still working on local cases and mainly leave the Throwsley lot to investigate themselves, but they split their time between here and the Hull station, leaving a civilian to man the desk.

When I think about it, I'm pretty sure Joy and Pudrow have greater titles than just "officer", but I can't remember what they are. Ever since we were twelve and too young to understand what a DI was when watching crime programmes on the telly, they've been "Officer Joy" and "Officer Pudrow". There must be other officers, somewhere, working on the case, uncovering evidence, following leads, but Joy and Pudrow are the only ones we talk to.

Maybe that's deliberate.

Maybe they want us to build up trust, a relationship, get to know the officers on a personal level. Chloe and Orla still have their parents in the room as they're only seventeen, but even so, I don't think I have a *relationship* with Joy. Being in a room alone with her makes my skin crawl, however friendly she may seem.

There's no one here now, however. The bell sounds throughout reception, shrill against the shell of a room, echoing against the Perspex screens.

I glance down the corridor, feeling my hands form

automatic fists, fingers curled inwards. There's a door at the end which I know leads to the interview rooms and a few other offices and such like, and Joy makes the tea there whenever Mum's here with me and asks for a mug. But the cells are also down there, brief holding rooms with tightly-locked doors and tiny square windows, the toilet, sink and single bed all in one.

I remember walking past those cells for the first time five years ago, when the four of us came here on a group interview. Officer Pudrow pushed back the door to reveal the boxy room to us, freshly scrubbed and bars on the windows just replaced. He gathered us together to peer inside. Orla was the only one who seemed even minorly interested, scrunching up her nose and gazing round at the neat facilities and brick walls, nodding in her head as though it all seemed familiar. Chloe, Kayleigh and I were too stunned to say anything, staring with wide eyes at the cell before us.

"Is this the kind of thing we could be kept in, if we ever get into trouble?" Chloe asked eventually, trying to play off her query by heightening her voice, raising an eyebrow. "It's so *small*."

"It sure is," Pudrow replied, patting his round belly and nodding. "For a night or two, at least, until you get transferred to the big prison near York, which is even worse. Criminals count themselves lucky every other night they get to spend in our cells."

Kayleigh's mouth couldn't possibly have dropped further.

I won't lie and say his words made a big impression on me, that he's the reason I've never been in trouble with the law since – until now, of course. I'm naturally a goody-two-shoes, too close to my parents to ever want to disappoint them.

But I never forgot those cells.

I wait a second longer, the bell still ringing in my ears, before pressing it again. This time, the shrill sound ricochets off the walls and reverberates all around, and, as I watch the corridor, a door opens halfway down and a curly head pokes round it.

"Ah, Lucy!" It's Officer Joy, at last, beaming at me as she raises her hand to wave. "It's so good to see you! Come on down, come on down... I'll let Pudrow know you're here, then we'll go on through to the interview room, yes? How are you feeling today?"

The interview room is only a short walk, through another set of double doors and before the cells. Joy keeps talking as I follow her, babbling something uninteresting about how her dog threw up all over her shoes this morning and left sicky footprints the whole way down her hallway, which her husband stepped in – or something along those lines. Thinking about Joy having any kind of life outside of work still feels alien to me. She knocks on the door of the biggest office and pushes down the handle to reveal her partner in crime prevention.

"Lucy! Lovely to see you again!"

Lovely, indeed.

The three of us unlock the interview room, a smaller one than last time, more close-knit, a tiny table in the centre boasting three hard-backed seats. I sit on one side, pulling off my gloves and hat and placing them on the table, Pudrow and Joy settling in and turning on the recording device, Joy pulling out her little black notebook.

"Right." She's still beaming, expression all plastic-niceness. Pudrow yawns, though I can tell he's trying to conceal it, as the recording device beeps to indicate that it's begun. "We're going to pick up from where we left off yesterday, if that's okay with you."

"Okay." I knit my hands together on my lap, nodding. Joy consults her notebook, then glances back up at me, expression gentler now, encouraging, like that's her tactic in order to get me to speak.

"So, Lucy. Let's start with your relationship with the victim, and the other two girls. Talk me through the run-up to the camp, when you first decided you were going, that sort of thing. Just talk us though that, if you can."

I swallow. Talk them through the run-up to the camp? Talk them through *my relationship with the other girls?*

My heart's pounding, stomach clenching. The quesadillas from earlier don't seem like such a good idea now, swirling round and round with the coconut milkshake like some horrible washing machine of cheap café food.

I can do this. I can talk about the girls, about the past, about our relationship.

If I do this – if I answer some of their questions, at least – it'll buy me more time.

And then…

Then I won't have to tell them the rest.

7

After leaving the local Guides group, age fifteen, there was never a question that the four of us were going to continue with Rangers. We started weekly meetings in year ten, just the four of us and a few girls from the year above who've since moved away to uni. Rangers isn't that different from Guides, if I'm honest. It's all polo shirts and badges and hikes through the countryside, but it's fun, and cosy. It makes you feel like you belong.

Sharon ran the local ranger group, too. It was only small, eight or nine girls, but it was fun, exciting. We felt like we were doing it for Lexie, and that's what made it feel so… *special*. Even as my social life grew and the other girls drifted, we had this one night every week to bring us back together. At Rangers, we were twelve years old again, little kids playing games and planning trips like nothing else mattered in the world.

We took a break from ranger meetings over the summer, between year twelve and year thirteen. Ever since Lexie died, we'd stopped the summer camps and activity days at water parks and on lakes, giving up on tyre swings and kayaks, on wild swimming and waterfalls. Sharon still loved organising activities for us all, but they were on land now. We always took August off in remembrance of Lexie.

We were used to seeing each other again after long breaks, used to not speaking for weeks on end. Now that everyone attended different colleges, getting along at Rangers was an entirely unique situation; we never used the group chat anymore, never hung out on weekends, but would act like normal every Wednesday, for Sharon's sake.

Towards the end of year eleven, alliances had shifted, following us into year twelve. Kayleigh was now the outcast, treated like she was below the rest of us, though she'd made plenty of friends at her new school and had finally learnt how to do her makeup and pluck her eyebrows. Orla was still the nerd of the group, top set for absolutely everything and dating wet-wipe Aaron, no proper friends to speak of. Then there was Chloe.

Chloe had always been cool, but she was now part of *that group* at school, the group everyone feared but craved to be a part of. She somehow swallowed thousands of Instagram followers, drew her eyebrows on in sharp lines, fake-tanned to a perfect shade of mocha, freckles glowing through her newly bronzed skin. She grew a proper figure, shifting from her pin-straight childish self to a *woman*, and forever gloated about the boys she was shagging, the older men who'd glance her up and down in the street, the brands contacting her online to model for them.

"I don't know what it is," she'd say, shaking her head in an attempt to act modest. "What do you think they see in me?"

Once upon a time, I never would've believed I'd be the girl Chloe respected most. Before Lexie, she seemed to view me as another one of her minions, little Lucy, too meek and timid and kind to be of note. Kayleigh was her favourite, the desperate tagalong, and Orla had always been respected for her quiet submission and brains.

But oh, how the tables turned...

Alicia, Nora and I were fairly well-liked in secondary

school, second to Chloe's group. We weren't scary, didn't answer back to teachers, didn't steal traybakes from the cafeteria... but my friends and I had a natural air of *cool* which kept us afloat. We wore the right clothes, did our makeup well, customised our uniform until it was the perfect level of rebellious and acceptable. We listened to the right music, did well in lessons, played sport and yet weren't defined by our success.

We talked to boys, got on well with teachers and students alike.

I wasn't Chloe – I didn't *want* to be Chloe – but I was enough for her to see me as a friend, an ally. She thought I was cool, though I never really tried to be. She saw my status as somewhere close to hers, and that spoke volumes.

So the dynamic at Ranger meetings altered, shifting from Kayleigh and Chloe to Kayleigh and Orla, from Lucy and Orla to Lucy and Chloe. None of us were that close anymore, but we had two well-established teams, which we'd switch into while playing games or completing challenges or going on days out. Things between Orla and I were stilted, awkward. I never knew what to say to her, and she'd never been one for small talk. If I asked her about the maths homework, she'd simply raise an eyebrow and tell me to ask Nora; she never asked me questions in return, knowing full well that Aaron had all the answers.

We didn't really speak, the four of us, the summer between year twelve and thirteen. I'd just finished my first year at sixth form without them all, and had a part-time job at a surf shack a short train ride away, on the coast. I spent most of my summer at the beach with Nora and Alicia, occasionally joined by Oli, Ethan and Kev, and barely noticed when Chloe and the others liked my Instagram posts or replied to my stories with heart-eyed emojis. Oli held parties all year round, but only for kids at sixth form, smaller affairs which felt more like the gathering of friends than proper bashes.

My old friends were never invited, weren't part of my new group, didn't associate with us in any way.

As the months went by, I somehow started to… forget about them.

And for the first time in five years, I almost forgot about Lexie, too.

The first Ranger meeting after the holidays was on a Wednesday, as usual, after school, at seven o'clock. Mum dropped me off, blowing me a kiss and waving to Orla's mum, who stood outside the chapel frowning and tip-tapping away on her phone. Orla was with her, head in a textbook, but her mum swiped it as soon as I approached. She switched to her normal smiley self, tucking Orla's book beneath her arm.

"Hello, Lucy!" she exclaimed, giving me a little wave. "Did you have a nice summer?"

Orla's mum was always nice to me, even when we first drifted apart back in year nine. Our families had always been close, even taking family trips to Center Parcs together when we were in primary school, but they never saw each other now, only when taking us to and from ranger events. Orla's family like Aaron a reasonable amount, but she'd lost all of her friends to be with him, shut herself off to spend every waking moment by his side. They knew that; I was never to blame for the fallout.

"It was lovely, thank you. And you?"

Orla had gotten out her phone during this exchange, and was focused entirely on it as I stood there, trying to smile at her. She wasn't interested in me. A name flashed across her screen as she tipped her head back to brush the hair out of her face: Ron-Ron.

Aaron.

"It was a… pleasant summer." Orla's mum tried for a smile, but it was all lopsided, eyes unfocused. "We went on holiday with Aaron's family, didn't we, Orla?"

That was when Orla looked up, blinking like she hadn't noticed me standing there, like Aaron was the only word able to get her attention.

"We did, yeah. Went for a week in the south of France."

I smiled, nodding, like it sounded as lovely as she made it out to be. Aaron's parents were a pompous couple who lived on the outskirts of Vibbington in a huge Tudor house, inciting his passion for politics and history and all things boring, and made the local papers a few years back for donating thousands to the restoration of Vibbington's library. Although Orla's parents were doctors and lived in a fairly big house a few streets from mine, they didn't act posh at all, and I couldn't imagine them happily spending a week with Mr and Mrs Robinson-Smythe.

The door of the chapel opened, and Sharon stuck her head out. She was wearing her trademark waterproof trousers and a fleece over her khaki t-shirt, and her face broke into a smile as she noticed us waiting.

"Welcome back, girls!" she announced, holding up her arms in welcome. "Are Chloe and Kayleigh not here yet? Come in, come in, I have lots to tell you about! How have your summers been?"

We said goodbye to Orla's mum, the two of us following Sharon into the chapel's main hall. It hadn't changed much over summer, the damp on the walls drying up and a few of the cracked floorboards now replaced. Otherwise, it looked identical, the same sad, empty space we'd inhabited since we were ten years old and shivering in our newly bought guide uniforms.

But we weren't the only ones here. There was another person stood in the corner of the room, sifting through laminated sheets of paper Sharon had clearly printed from PowerPoint, hovering awkwardly as though he wasn't sure whether he should greet us or not.

It was Steve, Sharon's husband of twenty years, a dishcloth of a man who ran a charity making sculptures from old, forgotten toys. We'd met him several times over the years, at Christmas fairs or parties, driving the bus when we went on excursions. He technically wasn't allowed to help with meetings as he hadn't done a DBS check or any kind of health and safety training. But since we were such a small unit, no one seemed to notice – or care.

Steve had always been awkward, a drab man, very bald and pink and scrawny. He was forever tagging Sharon in Facebook posts, calling her his dear, darling wife, creating their own anniversaries… from twenty-four years since their first kiss, twenty-two years since their first intimate moment, to twenty-one since they married. He was obsessed with her, and didn't mind if the whole world knew.

He gave us a shy smile now, which we both responded to with caution. The four of us never disliked Steve, but we always thought he was a bit… odd. Squirmy, wriggling, like a pig, always to be held at arm's length.

"Steve going to be helping us with the planning tonight, girls," Sharon explained, crossing the floor to take the laminated sheets from his hands. "We have some really exciting stuff to discuss!"

Chloe and Kayleigh arrived next, a few seconds between each other. Chloe had clearly jogged here, dressed in running leggings and a sports bra, pink in the face and hair scooshed into a high ponytail. Kayleigh looked bored, still a little dumpy for her height, face scrubbed bare of makeup, dressed in a fresh t-shirt and flared jeans which clung to her in all the wrong places.

"Gather round, gather round!"

So we did, forming a circle around Sharon, where she was sat with those laminated sheets. It was the same whenever we planned a camp, or any kind of trip out. We knew the drill, and this didn't feel any different to countless other meetings.

"We're planning another camp, an autumnal one, this time, creeping into winter." She shuffled the sheets, holding up one to show us. "It's at a field not too far from here, on the way to the moors, near the coast… just three nights of fun, of adventure and independence and learning."

"Sounds sick," Chloe said, flicking her hair behind her shoulder and crossing her arms, tapping her foot against the ground. "October… a Halloween camp, you mean?"

"Not exactly." Sharon gave a little laugh, though it wasn't really funny. "I thought camping on our own with spooky skeletons all around might be a bit creepy, so it's going to be more autumnal than… scary."

"I'll have to check I'm free that weekend," Kayleigh said, frowning. "My boyfriend's taking me away for a few nights for my birthday, and it's either that week or the one after."

Because Kayleigh had a boyfriend now, too. None of us had met him yet, but she'd posted photos with him online, and he looked like a nice enough guy. Brown hair, plain face, flat smile. Nothing extraordinary, but suiting Kayleigh to a tee.

"And I'll have to check it's well in advance of my mocks," Orla added. "I don't... I don't want to miss out on revision time, not this close to them. Cambridge ideally want at least one A*, but it's very competitive."

Chloe was rolling her eyes at me across the circle, and I couldn't help but smile back. She was still working full-time with her mum, and could easily request a few days off. She stated this now, to which Sharon sagged in relief, nodding her head.

"I do hope the rest of you can attend, too," she said, voice pleading. "This might be the last camp we ever get to do, what with your exams and university applications, etc…"

We all felt guilty then, noticing the desperation in her eyes, the way she so, so wanted us all to attend the camp she'd painstakingly planned and reserved a field for. The laminated sheets in her hand showed photos of her homegrown butternut squashes, garlands made from fallen leaves and twigs, and vegetarian s'mores, skewered like kebabs over a campfire. Even the plan was so Sharon, so hippie and authentic and cool.

She was right, of course, when she said it could be our last camp. University applications were imminent, and we all felt that things were changing. Chloe would turn eighteen next, then Kayleigh and Orla, weeks apart. Three quarters of us now had boyfriends, jobs, A-levels and projects and new friends, better friends. We wouldn't want to run around playing girl guides forever.

Looking round at the other girls, it was clear we were in agreement. We'd go to the camp, spend those three nights together… not just for Sharon's sake, but for Lexie's, for Macey's.

We had to make it epic, if it really *was* going to be our last camp.

We just didn't realise *why*.

8

The camp. Our final chance to remember Lexie, to commemorate her death, to have an adventure outside of school and work and our many strings attached. A final chance to be ourselves, the four of us, under the supervision of Sharon and Sharon only. No popularity contests, no drama, no boys and chaos and arguments... just me and Orla and Chloe and Kayleigh, life-long best friends, before we all split off in our different directions, pursuing the futures we'd always dreamt of.

Chloe, still working at her Mum's salon; Orla to Oxford or Cambridge; me to Durham or York, studying liberal arts or English or history; Kayleigh, finding some sort of job in the local area, still going steady with that boyfriend of hers.

Sharon led us through the plans for the camp, making tweaks to the dinner menu, snack list, activities we'd be doing. The camp was on a site by the sea, so a walk along the cliffs was prescribed for one day, with the intention of getting some fresh air and taking in the Yorkshire coastline. I could see Chloe's mind ticking over as she considered photos for her Instagram, Orla already losing interest, the thought of weak signal and not being able to speak to Aaron probably driving her crazy.

Kayleigh was the only one who seemed moderately interested, the two of us nodding along to what Sharon was saying, pointing out improvements in the plan here and there. At the ripe age of eighteen, I still loved the idea of a weekend in the countryside, a detox from society, from the stress of A-levels and boys and –

It was then that my phone buzzed, and, while Sharon was talking Kayleigh through the gluten free options on the menu, I tugged it from my pocket to examine.

It was Ethan, his Bitmoji all fluffy and smiley, gazing up at me from my phone. He'd sent a photo of his dog, Daisy, curled up on his lap as he sat on the bedroom floor, Minecraft lighting up the screen opposite.

We miss you, it said, accompanied by a sad-faced emoji and a dog emoji, and a further snap of a sealed tube of Pringles. **I'll be tempted to eat them without you if you don't come round soon. How's your ranger meeting going?**

I didn't know if I properly liked Ethan, at that point... not really. He was lovely, sweet and cuddly and funny, and we got on so, so well when I went round to his, playing video games and joking about the state of the government until it was time for me to leave. But that was it. We acted like *friends*, two people who liked each other a lot but would never develop that further, incapable of discussing our feelings.

I'd liked boys before, kissed one or two at the few year eleven parties we were invited to, back in the day. Ethan felt different. He wasn't my type – not traditionally, a little on the chubby side, and not really into fashion or media or pop culture the way I was – and yet we still had so much in common. Spending time with him was easy, relaxed, like I could just be myself and not worry about acting like a dork. He got me, and that was more than I could say for a lot of people... even Alicia and Nora, sometimes.

Ethan had had one serious girlfriend before, six months or

so ago, a girl we'd gone to secondary school with. *Lauren Accorn*. She'd broken up with him after trying to do long distance upon her move to Nottingham, but Oli and Kev told us it hadn't worked out, that Ethan had been crushed.

It played on my mind a little, knowing he'd been in love before, maybe even slept with her, and that I – if he even *liked* me – could just be a rebound, or someone to keep him occupied, now that he was single. I'd resigned myself to staying friends until he made a move, and stress about whatever feelings I may have for him *then*, should I need to.

Yet here he was, on my phone, gazing up at me with those beseeching brown eyes, waiting for me to say something. I couldn't say no. There was still time after Rangers to go round to his and work on our joint Minecraft world.

So I sent him a snap of my feet back, promising I'd be there in an hour, and requesting that he save the Pringles for me.

!!! can't wait – I want to build a swimming pool under the library and fill it with squid ;)

It was the winky face that did it for me.

I turned back to Sharon and the others now, slipping my phone into my back pocket so that I could give them my full attention with fewer Ethan-shaped distractions. Steve was standing behind his wife now, gazing down at the floor as though too awkward to make eye contact with any of us, and Sharon had completely filled her wheel-along whiteboard with the itinerary of the camp, sticking her laminated sheets to the plastic and scribbling all around them in red.

The first day seemed chill enough. A takeaway pizza in our newly erected tents, which were to be shared two-by-two.

Sharon usually let us pick our own buddies, but she insisted on switching things up today, claiming it'd be a great bonding experience for all of us.

Kayleigh and Orla, me and Chloe. Why not?

"Are we allowed our phones?" Orla asked suddenly, ignoring the new pairings and looking up from her screen for the first time all night. We'd had camps before where phones had been prohibited, handed over to Sharon upon arrival and hidden deep inside her tent. She was big on digital detoxes, but also loved the photos and videos we took at each camp, which often swayed her into allowing us to keep them.

"You are," she said now, cocking her head to one side. "But we'll be in the middle of the countryside, and they're doing maintenance work down the road that weekend, so there'll be absolutely no signal."

I think all of our mouths dropped open then, in a mix of horror and abject disbelief.

"No signal?" Chloe echoed, shaking her head. "But… isn't that against the rules, in case there's an emergency or something?"

"We've always had mobile signal at our camps, Chloe." Sharon was smiling as she shook her head, as though what Chloe was saying was completely ludicrous, like she was overreacting entirely. "And we've not had an emergency yet, have we?"

I guess we were no longer counting Lexie's missing body as an *emergency*.

"Don't jinx it," Kayleigh muttered, but nobody except me seemed to hear.

"I do think it's a bit irresponsible," Orla piped up. Forever the level-headed one, the sensible member, it was clear she was more concerned with not speaking to Aaron for three days than our possible safety. "Anything could happen, and we won't have the means to contact home…"

"There's a telephone on site – wired, so we'll hopefully still be able to use that, should the site encounter other problems." Sharon could still sense the unease passing between us, and added, "I promise you, girls, it'll be fine. You can take pictures and document the trip as much as you'd like, but there'll be no need to get online or text your cronies back home. It's just three days, three days of adventure and team-building and fun. If there is an emergency – which there won't be – I can easily call for assistance using the site's phone. They should have finished the maintenance work by Monday."

Three days. Three days without contact from the outside world, without social media and our friends and boys. Three days of camping, sharing a tent with Chloe, of all people, and not speaking to Ethan, to Alicia or Nora or my parents. Three days of what sounded like hell, hidden under the guise of another little camp, supposedly our last.

This whole weekend was beginning to sound a lot less appealing.

"It'll be fine," Sharon assured us, Steve reaching to put a hand on his shoulder behind her. "Nothing will go wrong."

Those famous last words.

9

"So... you knew Steve Jones?" Officer Joy is watching me carefully, eyes narrowed, mouth pursed. "Would you say you were friendly with him, given the circumstances?"

I blink, drawn out of my story, words stuck.

Steve. Bald-headed, wriggling Steve, stood in the corner of the church hall that day, watching us from afar, pupils unable to keep still, jerking from side to side, vibrating –

"No." I shake my head, tight-lipped and short, as the officers' eyes don't move from me. "He was just Sharon's husband. None of us were *friendly* with him."

"So you didn't have any problem with him attending camps in the past?"

That was the thing. He'd never really *attended* camps before. He sometimes drove the minibus there and back, or dropped supplies bought from the supermarket in his ancient Beetle, before scuttling back to their semi in Vibbington. I'd been there a few times over the years, to pass consent forms to Sharon or cheques for activity days and new uniform. It was a nice house – ordinary, neat, tucked-in, so unlike the couple – but it always felt cold, empty, lacking a heart.

"He was just Sharon's husband," I repeat, much to the dissatisfaction of Officer Pudrow and Officer Joy. "We never thought about him beyond that."

Just Sharon's husband. A pathetic man, no doubt, attention-seeking and whiney, desperately in love with his wife, but a husband all the same, someone it made no sense to question. Sharon was our leader, and she was married to Steve. End of.

Officer Joy switches tactics now, folding her arms across her chest. She's gazing at me with those impenetrable brown eyes, and it's all I can do not to move my eyes.

"What about the other man?"

The other man.

Another one of your friends is dead, and so are two more people.

I gulp.

"What about him?" I try to keep my voice light, cautious, but there's a slight tremor, a lump building in my throat, memories flashing through my mind –

A body, stark naked and stretched out across the grass, dark red spilling from below his chest. Blood, blood, blood on my hands, drip-drip-dripping, onto my shoes, crawling under my nails, causing spatters to form on my top, my neck, my cheeks, blood, blood, blood, blood –

"Did you know this man before the camp?"

Before the camp. Before everything went wrong, before I tumbled through the air and landed with a crash, all tears and sweat and chaos. I can't imagine existing in a time when this wasn't happening, when another girl wasn't dead, and two men, too, two men, one made of pure evil, the other...

"Did you know he had a record for GBH?"

Grievous bodily harm. We didn't know that, of course. We didn't even know he was camping with us, tucked away in a tent, until it was too late, until things were too far gone to ever reverse.

They only told us about his criminal record a week ago, when the body was identified. Carl Hall, they said his name was. Unmarried, with two little kiddies and a string of smaller offences... breaking and entering, stealing school shoes. He came from a dodgy part of Leeds, the BBC explained, and had only pleaded guilty to the GBH charges so that he could take the stint in prison and escape the rat race for a few years.

"Of the three bodies found on the campsite that morning, Hall was the only one to have ever been charged for offences of a violent nature. Police in North Yorkshire and the East Riding suspect him of murdering both a seventeen-year-old girl and an older man, but it's still unknown how Hall himself suffered the same critical injuries as his alleged victims."

That's what the reporter said, sat behind her desk in that nice, cosy studio, makeup perfected, hair straight, teeth white. That they suspected Hall of the murders, seeing as he was the only one to have ever been violent before – as far as they knew. I hardly noticed my fists clenching into balls by my sides as they replayed the photos of the victims, the girl I'd known all my life and that squirming, wriggling man –

"We only need short answers, Lucy." I'm drawn back to the present, to Officer Joy talking as she stares down at me, expression serious. "We need to know the truth about what happened that weekend, to set the record straight. Three people died, and we can only speculate on how they ended up that way. By the time you were able to get help, you and the other three girls were tired and bruised – but somehow scrubbed clean of blood. Unless the three of you plotted to kill these people – your own friend, and two older men you claim you barely knew – then there *has* to be another explanation, and none of you will speak."

But somehow scrubbed clean of blood. That's true, all right. Our clothes were ruined, tossed onto the fire, hair lank after showering thoroughly, bruises flowering on all parts of us, some inflicted, others mere accidents. Three dead bodies, side by side on the ground. And Sharon, our alleged fourth, unconscious in her tent, barely breathing.

"Answer me this, Lucy." Officer Joy is watching me again, those brown eyes dark and haunting, almost black to their core. Officer Pudrow is taking note of everything, but even he looks uncomfortable, shifting in his seat as I wait for the inevitable. "Did Hall kill the other two victims? Is he the man to blame?"

Silence. The lump in my throat keeps growing, getting bigger and bigger and bigger as I try to swallow. My eyes are slick with unshed tears.

"Lucy, it's not a difficult question. Did Hall kill those people? Did he assault Sharon Jones, and kill the other two because they found out about it, or caught him in action?"

I'd say I've never heard anything so ludicrous in my life… but it'd be a lie. The truth is crazier, far more horrifying, than Officer Joy has even begun to imagine. I can't shake my head, however, completely frozen in place, hands shaking. Officer Joy cocks her head and frowns.

"If he didn't assault Sharon, were they *together*?"

Another inevitable, one I've been expecting them to bring up ever since the examination at the hospital, when she was first taken in. Sharon's unconscious body was found with her trousers and pants stripped off, a condom on the sleeping bag beside her.

They had no idea whether what happened to Sharon was consensual, but it's obvious, with Sharon's steady job and loving husband and ordinary, middle-class ways, what the police were likely to believe.

Their theory was clinched when tests proved the DNA on the condom belonged to Carl Hall, not Steve.

And besides… a camp of girls, with no mobile signal and

no strong men to protect them, seemed like the perfect target for a rapist, even in deepest Yorkshire. It didn't matter that hardly anyone knew we'd be there that weekend, or the camp was securely locked and the only way in would be through the surrounding countryside and over the fence. Hall, with his criminal background, couldn't *possibly* have been having an affair with straight-up Sharon. It had to have been assault; there was no other explanation.

"Come on Lucy," Officer Joy adds, losing her patience now, eyes rolling back into her skull as she shakes her head at me. "You have to give us something to go off. If – *when* – Sharon wakes up from her coma, she'll tell us the whole truth. You might as well give in, tell us now."

It's a tactic, I know, one used by police to get suspects to spill. *You might as well tell. You have nothing to lose, and if you don't, it'll be so much worse for you when we find out.* That's true, of course... I'm not completely stupid. I know that, should the police find out what we're hiding, the punishment coming for us will be so much worse than it currently stands.

But I can't bring myself to do it. I can't bring myself to say it, to risk my entire future, my name, my reputation, my friendships and family and education. Not when there's still a slight chance that they won't find out what we've done, that they'll never, ever find out.

We could get into big trouble, too. They might not see it as self-defence.

My friends were right; they might not see it as self-defence, perhaps manslaughter, cold-blooded murder. And if that's the direction they take, our whole lives are screwed.

"I don't think you understand how serious this is, Lucy." Officer Pudrow speaks, for the first time in a good ten minutes. It's hard to take him seriously when there are boiled egg morsels stuck to his bottom lip and his blue eyes are watering. I try anyway, swallowing a burble of nervous laughter. "Your friend is dead, and, somehow, two men are. Do you have an explanation for that?"

The interview room falls silent, the only sound my beating heart, pumping faster and faster and faster as I stare at the officers before me. Joy then frowns, wrinkling her nose as she asks, "Did… did you kill Hall, Lucy? You and your friends? Did you kill Hall once you realised he'd gotten to Steve, Sharon, and the girl who, *and I quote*, was practically a sister to you?"

More silence, dragging on and on and on, as they await my response. I'm still trying to process what they've just said when Officer Pudrow asks, "Or did you kill all three of them?"

Me, a murderer…

Little Lucy, meek, mousy Lucy, Lucy of *top set* everything co-captain of the hockey team.

Plunging the knife we'd only just used to chop veggies for our curry into the chests of three victims, watching the blood spurt everywhere, covering my hands, my feet, my neck, my clothes –

I close my eyes, squeezing them tight, feeling the skin around them tighten and shrivel into rolls.

Me, a murderer.

Meek, mousy Lucy, *a murderer*.

"I think that's as much as we're going to get out of you today," Officer Joy says, pushing back her chair, letting it scrape across the floor. "Interview over."

10

I expect to see Mum waiting for me in reception when I emerge, hands shaking and heartrate ten times its usual capacity, but she's nowhere to be seen. I check my phone for messages, sure she was supposed to be picking me up, but there are no missed calls, no messages telling me she's caught up with work and can't get here in time after all.

It's not a long walk home.

I emerge from the police station into bright sunlight, blinking as it floods my vision, almost blinding me. I feel like I've been inside years, and the sky was overcast this morning, completely; it hits me now, the intensity of the sun and that cold, November chill, spreading through my body, the promise of December.

"Lucy!"

I turn, confused, lifting a hand to shield myself from the sun. There's a familiar red car parked by the wall, and a figure leans against its backside, tall and chubby and smiling.

Ethan raises a hand to wave me over, so I twist on my toes and start making my way over to where he's parked. Ethan passed his test a while ago, but only gets custody of his Mum's Peugeot at weekends, when she's not at work. I've only really been driven by him when our whole group would travel to visit the beach over summer, for picnics on the Yorkshire Wolds on pretty days, four of us piling onto the back seat in a fashion which wasn't exactly *legal*.

When I usually see Ethan, just the two of us, it's always round at his place, occasionally mine. His friends aren't entirely sure of what's going on between us, and mine only know that we kissed, once, haven't discussed it since. Parading round Vibbington in his Mum's car would definitely start rumours... and yet now, walking towards him, sunlight blaring, I couldn't care less.

"What are you doing here?" I ask, trying to sound stern. The relief in my voice is evident. I'm still trembling, mind reeling from what just happened in the interview room. Seeing Ethan calms me, causes my bones to meld together and my heartrate to increase tenfold, like it's going to flutter right out of my chest.

"I called your mum, told her I'd pick you up instead." He can't stop smiling as he says this. It's like he's so excited to be picking me up he can barely contain it. "I wanted to surprise you, so we're going out for pancakes, if you'll have me?"

If? Even though I'm still a mess inside, all sick and trembling and trying desperately to block out the bad, I can't help but grin back.

We climb into the car, him driving, me tucked beside him in the passenger seat. I push my hands between my knees to stop them from shaking, but being in his presence calms me, convinces me that everything's going to be fine, that I'm safe and happy and no one knows what happened that weekend, and I've gotten through another interview alive.

"So." Ethan pulls out of the car park, away from the station and down the street. He's a smooth driver, always careful, and takes care when pulling onto the main road. "How did it go in there?"

I shrug. Feeling my hands grow clammy between my knees, mouth runs sour with the taste of guilt.

How *did* it go? I got out without any more accusations being thrown at me, and that's all I care about right now. I hesitate before answering, ears ringing with the sound of silence.

"It was fine." I don't know what else to say, so Ethan doesn't push, carries on driving as though I never said anything. He switches the radio to the kind of 80s and 90s pop he loves, nodding his head in time to the beat of Madonna, Whitney Houston, Michael Jackson. I try to focus on the music, but my mind keeps wandering, eyes flicking back to Ethan, time and time again…

Ethan Morgan is possibly the prettiest boy ever to exist, I realise as I stare at him, trying not to make it obvious, texting at the same time, mumbo-jumbo nonsense to Nora and Alicia about how the interview went, how I feel now, informing them I'm off out with Ethan and that I'll see them tomorrow for a study session, as planned. I have hockey practice for the first time in weeks, my kit all washed and ready to go at home, trainers aching for me to throw them on again. But every few seconds, I can't help but glance at Ethan, breath catching in my throat…

It's no good, I tell myself, shivering and turning back to my phone. It's fine doing stuff like this – playing Minecraft, going to get pancakes, hanging out with our friends, as a group – but it can't go beyond that. Being around Ethan makes me forget what I did, what I'm capable of, but Ethan has no idea what I'm really like, what damage I could cause to him. He thinks I'm just *little Lucy*, like everybody else does. Little does he know…

I don't want to hurt him. I don't want him to get the wrong idea, or for me to unknowingly lead him on. I want to be his friend. Just his friend.

He's humming along to 'Vogue' now, doing all the little poses and sticking his tongue out as he tries to still focus on driving. If it were any other guy doing this – miming to Madonna, jigging away as he drives us to get pancakes, dressed in a lilac hoodie, face clean-shaven and brown eyes all melty and delicious – I'd get the ick, right? He's not my type in any way, yet there's something about him which just feels *right*.

Only he's not right. He can't be. *Nobody* can be, not for me.

Especially someone as perfect as him.

We pull off at the next town over, where a row of brightly coloured cafés and restaurants light up the centre. It's a hub of local food and produce, the sophisticated sister to Vibbington, and Ethan parks outside the Soho Pancake House and turns off the engine. We sit there for a moment, unspeaking, the radio still blasting 80s pop as we wait for the other to make the first move.

"You ready?" he asks eventually, reaching to place a hand on my knee. My whole body retracts at his touch, and I try for a smile, nodding.

The café is small but quaint, following the layout of the original terrace house it used to be, all interconnected quirky rooms going off the central corridor which leads down to the kitchen. The waitress seats us on a table for two in one of the front rooms, by the bay window, and tells us she'll be back in five minutes for our orders, placing two menus on the cloth before us.

"Thanks!" Ethan exclaims, grinning as she moves away, then he turns back to me and taps the menu. "Doesn't it look great?"

It does, I suppose. The pictures are all dusted with icing

sugar and fruit, drizzled in chocolate and Nutella, decorated liberally with sprinkles and candy and little marshmallows. There's a sweet, sickly scent circulating around the room, which is empty bar us. It's faintly nauseating.

The pancake stack with natural yoghurt and winter berries sounds most manageable. The picture depicts a dish lacking furious embellishments and extra sugar. Ethan chooses a strawberry cream crêpe, of course, with extra strawberry sauce and glossy cream squashed beneath more strawberries. He leans back in satisfaction when the waitress takes away our menus and asks if we'd like drinks.

"Two hot chocolates," Ethan says, before I can object. "With extra squirty cream, of course." Then he smiles at me, nudging my foot gently beneath the table. "You deserve it."

Even though I don't want the hot chocolate – even though I don't want to like him, or for him to treat me like this, like I need looking after – a part of me breaks when he says that.

We're submerged in quiet again, cloying around us, thick and dense and angry, like fog. It's my fault, of course; I'm not saying anything, not making any effort to start a conversation, and Ethan looks lost without it. I don't want to be rude, but the awkward silence is getting under my skin, so I whip my phone out of my pocket, pushing it onto the table before me so that he doesn't think I'm being secretive.

As soon I tap the screen, my heart stutters.

It's that group chat again. The one with us five girls in it, now reduced to three active, two dead.

There are 18 messages unread by me.

"What is it?" Ethan asks, keeping his voice light, steady. "You look like you've seen a ghost…"

If only.

The police were proper grilling me this afternoon. They're convinced the guy shagging Sharon – Carl Hall, or whatever his name is – killed the other two, so we killed him to avenge their death or some shit. And that Sharon got injured somehow when Hall assaulted her and the other two intervened. It's a load of bullshit – but if we don't tell them what really happened and risk a manslaughter charge at best, we'll go down for murder. Either way we're gonna get stuck with a load of shit.

I don't breathe for a few seconds, staring at the message, reading it over and over and over, trying to make sense of it all.

They genuinely think we killed him – killed him deliberately, as part a cold, calculated murder. They think we conspired to stab him to death to avenge the deaths of two people it wouldn't even make *sense* for Hall to have killed.

There's no point saying anything yet. They have no evidence that we took part in the killing, so they can't do us for the murder, and they'll only figure out what actually happened if we let on. We got rid of the evidence well, remember?

We did – we were careful about that. The bonfire was still blazing, stocked up with smaller sticks and twigs, flames raging high into the sky. Everything was burnt that weekend. Everything we thought might be incriminating, even if it wasn't in the slightest.

We kept our clothes, however. The blood-stained t-shirts and jeans, the soaked leggings, the ripped coats. We had to make it realistic – we couldn't just pretend we'd been nowhere near the three dead bodies, or they'd be even more suspicious. We were three traumatised teens, found on a campsite near one of our murdered friends, and two older men with gruesome wounds. For us to be covered in their blood seemed almost... expected.

I know, I know. And all of this is just theories – they don't have any proof of anything, just ideas. Even if they get hold of our message records, there's nothing incriminating here.

It feels like a reminder that someday, someone will read over these texts, flick through our Snapchat memories, go into the archives. We make sure our messages delete after twenty-four hours, but they have ways to find them, right?

I know.

That message feels like the end of a conversation – there are a few more short ones, back and forth, before:

I'm still worried they'll find something. A fingerprint on the wrong branch, bloodstain splatters of a certain velocity on one of our shoes... I don't know, it seems too risky. We're basically lying at this point, by not saying anything. We're telling them, in our own way, that we didn't have anything to do with any of the deaths. If they think otherwise, they'll say we've been deliberately withholding the truth, and we'll likely get an even more severe punishment.

The message feels comforting, and I sag back against the chair in relief, trying to believe what she's saying, to agree, somehow, that everything will be fine, that I'm safe, that *no one's ever going to find out*.

They've done so many tests of everything which came

> **out of the camp, and site isn't closed off for examination anymore. You can't keep stressing over stupid things like that – it's not doing us any good.**

I inhale sharply at that, the insult stark. Somehow, despite us no longer being close, I expected this to bring us all together, to unite us in grief and guilt.

Instead, it appears to have done the opposite.

> **Do you think we should meet? Discuss what happened, figure out what to do next, you know?**

> **Don't be stupid – they know none of us are friends, so why the hell would we meet for a chit-chat?**

> **I just thought it might help…**

I close my eyes, focusing on my breathing, Ethan tense across the table. He reaches out to clasp my hand and I latch on, desperate to feel him beneath me, despite him not knowing what's happening, why I'm such a psycho, why everything's going wrong –

> **Don't think. It's your fault I'm even in this mess now, and another one of us is dead – you two and your grand ideas, as usual. All. Your. Fault.**

All my fault,
    All.
    My.
    Fault.
    Every word feels like a stab of truth.

11

Cold air whips around me, making my cheeks tingle, hands sting. There's a faint waft of exhaust fumes in the air, traffic sounding behind the fence, the gentle thwack of a hockey ball being catapulted into the air, breaking the silence –

"Lucy!" comes a cry, and I turn just in time to see the ball whizzing towards me at a rate of knots, spinning, twisting round and round across the AstroTurf. I whack it back to Nora as she pushes it forward, rushing towards the goal. She smacks it forward, letting out a shriek as it hits the back of the net.

"Fuck yeah!" she screeches, running to high-five me, as the coach whistles to signal the end of practice. "And that, Lucy, is why we needed you back!"

It's Sunday morning, and I'm still in a state of shock from yesterday. I never replied to the messages in the group chat, but the debate went on long after Ethan dropped me back home, giving me a kiss on the cheek that made me shiver for all the wrong reasons.

I'm trying to avoid my phone now, to not think about the messages and the investigation, how the police have asked me to go into the station every day after school for the foreseeable future, to, and I quote, "Work on your story, Lucy."

It's near impossible to ignore my phone as we enter the changing rooms, however, to spot it face-up and buzzing with new messages, perched on a pile of my clothes and lighting up every few seconds in vibrant yellow.

"The Very Best Group Chat –" Nora reads, cutting off as I snatch up my phone and thrust it into my bag. "What's that?"

In all the years we've had that chat – almost seven, I think, longer than I can even remember – we've never bothered to change the name. What seemed cool to ten-year-old Chloe seems more than pathetic now, but to alter it seems almost blasphemous, like admitting that we've grown up and changed, that five has decreased to three.

"Just… just ranger stuff."

I start to unfold my clothes, a fresh pair of socks hidden beneath the same baggy jeans and hoodie I had on yesterday – and the day before. I give them a suspicious sniff before pulling tugging the hoodie on over my hockey shirt, tugging down my shorts and rustling about in my bag for the fresh pair of leggings I grabbed before I left this morning.

The Lucy of three weeks ago would be repulsed.

"Are you not showering?" Alicia's voice sounds from behind us, startling the life out of me. I jump, pivoting to see her stood, hair slick with sweat, wrapped in a towel and still red-faced from practice. "You're gonna *stink* if we go back to yours."

"I'll shower when I'm home." I turn back round, tugging the leggings on over my thighs, then my pants, concealed by the baggy hoodie. "I'll wait for you guys here."

Showering after hockey is common practice at Vibbington. The old school building still has a row of communal showers, and the team have known each other so long that it's not weird getting naked in front of each other, something we don't think twice about. I can hear Nora behind me, tugging off her kit and unclipping her bra, reaching into her bag for her towel.

"Fine." Alicia raises an eyebrow, but claps me on the back anyway, before turning towards the showers. "Well played, by the way. We've missed you out there."

I smile back weakly.

They're only saying that to be nice. I was useless on the field, passing the ball back as soon as it came my way, too exhausted to even attempt a goal, for fear of it stopping before even reaching the goal line. It's like half my Lucy-ness has been zipped out of me. Lucy, the star hockey player and near-girlfriend of Ethan Morgan, would never act like this. She wouldn't sit in silence over a lunch of expensive pancakes and hot chocolate, wouldn't feel too self-conscious to take a shower, worried that everyone would notice the blood splatters on her skin, staining her stomach, her thighs, exploding across her chest. She'd simply exist, like everybody else, without thinking.

If I'm not Lucy anymore, what am I? A mess, that's what I am. A splodge of brown, sludgy mud, stamped on and embedded into the ground, a waste of space, barely worth acknowledging.

I close my eyes, hands gripping the bench, as my phone vibrates in my bag once again.

Piss off, piss off, *piss off* –

Nora drives us back to mine. I've always sat up front, Alicia navigating the playlist from her phone in the back, but the dynamic has clearly shifted. I'm barely even aware of what they're saying as we drive, focused only on the buzz, buzz, buzz of my phone beneath me, vibrating in my hand.

Make. It. Stop.

Mum greets us from the living room once we're back, telling my friends to leave their stuff by the door, she'll get their kits washed before they go home, that she'll bring up a cuppa in a minute; she's just catching up with Strictly on the TV. Nora and Alicia both love my mum, but she's the reason they never want sleepovers at mine. Being an only child means you get special attention from your parents, and being waited on beyond reason loses its gloss after a while.

"How was practice?" She directs this at all of us, but we all know the question is directed at me. My friends reply amicably before turning their attention to me, waiting for me to speak.

"It was fine," is all I can say.

Nora and Alicia let themselves into my room; we've been friends for so long that it's as much their house as it is mine. I disappear into the shower, determined not to take too long, to wash without dwelling on the damage left by the that weekend. I refuse to look down as I stand there, under the stream, counting to ten between washing off my shampoo, conditioner, shower gel. I'm even quicker in pulling on a change of clothes and wrapping my hair in a towel, out and shut inside my bedroom again in under five minutes.

"New record," Nora says.

Mum brings up a plate of biscuits and three steaming mugs of tea a few minutes later, on one of the Emma Bridgewater trays she only ever brings out for guests. She places it on my desk and shakes her head at the state of us all, lounging about on the bed with our textbooks open and unattended, phones out, Nora swiping through TikTok.

I'm staring at my home screen, heart thudding. It's a selfie Alicia took of the three of us, stood in the mirror at Maguires, smiling, laughing, posing for Instagram. In the corner of the screen, the little ghost indicates new messages from Snapchat. I don't click it.

"You girls," Mum's saying, shaking her head as she goes to

leave. "So antisocial…"

She shuts the door with a click, and the three of us listen for her footsteps on the stairs, ears pricked, eyes on the handle.

There's a familiar creak as she reaches the second-to-last step, and we all let out a collective sigh.

She's gone, meaning the coast is now clear to talk.

My friends are silent for a moment, still clutching their phones. Usually, Mum's absence would be a sign to break into chatter, snorting and taking silly photos and spamming the group chat with videos. Not today. Nora glances up at Alicia and the pair share a look, one I can't help but feel uneasy about.

"So…" Alicia starts, voice trailing away. She's sat on my pillow with her back to my headboard, makeup-free and tip-tapping her false nails against her phone. Both my friends are obsessed with mango shower gel, and I can smell it now, wafting around me, filling my nostrils, my head. It smells like blood. That's something you don't think about until you've smelt the tangy scent of somebody else's. "This is a bit awkward, Luce. We wanted to talk to you about…"

Glancing at Nora for help, my best friend picks up where Alicia left off, turning to me and pulling a face. "We want to talk to you about the camp, Luce. I know you don't want to, but… seeing as the police aren't getting anywhere, we thought it might help if you could talk to us about it, about what you went through."

Silence.

I didn't think they'd ever ask… and in a way, that's what I was hoping for. Just one space, one space free of the memories, the questions, the blame, is all I wanted.

Now, even that seems impossible.

"We're not touting for gossip, Lucy, you know that," Nora continues. "We genuinely do just want to help. Neither of us can imagine how traumatic it was for you to have to go through that, and see... see those people die."

It's funny, but seeing three dead bodies wasn't even the most damaging bit. Although we never saw Lexie die, knowing her, hearing that her lifeless corpse was found, bloated and blue in the river, sort of... accustomed me to death, prepared me for the brutality of the world to take such a young life. *Three* dead bodies is just an exaggeration.

But the way in which they were killed, and all the blood, and the sound, that horrid, bone-crunching crush of flesh and sinew and skin beneath the blade of the knife...

Those are the traumatic parts, the parts I can't stop thinking about, dancing round my mind.

"I'm honestly fine," I say. I try my best fake smile, which I almost think is working until Alicia frowns at me, sitting up and reaching out to put a hand on mine. "It was just a lot to process, but I'm working on it, and I feel a lot better after hockey this morning –"

My phone chooses the worst possible moment to buzz, screen lighting up with a new notification. I grab it as soon as it vibrates, thrusting it into my pocket, but not quick enough that Nora doesn't see it, doesn't see the name flash across the screen.

"The Very Best Group Chat," she repeats. "That's the one with your ranger friends, isn't it?"

There's no point denying it. I told her so just hours ago, in the changing room, when Snapchat gave away my secret again. The Very Best Group Chat. Seven years, three fifths of what it once was.

Silence. More silence. Silence so thick you could drown in

it, if I wasn't treading so hard to stay above water.

"What's going on, Lucy?"

I don't like Nora's tone. It doesn't sound like Nora. It's too hard, too cold, too suspicious. Nora knows me better than most people, and yet the way she says that – says my name, *Lucy*, with such confusion – makes my skin crawl, my fingertips tingle, every nerve in my body ready to respond.

"What do you mean?" I ask, but Alicia too has put down her phone and is gazing at me with that same bemused expression.

"Why haven't any of you told the police what happened that weekend?"

The question comes as a blow, another kick in the gut. Alicia is always direct, but I didn't expect her to put it quite so bluntly, so very clearly accusing me.

"You three were *there*. If you'd told the police exactly what happened, they'd have stopped interviewing you by now, and probably released a statement saying exactly how those people ended up dead."

Blood – blood everywhere – drip, drip, dripping. Wind, whipping round our tents in the middle of the night... Shouts and cries and a horrible, thumping stab... Blood dripping down my hands, my neck, my ankles... A seventeen-year-old's screams erupting into the night as she –

I stand, whole body shaking beneath me. Alicia and Nora have stopped, but are now staring at me like I'm the one who's out of order, twin frowns on their faces.

"I feel sick." I hear the words before I register speaking them. I don't feel sick – but I want them to leave. "I think I must be coming down with something... a bug, picked up from hockey this morning. I need rest, but you two should probably leave."

Alicia and Nora exchange confused glances, still sat on my bed, textbooks spread everywhere, waiting to start our study session.

"Luce, we were just trying to –"

"Please. I want to sleep."

I stand, hand propping the door open, until they've packed their stuff away, both friends unspeaking. I stand, hand propping the door open, until they've left, waving goodbye and shouting thank you to Mum from the front door. I stand, hand propping the door open, until my legs give way and I fall to the floor, tears rolling down my cheeks, the whole world falling to pieces around me.

12

I probably shouldn't be doing this. I know it's wrong as I pull on a fresh set of underwear, the new mom jeans I bought about a month ago but haven't had chance to wear yet, the rainbow jumper I thrifted with Nora over summer. I know it's wrong as I straighten my hair, tugging a hand through the knotted parts and brushing the caramel-dipped edges. I know it's wrong as I apply mascara, lip gloss, sitting and staring at myself in the mirror for a good twenty minutes, not moving a muscle.

My phone is virtually dead, but I have just enough battery left to text, sending a single message before placing it back on the floor beside me, face-up. It buzzes with a reply just seconds later.

of courseee x

Which is why I'm now sat here, staring at my reflection, at those wide grey eyes I've always hated, at my button nose and slightly pointed chin, at the spot on my temple – a stress-spot, according to Mum – and the freckles over my nose and cheeks. Lucy. I'm Lucy, and everything's going to be fine.

"Lucy?" Mum's voice sounds from the living room as I hit the creaky second-to-last step, on instinct. "Where are you going?"

I push open the door a crack, peering round the edge to

where my parents are both sat on the sofa, curled up together, arms round one another. They're watching some cooking show on the TV, the blinds closed to block out the blinding setting sun, decorating the room in an orange glow.

"I'm just off out for a few hours," I say, gesturing to the front door, as if that isn't obvious. "I'll be back before eleven."

"Ten," Mum corrects, narrowing her eyes. "You *are* going back to school tomorrow, aren't you?"

Of course. Tomorrow's Monday, and I've already had the requested two weeks away from sixth form. I swallow, nodding and attempting a smile, as Mum sags in relief and waves her hand at me.

"See you at ten, then." She only says that to reinforce the fact I'm *going* to school, that there are no excuses this time, that I have to get back into the swing of things somehow. "Text me if you need picking up, okay, Lucy?"

My phone's now completely dead in my pocket, squatting like a brick against the lining of my coat. There's no point even bringing it, really. But I nod again anyway as I say my goodbyes.

The walk only takes ten minutes or so, but Vibbington is already getting dark. It's cold, too; give it another week, and Christmas will be in full swing, lights erupting in the surrounding neighbourhood and high street filling up till way past nine. Across town, families will be buying presents, shopping for candles and dolls and fucking mango shower gel. Most families, that is. At least two families will sit in silence around a dinner table, the first of many with one piece missing.

I forgot to grab a coat, and the wind whips under my thin jumper and tickles my skin. The sun has almost disappeared behind the row of houses up ahead. I go to turn on my phone, check for messages, but it's still dead, screen sunk to black. I take a piece of gum and place it between my front teeth, sucking the first layer of minty goodness. Chew, chew, chew.

I look good. Pretty. Put together, for the first time in weeks. Nice, normal outfit. Concealer covering that one spot. Mascara, closing the gap between my wide eyes. I look good, but that's not enough to make me *feel* good.

The road is approaching, a turn-off onto a main avenue of houses leading towards the very edge of Vibbington. Houses here are average in size, all cream carpets and sage green front doors, the homes of teachers and social workers and people who write reports about the aforementioned. It's a nice area, a respectable area, and I feel like I'm tainting it just by walking through.

I glance behind me, at the pavement and beyond. Red footsteps, jagged, splatters of crimson here and there. Evidence, clear as day, imprinted on the ground as I move.

Someone's going to notice.

Someone *has* to notice.

Number fifty-one. A clean house, a house with little to hide. I stand at the bottom of the drive for a few moments too long, taking in the front door, newly painted duck egg blue, and the curtains, pulled closed to block out the road in front. A dog barks, heard from within those thick walls, dense with insulation. It's a house not unlike my own, and yet I feel so guilty even turning up here, traipsing someone else's blood through their house –

I knock three times, as usual. There's a shuffling as someone moves something to get to the door – probably Daisy, who's only a few years old, still as boisterous and friendly as a pup. The door opens, peeling back a tad to reveal a sliver of Ethan's perfect face and the even more perfect face of Daisy, who's trying to get out onto the street.

Ethan. My Ethan.

Seeing them stood there – the two things which have started to feel like home these last few weeks – is almost enough to make everything else go away.

"Lucy!"

Lucy. I can't help but beam as he says my name, his expression equally lit as he pulls back the door a crack and hurries to scoop up the excitable Daisy.

"Grab the door and shut it behind you, and come straight upstairs – Mum and Dad are out for the evening with Grandma and her new carer, so they won't be back till late."

I take off my shoes at the door, confining all that blood to his entrance hall, which is as spotless and creamy as the rest of Ethan's house. I know I shouldn't be here, that I'm tainting his house, his family, his heart, by continuing any kind of friendship between us. But I can't help it. I'm being selfish, listening to my heart, the voice inside me insisting it's the only way I'll be okay.

Ethan disappears into the kitchen for a moment, the sound of running water suggesting he's filling up Daisy's bowl and pouring some food to keep her occupied. I'm halfway up the stairs when he appears, shutting the door behind him and leaving Daisy to her evening meal.

"She's super hyper tonight," he explains, as I hang back, waiting for him to join me. "We wouldn't get a word in edgeways…"

I watch, silent, as Ethan passes me. His bedroom door is ajar, the familiar scent of his deodorant wafting across the landing, peppery and full of citrus, the kind they market as *masculine*. He gestures for me to follow, but I can't help smiling, struck by how very Ethan this all is, how sweet and innocent and hopeful. The fact he's very clearly doused himself in deodorant upon my arrival, and made sure to lock Daisy out of the way so we can talk properly.

There's no blood left behind me as I check the carpet, trying to avert my gaze before Ethan catches on.

It's clean, barely even a footprint in sight.

"Shut the door behind you," he calls.

I obey.

Ethan's room has always been messy, but in a typical boyish way rather than a way which seems unclean. He's remembered to hide any dirty laundry and make his bed somewhat, but the floor is still scattered with cushions from where he's been playing Minecraft with Daisy, who's left the carpet covered in fur.

I take a seat on the floor, in my usual spot. There's a tube of Pringles beside me, unopened, a discount sticker from the corner shop still stuck above the logo. They're the green ones, of course. Sour cream. The best flavour.

From where I'm sat, I get a perfect view of the rest of his room, of the bed and its underside, of the walls covered in posters and revision and photos. Unlike me, Ethan always remembers to take pictures of everything, capturing our entire summer in a montage of fish and chips, surfing, blue waves, green fields. He's made posters for every Tudor monarch in preparation for our mocks, and there are digital print-outs of each Minecraft monster alongside these – definitely not for an exam.

Under the bed, amid dust and childhood boxes and forgotten chunks of Lego, lies a single pair of crumpled boxers. Ethan clearly forgot to pick them up as he tidied his room, and so they sit, fusty and used, directly in my line of sight. I feel my cheeks burn as Ethan bustles around, tidying away the revision on his desk and grabbing us both a diet coke from his mini fridge.

Just friends.

That's why I'm here, right?

"Anyway." Ethan pushes the desk chair under and whips past it to get to me. He bends to sit on the floor beside me and passes me one of the diet cokes, already opened. I shuffle backwards to give him space and he leans back, head touching the wall and soft body moulding to fit the cushions.

We've sat in this position so many times that it almost feels instinctive, piecing together like this is how the story's meant to go, how we're meant to be. His hand reaches for the Pringles without thinking, and I take a handful, even though I'm not hungry. Like I said, it's instinct. Ethan is my instinct.

"Anyway," I echo, a smile rubbing the edges of my mouth. "Anyway…"

Usually, we're full of things to say, unable to stop talking.

Today, we can't even start.

Awkward silence ensues, whirling around us, filling the space. There's an elephant in the room; the kiss we shared, all those weeks ago, before everything went wrong, before I ruined whatever could've happened. Ethan breaks the silence by taking a Pringle from his pile and crunching down on it, slowly. I want to laugh at how painful it sounds.

I do the same, the two of us munching without speaking. Munch, munch, munch. Ethan's eyes flit round the room to avoid meeting mine, while my own can't help but settle on his face, the curve of his soft chin, those brown eyes, dark lashes, button nose.

He must have noticed the boxers, the dirty pair lingering beneath his bed, ones he forgot to pick up. I know that because his cheeks have gone all pink and he's squirming as he takes a final Pringle, before turning back to me.

"Lucy…"

Lucy. Even hearing him say my name makes my heartrate speed up, my hands tremble and every inch of my body scream *yes*. I gaze back in as calm a way as is possible, despite the rollercoaster rushing inside me.

"I think we need to talk about what happened the other week. When you… when we kissed."

I hear the words as they enter my brain, but I don't fully register what he's saying until I meet his eyes and they hold, green on brown, that unbreakable gaze.

"Why?"

Ethan frowns, wrinkling his nose. "Because… I don't know. I don't know how you feel, or what you want to happen next, or…"

I can hear my heart pounding in my eardrums, faster and faster, an electric beat that won't stop. Ethan's expression is so innocent, so hopeful, and –

I'm still trying to process my next sentence when he kisses me.

It comes out of nowhere, an explosion of sour cream tinged lips and button nose caressing mine, his eyes closed and lashes brushing his cheeks, mine wide open and staring, too shocked to do anything. I can't even kiss him back, frozen, locked in place before him.

He pulls back the moment I flinch.

"Sorry," he says at once, shaking his head and staring at me in horror, like he's only just realising what he's done. "I shouldn't have –"

"It's – it's fine."

Silence. More silence. Silence which drips from the ceiling

and splashes all around us, covering us in a double dose of more silence, thick and gloopy and –

"But I think we should just be friends."

Before me, Ethan's expression drops. He stares at me for a moment, unsure of what to say, as guilt begins to writhe in my stomach.

"I don't think it would work," I continue, though that's not the reason, not even a little bit.

All the blood... The sound, that horrid, bone-crunching crush of flesh and sinew and skin beneath the blade of the knife...

I can't do it to him. I've been going back and forth, back and forth, trying to figure out what would be best for him, what would be kinder... but I can't let him date a psychopath, a girl full of secrets, a girl who, at any moment, could be carted off to jail on the grounds that three people are dead and she knows more than she's letting on.

I close my eyes, squeezing them tight, as the sound of Ethan's breaths grow shorter, faster.

"I don't... I mean, if that's what you want, then I respect your decision, but... I thought..."

He thought I was normal. That I wanted what he wanted, and that we could be a sweet little sixth form couple, despite everything that's happened over the last few weeks, despite what I've *done*.

"I should go," I say, standing to leave, tipping the tube on its side as I go. There's a horrible splintering nose as tens of Pringles crash together, snapping and cracking and crumbling across Ethan's hair-strewn carpet. "I'll see you at school, yeah?"

"You don't have to go!" He jumps to his feet too, but something is already broken, ruined, the elephant in the room almost doubled in size. "Honestly, Luce, I'm so sorry I took it the wrong way…"

"Bye, Ethan."

The footsteps are back, following me as I walk to the door. Bright red, stark against his deep blue carpet, imperfect, splattering across the floor.

"I…"

I even leave a bloody handprint on the handle of his door.

13

"Lucy? Lucy, it's already eight, and you're going to be late for school…"

Bright lights. Bright, blaring lights, streaming in from between my curtains. It's freezing, and someone's tugging at my sheets, trying to pull them off me.

"Mum!" I open my eyes properly to find Mum there, attempting to wake me by stripping off my duvet. She's right. My phone tells me it's gone eight, and I have six billion messages from Nora and Alicia, telling me they'll be outside to pick me up in fifteen, that I need to be ready by then or they'll leave me behind. There's even a message from Ethan, an apology for what happened last night, but I swipe the notification away so that it's one less thing to think about.

"I'm not going to school today."

Mum frowns, letting go of the duvet and stepping to face me. "What do you mean, not going to school? Two weeks, Lucy. That's what the school promised you, and that's what you're having."

"I'm not going to school today." I hold my phone above my face, covering my expression as I insist. "I'll phone Mr Roberts later, and catch up on the work from the last few weeks."

Mum frowns again, deeper this time, and gives me a little shove so that she can sit on the bed beside me. I don't let my eyes move from the screen, blindly scrolling through

Instagram, trying not to catch her gaze.

"What's the problem with school?" she asks, gently probing. "Is everything okay with Nora and Alicia? Or… is it something else?"

"I'm not ready." Which is the truth. I thought I would be, by now. I thought I would've processed things enough to at least attend my lessons, even if I'm not the life and soul of the party.

But I can't. The thought of "going back to normal" makes me feel faintly nauseous, like yesterday at hockey practice, everything upside down, life not what it once was.

And Ethan. I've messed things up with him, as I should, and I don't have a clue how to face him again.

I can't. I *can't*.

"Are you sure?" Mum looks so concerned that I almost want to cry. She feels sorry for me. I don't know how much I deserve her sympathy, if at all. "A day or two more, if you have to… then you're definitely going back on Wednesday, yes? No compromises. I'll call Mr Roberts for you. You go back to sleep, and make sure you catch up on your work from earlier, yes?"

I nod obligingly as she stands and crosses over to the door, waving before shutting it behind her.

Wednesday. I can do Wednesday.

I nestle back under the covers now, taking my phone down with me, tucked into one hand beneath the sheets. It's still freezing, but I'm filled with relief now, shoulders relaxing as I click back onto my messages.

I need a few more days off to process things, but I'll be back on Wednesday. Sorry about yesterday, I'm just still trying to deal with everything, but it's really hard.

Nora and Alicia pop back up immediately, telling me it's fine, that they understand and they totally don't care about yesterday, that it was clearly just a hard day for me with things starting to get back to normal and everything, and that I should be less hard on myself. They're being lovely, as usual. I don't know how much of what they've said is the truth, or simply them trying to be nice, to not cause conflict.

I leave a comment on Alicia's latest Instagram post to prove that I really *am* sorry, that I didn't mean to act that way yesterday. It's a compilation of selfies and outfit pics, Alicia looking ridiculously cool in her early 2000s inspired baggy jeans and bold eye makeup, staring sultrily into the camera with her hand tugging the waistband down. I even share it to my story, captioning it with something cringy about how gorgeous my bestie is, and she replies with an abundance of heart and aubergine emojis in seconds.

So that's *that* smoothed over.

I message Ethan next, clicking onto his funny little Bitmoji and scrolling through the string of apology messages he's sent me. They're all pretty much a variation of the same thing, apologising for the kiss and for assuming I wanted to be anything more than friends when I'm clearly going through a lot right now, which is the understatement of the century. He's as sweet as ever, just like my friends, clearly feeling horribly guilty about it all. But I can't go back on what I said last night.

He's too good for me. Far too good. Far too good for… for what I've become.

I tell him I'm sorry too, but that I hope we can just go back to being friends. I tell him I'll be back at school on Wednesday, that I'll see him then. That I'm sorry I spilt his Pringles.

Hey, don't worry about it! Of course we can, you're one of my favourite people, silly. I'll see you Wednesday, Mr O'Flannel is expecting us to have full essay drafts ready for the last piece of coursework, so beware… x

How can anyone ever deserve someone as perfect as Ethan Morgan?

I lounge in bed for a little later, unable to bring myself to move. There's nothing else interesting on Instagram or Facebook or TikTok as I scroll through each for the hundredth time, watching Nora's Snapchat selfies another thousand times before giving up. There's a collection of emails from the universities whose mailing lists I've signed up to, but nothing appeals to me less right now than finishing my personal statement and browsing through undergraduate courses I'm too scared to apply to.

The Very Best Group Chat has been inactive over the last few hours. I don't know why I do what I do next; I don't know why I click it. I don't know why I scroll down in the chat options, to where all past media has been saved, locked away in a Snapchat folder that we once thought would last the test of time.

Seven years of photos. Seven years of memories, of photos turned grey with one click.

Seven years of us, the very best of friends, the group that was meant the last.

The most recent saved photos are from a good few months ago, before summer, on a day out we had to the beach one random day in June. Silly selfies taken by Chloe, or more posed shots for her Instagram, thong-split bum stretched towards the camera as waves splash against her thighs. The four of us, stood in a row, grinning at Sharon as she took the photo, all of us in bikinis and holding up peace signs to the sky.

Instagram never saw any of these, unsurprisingly. Chloe, Orla, Kayleigh and I have always kept our friendship completely offline, since Lexie died and we began to drift apart. I don't know if we were embarrassed to admit that we still knew each other, or whether it didn't fit our aesthetic. Chloe's Instagram is too Chloe to include any of us, filled with selfies and underwear shots, photos taken on her tripod against concrete backdrops or in bars, restaurants. The rest of us are more lowkey. The odd selfie when we're really feeling ourselves, and photos with friends, prom and results day and birthdays, at a push.

I scroll further, onto other outings, still as a four, like we have been for the last five years. Occasionally, Sharon will pop in, her head taking up most of the screen within a cringy selfie or landmark shot for her Facebook, or to send to Steve. Steve himself even took a few of these photos, the ones including the four of us and Sharon, stood by road signs after a hike, or pointing at the car, filled with goodies, ready to drive off to a camp.

I'm scrolling so, so far – too far – and soon I'm in dangerous territory, so far within the chat that four turns into five, teens to children. Lexie's grey-eyed stare penetrates the camera, those tiny, inward-bending teeth and wispy hair, the way she always looked out of place, never really felt like one of us. I'll admit that, now. As much as we liked her – or I liked her, more like – she never really *fit in*.

I'm at the bottom now, the very first photo we ever took as a group. It's just a selfie in someone's room, heavily filtered, but we're all smiling, looking almost *too* happy for

once.
 Lexie. Chloe. Kayleigh. Orla.
 And me, little Lucy, stood in the middle, smiling wide.
 Smiling wide, like she could do no fucking wrong.

14

I manage to catch up on quite a bit of work, somehow. I force myself to write until my hands both ache and so does my head, and I can barely focus on the textbook for my eyes darting back and forth. I go downstairs to make some cheese on toast at eleven, slicing the expensive stuff Dad buys because no one's here to stop me, placing four thick slices under the grill, watching the oven as my stomach grumbles.

I eat it sat at the island, sunlight pouring in through the window, with an apple, to balance it out. Another three spots have appeared across my hairline since yesterday, probably due to my stress now skyrocketing, and the cheese on toast just makes me feel even more greasy, disgusting. I lick the oil off my fingers to hide any evidence, but it's not enough to stop me from snaffling a bag of cheese and onion crisps, Mum's guilty pleasure, from the carousel.

I get dressed, too, into leggings and a hoodie I'm pretty sure used to be Nora's, and squirt a load of dry shampoo into my hair to hide the grease. It's twelve, now. There are three hours to kill until I have to leave.

I end up with Netflix on while I wait, the same old shows repeating, not taking much in. I keep scrolling through Instagram, expecting something to change, someone new to pop up, but it's the same as ever, insisting I'm "all caught up".

One.

One thirty.

Two.

Two thirty…

I set off early, heading out of the back door and leaving it unlocked for me to get back in later, if Mum and Dad are still out. I lost my keys a few weeks ago, and they still haven't had time to find me a replacement. Instead, I check no one's watching and slip out of the side gate, just in case. Then I set off down our road and into Vibbington.

The police said they wanted to speak to me every day after school this week, as soon as I could get there, from three thirty onwards. Extended questioning, until they get to the bottom of what happened. The other two girls can't get there until later, and so have their interviews in rooms set side by side, with separate officers. In a way, I wish I didn't live so close to the station, didn't still attend Vibbington Secondary… I'd quite like to be interviewed with the others, see them in the waiting room before and after. It would transfer a little of the guilt from me to them, if anything.

It's a half an hour walk, at most, but the day is cold and I'm slow on my feet, which are numb and frozen in my trainers, like icebergs. Wind whips up my jeans and the hoodie which most definitely seems borrowed from Nora – there's a pizza stain on the sleeve, and train tracks where she's previously wiped her nose – and I have to fish about in the pocket for a pair of gloves, convinced my fingers will otherwise drop off.

The waiting room is empty, as usual, no receptionist behind the desk, even the bell removed from where it usually sits on the other side of the Perspex screen. I know where to knock this time, however, so I try Pudrow's room, using three sharp raps to get his attention. It only takes a few seconds for movement to be heard on the other side of the door, and for it to then creak open, that familiar potbelly appearing in my sight.

"Lucy!" he greets me, holding out a hand to shake mine and grinning, like he wasn't expecting me to turn up so early. "Come through to the interview room, I'll get Joy. We've got some developments to talk you through…"

Which is the exact point at which my stomach drops.

Developments.

They've found something out, found something on one of the bodies, on the DNA lifted from nearby objects, the surrounding woodland, the clifftops. They've found something to incriminate us, something which says we had more part to play in one of those deaths than we're letting on, than we want anyone to know –

I keep my breath held as Pudrow knocks on Officer Joy's door, waits for her to come and join us in the corridor before unlocking the interview room. That familiar box, each surface painted cream, table slap-bang in the centre, waiting for us to take our seats.

So I do. I sit central to the table, Pudrow and Joy opposite, as usual. They're not recording. The whole thing feels informal, almost friendly, like we're having a cosy chat over a cup of tea.

"So…" Officer Joy begins, pulling out a sheet of paper from her file, placing it flat on the table before us. "We have official post-mortems back from all three of the victims, which is huge progress. It took so long because in cases like these, we need to be certain. All have been positively identified by family members, but now that we have the causes of death and times of death verified, we can really start to ramp up the investigation."

Her finger jabs the photo of Steve first, frowning down at

it, like she can't quite understand. "The most troubling part of the results is undoubtedly Steve Jones. We think he died last, which doesn't line up to the idea that Carl Hall killed the other two victims, as we originally suspected. Steve Jones suffered critical stab wounds to his lower abdomen and kidneys, several on both his left and right sides."

I close my eyes as she says this, trying to control the blood pulsing round my head, faster and faster. *Critical stab wounds. His official cause of death.* Hearing that makes me feel ill, physically ill, throat thick with bile and guilt, memories flooding back, unstoppable –

"And then there's Carl Hall. He also suffered stab wounds, but is estimated to have died at *least* twenty-four hours prior to Steve, which really makes no sense at all. He's the only one with a violent criminal past, so for him to have died before Steve… unless Steve's injuries kept him alive for hours before he eventually stopped breathing, which the evidence suggests wasn't the case, we have a real conundrum on our hands." Officer Pudrow says this without his eyes leaving my face, as though to try and spot any changes to my demeanour, to the way I respond. "Unless you three had a part to play in Steve's death, after the murders of our other two victims, we really have no other explanation."

"Finally," Officer Joy takes over, shaking her head, "is our youngest victim, your friend. Strangulation. Then three blows to the head, which we believe finished her off – and a stab to her chest, which missed her heart and any vital cords. But you already knew all of this, didn't you, Lucy? You were there, after all. You saw exactly how they died."

I can feel my eyes filling up with unwanted tears before I have a chance to eject them, shaking my head, heart heavy and hands clenched into fists. The times all match up a little too perfectly, spelling out exactly where we must've been that night, and the next, how we can't deny that Steve died almost a whole day after the other two... meaning, like Pudrow said, he was either killed by the three of us, or his wounds took twenty-four hours to kill him, while the three of us lay around the camp with two dead bodies and Sharon's unconscious lump before finding help.

If this wasn't all speculative – if the three of us weren't staying quiet – they'd be able to join each of the dots they're trying so hard to loop together. They'd know why the times don't match their theories, why four girls and their leader went into that camp and three came out alive, Sharon in a coma and two other men dead. They'd know why Steve and Carl were present, even, and why Carl's DNA was all over Sharon –

"Lucy." Officer Joy switches to her serious voice now, the one she uses to prove that she's not messing around. She's watching me carefully, eyes narrowed, and Pudrow is doing the same, only not so... *accusatorily*. "Lucy. We really need to find out what happened to those people, so that we can get justice. We're being given another week to follow our leads, before the high level officers come up from London to help on the case... and anything you're hiding, they will find. We only want justice, Lucy. Justice for your friend, and for Sharon, and for her husband. Even justice for Carl Hall, should he deserve it."

"We didn't want to interview you any further today," Pudrow continues, taking the papers from Joy and shuffling them in his hands. He perfects them until each aligns in a rectangular pile, then stands, pushing back his chair so that it scrapes against the floor. "We'll continue tomorrow, once you've had a time to process this. Go home, talk to your parents, and come back tomorrow evening, okay?"

I nod. There's nothing else left to say.

Outside, I say goodbye to Joy and Pudrow before I make my way into the car park and out onto the road. I wait until I'm on the street before stopping, taking shelter behind a short brick wall and crouching down while I type my message, hands trembling.

> **We need to reconsider our stories. They know the others died twenty-four hours before Steve, and so they suspect that we killed Steve. The only other option would be that Steve was killed by an outsider, someone who maybe came into the camp and killed the other two, as well, before trying to get Steve, too. We called for help before he could kill any of us, too. It sounds ludicrous, but I don't know what else we're supposed to say. It's that or maybe that Steve and Carl fought, killing Carl and injuring Steve, and that Steve then died the next day from his injuries. Shall we meet to talk about it, or do a group call? They won't ask any questions tonight because they're just updating us on the post-mortem results, but don't say anything yet anyway. Delete this message as soon as you receive it.**

I stand, pocketing my phone and leaving the station as though everything's under control.

15

My phone finally buzzes with a response while we're eating tea that night, curled up on sofas in the front room, quick jacket potatoes with an abundance of filling dumped on each. My parents are focused entirely on the screen, and don't seem to notice as I slip out my phone from within my pocket and frown down at the screen.

One new message from The Very Best Group Chat.

We can't meet up or do a group call, that's literally the most suspicious thing ever. If us three even interact outside of snap, they'll know something's going on, stupid.

One of the four icons at the bottom of the screen is bobbing up and down, indicating that she's still typing, that she has more to say.

The idea that there was another person who came onto the camp and killed them all is stupid, because we would've just said that in the first place. There has to be a reason we haven't wanted to say anything about how they died, but something that won't actually incriminate us.

Mum and Dad still haven't noticed, laughing out loud at the quiz show on the TV, backs to me. Dad reaches over to pat Mum's hand as they continue to watch, so sickeningly pure that my stomach flips over.

Something that won't actually incriminate us… but that we were scared to say all along, just in case it would.

I start typing, fingers fast as they race across the screen.

The only option is that Steve took longer to die but got injured in a fight with Carl, because… because he assaulted Sharon, and Steve caught him. They fought, and we all tried to intervene, but one of us got stabbed in the process. We were trying to keep her and Steve alive and didn't want to call for help because we were terrified, and didn't tell the police before now because we were worried us waiting longer than we should've is what caused all three to die???

My story doesn't sound *completely* ludicrous. The police know Carl had sex with Sharon, whether it was consensual or not, and that – according to them, though the thought makes me feel sick to my stomach with guilt – could have been enough for Steve to fight him, with a knife, and fatally wound him.

But then there's the third death, the death of one of us, the harmless rangers, camping there that night. Strangulation. *Three blows to the head, which we believe finished her off – and a stab to her chest, which just missed her heart and any vital cords.* That's no accident, not something harmless intervention could cause.

That would make no sense, given her injuries. The reply is instant, echoing my thoughts exactly, ones I wish she'd just ignore. **Strangulation and multiple blows, including a stab wound, points to murder. We're in a hole, Lucy. Whichever way we turn, we've blocked ourselves in.**

That's when the third party joins the chat, two little faces peering up at me instead of one. I pause – and start typing again.

Then we tell them about a stranger… a man, say, who killed Carl and injured Sharon, then came after us and Steve. He managed to kill one of us and stab Steve, and then fled the scene because we'd already found the phone box and called for help. We were too scared to tell the police until now because he's still out there, and could kill more campers. He was just a psycho, a crazed madman who wanted to stab some innocent people that weekend.

It's not the worst idea we've had. It ties up all of the loose ends, puts a stop to the theory that we had anything to do with the deaths, that we're to blame in any way. It gives everyone answers – answers they deserve.

Because a psycho did kill one of us that weekend.

He just wasn't a stranger.

The other girl is typing now, feeling the need to put her two cents in, as usual. My eye roll is so big you can practically hear it. I realise then that I haven't taken a mouthful of my tea in at least five minutes, and it's already going cold.

Baked potato, skin crispy and seasoned with salt and pepper, covered in warmed-up chilli con carne and heaps of cheese. I play with pieces of lettuce and tomato as she continues to type.

The chances of a serial killer in Yorkshire getting onto our campsite and creeping into our tents to kill us, even though he was so outnumbered, is pretty much zero to none. Plus, why were Steve and Carl on the site? As far as the police know, five people went on the camp that weekend… us four, and Sharon.

She continues, though each message is making me feel even

more sick, chilli swirling through my stomach.

They had no reason to connect Sharon and Carl, because there isn't even a record of the two messaging. They're literally just Facebook friends and that's it. And why was Steve there? He wasn't supposed to be. A camp for four rangers and their leader, and the leader's husband just happens to turn up out of the blue, find another man in his wife's tent... and then a psycho serial killer turns up and tries to kill all three of them.

A final message, the most blunt, putting an end to all of our ideas:

Whether the police think Sharon was assaulted or that she was having an affair with Carl is up to them, but either way, it gives Steve a motive for wanting him dead. If they figure out Steve killed Carl, it's maybe feasible that they fought and both were injured, it just took longer for Steve to pass away. But who killed one of us rangers? Strangulation, blows to the head, and a stab wound. Murder. They'll either think it's us, or that Steve or Carl killed her, and that we killed them in return to get revenge. It's the only way things work, and we'll be in deep shit if that's the conclusion they come to.

I hate how pragmatic she sounds, how she's gone through every final detail to see where the police could find loopholes, where they could tear our story to shreds.

But she's right. Even though the police are so lost, so confused about what really happened that weekend, they have enough evidence to say what definitely *didn't* happen.

So... what do we do? I type. **What are we going to say?**

Nothing. Another instant reply, lighting up my screen. **We say nothing.**

Nothing. Saying nothing is easier said than done. You can't simply deny the fact that three people are dead and we know what happened, when we were there and saw the blood run from all of those stab wounds, skin turn pale and waxy, eyes roll back into skulls. They know we were there, and they know that we know what happened, no matter what they say. Denying the fact that we have all the answers will only make them more suspicious.

What happened that weekend?
Nothing.
What did you see?
Nothing.

16

The next day is spent in pretty much the same way. Catching up on work, emailing teachers to pass on assignments I never got done the weekend everything happened, and eating junk food in front of Netflix. I still have mocks coming up over the following weeks, but thinking about impending university applications and subsequent rejections makes me feel beyond queasy. I call the station to ask if I can go in for my interview a little earlier today, and Officer Joy says that's fine, that they're looking forward to seeing me as usual.

So I do. I walk there all by myself, dressed in skinny jeans and little ankle boots, a nice top, hair straightened. I walk straight there and press the bell, one, two, three, four times, ring-ring-ring, until Joy appears from within her office and gives me a little wave. She's wearing a thick scarf over her uniform today, fluffy socks peeping over her police boots, and offers me a cup of tea as I approach – "The kettle has just boiled!"

It's becoming familiar, the ritual of going into the station and taking my seat, opposite the two officers, smiling and nodding, hands gripped together beneath the table all the while. But not today. I unlatch my fingers and wrap them around the mug, taking long, forced gulps of the murky brown liquid labelled "tea" by Joy.

It's cold. December is sneaking up faster than expected, and both officers are prepared for the impending chill. I'm wearing a puffer coat, but am tempted to take it off as I stare at them. My face grows hotter and hotter and hotter.

I'm going to say nothing. It's already been decided. All of us, the three survivors, are all saying nothing. I don't fully understand the logistics of that, but it made total sense last night, and I'm holding onto that. What happened, Lucy? Nothing, nothing, nothing –

"So."

Joy goes through the usual, reeling off what happened, the evidence they have so far, why certain parts don't make sense, why they're confused. She's poised to ask the same questions they always ask, gazing at me across the table as though to read every slight change in my expression. I stay silent, face neutral. Neutral.

Dad is making tacos tonight, with homemade guacamole and a veggie chilli. I focus on that; it's easier than trying to keep my mind blank. I promised I'd stop by a shop and pick up some avocados on my way home, ones that are perfectly ripe. Soft to touch, but not so squishy that the flesh beneath is bruised and brown, turning from sage to olive.

"Shall we pick up from where we left off yesterday, Lucy?" Officer Joy asks, smiling and cocking her head to one side. "We were talking about the injuries the victims suffered, which led to their deaths, in some cases. You didn't seem surprised when we told you about each, so we assume you already knew those facts."

As far as officers go, I don't think Joy is very good at her job. I didn't think they handled Lexie's death well at all, all those years ago, but this investigation is even more of a shambles. *We assume you already knew those facts.* Putting words in my mouth, Joy. You're putting words in my mouth.

When Lexie's body was confirmed to be drowned, they

could tell that she'd fallen from the tyre swing. They disregarded her death as an accident immediately. She was found in a lifejacket, floating downstream, far away from the camp, blue and limp and lifeless. The tyre was swinging above the river, instead of in its usual holding space, on the decking.

What they failed to recognise is that for Lexie to fall from the moving tyre swing, someone would have had to hoist her up, over the river, high enough for her to drop and hit the centre of the river, which was moving so fast it would've been impossible for her to be saved.

Someone else had clearly been with her that night, but that was never considered, or even seen as important to the case. Lexie's death was viewed as an accident by everyone other than her family and the four of us, who felt too guilty about the torture we'd put her through to say anything to the contrary. We felt awful enough about the reason Lexie was up on that tyre.

We'd all taken turns that day to swing over the river, whooping with laughter and tipping back our heads as we soared through the canopy, hair sailing out behind us. Chloe, Kayleigh, Orla and I, braver than expected, shrieking and insisting the experience had been complete and utter bliss as we discussed it in our swimsuits and life jackets, the hot August sun beating down through the trees.

We all had a go, taking turns, patiently waiting in the water below.

Except Lexie.

She was too scared, terrified of falling. We all knew it. Chloe teased her mercilessly, daring her to have a go later that evening, black eyes glinting. But Lexie was sensible. We never would've expected her to go back that night and attempt to take the tyre swing all by herself...

Expect the unexpected. Trust no one – not even yourself. Two things I've learnt over the last two and a half weeks, things I wish I could unlearn, strip my mind of. Paranoia and doubt. I feel like I'm drowning in both.

Officer Joy stares at me all the while as I think, lips zipped firmly shut. Pudrow does the same. I knit and unknit my fingers on my lap. I'm saying nothing. So are they.

Until Joy tips her head to one side again, frowning at me, and jabs at the table with a finger.

"Okay, Lucy. If you won't cooperate, here's a new tactic. We're going to recount the weekend from start to finish, as far as we know what happened, and you're going to cut in and correct us whenever we get anything wrong. Is that okay?"

I say nothing still, holding her gaze steady. I don't like that plan. It sounds too good to be true, too much like a trap. Not that I can cut in and correct her, anyway. There are too many details which would give something away.

Joy lowers her voice then, gazing at me intently, her expression screaming, *Trust me!*

"We're not accusing you of anything, Lucy," she adds. Pudrow nods, the two of them with eyes fixed on me, still monitoring my expression so closely. "Innocent until proven guilty, as I'm sure you've heard. We don't think you're a bad person, but there's something you're hiding about that weekend. I've known you five years, Lucy, and you've never been uncooperative before, have you, now? Let's not make this a first."

"Okay," I say. "Fine."

"Let's start at the beginning," Joy continues. She has a stack of papers which smell fresh from the printer, and droop in that still-warm fashion. She angles them upwards so that I can't see a thing.

Then she starts reading.

"So, Lucy. You started the camp with Chloe Alize, Orla Lloyd, and Kayleigh Kettering, on November 8th, a Friday evening. You all caught a lift with Sharon Jones, with the tents and extras travelling in a separate car, driven by your own mother. Is that correct so far?"

The date. Dates aren't something I tend to remember. I know we all drove there with Sharon, of course – arguments about music choices, the lack of mobile signal, food, Chloe boasting about the boy she's still dating now – and that Mum followed behind with the food and tents and firewood.

But I don't remember the date.

I shrug at Joy, nonchalant.

"You were having an autumnal themed camp. Sharon had grown her own butternut squashes, and you were going to be carving them first, like you would pumpkins, then cooking with them over the fire. Am I right? You arrived there that night after school, and unpacked the tent and things – we have photograph evidence from Chloe and your mum, obtained the following Monday when police arrived."

Joy turns onto the next page, eyes flickering up to me before continuing. "You slept in three tents that night. Sharon had one, you and Chloe another, Kayleigh and Orla a third. As far as we know, it was just the five of you there that night. The next day, we have photos of a breakfast buffet cooked over the fire, and of an early morning walk to see the sunrise over the cliffs. You hiked there and back through a forest, then spent the morning doing team-building activities back at the camp. Soup for lunch, and another hike in the afternoon. Sharon left the camp around six to collect pizza, and we think she left the gates to the campsite open when she returned. You ate the pizza, then she left you alone around the fire before you went to bed a while later.

"We have photos of Chloe and you – selfies, amongst racier shots – from inside the tent around eleven. Can I confirm that I have the day correctly documented so far, Lucy?"

Again, I shrug.

Does she? Who knows.

"This is where the documentation dies. Chloe doesn't take another photo after you and her enter the tent on Saturday night. Not a single one. You aren't found by the police until Monday afternoon."

Does she mean to sound this thick?

"Somehow, Carl Hall enters the camp on this Saturday night. To recap, he has a record for GBH, and is known for being – for want of a better term – *dodgy*. The gates of the camp appeared to be open, so we assume Sharon either forgot to close them, or left them open. She either left them open for Carl to enter – or for Steve, who arrived shortly after Carl.

"Sometime during the night, Carl and Sharon had sexual intercourse. We still can't establish whether this was consensual. All we know from this point onwards is that Steve Jones, Sharon's husband, entered the camp, and both he and Carl died – Carl first, presumably that night, sometime after midnight. This is also assumed to be when Sharon ended up unconscious, Steve dying from his injuries twenty-four hours later, early on Monday morning."

She's just recounted things we've been over a million times before, things she doesn't actually need to say. I know what's coming next. It's obvious. There's no need to wait around, to beat about the bush, for want of a better phrase.

"Your friend also died during this time frame, sometime during the night, early on Sunday morning, around the same time as Carl Hall. We don't know why, or who inflicted her injuries, but it was clearly murder, a deliberate attempt to end her life. We don't in any way believe that you three aren't aware of how that happened – you were all there, and either had a part in her death, or at least saw what happened in some way. Do you have anything to add, Lucy? Do you want to tell us how your friend died?"

"She has a name." That's all I can say, all I can manage to croak out. "She has a name, and you can say it without triggering me."

Officer Joy exchanges a glance with Pudrow, one which speaks wary volumes. Then she turns back to me. We hold eyes for another moment or two before she opens her mouth, my eyes trained on her lips as she speaks.

"Okay, Lucy. Do you want to tell us how Kayleigh died?"

17

Kayleigh Kettering. Brown hair, thick eyebrows, a sludgy, badly tanned complexion. She was the kind of girl to always chew gum and smother herself in foundation, painting her nails in cheap polish or sticking on Primark falsies with a ton of nail glue. I've known her my whole life, watching her grow up beside me into a complete mess, falling apart six hundred times before finally piecing herself together again, just months before she died.

The four of us technically went to primary school together, though I can't remember much about our first impressions. I still have all our earliest class photos, years before we became best friends, a tight-knit group of four. Kayleigh was chubby as a four-year-old, all dark hair and frumpy pinafore-clad body, a frown already etched across her face. A wannabe. She was desperate in every sense of the word.

Starting with our friendship, with the creation of The Very Best Group Chat. I was never that close to Kayleigh, not even after sleepovers and parties, after we'd all dressed in the same room, shared innocent kisses during truth or dare. She was the girl I got on with least, out of the three of them. Orla was my bestie, my ride or die, and Chloe I looked up to, like we all did. I always thought Kayleigh was pathetic, if I can admit that now. She was just so… bland. She wanted to fit in so much that the desire to be liked consumed her completely, stole any personality she'd once had.

She'd mock Lexie along with Chloe, agree with Chloe's jibes at the other girls in our class, copy Chloe's every move, every word. We were all a bit like that, but Kayleigh took it to the extreme. It was like she was terrified of anyone knowing the real her, so much so that she folded into a ball and stayed like that, all wrapped up, the whole time I knew her, all those long years.

From being four to being seventeen, growing up together, side-by-side, through thick and thin… I might not have been emotionally close to Kayleigh, but we weren't exaggerating when we all agreed she was more like a sister to us than a *friend*.

It's usually cringeworthy, seeing someone try so cripplingly hard to fit in, to be liked. With Kayleigh, it was just painful. Especially after Lexie died.

In some ways, I blame myself for the way Kayleigh shifted that following year. After Chloe ditched us for a group more popular, a group with more influence and a matching reputation, Orla and I never made an effort to include Kayleigh in our own pair. With Chloe gone, we didn't have anything in common with the brown-haired tagalong we really knew next to nothing about, and did everything we could to show her we maybe weren't the ones for her.

That was when Kayleigh met Ben Margate.

Chloe's ex-boyfriend, the boy she'd lost her virginity to at just thirteen years old. The prospect of sex seemed so alien to us as innocent little year eights, listening with wide eyes one night at a Guides' meeting as Chloe told us what she'd done, how it had happened, how much it had hurt. Kayleigh had been the most shocked, mouth open wide as Chloe talked, clearly unsure of how to take it and yet still so in awe.

None of us should have even been considering sleeping with boys at that age. Ben Margate was in year ten, and the fact he'd even taken advantage of such young girls is awful enough – it's easy to see that, now. When he broke up with Chloe, she acted like she wasn't bothered, like it was his loss, but it was clear that it had hurt her more than she ever let on. She wasn't used to rejection. Everyone liked Chloe, wanted to be her friend.

I don't know whether Kayleigh approached Ben or Ben approached Kayleigh, but soon they were an item, splayed across Kayleigh's Instagram in the form of heavily filtered selfies and photos and comments. Ben Margate, kissing her neck as she pouted at the camara; Ben Margate, hands on her waist, posing in the mirror; Ben Margate, Ben Margate, Ben Margate.

Kayleigh told us she'd slept with him just a few weeks after Chloe, in a sudden move which shocked us all. Chloe had been thirteen, sure, but *Chloe* at thirteen was a completely different person to Kayleigh at thirteen. Kayleigh still struggled with times tables and spelling, and used "ur" and "tbh" in English essays. She was in year eight, for God's sake. I'm almost finishing sixth form, and still haven't even come *close* to having sex.

I still remember Chloe's face as she told us this, divulging the information as though it was something she didn't see as surprising. "He stayed at mine last night, snuck in through the window after Mum and Dad went to bed. I don't know what you were on about, Chloe. It didn't hurt at all."

Part of me always wondered if she was lying.

I don't know how what happened next actually came about, but Orla and I always speculated that Chloe was still seeing Ben behind Kayleigh's back. Kayleigh didn't really seem that interested in Ben, perhaps more interested in the spectacle of having a boyfriend than in him as a *person*, but was so desperate to keep him as hers that she was prepared to do some pretty stupid things.

We were all on Snapchat by then, used to taking "sexy" selfies. They usually comprised of pouts and too much mascara, maybe a bare shoulder at a push, but some girls – and some boys, some very stupid boys – went a step further, taking inappropriate photos and banking on the fact they'd be deleted. We had assemblies in school about how wrong this was, how, since we were still children, this was classed as child pornography, a concept we couldn't really get our heads around. We didn't feel like children. We felt so… grown-up.

Kayleigh wasn't just stupid – she was downright thick. She didn't send her nudes to Ben Margate over social media, deleting themselves the minute he opened them. She sent them as a text. She sent them as a text, where they downloaded to his fucking *gallery*.

There was never actually any evidence that it was Chloe who leaked the photos, using an anonymous Instagram account. Ben might have been a weirdo, but he wasn't malicious. He genuinely seemed to like Kayleigh, and wouldn't have wanted to admit to the world that he was seeing a thirteen-year-old and receiving explicit photographs from her at age fifteen. The photos were only up for a few minutes, but that was enough time for the owner of the account to follow as many kids in our year as they could think of, and for said kids to circulate the link until it was rendered unfound.

Her parents had to get involved, and the school administration… Ben Margate's family, the headteacher, probably even the police, though if it really *was* Chloe who posted those photos, we never saw her in trouble. I can't imagine the embarrassment Kayleigh must've faced, and I can't say I blamed her for it. We all do stupid things when we're kids, though Kayleigh took it to a whole new level. She trusted Ben. She was *thirteen*, and had no prior experience of talking to boys, of playing trust in their hands. It could've happened to any of us; Kayleigh was just unlucky.

Going to Throwsley High changed her for the better, though she was still just as eager to be liked as she always had been. No one there ever found out about the scandal to our knowledge, but some kids in Vibbington kept screenshots as ammunition, and would taunt Kayleigh with them in the weeks before she transferred schools. It was hard to view her in the same light after we'd seen the photos, anyway… Orla and I both felt that. Even though we'd known her almost all our lives, seen her getting dressed before, there was something horribly intimate about the pictures, the pose, the soft lighting, the intention behind them. It felt like something we really, really shouldn't have seen.

She didn't have another boyfriend until this year, as far as I know. She started posting pictures of him back in March or April. Brown hair, flat smile, soft hoodies and too-baggy jeans. He looked nice, simple, safe. Comfortable. His name was Dan, and they would pose together in photos, smiling pristinely as she held him down. She almost couldn't come on that camp, but it turned out her boyfriend was taking her on a weekend away for her birthday the previous weekend, which felt like good luck. I wonder whether he's kicking himself as much as we are, now.

He was at the funeral. It looked like his parents had bought his suit, which hung a little awkwardly, too baggy around the bum and sleeves. We introduced ourselves, the three survivors, and his cheeks were stained red as he shook our hands.

"Kayleigh told me so much about you," he said, trying to smile. "She... I think she really liked you all. She showed me the pictures from the camps you used to go and stuff. You seemed really close."

"She was more like a sister to us than a friend," Chloe said, falsely. That was where the phrase was first penned, flying out of Chloe's mouth as we stared at her in disbelief. Dan didn't seem to question this. Kayleigh clearly hadn't confessed to him about the photos, about the part Chloe had played in forcing her to move schools. "I'm really sorry for your loss, Dan. She told us a lot about you, too. She must've really loved you."

Another lie. Kayleigh never really brought him up, probably conscious that the last time she boasted so much about a boy, it completely blew up in her face.

"Hopefully they get to the bottom of what happened to her," he added, eyes softening, shoulders relaxing. He clearly thought we could be trusted, like we all had a shared love for his girlfriend – ex-girlfriend. We nodded back at him, though there was an uncomfortable level of truth running between us.

Hopefully they won't get to the bottom of what happened to her, is what we were all thinking. Hopefully. Nothing is guaranteed.

It was a nice funeral. Her parents stayed strong, Dan stood beside them throughout, controlling his bottom lip. There was only one sibling to comfort, a sister a year younger than us, silent and mature, the picture of composed. There were no grandparents nursing squash or biscuits with tremulous hands, few aunties and uncles and cousins, hardly any friends.

Both grandmas were dead, and her only surviving grandfather lived in Australia, streaming the service online.

None of our parents attended with us, unlike Lexie's funeral. I won't say it was because they cared less – they'd known Kayleigh for much longer than Lexie, after all – but maybe the spectacle had worn off. They'd already attended one friend's funeral. Why get the day off work for another?

Kayleigh Kettering was cremated; Lexie was, too. Both ashes were scattered into the surrounding countryside, some left to bury at the foot of a simple headstone in Vibbington's cemetery.

Kayleigh Kettering. Beloved friend, daughter, grandchild, niece.

Sorely missed and loved by all.

18

Officer Joy watches me, trying to gauge my reaction to her saying Kayleigh's name out loud.

"Okay, Lucy. Do you want to tell us how Kayleigh Kettering died?"

No. No, I don't. I don't want to tell her how Kayleigh died. I don't want to tell her anything. What right does she have to know? The person who did it is *dead*, the sequence of events leading to her murder already put to bed. It won't bring Kayleigh back. Nothing will. She was cremated, her body burnt, ashes now flying through the wind as we speak, blown away across the universe.

And, like I said, what right does she have to know? That's something people don't seem to question. Why do we give the police so many answers, tell them the truth about things they're not involved in? Unless they can help us serve justice, what gives them the right to be so pompous and self-absorbed, to assume they deserve *answers*?

"Then how about you tell us your version of events, Lucy? Talk us through what happened that weekend, and how your friend ended up in the position she did. Tell us the proper timeline, and we can talk it through, make sense of things. You're not in any trouble, Lucy, and things will be so much better for you if you just tell the truth. We're constantly finding new information all the time, increasingly incriminating on all fronts. If there's anything you're scared to tell us, it'll be so much better for everyone if it comes from you first."

What happened that weekend?

Nothing.

That's what we agreed. That's what we agreed to say, what we all decided was best. Now, more than ever before, I'm tied to Chloe and Orla in a way that means I don't want to go against their promise in any way. We've seen so much together, done so much. They know the truth of what I'm capable of – and vice versa. We owe it to Kayleigh to stay quiet.

"Shall I take you through the timeline again?"

Officer Joy doesn't give me chance to reply before bursting into another spiel, going into detail about Sharon's plans for the camp, the photos Chloe took, the timestamps they've been able to establish. She even turns her pages round to face me so that I can see for myself the photos, the ones they've printed. My eyes sting as I stare at them taking in those first two nights of the camp, the first full day of fun.

We look so happy. So… unbothered. It really was just a camp to us, like any other.

I carved a castle scene onto my butternut squash. I remember using the tools Sharon had borrowed from Steve to etch turrets and a huge door, trees and bushes and flowers, a fountain before it, using any skills I'd acquired from my art GCSE to recreate a scene which appeared rather Disney-esque. Kayleigh carved a face, a scary expression which eerily resembled John Lennon, and Orla went for something intelligent none of us really understood. Chloe carved herself, of course, a self-portrait based off of one of her perfect selfies.

We cooked on the campfire, took turns chopping veg and stirring the pot. Sharon took a photo of us on Chloe's phone of us sat round on camp chairs, toasting veggie marshmallows for s'mores. There are more photos from the next day, the four of us hiking through forests, over the clifftops, laughing and singing and gossiping.

Later on, on Saturday night, are the last photos we took. Chloe, posing in a bikini top and tiny shorts, as I took photos with the flashlight, ones she could later post to Instagram. She has thousands of followers to feed, but due to what happened, it's no surprise that these particular shots never made the 'gram.

"Can you remember taking these photos?" Officer Joy asks, frowning. "Chloe told us in her interview that these photos were the last ones you took before everything went down, and that they were for her Instagram. Due to the racy nature of these shots, we need to confirm that they had nothing to do with…"

I blink. "Racy? She was wearing a bikini top. Have you seen Chloe's Instagram?"

"Did you take these photos, Lucy?"

I nod.

So much for saying nothing.

"Thank you." Joy glances at Pudrow, who still isn't saying anything, as though to say they're finally getting somewhere, that I'm cooperating at last. I want to kick myself for giving in… but maybe it's safer to give them a little bit, rather than infuriate them by showing nothing.

I pretend to check my phone for the time then, slipping it out of my pocket under the table. There's a message from Alicia waiting, another snap from Nora I don't dare open.

We heard you rejected Ethan and I SO WANT TO BE MAD AT YOU but Nora says we have to hear you out first, but OH MY GOD BESTIE WTF ARE YOU DOING?!

Btw we're all going to MAGUIRES tonight hehe and you're coming too. And it'll show how difficult it is to just be friends with Ethan when he literally gets hard just looking at you. We'll pick you up at five, k? Don't bother eating – we'll share some wings and I'm gonna drink a pot of barbecue sauce xoxoxo I love you but again WHAT ARE YOU DOING?

"It's coming up on an hour," I say, glancing back up at Joy and Pudrow. "I need to be getting home, I have revision to be getting on with. Mocks in a few weeks, remember?"

At the start of the investigation, the officers made it clear they wouldn't jeopardise our education when there's no evidence of what happened that weekend, and whether we were a part of that. My applying to university has to come equal to interviews and questioning. They get up to an hour of my time every day after school, but that's it.

"Fine – we won't keep you any longer." Officer Joy shuffles her papers into a pile, nodding at me and gesturing that I can stand to leave. "Today was much more productive, I'd say, Lucy. But tomorrow, you'll be required to recount the weekend in your own words – or at least the first two days, if the whole thing is too much for you. Get things straight, then tell us what happened in as much detail as you can. I know this is a lot and it's probably traumatic to look back on, but we need to start moving forwards in this investigation."

Twenty-four hours to get my story straight, to figure out what the hell I'm supposed to tell them about those first two days of camp...

I swallow, but nod back. I can do that. It'll give me one more day, at least.

"The other girls will be asked to do the same, so we ask that you don't contact them over the next twenty-four hours, in case there's any collaboration over your stories. Thank you, Lucy. We'll see you tomorrow."

19

Alicia and Nora knock on my door just before five. Mum answers, but I hear from the kitchen that it's them, shoving past Dad to make my way into the hall.

"Lucy!" Alicia calls, beaming and waving. "Your mum just told us you're coming back to school tomorrow, for definite?"

I glance at Mum, who's giving me that look, one that tells me I am *going* to school tomorrow, whether I like it or not.

"I thought I would, but I'm not sure now." I feel a little guilty at my best friends' disappointed faces, Mum's surprise. "I just… I have quite an important interview tomorrow night, and I need to make notes and stuff. I'll catch up on the work at home again."

"I might have to have a word with those police officers," Mum says, frowning. "You're putting an awful lot of time into the investigation, Lucy, and although it's important, you have so much else to be thinking about…"

"Roberts wants us to send off our UCAS stuff over the next two weeks," Nora adds, not realising it sounds like she's on my Mum's side and not mine, probably thinking she sounds helpful. "At least before Christmas, anyway – January is the deadline, and you'll be pushing it then."

"I didn't realise it was so soon." Mum looks suddenly panicked, glancing at me. "Have you finished your personal statement, Luce? God, I don't even know which courses you're applying to, or which universities. Are you still considering law, or something with English and history?"

The irony of me doing law is too much, and I can't help but snort. The three of them stare at me in bewilderment.

Only Alicia senses how uncomfortable things are, and grabs my arm to tug me out of the door.

"Come on, girls, we're going to be late!" She smiles at Mum so as not to be rude, but Mum's expression is now one of worry, a million thoughts whirling round her head.

"I'm going to contact the station, Lucy, this is really starting to worry me…"

"You don't need to do that!" I tell her, but Alicia and Nora have hold of both my arms now, and it's a struggle to push my shoes on as we collapse out of the door. "I won't be late back."

"We'll talk about this later!" is the last thing Mum says before Alicia slams the door.

***

Maguires is surprisingly quiet tonight, even for a weekday. There are a few older men sat at the bar supping beers, a group of pensioners cluttered in a booth, and Ethan, Oli and Kev waiting in the next, saving our seats.

"And how are the three most gorgeous girls in Vibbington?" Oli greets us with a grin, scooting over to make room for Alicia and I. Ethan is sat by the window, furthest from me, and yet I can't help but catch his eye as I take my place on the bench opposite. Kev is next to him, Nora opposite me, winking as she clicks onto the app to order her first drink.

Nora, Kev and I are the only ones old enough to drink, but the staff never bother to ID us if we're with the boys, who all look legal. Nora picks a lurid blue pitcher of alcohol and juice, asking for two extra straws, and the three of us take it in turns to sip, the jug taking up the table between us.

Kev orders three beers for him and the boys. I know that Ethan isn't a fan of beer, that he prefers cocktails and sweet cans of cider, but he takes it politely enough, supping with an almost straight face. Seeing him again makes my stomach flip, guilt writhe deep within me. *You don't like him, so it doesn't matter!*

I don't know who I'm kidding.

The six of us chat for five minutes or so, like old times, avoiding the elephant in the room – Ethan's recent rejection. Alicia's message said they'd all heard about it, so no doubt Ethan told the boys what happened, and one of them relayed it back to my best friends. I squirm just thinking about the fact I didn't tell them myself. What's changed? Just weeks ago, I couldn't go a day without relaying every detail of my life to Alicia and Nora, insignificant as each may seem.

Then again, Ethan and I used to be the same. He's the only guy I've ever been that close to, unable to go even a few hours without spamming his phone with messages. We talked about everything, every conversation somehow finding a way to dig deeper, sometimes way too deep. What's changed with in him, too?

Have *I* changed? Probably. I discovered a part of myself I never knew existed. I discovered what I'm really like. Why I don't deserve this – any of this.

The pitcher tastes sour as I go for my next sip. Everyone's looking at me. I must've zoned out, because they're waiting for me to say something, to answer them.

"What food are we ordering?" Nora asks, her tone suggesting it's not the first time she's said it. "If you get chips and garlic bread, me and Alicia will get the meat, yeah?"

Nora calls herself a vegetarian half the time – occasionally vegan. The other half is spent in Maguires, unable to resist their chicken strips and dirty wings, the extra large pot of barbecue sauce Alicia will slurp by itself.

I'm ordering the chips and garlic bread when as Oli's voice comes to my attention. I click "pay" as I glance up to find all eyes on Ethan, Oli deliberately speaking far too loudly, intending for me to hear.

"So, Eth. What are you going to do about Lauren's message?"

My body stills.

Alicia and Nora are looking at me. I take a sip of my pitcher, acting like I don't care, that I feel as blasé as I'm pretending to.

Lauren. Ethan's ex, the one he dated for a good year or two before they broke up towards the end of year twelve, following her move to Nottingham which make it increasingly difficult for them to see each other. Oli and Kev said he was crushed, though he doesn't talk about her much. She was gorgeous, all blonde hair and good grades and straight teeth, a mutual friend of Alicia's from their tennis club. She was on the hockey team throughout secondary school, so we were acquaintances, kind of. Lauren was nice – too nice. It made her impossible to hate.

I know they're only talking about her to make me jealous, and to make me realise that I do like Ethan, that I do want to be with him, that I made a mistake.

But... what message are they talking about? I thought it was Lauren who had ended things, sick of long train journeys and phone calls. There were rumours that she met someone else over summer, that the picnics and late night trips to

McDonald's she'd post on her story were with this new man. Why would she message Ethan, after all this time?

I can't help but take a sneak glance at his face, my own cheeks flaming. He looks uncomfortable, like he doesn't want to discuss this in front of me, aware of what his friends are trying to do. I take another sip of the pitcher, determined to act unbothered. If he wants to get back with Lauren, that's fine by me. So unbelievably fine.

"I don't know," he says eventually. "I was just going to tell her I was busy, but now..."

Now that I've rejected him, and he's free to do what he wants.

"What did the message say?" Nora asks, curiosity getting the better of her, and there's a short pause as Ethan fumbles with his phone, pulling it from his pocket and twisting it round to show us.

> **Hey, it's Loz. I'm back in Vibbington this weekend, visiting my dad, and I was wondering if we could meet for a coffee? I know this probably isn't appropriate and I just want you to be honest with me, but I feel like we didn't really give long-distance a go, and I've missed you a lot while I've been in Notts. I'm applying to uni in Hull, so I'll be back in the area a lot more come September. God, I sound delusional, expecting to still have a chance with you. I just miss you so much, Eth. Let me know if you're down for coffee, even if it's just as friends. xox**

I don't know what my stomach's doing. It's flipping over itself in some sort of dramatic gymnastics routine, and my friends are sneaking glances at me, trying to read my mind.

"That's..." Alicia takes a deep breath, tearing off a segment of chicken strip. "What are you going to say to her? I thought you were over her."

She only says that for my benefit. We have no idea whether Ethan is over Lauren or not, when he barely talks about her and unfollowed her on Instagram due to the number of selfies she posts of her looking drop-dead gorgeous. We only found out they broke up when Oli and Kev let us know, one day on the beach in June, when Ethan was being suspiciously quiet and hadn't checked his phone once. He disappeared off to buy us all ice creams as Oli said, "Lauren dumped him. She called last night – she didn't want to wait until she next came up to see him."

I liked Ethan a little bit at the time, but only in an I-think-you're-cute-but-would-never-try-anything kind of way. Not even Alicia or Nora knew this, though. Hearing Oli talk about the break-up, I could only feel sorry for him.

But not now. I feel my cheeks flame again as I take another sip, a long one, almost draining the pitcher. Nora raises an eyebrow at me and says, "Another?"

Ethan's frowning. He can't catch my eye.

We're all waiting for him to speak.

"I don't know what to do," he says eventually. "I don't think getting back together would work, and she shouldn't have broken up with me if she ever thought it would." He shakes his head, the froth on his beer sloshing over the edges of the glass. "And besides… a lot has changed since then."

Every head on the table turns to face me then, except Ethan's. Even Kev, pragmatic and quiet and a master at steering clear of gossip, is watching me with narrowed eyes.

They all want me to say something. To convince Ethan that he shouldn't text Lauren back, and that even meeting her for a coffee is a bad idea. They're routing for us, for Lucy and Ethan, a cute little sixth form couple-to-be.

They shouldn't.

"What?" I object, face still bright red. "If he's even considering texting back, he should. What harm would a coffee do?"

Oli and Alicia shake their heads in exasperation, and even Nora and Kev look disappointed.

"Eth, if you were finally getting over her after all this time, maybe that's a sign that you shouldn't see her again." Oli, once again, is talking way too loudly. He's addressing the entire pub, not just our booth. "Plus, remember why you broke up. She couldn't handle the lack of sex being long distance, and sucked at messaging. In the end, you were calling, what, two or three times a week, sometimes less?"

My cheeks really are red now, as Ethan nods.

So he did sleep with her.

God.

I have no idea why that makes me feel so *jealous*.

It was to be expected. They were together for a year, after all. But I assumed, and hoped, that maybe they hadn't yet, that maybe long distance had killed off any hope that they might have ever had sex. The thought makes my stomach twist, my palms ache.

Lauren's beautiful, the definition of gorgeous, and knowing they shared that moment makes me feel a little sick. Not only am I a terrible person up to my neck in secrets, but I've never done anything more than kissing, politely, without tongue. I'll never quite be Ethan's first the way he would've been mine.

Not that it matters. I don't want to be with him. I *can't* be with him.

And if being with Lauren instead makes him happy, I should let him get on with it.

"Honestly," I continue, draining the pitcher, the racket I make as I swirl the ice cubes round acting as a distraction from the awkwardness. "You're not doing me any favours by not messaging her back. We're just friends, remember?"

Ethan looks as though he's been kicked in the teeth. Even our friends are gobsmacked, unsure of how to react, shocked that I've actually said that out loud.

But why? Why are they shocked? They know I just want to be friends, that it's never going to work. They know I'm damaged, surely. They know I'm being interviewed by the police each night, that I haven't been to school in weeks, that I've spent the last fortnight proving that I'm mentally unhinged.

I stare around at them all, but they just look... sad. Disappointed in me, expressions magnified. Like I'm making a mistake, and they don't know how to stop me.

"Message her back," I say, desperate this time, speaking with so much less conviction than before. "Please, Ethan."

No one follows me as I stand to leave.

20

It's cold out, so freezing that my teeth chatter and goosebumps spring over my arms. The smokers' corner is empty, concrete seats clear aside from cigarette stumps and crisp packets. It's only ever used at the weekends, when men from the chavvier parts of Vibbington come to smoke and drink and start Facebook drama, posting blurry selfies and shouting, "Slag!" at the waitresses. The staff haven't moved a tray of pint glasses back inside, and by the morning it will've shattered in freezing temperatures, frost littering the shards.

Did I say the wrong thing in there? No, of course I didn't. I was honest, and that was what Ethan deserved. Lauren is smart and beautiful, sporty and fun, and they've already slept together. Unlike me, unexperienced to the extreme, lacking that connection with him. He'd be better off with her, his first love – a cookie-cutter girlfriend, perfection by its very definition.

I imagine them playing Minecraft together, curled up on the floor of Ethan's bedroom, the bedroom I used to think felt so special, so secure. His double bed, the one I always felt awkward perching on, the bed he probably lost his virginity in. The thought of Lauren seeing him naked makes me feel nauseous, the thought of him caressing her perfect body, golden skin and boobs… I breathe in and out, in and out, trying to calm down.

Like I said, he'd be better off with her. Lauren would

never get involved in murder, would never even get called into a police station for as much as shoplifting, or witnessing a crime. She's so *good*, the way I thought I was, once. The way I really truly felt, before I discovered that dark side of myself, the part of my soul shaded in black –

I'm a bad person. I've seen bad things. I've done bad things, felt blood drip from my hands, left those notorious footprints all down the street. I'm a bad person. Ethan is *not* a bad person. The two aren't compatible.

I fumble for my phone now, clicking onto Lauren's Instagram. It's so cold my fingers are almost numb, but they work enough for me to scroll down, down, down, taking in all of the posts I liked but never really took in, the perfect photos I've breezed past a hundred times over the last few months. She posts a lot, but not in an obnoxious, show-off kind of way. People genuinely want to see her photos, want to view her new life in Nottingham, the cocktail bars and museums and outfit pics. Each individual post has at least two hundred likes.

Blonde, messy hair, layered and highlighted, the kind of hair you only really see in shampoo adverts and on daytime TV. Freckles, the perfect amount, scattering her cheeks and nose. Expensive clothes, with a tad more individuality than anything I'd ever wear, and funky makeup I'd never even attempt to pull off. Blue eyeliner, bright mascara, ombre lipstick…

I try to imagine her in my place, stood by the open flaps of a tent, holding a knife. I try to imagine blood dripping onto those expensive trainers, staining the fabric she's somehow kept pristine. The splatters would bounce right off her, unable to stick, to make a single mark.

I try to imagine her face – her lovely, kind face – as she

pushed said knife into flesh, stepping back as blood squirted over her hands, her tiny *Bratz* top.

I try to imagine her turning her back on the scene, turning her back as though it was nothing... but I can't.

Lauren isn't like me. She's not a psycho.

She wouldn't be able to hold it together this well, sit across from the police and say nothing, nothing at all. She wouldn't be able to go to Maguires and sit around a table with her friends, knowing what she'd done, what she'd seen. She wouldn't be able to hide it – not many people would. Not many people are so false, so capable of being *fake*. I didn't think I was. A few weeks ago, I couldn't even keep a kiss secret from Nora and Alicia... let alone a murder.

Is there something wrong with me? With Chloe, with Orla? Is there a reason we walked away from that camp with barely a scratch on us, three dead bodies lying beneath the trees, our clothes burnt on the bonfire, ashes sprinkled far, far away, where the police would never find them? Is there a reason we could call the police so calmly, like there was nothing wrong, then stand back and laugh our relief, knowing Kayleigh was dead?

Of course there's something wrong with me. There probably always has been. I'm not like Lauren, with her genuine heart and soft smile, perfect clothes and hair matching a perfect personality. I'm not even like Nora and Alicia, effortlessly *good*, the kind of girls everyone likes and trusts. I thought I was, but I was really just buying time, trying to fit in, to be normal, while the past continued to creep up on me, to take me – us – by surprise, all over again.

I knew what I was really like all those years ago, when Lexie died, but hoped I could ignore it. We drove her to her death, one way or another. Chloe, through the incessant bullying; Kayleigh, through the teasing and gentle jibes here and there, the fact she couldn't seem to stop; Orla and I for complying, for not sticking up for Lexie, for not getting help, telling people sooner.

This was supposed to be our punishment. The universe's way of saying, "Eff you. You never paid for what you did to Lexie, so here's a weekend of hell for you to enjoy."

Only the evil it bestowed brought out further evil *within* us, bad fighting bad, the three of us feeling all high and mighty and assuming we were on the good side.

We were *never* on the good side.

I'm evil. Pure evil. Said evil took over the minute I picked up that knife, knowing deep inside what I intended to do with it.

Ethan must be delusional if he can't see that. If he wants me instead of Lauren, the girl who fits him perfectly, who'd have another happy, long-lasting relationship if he'd let her, who's clearly willing to put up with not seeing him often just to be his again.

I hope they're happy. It's the least they deserve.

I don't deserve to be happy.

I don't deserve to feel a shred of happiness ever again.

21

I refuse to get up in the morning. If I wait until Mum goes to work, she can't *force* me to go to school. I'll email Mr Roberts for an extension to my absence, given the circumstances… I can't face going back to sixth form after last night, can't face the idea of Ethan obsessing over the prospective catch-up with Lauren in all its gory details.

And besides – I have tonight's interview to prepare for. They want me to recount everything that happened those two days of camp, and I can do that, easy. It might not constitute saying nothing, but it'll at least *look* like cooperation, if that counts.

I get up around eleven, once the house is silent and my parents are both safely away at work. I dress in nice clothes, understated enough to get me through the day, and pull out a piece of paper from the printer in Dad's office (a glorified junk room). I take a seat at my desk, frowning, and draw a little picture of a tent in one of my old felt-tips, the ink faded and scratchy.

The camp.

I take out my phone next. Joy and Pudrow asked us not to contact each other before recounting the events to them, but a few messages won't make a difference. I toggle with the settings of The Very Best Group Chat. "Delete messages after viewing." Easy.

In my head, I know they don't *really* suspect that three

teenage girls had anything to do with the murder of their friend and two older men. They know there's something more sinister going on, that we're probably just too traumatised to say what *really* happened. For highly trained officers, they're not exactly brilliant at investigating. If they actually thought we had anything to do with the deaths, they'd have gotten copies of our messages by now, dug deeper into our phone logs and history, scoured further afield on the camp, noticed how much of our clothing and essentials were missing. Only three of us had sleeping bags still, for God's sake – the other was burnt to a crisp, and was now in fragments floating away in the sea below.

I'm going to tell as much truth as possible about the first two days of camp, I type, fingers shaking. **We need to show cooperation or they'll think we're being deliberately insolent. As for saying nothing… we need a reason for saying nothing, not just that we can't be bothered with the interview and that we want to make things difficult.**

The reply comes instantly.

We'll act like we're too traumatised to tell them what happened, one of them types, the other agreeing. **That's the only way it makes sense.**

I push my phone back down onto my desk, focusing on the piece of paper before me. I need to get my story straight before I turn up there tonight, and take a picture to send to the girls, to make sure we have exactly the same version of events.

This is going to work. It *is*. They'll give up eventually, or make their own assumptions about what happened at the camp… and there'll be no one to arrest or even accuse, since their two suspects are dead, dead, dead.

What are we going to do when Sharon wakes up?

I feel like the worst person in the world for hoping she never does.

**

Officer Joy makes me another cup of tea. It's stronger today, and she doesn't use much milk. I take a grateful few sips, enjoying the way it scalds my tongue, numbing the tastebuds in my mouth.

"Come on through!" she says, grinning at me. She's in unusually good spirits today, and even high-fives Pudrow as he tells her something about report he's finished, how proud he is. They're both smiling, perhaps because the sky is blue and the sun is bright in the sky, warming up Vibbington's November chill and casting the police station in warmth.

"Isn't it a beautiful day?" she says to me, and I feel obliged to nod and smile back. It's sunny. There's nothing particularly beautiful about today aside from the fact the sun is shining… which isn't exactly an uncommon phenomenon, even for Yorkshire.

The interview room is less cold than usual. The cream walls feel warming, soft, subtle. I'm sat in my usual seat, clutching the piece of paper in one hand. I covered it in scribbled biro notes and tiny felt-tip illustrations, covering the whole sheet, and sent a photo to The Very Best Group Chat before I left. It looks like a child's plan for a story they're writing in school, but it'll help me keep my head straight, at least. And it'll make sure I don't miss anything important.

There are arrows connecting each note, each little explanation and anecdote. I worked on it all day, neglecting my UCAS application for another day, completely forgetting to do the rest of my English notes. Maybe it won't be such a terrible thing if I fail my mocks in a week or so… at least it'll make choosing a university easier. The thought of me, Lucy, attending anything less than a Russell Group makes me snort with disbelief.

"So," Officer Joy begins, grinning again. Her eyes fall to the piece of paper clutched in my hand, and she frowns, as though trying to figure out what it is and why I might have it with me. "Is this…"

"It's some notes," I explain. "So that I can recount the first two days of camp accurately."

I hear the words coming out of my mouth and writhe with pride. I sound cooperative, like I really want to help them figure out what happened but can't say the words myself.

"Okay, that's great!" Joy replies. "Just keep talking, Lucy, until we get to the parts you find too hard relaying. We can go over those today if you feel ready, but I don't want you to feel… uncomfortable."

She's only saying that to butter me up, to make me feel like I don't *have* to say anything real today. I know what they're thinking. That I'll spill enough by recounting those first two days of camp for them to figure out at least some of what happened that weekend, before I have to tell them myself. They think they're being clever, but the sheet in front of me isn't incriminating in the slightest. If anything, it's the *opposite* of incriminating, neat and precise, each tiny note written with intention.

"Shall we start with the date of the camp?" Joy suggests. "We need to get that as part of the recording, so that we can prove you're telling us about the correct day. Is that okay, Lucy?"

I nod. "It was... I think it was November 8th, a Friday evening. Yes – that's right. The weekend after we went out for Halloween. It was an autumnal camp because of that."

They already know this. They have the photo evidence, the laminated sheets Sharon made to plan the camp. An autumnal camp seemed fun, unusual, as we'd initially planned it in the chapel that night. Maybe a little spooky, being a week after Halloween, but Sharon promised a frightened Kayleigh that there'd be no mention of ghosts and ghoulies.

Since we'd held our Guide meetings in the same chapel for years and years, we'd never been allowed to celebrate Halloween anyway. It was because of paganism, I think. Something like that.

"November 8th, yes," Joy says, nodding. She's jotting down notes of her own, then goes to take a sip of her scalding hot tea. It's almost as though she's excited to hear what I have to say, all set up with her steaming mug. I'm about to read them an audiobook all about the events that weekend, a story set to send them to sleep, put their doubts and suspicions well and truly to bed. I'm going to hypnotise them. That's the reason for my precise notes, for the well-planned story, the story they're *dying* to hear.

"Okay, Lucy," Officer Pudrow says, smiling and fiddling with the buttons on the recording device. Today, I'm recounting a proper tale, a long series of events they'll piece together, bit by bit, with fragments of Orla and Chloe's own interviews. "Begin when you're ready."

I smile and nod, glancing down at the paper.

I can do this. Three, two, one... *Go.*

22

We all got a lift with Sharon to the camp. We often did, especially as we got older. Only Chloe could drive, and she didn't want to leave her car on some "grimy old campsite" in the middle of nowhere, especially after three weeks of non-stop rain, the ground punctuated with spots of water. Even the roads were a nightmare, wet and slimy and slippery, and there was more rain forecast for the weekend ahead – or so she said.

We congregated at mine after school on Friday the 8th, all four of us. Kayleigh and Orla had just gotten the buses back from college, and Chloe had finished work at her mum's salon, lugging a bright purple suitcase through the backstreets of Vibbington. We all lived fairly close by, so it wasn't much of a fuss. We'd packed before school that morning and everything was ready to go by five o'clock, squashed into Mum's car.

We still had a whole load of other things to carry, like food and bits for the campfire, the three tents and sleeping bags, fairy lights and blankets and cushions. Chloe went overboard in order to get photos for her Instagram, grinning as she tucked a fluffy throw and some plastic lanterns into Mum's boot, beside her huge suitcase. I didn't have a clue what was in there, what she could possibly need for a three, four day camp, one which didn't include boys or parties or alcohol.

"Sharon will go bonkers if she sees that," I told her, as the four of us continued to pack Mum's car while she waited at the bottom of the street to guide Sharon. Chloe had a carrier bag filled with bottles and cans, vodka and apple Tangyz and WKD, and was giggling to herself as we helped her hide it. "Is it *really* necessary?"

"Of course," she said, rolling her eyes. "God, you are boring. It's a sleepover, Lucy. What do people do at sleepovers?"

"It's a *camp*, not a sleepover," Orla cut in, to which even *I* had to roll my eyes. "And I don't drink."

"Live a little!" Chloe retorted. "You can shot Tangyz, Orla. It's like… special juice. Sour, alcoholic juice."

She licked her lips deliberately.

It was at that moment that Sharon pulled into the drive, her little car making the most alarming sounds as it came to a stop beside us. She'd had it years and years, and it'd been trying to break down and leave her stranded for at least the last ten. We made sure the alcohol and Chloe's excessive blankets were tucked out of sight before pushing down the boot and standing against it in a row, smiling at Sharon.

We were all dressed for the camp, four perfect rangers, and Sharon couldn't help but look relieved as she stepped out of the car. For our last camp, and a cold one at that, we'd all made the effort. Hoodies and sensible leggings, rucksacks and bare nails. Even Chloe had taken off her makeup and picked a pair of waterproof trousers, though they were probably ridiculously expensive, baby-blue, costing more than my entire outfit put together.

"You girls look wonderful," she said, nodding her approval. "Shall we get these cars packed up?"

We managed to stuff the remaining tents and bags onto

the backseat of Mum's car, as Sharon's boot space was limited. There was room for me to travel with Mum, but she insisted I go with the other girls, start the camp as I meant to go on.

"I'll say goodbye properly when I get there," she said, planting a kiss on my forehead. "You'll be okay, won't you?"

"It's just a camp," I said, rolling my eyes for a second time. Just a camp.

The drive took forty minutes or so, filled with stilted conversation and terrible country music on the radio, a station Sharon insisted would get us in the mood for autumn. After five minutes or so of trying to ask her questions about the camp and all our activities while she tried to concentrate on driving, Chloe took over, telling us all about her life, the brand deals she was doing for underwear companies on Instagram, the holiday she'd been gifted to the Bahamas.

"Hashtag gifted!" is what she actually said, doing the little hashtag sign with her hands. "I'm going in January with Tobes, and it should be so fun!"

Tobes, or Toby, was the boy she'd recently started seeing. I'd noticed his profile pop up on Instagram, all gym selfies and bulging muscles, chiselled jawline and beauty spot below his left eye. He was half-Italian, Chloe explained – like Nora, I thought. I'd have to send her a link.

She started flicking through pictures of him on her phone, clearly bragging. Kayleigh was sat up front with Sharon, and barely said anything the entire journey, contributing only with some nondescript grunts and nods when we asked her questions. Orla was too engrossed in texting Aaron to respond to much, but after twenty minutes ago she stopped typing and took to checking every few minutes for a reply. He'd clearly gone AWOL.

The photos Chloe showed us were kind of... weird. Toby

and her, dressed up to go to some fancy restaurant, looking at least five years older than us in their expensive dress and Toby's suit, chest puffed out. Chloe had undoubtedly grown up masses since leaving school and going into business with her Mum, but here, she seemed to have aged *years*. Bikini pics with Tobes leaning on her arm on a beach somewhere; photos for an underwear ad, the kind of sexy lingerie they usually bring out for Valentine's, Toby's hands covering her; Tobes and her, topless and covered by the sheets, Chloe snuggled up to his chest.

"I'm going to compile these photos into an album for him," Chloe said, grinning to herself. She seemed so happy, so deliriously in love, that it felt... odd. Chloe didn't do love. She did shags in the school toilets, inappropriate Instagram posts, affairs with older men.

Rumour had it she'd snogged our English teacher, Mr Cole, and *that* was the reason she never joined sixth form, but I really hoped it was just that – a rumour.

"Look at this one," she said, giggling. Even Orla looked over her shoulder at it. The photo was of Chloe and Tobes outside a bar somewhere nice, maybe York, in nice clothes and perfectly styled hair.

But as we looked closer, I felt myself blush. Tobes had a very clear bulge beneath his black jeans, which Chloe thought was hilarious.

"Obviously couldn't post that one..."

It was a relief to finally arrive at the campsite, Chloe's phone tucked safely into her pocket. We all tried for signal upon arriving, but Sharon had been right. There was absolutely no way we could call or text here, or even connect to the internet via our 4G. Orla looked like she was about to cry.

"It's just until Monday," I told her, trying not to sound unsympathetic. As much as I loved my friends, I could easily last a few evenings without talking to them; we weren't *completely* attached at the hip. As for Ethan... I still wasn't sure what I was going to do about him. We'd talked since the kiss but never acknowledged it, and I thought that maybe a few days away from the situation might bring clarity for the both of us.

Mum helped unpack the cars, Chloe artfully hiding the alcohol between her suitcase and canvas bag filled with snacks and accessories. She even stayed to put the tents up, which took a lot less time than usual. Chloe snapped photos the whole way – she couldn't seem to help it – while Mum and I slid the poles in, helped bend them into shape, twisting the material so that it slipped over the metal and filled the gaps. We'd had so much practice at putting up tents that it felt like second nature.

Chloe strung fairy lights around the door or our tent, her only contribution. The campsite was nice, big and round and surrounded by trees, pathways leading off here and there to the cliffs, into the forest, to different areas of the countryside. We were slap-bang in the middle, the cars parked all the way down by the gates.

"It's a lovely spot," Mum said, turning to give me a hug. "Have fun, won't you? I love you, Luce. If there are ever any problems, ring me on the site phone, okay?"

There was a phone wired into the office, which sat a little way from our camp, by the trees. It was only a portacabin, but had electricity to charge our phones and a working fridge and toilets and shower cubicle. I waved and waved until Mum was out of site, driving through the gates and padlocking them behind her. She and Sharon had the code.

Chloe and I had the perfect tent, both inside and out. We'd tossed a coin a week ago, landing us with a brand-new blue one, Orla and Kayleigh with a slightly mouldy pink version. Sharon had her robust one-man thing, a little green bug which looked like an alien spaceship.

We'd decked out the inside perfectly, of course. Chloe's blankets and cushions came in strong, in all kinds of colours and fabrics, fluffy and shaggy and warm. The plastic lanterns were a perfect touch. The finished interior was bright, indie-inspired, and Chloe insisted I take photos of her in it for her Instagram.

"I'll post everything when I'm back," she explained. "Tomorrow, we need to take some bikini pics, because I was hashtag gifted some last week, but for now, let's get some outdoorsy ones in these trousers. They're from ASOS, but they were this expensive brand I've literally never heard of – apparently *all* the hikers wear it – and they were on sale for sixty pounds! Honestly, what a bargain. Yes, move back a little bit, you need to get my bum in... I love that, do more... I feel like these give me a really natural, down-to-earth vibe, you know? Like, I'm gorgeous, but I also love camping and no makeup days. Pics like this can blow up big time!"

I don't think anyone would ever describe Chloe as natural or down-to-earth, but I nodded and smiled as I snapped picture after picture after picture. I was used to taking outfit pics for Alicia's page, which was filled with fashion and funky photography, and Chloe gushed when she saw the end products, insisting I should take *all* her photos from now on.

She was out of the waterproof trousers in a flash the minute Sharon told us we were going to start carving the squashes, pulling on some gym leggings, unzipping her hoodie to reveal a sports bra beneath. We met Sharon and the others by the camp table outside, which had been covered in newspaper. This trusty thing had been taken with us for years now, used to chop veggies and carry out activities across the last half-decade. It was crusty with use.

"Okay!" Sharon started, smiling round at us all. She was in full organisation mode, clutching those laminated cards to her chest and beaming. "You've each got a butternut squash in front of you – homegrown by Steve and me, might I add – and I want you to carve a face into each using his tools. Unlike pumpkins, there's not enough flesh to hollow out the insides... I think it'd be best if you'd just carve the skin, rather than cutting out chunks. We're going to be using them afterwards for our tea."

The squash carving was surprisingly fun, and even Chloe and Orla got into it, though Chloe was fussing about getting her hoodie dirty and Orla couldn't stop lifting her phone up as though she would've received a text from Aaron on this signal-less campsite over the last five minutes.

Kayleigh was good – really good. She'd done art at Throwsley High, she explained, receiving a seven at GCSE. The face she carved was horribly realistic in a creepy, twisted way, and reminded us all of John Lennon, with that narrow nose and hollow, glaring eyes. Chloe carved a miniature version herself, big bum and all, and Orla put extra care into creating some sort of mathematical symbol, claiming she'd take a photo of it to send to Aaron. I made a castle. It looked Disney-esque, but could've been anywhere, anything, surrounded by trees and flowers. It didn't have a meaning. That wasn't the point of the activity.

It was nice, peaceful, sat side by side and chopping away at the squash. Sharon was busy in the portacabin sorting something on the phone, so the four of us chatted amicably, like we always used to, polite as ever, getting along almost *too* well.

We lined the squashes side by side once we'd finished, so Chloe could take a picture. They looked good. Funny, even.

"Don't you think they perfectly represent our personalities?" Kayleigh asked innocently, as we all agreed, even Chloe joking about her own narcissism.

I wasn't going to overthink it. The chilled atmosphere, Chloe's laughter, the way we were all getting *on*.

Maybe – just maybe – this camp was going to be fun after all.

23

Sharon went to bed early that first night. She had dark circles under her eyes and kept yawning as we ate the now mushed-to-a-pulp butternut squashed, with heaps of bread and butter, chocolate coins for afters.

"I trust you girls to take yourselves off to bed," she said. "And I suppose you're too old now for me to give you a curfew. Just remember that we have a long day of activities lined up, and you'll need a good night's sleep if you're to make the most of it."

Which was basically her saying we had free reign of the camp for the rest of the night, since she was too tired to do anything. We grinned around at each other, nodding and hastening to finish our soup. This part of camp always signalled *fun*.

Sharon kept glancing over at the gates as we went into our tents to wrap up warmer, the November air now biting, the sky an inky shade of dark blue. I didn't think anything of it at the time. I assumed maybe she was just checking it was all locked up and we were safe, the camp secure.

Not now.

The police only know about the two men – Carl Hall, and Steve – attending camp on the second night, Saturday the ninth…

But I think one of them was there on Friday, too.

I don't tell them any of that, now. I carry on the story, eyes fixed on the sheet of paper, hands held firm.

Sharon was zipped up in her tent by ten on the dot, the four of us wrapped in hats and scarves and big coats. Chloe looked good even straddled in knitwear, and her tanned stomach somehow survived the cold as it stared out from beneath her jacket. It was designer – I could see the Balenciaga logo peeking out from under her collar – but the rest of her clothes were ordinary, made fancy by being on Chloe alone.

Orla and Kayleigh looked fairly normal, too. Orla had on leggings and a fleece which no doubt belonged to Aaron, a pink scarf round her neck and some nerdy fantasy t-shirt squeezed across her frame. She'd always been straight up and down, but over the last couple of years had developed proper boobs and hips, transforming her from a geeky maths extraordinaire to a preppy catch. I was pretty sure Aaron had no idea how lucky he was, despite how loved up Orla was.

Kayleigh was in an oversized hoodie, which also probably belonged to her boyfriend, Dan. It occurred to me then that I was the only girl without one – a boyfriend, that is. The only girl still single, five years after we started dating, started meeting boys and *really* caring what they thought of us. Even Chloe was starting to settle down.

Kayleigh noticed me staring and smiled, clearly self-conscious. She'd lost weight since being the "tubby" one of the group, as Chloe always loved to point out, but was still naturally bigger than us, her frame gaunt and sagging. She was wearing leggings, too, but her legs looked knobbly and awkward beneath the hoodie, like they weren't sure how to stand.

"Okay, ladies!" Chloe said, eyeing us up and flicking on her flashlight. We each had ones we always took to camp,

Orla the only one bypassing this and sprouting a headtorch. Out of all of us, Orla was always more likely to forego fashion for practicality; her glasses were still stuck over her nose, steamed up from the fire and the icy air.

"Where are we off to?" she asked now, frowning at Chloe. "Just for a walk around the site, or to play hide and seek?"

Hide and seek was still a tradition, even after all these years – that or sardines. Both were a guilty pleasure, games we'd never admit to enjoying in the real world.

"You'll see."

Chloe set off walking, the three of us following behind. All were in trainers, but the ground was slick with just-wet mud beneath our feet, and I could feel splatters hitting my ankles and the shins of my leggings as we made our way across the site. The field we usually used – the one we still used for convenience, even after what happened to Lexie there – was surrounded by trees and forest, and this was no different. Tall firs and silver birch loomed above us as Chloe led the group to the edge of the field, away from Sharon and the camp, away from the loo block and the landline and everything safe.

"Torches on, ladies," she said, and I could sense the grin in her voice. I don't know why she always called us ladies. It made us sound older than we actually were, more mature than she really found us.

The forest was dark and wet and cold, but silent, so silent. There was virtually no wind and the rain had long stopped, more due across the weekend. Each step was slimy, unstable, the ground slick with autumn leaves and twigs, the greenery of the forest floor wilting.

Chloe led the way, following a path of loose gravel and wooden markers. There were several walks leading from the camp; unlike our usual site, it wasn't fenced off, so anyone could technically make their way through the trees and reach us, which had freaked my parents out at first. Sharon had made us all print a map before we set off. She explained, pointing at the patch of dark green, that the forest surrounding the field was so thick and dense it was impossible to navigate, more use than any fence.

Half the paths led west, into the surrounding countryside to farms, villages, valleys. One led slightly north, up onto the moors, desolate and windswept and cold. A few more led east, to the coast, where rugged cliffs were sliced from the countryside between East and North Yorkshire. I should've studied the map more closely, clearly, because I had no idea where we were going.

Neither did the others, I realised, glancing at Kayleigh and Orla. Orla was barely speaking, lips zipped tight as we wandered on, but Kayleigh looked content enough, taking in her surroundings and flashing her torch into the forest around us. I wished she wouldn't do that. With all four torches pointed on the path ahead, it was easy to forget that the forest around us existed, that it was anything more than blackness.

We might be from Yorkshire, girl guides our whole lives, but we weren't exactly country people. Vibbington was a small settlement nestled into the Yorkshire Wolds, but a town all the same, all tarmac and charity shops and car fumes. The closest we ever got to being in nature was picnics in the park during study periods in year eleven, listening to traffic as we munched on scotch eggs and Pringles.

Hence our lack of outdoorsy clothing and navigation skills, our affinity for takeaways and Wi-Fi and squeaky clean shoes. Orla might have sprouted a headtorch and explored the

French countryside from the safety of Aaron's *maison*, but she was just as useless as the rest of us, checking for signal every time we reached a clearing.

"I think we should be getting closer…" Chloe mumbled, stopping short so that Kayleigh went flying into her. An owl chose that moment to go shooting through the trees away from us, and we all flinched, its hoot-hoot echoing all around.

"That was creepy," Orla said, pulling a face. "I *hate* owls."

"You hate everything." Chloe had her phone out, zooming in and out of a photo. It was the map. She must've taken a photo before setting off, so we wouldn't have to bring it with us. "Okay… I think I know where we are. The path forked and we didn't notice, but we *should* just have to follow this little section of bark and we'll hit the destination!"

The destination – as if it was something exciting, something more than just countryside. Where on *earth* was she taking us?

I thought I could hear it then, just. A low rumbling, a crashing, repetitive and dull, slow against chalky rocks.

The sea.

Chloe was taking us to the *sea*.

We walked on, faster, desperate to leave the forest. It wasn't so silent now, the ocean beyond sending a ripple of sea breeze through the trees, the wish-washing of waves trilling. Orla was so tense I could practically feel the magnetic field around her, and even Kayleigh fell silent, no longer pointing out weirdly shaped trees or spidery branches.

The trunks were thinning now. It was colder, but not yet biting, and the air tasted of sweat and tears, salty and hard. I wrapped my hoodie further round myself but still couldn't stop shivering.

"Three, two, one…" Chloe breathed in just at the right

moment, opening her arms wide as the trees finally came to a stop.

There, stretched before us in a dim, stodgy line, was the sea.

It was only just possible to make out where the cliff broke away and the ocean took over, moon dancing across wave tips and sparkling pale grey. They were loud and crashing, but it still wasn't windy enough for them to seem threatening, and we all stood there for a moment, taking them in. Breathing, staring. Eyes floating over the landscape, the never-ending pile of water, the jagged cliff edge which seemed too far away to be real.

"This is where the fun starts."

We all turned to face Chloe, half expecting something horrid, some awful dare or challenge involving the cliff before us, but she just grinned. Wind had blown her hair into a mad frenzy and yet she still looked perfect, pouty and pretty and so much older than the rest of us. I felt like a child, looking at her. Small, immature, pathetic.

"It's about a mile walk up the coast, but I googled the area before I came, and there's supposed to be a really cool pop-up festival on tonight – completely free if you walk in from the clifftops. It's been on all week, packing up tomorrow morning. You up for it?"

A pop-up festival, a mile away, in the middle of nowhere...

It was already late, but the three of us were too scared to say no, conscious, as ever, of spoiling the fun. I could see Kayleigh twitching anxiously, my own heart racing, but Orla was nodding her enthusiasm, and Chloe took that as a big fat yes.

"There'll be Wi-Fi, right?" Orla checked.

Chloe nodded, a smile creeping over. "Yep. Your last chance to contact the outside world until Monday morning, ladies! It's a hefty walk, but I *promise* it'll be worth it."

"What if Sharon wakes up and finds us gone?" I didn't want to be the party-pooper, but I couldn't help it. The idea of walking along the cliff edge late at night to some random festival in an area we didn't know, far away from Sharon and the campsite, probably to have to walk back again late, late, late, just seemed so… stupid, pointless. It was a camp, our last ever, and using it as an excuse to creep away to some festival felt *silly*.

"Think of the Instagram pics, Luce," Chloe said, as if that was going to sway me. "I'll take a load for that dozy Ethan, if you like."

I flushed. How did *she* know I liked Ethan? He was hardly one of the popular kids back in school, and it had been a year and a half since we all left year eleven. The others smiled knowingly, suddenly seeing the fun side to what Chloe was saying, and so I couldn't help but sigh.

It was just a festival, some crappy pop-up on the side of a cliff in Yorkshire.

What harm could it do?

24

"You already know about the festival, don't you?"

Officer Joy and Officer Pudrow exchange sheepish glances. It doesn't take a mind-reader to figure that out. They haven't even blinked over the last ten minutes ago, as I described walking through the forest that night, towards the cliff edge. They're still unphased now, as Joy nods.

"I… yes, we did."

When I spoke to Orla and Chloe this afternoon, we all agreed to tell them about the festival; keeping it a secret made no sense. They knew the locations our phones travelled to, and must've seen our excursion along the coast that night, despite not mentioning it. There were the photos, too, photos Chloe took, photos *I* took, even Snapchat memories of Orla and Kayleigh's. They took every photo and video from our phones of that weekend, forming a patchwork quilt of events, a timeline they could pinpoint each death within. They didn't mention the festival, though – probably waiting to see if we'd mention it ourselves.

Do they think it could be relevant to the case, somehow?

I don't see how.

"Tell us about how you felt, Lucy," Joy continues, resting her chin on her hand. "How you felt when Chloe brought you away from the camp in the middle of the night, to attend a festival *she* wanted to go to, a festival you had no idea about."

It wasn't the middle of the night, but that feels like a minor detail.

I felt betrayed, in a way. Angry, too. I didn't *want* to go to some festival. I was tired and cold and aware of the time, of how late it'd be when we eventually walked back along the clifftops, but Chloe didn't seem to care. She'd brought us here knowing full well that once she sprung the idea on us, we couldn't *possibly* say no. You could see this on her face as she watched us, waiting for a reaction. She was gloating. Gloating, because she knew she had us trapped.

"Fine," I said eventually. Orla and Kayleigh were still cautious, and so I knew I'd have them onside as I added, "But if you're not ready to leave by one, we'll walk back without you, okay?"

"Deal." The grin on Chloe's face was electric. She clearly didn't think we meant it, and I wasn't too sure either.

The mile walk along the coast dragged on and on, later into the night, darkness descending and the moon covering itself in fog. Our torches were more necessary than ever as we picked our way down the path, which was rough and stone-scattered. It was a good job we weren't walking right on the edge, because Kayleigh kept tripping and stumbling in her too-big trainers. She dropped her torch twice.

We didn't speak. It didn't feel right to. We were so focused on making it to the festival and not looking at the crashing waves and forest, at how high up we were, that everything else melted into the background.

Chloe was in front, of course. She spotted the festival first. Bright lights in the distance, fairy lights strung across tents, and that thump, thump, thump, the thwack of music bursting from speakers as we got closer. Thump, thump, thump. Thump, thump, thump.

Was I just being boring, feeling apprehensive about the music festival? Probably. We were seventeen years old, miles and miles away from home, where no one knew us or could stop us from attending a festival (free) on the coast, late at night, where there'd probably be booze and boys and fun. Most girls my age would *kill* for an opportunity like this, a chance to really let loose.

But something felt… off.

Chloe sped up, hurrying along the path with her torch flashing the ground in case she tripped. Orla still couldn't get signal, and Kayleigh was shivering, face a little too blue and breath coming out in huge, steamy wafts.

This wasn't how this weekend was supposed to go. We were meant to be tucked up in our tents, maybe playing truth or dare or whispering about our – *their* – boyfriends. I tried not to think about the last time Sharon went to bed early at a camp. Maybe that should've been a sign, a sign this wasn't going to end well.

The festival wasn't gated, not even on the clifftops. There was no point. We hadn't passed any houses on our way here, and there was no road, just that long, stone-scattered pathway leading all the way down the coast, flanked by trees on one side and gaping cliffs on the other. The music was more eclectic than my own taste, coloured lights and canvas pyramids spelling out exactly what kind of festival this was. We were all trying not to wrinkle up our noses as we noticed the smell. Soft, sweet, earthy, almost musty, indescribable unless you'd experienced it first-hand; I'd lived in Vibbington long enough.

"Are you *sure* we won't need tickets or anything?" Orla asked, to which Chloe clearly thought was such a stupid question it didn't warrant a reply. We were all cold now, so cold we were shaking, that even pondering the possibility of refusal seemed barmy. But we didn't need tickets. No one even looked at us as we wandered in.

We passed a few actual tents first, with families and hippie-type groups smoking and dealing out cards, their own music blaring from speakers attached to canvas rooves. They didn't look at us, so engrossed in their own activities that four teenage girls covered in mud and armed with torches hardly fazed them. Most were adults, but one family had a little girl with them, eight or nine, who sat on an older man's lap and held his cigarette between puffs.

"What kind of festival is this?" Kayleigh hissed, pulling a face at me, and I shrugged. Even Chloe was starting to look worried.

The main area was bigger, more impressive, the stage in the middle sporting high-tech speakers and lighting, band lit up in all colours of the rainbow. They were playing a sort of BTEC Coldplay set, attempting to jump about and screech into their mics, but fell short, crowds thin and uninspired.

Most people were gathered around the smaller stages, where random acts were playing by themselves, without the lights and production. Girls our age with guitars and nipple piercings, and slimy middle-aged men, sat by drum sets and singing about broken hearts. Chloe stopped to stare at a boy in his early twenties for a few seconds, eyes narrowed, swaying a little to the sound of his depressing trill.

"I'll find him later," she said.

None of us had brought any money, but Chloe and Orla had Apple Pay set up on their phones, and we promised we'd pay them back for drinks and food. The man who'd employed me over summer was old-school and always paid in cash, but Chloe didn't seem to care about splashing out, waving her phone around in the need to show off. Brand deals, ambassador positions, AdSense. Blah-blah-blah.

She bought us each a taco, even though Orla insisted she was trying to give up red meat and Kayleigh said she wasn't hungry. Three-bean-and-beef-chilli, plenty of lettuce and guac, a healthy amount of cheese sprinkled on top. I took a picture, making a mental note to send it to Alicia later, our resident taco-superfan. I felt a pang of guilt then, remembering my friends and how they'd told me they'd be bored this weekend, Alicia resigned to visiting her family in Hertfordshire and Nora to bowling with Oli, Kev and Ethan, who always beat her. They'd have loved the festival. That being said, I'd have probably loved it too if they were here, too.

Chloe bought us cider, the strong kind, the kind made from more than just sugar and additives. I'm pretty sure there was more than just cider in the cups, but I drank it anyway, grateful for the warm feeling it spread through my stomach. A taco, a few drinks, then we'd go home.

That was the plan.

We made our way back to the main space, where that boy was just finishing his set. He must've been at least twenty-one, with a short brown beard and muscles bulging from his white shirt, and got a ferocious clap from the audience, who were mostly middle-aged women and grannies wearing tie-dye and cowboy boots. He wasn't even that good-looking. Maybe in an obvious way, which he was clearly aware of, but not... properly. Then again, my friends would say Ethan wasn't typically good-looking, either. Maybe I just have a *really* specific type.

"Don't even bother," Orla whispered to Chloe. We were stood in a line, watching him, eyes narrowed. Each of us were thinking something different.

"Why?" Chloe hissed back. "He's fit. And not that much older…"

"But you have a *boyfriend*," Kayleigh added, to which we all rolled our eyes.

As if *that* would stop her.

She made her move while we stood there, watching. Forced her way between the grannies and tapped him on that sculped biceps, scrunching up her nose and beaming. She congratulated him on the set, on his excellent playing. *Did you write the songs yourself? Was your girlfriend the inspiration? Oh, you don't have a girlfriend. What a shame.*

She beckoned to us as the boy started leading her away, gesturing that we should follow. We did. Kayleigh was shaking her head in disappointment, and I felt a little sceptical, though thoroughly entertained. I had little sympathy for poor Tobes, who most likely did the exact same thing to Chloe every chance he got – but maybe that's presumptuous of me.

Orla was harder to read. She was staring at Chloe so hard that she almost made holes in the back of her head.

He was leading us back to where the tents were set up, in little clumps, dozens of them. The children had long gone to bed, and the stench of weed was stronger than ever. The boy had a firm grip of Chloe's bum now, squeezing so tight the fabric of her leggings was stretched to the max. All three of us couldn't help but stare.

We found his tent eventually. It was open, the door hooked backwards and fairy lights strung all around. It wasn't done half as artfully as the others, the lights harsh blue and the blankets spilling out dragged straight from a boy's bedroom, and the weed smell was most concentrated here, so pungent we could feel it coming from the tent in waves.

"I don't like this," Kayleigh said, as Orla shook her head in agreement. Both looked curious, though. Probably as curious as I felt. Chloe had ventured inside now, the boy on her heel.

We followed.

There were three other boys sat inside the tent. They all looked about twenty, though one was clearly younger, seventeen or eighteen. They were all smoking, but the rolls in their hands weren't tobacco. The biggest one, a ginger with a potbelly and face of scratchy orange freckles, grinned at us. His teeth were so yellow they almost matched his hair.

We sat. Kayleigh and I made sure to stay by the entrance, Chloe taking a seat on the first boy's lap, where he now had a firm grasp of her waist and was making slow, sensual movements, like he was grinding against her from below. It was obvious he was already high. The other three looked even more out of it, though the ginger was by far the worst, swaying and spitting every time he tried to speak. He was staring at us properly now, sizing us up, picking his favourite.

Roaming across us, our chests and legs and lips, he came to a stop on Orla. Watched her for a moment, taking in the fact she was specky and awkward-looking, with her head-torch and solemn expression. Then he smiled. It was a horrible smile, leering and cold, like he was deciding his prey.

Then Orla. Smiled. Back.

We did nothing as the ginger rose, trying not to trip up, and held out a hand to our friend. She took it unflinchingly, and stood with him, letting him lead her from the tent. Her cup of cider fell to the floor.

It was empty.

"She doesn't drink, does she?" Kayleigh asked, eyes flashing, and I shook my head back. It was pointless doing anything – Orla had already gone, rushing off through the campsite with that lumbering ginger on her tail, giggling and singing along to whatever George Ezra number was playing right now. We knew she wouldn't do anything stupid, that she was completely in love with Aaron and desperate to stay that way.

Right?

The boy whose lap Chloe was perched atop took a joint from the younger lad, lighting it and pushing it between his teeth. It was pointless worrying about Orla now. Kayleigh was offered one from the lad, but neither of us had ever smoked before, especially not weed, and she shook her head firmly. Chloe rolled her eyes, though, taking the joint from the boy beneath her. She placed it between her own lips, not taking a puff until she'd said, "You girls need to live a little!"

I think we both knew then that everything was about to go horribly wrong.

25

We waited a half hour in that stuffy tent before things started tilting sidewards. I was getting dizzy, gripping Kayleigh's knee to stop myself from flopping, and suddenly had the urge to giggle for absolutely no reason. Kayleigh shook my arm a little too firmly, breath hot against my ear.

"We need to go and find Orla," she said. Despite my blurred vision, I could make out the urgency in her expression, how serious she was. "It's been too long, and she's not used to being tipsy. What if she's done something she'll regret? Or what if… if that man has done something to her?"

Man. Because that was what he was. A man. A man, who'd run off into the dark with our tipsy friend, high out of his mind.

I focused on Chloe for the first time in at least ten minutes then. We'd been chatting to the two other boys, who actually seemed okay, about the festival and where they came from, how they were travelling the country in support of their singer friend, who was going to be the "next big thing". I wasn't so sure about that.

He was groping Chloe, I could just make out, one hand on her back and the other stuffed down her leggings, feeling about. Not that she minded. She just kept giggling, nuzzling his neck and crowing, "More, more!"

So much for being in love with Tobes.

"Chloe," Kayleigh said, interrupting the pair. Music was

still thudding from the main stage, but it had quietened down a little as the first few campers drifted off to sleep. "Chloe. Chloe, we need to go."

Chloe detached herself from the boy then, glancing up at us with bleary eyes. "What? No, no, I don't need to go. You go. I'm staying here with…" She started properly laughing, head tipped back as the boy was jerked into reality, taking his hand from her leggings and wiping it sheepishly on his jeans. "I don't even know his name!"

"Chloe, we're leaving," I cut in, grabbing one of her arms. She was surprisingly heavy for someone so slight, but the weed made her easier to manoeuvre, and Kayleigh swooped in to take her other as we lugged her outside. The cold air helped shock me back to normal, but Chloe was still floppy and delirious, barely even shivering. "Chloe, you need to stand up straight and walk, okay?"

She could – just – and managed to make it a few steps before collapsing into me again. We just had to make it out of the campsite, that was all. Make it out of the campsite, and back into the festival, where we could find Orla and get Chloe some water and try to find our way back to Sharon. Maybe we could get a taxi? But as I checked my phone, I realised we still had no signal here, and Google just kept loading and reloading, unable to connect. What happened to the promise of free Wi-Fi?

"Kayleigh, I'm going to have to leave you here while I go look for Orla."

Kayleigh frowned, clearly not desperate to be left in charge of Chloe, but nodded bravely.

"Be quick, yeah? And try get something to eat for Chloe, something to soak up all this drink…"

I left the two of them collapsed by a gatepost as I started to run towards the main stage, the lights of which made it easy to follow. There weren't any performers on now, and the stage itself was bare, music thumping from the speakers just tinny radio crap. If I could make it onto the main stage, maybe – just maybe – I could spot Orla and the ginge from up there. I'd have a good view of the whole festival, and if they were stood somewhere, soaking in the atmosphere, I was bound to spot his bright hair and freckles; his teeth alone were pretty luminous.

There was no one manning the stage, so I hopped up the steps with ease. No one even looked at me as I took my place in the centre, gazing out over the site. You could see right out to sea, to the moon rippling against the waves, could see the tents and food stands and few performers still going, trying to earn more tips... but no Orla.

I tried a new tactic then, rushing round the site in a spiral, closing in on the centre as I did laps. The main part was quite small, so there was nowhere really to hide, but I was still hoping she was somewhere, huddled up to the ginge as they supped cider and soaked in the atmosphere. I couldn't see her even when I'd lapped two, three times, covering every stall and stage. Where *was* she?

This was my old best friend we were talking about. My Orla. I knew her better than most, remembered every little detail about how she acted, how she spoke, how she thought. One thing I knew for sure was that there was a lot more to Orla Lloyd than met the eye. There was nothing she loved more than to surprise people.

She wasn't on the campsite in one of those tents, I knew that for sure. The ginge and his friends shared one between them, and they'd run away from the camp initially, towards the main stage. Where would two people go if they wanted to be alone – presuming, at this point, that they were alone – at a busy festival?

Then it dawned on me.

I rushed to the food stalls on the right side, where the main entrance was. Vans and marquees were set up to serve hot dogs and beer and overpriced cider, and the whole place reeked of fried food and stale burps. What was it that boy had said back in the tent, about how the three of them made enough money to follow their friend all around the country as part of his tour?

They had an *ice cream van*.

Sure enough, there was a lurid lilac ice cream van squatting beneath a tree, between two caravans selling jacket potatoes and sticky coleslaw. Metal covered the windows and the doors were all shut, so it was impossible to tell if there was a light on inside. I had to trust my gut.

The door wasn't locked. I could tell straight away as I tried the old handle, which swung through the air with ease. I pulled it back just a crack, enough to let my body slip through, the other vendors oblivious.

I heard her before I saw her. Heard her giggle, the one I knew so well, and a little moan, followed by another giggle. I heard her, and I think I knew straight away what was happening in there.

I shouldn't have turned on the light.

Orla was laid atop the ginger man, and spun around in horror as the lights flickered, flooding the van with the harshness of LEDs. My own jaw dropped. She had her leggings pulled down to her knees, bare bottom staring back at me, moon-white and mottled with cold. The ginger had no clothes on at all. He was hairy all over, the hairs just as orange as the ones on his face, and I got a full flash of his body as

Orla rolled off him and started hurriedly pulling up her pants.

It sounds stupid to say it now, but that was the first – and only – time I'd ever seen a *you-know-what* in the flesh. There, at the festival, like that. Ginger and speckled, like a great orange sausage. In a *lilac ice cream van*.

I didn't have much time to stare, because Orla grabbed my hand and started pulling me away, down the steps and back out into the cold. I was still in shock, so much so that I couldn't do anything but follow her, mouth hung open wide.

"Orla!" was all I could say, the horror in my voice evident. "Orla!"

Kayleigh and Chloe had somehow managed to make it to the festival again, from the campsite. Chloe had a cup of water and was sipping at it as we came to a stop beside them, trying to catch our breath. They were sat by the main stage, which was still unoccupied, and the crowds were dwindling, most either heading home or back to their tents for the night. I still couldn't speak, staring at Orla with wide eyes.

"Orla!" I repeated.

And Orla started to laugh.

It was high-pitched at first, the same giggles as when she was in the ice cream van, before I turned on the lights. But soon the laughter turned to sobs, harsh and heavy and so desperately *sad*, that even Chloe had looked up from her disorientated state to frown and prod Orla's leg.

"What's up with you?" she asked, clearly still out of it.

Only Kayleigh seemed to understand. She grabbed Chloe's arm again, tugging her to stand up. I did the same to Orla, linking the four of us, a solid line, us against everyone, now stronger, united.

"Shall we go back to the clifftops, away from... all this?"

I nodded at Kayleigh, replying, "I think we need to."

***

The clifftops didn't seem so far away, and it was a relief to leave the thumping music and the stench of weed that seemed to clog every corner of the festival. We collapsed onto the wet grass a good few metres from the edge, careful to sit Orla and Chloe furthest away, where it seemed safest. Chloe said nothing, slumped in her sports bra and leggings, somehow now without a hoodie but too high to notice the cold. Orla was still crying. They were silent tears, the kind which still wracked her body, spilling from her eyes and gaping mouth as she stared at the ground.

"Would you like to talk about it?" Kayleigh asked, reaching to take her hand.

I wasn't expecting Orla to say yes.

"Basically, Lucy just found me shagging that guy in... a fucking ice cream van."

I blinked at the language; Orla never swore, *still* never swears. But Kayleigh didn't flinch. She just continued to hold Orla's hand as though what she said was the nothing out of the ordinary – as though Orla slept with random guys all the time, in equally uncomfortable places. I didn't know when she'd gotten so *mature*.

"Okay," she replied, nodding. "And... what's the problem with that?"

She was going to make Orla spell it out for her.

Which she did.

"Aaron's the problem, obviously." Orla's voice broke as she said that. Aaron was the problem – obviously. Like Aaron was *always* the problem.

"Okay." Kayleigh nodded, glancing at me for help. I didn't know what to say, though. Orla wasn't *that* drunk, surely. Or maybe... maybe I didn't know her that well, after all.

"I've messed everything up," Orla continued, eyes filling with tears again. "I've messed everything up so, so bad –"

"Hey, hey!" Kayleigh squeezed her hand, and I watched the blood leave her fingers, flood to them again. "It's not a big deal, really. You can explain to Aaron that you were drunk, or not even tell him at all – and it's not as if it was your first time, was it?"

"That's the point," Orla said, and a few more tears escape her lids, rushing down her cheeks. They too were mottled, reminding me horribly of that moment in the ice cream van, pushing open the door to find Orla's bare bum staring up at me from the ground. I shuddered, trying to push the memory from my mind, as Orla added, "It was my first time. Aaron and I have never... done it."

"Oh."

I don't know what else there was to say.

"We tried, but Aaron's just... I don't know what's wrong with him, or me, but we *couldn't*. He couldn't get it... you know. He just kept trying but it just stayed..."

Just the thought of Orla saying the word made laughter burble up in my throat, though I tried my best to suppress it. Chloe couldn't. She let out a snort, patting Orla rather viciously on the back and shaking her head as she giggled.

"I always knew –"

"It's perfectly normal!"

"Sorry, sorry! Sorry, Orla. Erectile dysfunction *is* perfectly normal, but –"

"It was tiny, too." I was pretty sure this wasn't just tipsy Orla talking now. It was years of pent-up despair over Aaron, years of having to act like he was the perfect boyfriend, like they were made for each other, like he could do wrong. It was years of not being able to confide in anyone, of only having Aaron to vent to... and she obviously couldn't vent to him about this. "Like, literally miniscule. I've eaten bigger cocktail sausages."

This time, I really couldn't help the laughter which escaped me. We were seventeen, well past the age of giggling about body parts and doodling them in textbooks... but with the girls, I was twelve again, at a past camp, snorting as we sat in a tent under the light of a torch. It seemed to infect Kayleigh too, because soon all three of us were giggling so much we couldn't stop, and even Orla was trying her best not to join us.

"He – we tried *so* many times, but it never gets past mouth stuff, and he's terrible at that too."

Again, whether it was the weed or just the situation, I couldn't tell. All I knew was that the idea of Orla and Aaron doing anything other than maths homework made me laugh so hard I wanted to throw up, leaning on Kayleigh for support, all four of us now dissolved into such peals we could barely catch our breath.

"I mean, you're right, Chloe. It's perfectly normal, but I... I just... combined with everything else..."

Chloe stopped laughing, then. She sat up perfectly straight and said, in such a matter-of-fact voice that I almost thought she was going to recite deforestation facts or read the news to us, "Toby's bends to the right. It's like... wonky."

The way she said it – so calmly, like it was only just dawning on her – was enough to set us off again. We laughed and laughed and laughed, there on the clifftops, the four of us together, for so long the memory has turned hazy, blurred, almost like it never even happened. I can picture the scene as though I wasn't really part of it, drifting above Lucy, Orla, Kayleigh and Chloe. Four girls, laughing until their sides hurt, a little high and a little tipsy, unaware of everything that was about to happen to them.

I thought, at the time, that Orla's confession would bring us closer again. Despite walking in on her losing her virginity to a complete stranger, I thought, maybe, it would change something between us, tie us together in a way which wasn't strong enough before. Her relationship with Aaron wasn't perfect, not by a long shot, and she needed a friend – a proper friend, a friend who wasn't her boyfriend or mum. Though it pained me to admit, I'd missed Orla. I'd missed my best friend.

In a way, that night on the cliff seemed like the perfect goodbye. If we weren't to have a camp again, maybe ending on such a high, giggling about such personal things, sharing secrets, huddled together by the sea, was the best way to end things. Seven years of The Very Best Group Chat, coming to a close in such an intimate way. It felt right. Like this was the end of an era, but the beginning of another, one which would perhaps be... *better*.

It was Kayleigh who spoke first.

"Dan... I think he might be the one."

She didn't say it in a way to spite Orla or Chloe, wasn't trying to gloat about the fact she was with the love of her life while Orla struggled with erectile dysfunction and Chloe with a wonky willy. She really meant it. She thought Dan was her soulmate, that he was it for her.

And in a way, I guess he was.

"I'm really glad," Chloe said softly.

We were all thinking the same, I think.

That despite everything that had happened in the past – on both Chloe's end and Kayleigh's, and on mine and Orla's, for not sticking by her when the photos were first leaked and Kayleigh was left all alone – we were just so glad that she was happy. That she'd found someone who loved her for who she was, and who she loved, too.

I'm still grateful for that.

26

I don't say all of this to the police, obviously. The bits about Chloe getting touched up by some guitar player in his tent; the bits about the weed, how we were all a little tipsy and high as we made our way back along the cliff path to Sharon and our own campsite; the bits about Orla and the ginge, writhing on the floor of a lilac ice cream van. I don't tell them about Aaron's erectile dysfunction, either, though he probably doesn't deserve my protection.

Orla continued to talk about him as we got back to the site, the four of us nestled into mine and Chloe's tent, lit up with fairy lights and a lantern which hung from the centre. It was freezing, but Chloe had enough blankets for at least ten more people, and we all perked up when she brought us doughnuts. Proper doughnuts, with a sticky jam centre and a healthy sprinkling of sugar. Kayleigh licked out all of the jam in hers, then spent a good half hour nibbling through the doughnut itself, lips encrusted in sugar.

We found out that Aaron had been a pretty rubbish boyfriend from the beginning. He had a thing about body hair; he wasn't a bushy guy, and the hairs on his legs were fine and wispy and barely visible to the naked eye. He made Orla shave every hair which sprouted from her body (aside from eyebrows, head-hair and eyelashes, which he deemed acceptable). He wouldn't go near her unless she was perfectly clean shaven.

He was mildly autistic, Orla explained, which was why he was so particular about things. Not that it explained his control over Orla – not in the way she thought it did – but it helped her make excuses for him, in a way.

"I think I've been blaming every little thing he does on his autism," she tells us, wiping her eyes. "And yes, he struggles, says things he doesn't mean, and I completely understand that. But… sometimes, I think he might just be a not so great guy."

Then there was the issue of grades. Orla told us how he put more pressure on her to succeed than even her parents did, which made me feel queasy. Orla's parents were big on school, and wanted Orla to go off and do great things after her A-levels. Aaron, however, had insisted on the fact they were both going to Cambridge. Him to study mathematics, her chemistry. It was the only way he could envision their future.

"I already know I didn't get an interview," she said, gritting her teeth. "I haven't told Aaron yet. I just said that chemistry must take longer to release its final verdict than mathematics. I don't know how we'd survive going to different universities. Aaron hates texting. He says I'm too clingy, trying to contact him all the time. But even he knows we'd probably break up if I went elsewhere. We couldn't do long-distance."

I remember thinking about Ethan, then. Thinking how he and Lauren had broken up after trying to do long-distance, but how it had actually worked in their favour, as he'd now met me, and things were possibly going to happen between us instead. Everything works out in the end, I thought.

How naïve was I?

We talked and talked and talked until late into the night,

Orla about Aaron, Chloe about Tobes, Kayleigh about Dan. Aaron had a peanut-shaped mole on his left shoulder blade which repulsed Orla. Tobes was very physical, and made Chloe feel guilty for sometimes just wanting to watch TV and chill (I'm ashamed to say, I assumed would be the other way round). Dan was awkward in that department, but maybe that was better for Kayleigh, because he always asked her permission before touching her and had checked about a dozen times before making sure she was ready to go further.

"How did he feel about you already shagging Ben?" Chloe asked. She was only echoing what Orla and I were wondering, though we never would've brought it up. The Ben Margate situation was always the elephant in the room, though we knew Chloe would never own up to leaking the photo.

Kayleigh shrugged. "That was… a long time ago. I've almost completely pushed the memory from my mind. Dan knows I slept with Ben, of course, but as far as we were both concerned, we lost our virginity to each other. I was so young when I knew Ben, didn't know what I was doing. I know we were both underage, but Ben should've known better. He took advantage of me, and of my innocence. I don't really count it as… you know."

I liked that about Kayleigh. She didn't seem to be dwelling on the situation. It clearly still pained her, but she'd moved on, allowed herself to be vulnerable again, let her guard down. She'd let Dan in, and so far, the gamble had paid off. She was happy. He was happy. They were in love, and would be for as long as they both had left.

The girls turned their attention to questioning me after a while. The only virgin in the group. Looking back to when we first met, all those years ago, I wonder if it was obvious that I'd be the last – not that it even matters, I suppose. I've always just been innocent little Lucy, who wouldn't say boo to a goose.

Probably. Even Orla had more to her than me, a reckless side she didn't let many people see.

I was the boring one. The boring, good one.

So we all thought.

"Do you *really* like Ethan Morgan, then?" Orla asked, frowning at me. "I thought he was dating that Lauren girl, anyway. You know – the one with the boobs who plays every sport under the sun."

"They broke up," I explained, though my cheeks went pink talking about it. I felt a weird sense of loyalty to Lauren, in that moment, which made no sense. "It wasn't right anymore, for either of them. We're just friends, anyway. We revise and play Minecraft and eat Pringles together. It's nothing... more."

"Have you kissed?"

The look on my face gave the answer away.

"Lucy! Oh my God, you dumb bitch, get with him already!" Chloe squealed, thumping me on the back.

"It's not as simple as that!"

I hated the way I said it, like I was thirteen years old again and discussing drama on the school playground, overcomplicating everything just to feel like I was a character in a soap. *It's not as simple as that*. But it really was. I was seventeen, too busy with school and exams and university applications to worry about anything serious anyway. As far as normal people were concerned, there was a fairly easy solution. I liked Ethan, he liked me. We were both single. We should get together. Was that not that obvious?

"He's fitter than you initially think, that Ethan," Chloe cut in, expression pondering. "Like, he's just a chunky, brown haired guy, on first glance, nothing special. But those big brown eyes... I think you'd be stupid not to go for it, Luce. That's my opinion as an expert on men, by the way."

"Thanks," I replied. "That's cleared *everything* up for me. Shall I just go round there now, bang him on the doorstep? You make it sound so... simple."

Chloe rolled her eyes. "Sarcasm certainly won't do it."

We handed round a second helping of doughnuts. These ones had chocolate cream stuffed inside them and were drizzled in pink icing. There were rainbow sprinkles scattered across the tops, and they smelt warm and unhealthy, the perfect anecdote.

"Mmm," Kayleigh said, licking her lips as she took a great big bite. "These are so, so good."

"The epitome of a chocoholic's wet dream," Chloe added, nodding her head.

"Delicious." Orla's contribution included such a huge bite that a load of chocolate cream spilt out and down her front, almost certainly leaving a stain.

"Lexie would've loved it." My response left everyone silent, munching slowed and breaths held. Lexie *would* have loved it. The doughnut, the chocolate cream, the blankets and the fairy lights and rainbow sprinkles...

"I think about her a lot, you know." Kayleigh. Eyes down, guilt evident in her expression. "What she would be like now, if she was still here. Whether she'd... have a boyfriend, you know. What A-levels she'd be doing, or where she'd be going to university next year. I still think about how easily it could've been one of us. She was the unlucky one."

That was a lie. It couldn't have easily been one of us on the tyre swing that night, because we all knew better. And because none of us were being bullied – not like Lexie was.

We had nothing to prove.

Not that we said that now. We just nodded along with Kayleigh, sharing in her guilt, a fragment of Lexie's death still stuck into each of us. Even Chloe. If you think Chloe doesn't feel pain, you're wrong. She feels it sharper than the rest of us, for all her sins.

"I bet she would've had a boyfriend," Orla said. "A really arty type. Remember how Lexie started getting into painting and stuff, right before she died? She made me a card when my granddad died, with a bunny on the front in a little funeral dress. She wrote some really nice things inside, even though we were never really close. She was just like that, wasn't she? Kind. Forgiving. I think I've probably learnt a lot from her."

We all nodded again. It was true. Lexie was kind, kinder in a way none of us really were. Except maybe Kayleigh, now. Although Orla claimed to have been influenced by Lexie, I could only really see the shift in Kayleigh, in how she acted, how she spoke. She was still the same slightly unsure girl we'd known all those years ago, but her values were brighter now, more of a priority. She stood up for what she believed in, for what she felt. She spoke her mind.

"I know you all think I'm a bitch for how I treated Lexie." Chloe. She spoke in a low voice, staring down. Her eyes were glistening, though I could see she was determined not to cry. "I beat myself up about it every day, you know. Thinking how I could've done things differently, so she'd… still be alive, I don't know. Even if Lexie was meant to die that night, maybe I could've made her last few months easier. Maybe."

None of us agreed with her, though it was true. She could've made a difference to Lexie in so many ways. But so could we. We could've called Chloe out, showed Lexie some solidarity. It wasn't Chloe who killed Lexie, but all of us, together. That was just something we had to live with. A consequence of our actions which would never go away.

"I miss her, you know." The sound of my voice surprised me. Did I miss Lexie? In my own weird way, I think maybe I did. I missed Lexie for the glue she was within our group, for the person she was inside, the person we all knew we should be, deep down. I didn't remember much about the girl who died five years ago; I still don't, not really. I've pushed out the memories, pushed them far, far away, out of my mind. But I knew, in that moment, that I missed Lexie for the friend she'd been to twelve-year-old Lucy. For the friend she would've become.

"To Lexie!" Kayleigh held out the remaining chunk of doughnut in her hand, and we all raised our own in solidarity, clinking them in the middle. They joined in a mishmash of chocolate cream and icing, runaway sprinkles. They joined, sticking together, as though they were all one doughnut, meant to be.

"To Lexie!" we all echoed.

In the end, it was Kayleigh who ate our newly formed doughnut, the four chunks stuck together. She licked every last bit of chocolate cream from her fingers, murmuring her appreciation.

Just like Lexie would've done.

27

Sharon awoke us the next morning, far too early, before the sun had even begun to rise. We only got two or three hours of sleep in the end; Kayleigh and Orla crawled back to their own tent after polishing off the last of the doughnuts, and Chloe and I only had enough energy to chat for a few more minutes before falling asleep ourselves. Sharon did her classic whack-a-saucepan wakeup call, startling us out of our dream worlds and into the cold darkness of the camp.

"Come on, girls!" she shouted, thumping the pan with a wooden spoon over and over, as though she thought we hadn't yet heard her. "It's a gorgeous, cool Saturday morning, completely devoid of rain! We're also about a half mile from the beautiful east coast of England. And what happens on the east coast?"

I don't think she was actually expecting us to reply.

"The sun rises over the east coast, that's what!" She banged the pan a few more times before a clunk indicated she'd put it down, and I relaxed back into my sleeping bag.

The shouting continued.

"Come on, come on, get dressed and out here before I come in and dress you myself! I've got a lovely breakfast buffet set out for you... I think you'll really appreciate the selection. Pains au chocolat, strawberry éclairs, yoghurt and granola... I might even throw in a few fresh blueberries if you're out here in five!"

That did it; she knew what a weakness Kayleigh had for blueberries.

Chloe took the longest to get dressed. I was in fresh leggings and a baggy t-shirt before she'd even had the energy to tug off last night's clothes, writhing in her bra and thong and complaining about how early it was, how she'd barely had any sleep, how she still felt a little drunk. I wanted to tell her how it was all her fault, but I was still on a delirious high from last night, ridiculously grateful for the camp and for my three oldest friends that I didn't want to do *anything* to jeopardise it.

Looking back, Sharon was in a weirdly perky mood that morning. We'd come back in the early hours of the morning, so of course we didn't hear anything coming from Sharon's tent... and even if we had been there that night, she was Sharon. She'd die if we ever heard a sound coming from the green canvas walls.

I never thought anything about the fact her tent was firmly zipped up, the fact that she only opened the door a crack when she crawled in to pull out her hiking boots. Hindsight is a wonderful, wonderful thing. I didn't question her random little smiles, the way she'd chuckle to herself when she thought we weren't watching. It didn't cross my mind that maybe Orla wasn't the only one to get lucky that night. Why would it?

We set off through the trees after clearing up the breakfast things in a hurry. Sharon was desperate not to miss the sunrise. Even after living on the east coast my whole life, I'd never seen a proper sunrise over the sea, and felt that was an integral part of the Yorkshire experience I should try and look forward to. Orla, Kayleigh and Chloe were like zombies, traipsing through the trees with their heads down and their feet dragging, but I was as bouncy and cheerful as ever, bounding ahead, retracing last night's steps towards the coast.

The sun was still hidden by the time we arrived. The dark blue horizon was just turning orange, a light scattering of gold covering the waves furthest from us. We settled near the edge on picnic blankets and with cushions propping us from behind, Chloe and I nestled together, Kayleigh and Orla to either side. Sharon sat a little way off, where she could smile and giggle as much as she desired without us paying her any attention.

We didn't talk much as the sun rose. It didn't feel right to. We were all so engrossed in watching the pinky yellow light burst from beneath the horizon line that nothing else seemed important.

Colour, erupting from beneath the earth; pastel shades, indescribable, blues and primrose and violet. And that orange. A vibrant, almost fluorescent shade I'd never seen before, not even as part of a sunset over Vibbington. We were engrossed completely, staring up at the sky, a rainbow reflected in each of our eyes.

Once it had settled, Chloe held up her phone to take a selfie of all four of us. She took it straight on Instagram, despite not having Wi-Fi, so she could save it to her drafts to post later on. We were all beaming, faces lit up by the sunrise, colours dancing on the grass behind us. Chloe never shared any of us with the world of social media, so it felt like a huge step, somehow. An indication that last night really had pulled us closer together, like never before.

I don't have a copy of that photo, of course. I kind of wish I did. It was one of the happiest moments of my life, posing for that image, sat on the clifftops with some of my favourite people as the sun rose in all its most vibrant shades, right over the east coast of Yorkshire. My land, my friends, my smile, all of my smiles. It couldn't have been more perfect.

Sharon started leading us back after the sun had long made its appearance and was now dancing across the sky in all its glory. Blue sky, stretching on for miles. Chloe was clearly wrong about the chance of precipitation – that's what we all thought.

In reality, we had approximately twelve hours left of cloudless skies before it started to rain.

Twelve hours.

That was it.

Twelve hours, until the first domino fell on our sequence of events.

28

Back at the camp, Sharon instructed us to get dressed into our trainers and comfy clothes – we needed to keep our hiking shoes dry for this afternoon.

"Come on, chop chop!" she called, as we re-dressed in our tents, complaining all the while. "I've got some great activities lined up for you all. It'll be so much fun!"

Fun, by Sharon's definition, had shifted hugely throughout the years. From innocent childhood games, ignoring the fact one girl could be left out, the idea that arguments might break out, tensions arise. Everything now was about teamwork and telling the truth. We'd had several "circle time" sessions during our weekly meetings, Sharon attempting to break down our walls and get us talking.

Chloe and I agreed on leggings and hoodies, though it was colder outside than we were expecting, a November chill high in the air. Sharon waved us over to the table where Kayleigh and Orla were waiting. In the cold light of day, Orla looked pale, frustrated, like she was well aware of what she'd done wrong last night and already starting to regret it. She didn't check her phone once. That was an improvement, at least.

Sharon started us off by splitting us into two teams. She artfully picked Orla and Chloe to go together, aware of the tension between the two and how Chloe always disregarded the nerdier of the group, and Kayleigh and me, who got on fine but weren't exactly close. We started simple, as usual.

That game where one girl stands behind the other and has to catch her as she falls, testing trust and our ability to take risks, to let go. I caught Kayleigh without a worry, and she did the same for me, laughing as I fell back into her arms. Chloe and Orla found it more difficult. Orla was gangly and on edge, and Chloe lost patience, pretending to try and catch her and acting shocked as Orla fell back onto her bum.

"Chloe!" Sharon scolded, though she couldn't tell if the failure had been deliberate or not. "Orla, get up, dear. Chloe... I'm disappointed in you! Orla could have seriously injured herself!"

Next was a sandwich competition – timed. Again, Sharon wanted to test our teamwork, and make packed lunches for later at the same time. She gave both teams a recipe for a BLT and set us up on the camp table, with ten minutes to present the perfect sandwiches. I fried the bacon; Kayleigh chopped the veg. We finished in five minutes, while Chloe and Orla were still arguing over wholemeal or white.

"To hell with this," Chloe said, rolling her eyes. "Are we gonna do something worthwhile today, or what?"

Chloe was always like this if she was losing; she just couldn't take it. It didn't help that Kayleigh and I couldn't help but snigger, Orla joining in as we saw Chloe's fuming expression go from mad to worse. Smooth skin disrupted by angry red cheeks and a pulsing vein; eyebrows furrowed in annoyance.

Sharon did have something worthwhile planned, it turned out. A game she called "spy" – apparently one her niece and nephew had come up with as children. A game demanding stealth, in need of concentration and skill, something we all severely lacked at camps.

"One team will be the spies, the other the bad guys," she

explained, pointing around the camp. "Just pretend you're 007 with one of his lady friends. I'll be Miss Moneypenny, or maybe 'M'. Chloe and Orla, you're the spies first, and Kayleigh and Lucy, you're the bad guys. The bad guys have to walk around the camp – you can't stop, you must keep moving – while the spies follow them, trying to catch them in the act. As spies, you must capture five images of the bad guys in five different locations before you can report back to me. The game is over if one of the bad guys spots the spies."

The game sounded simple – kind of. Kayleigh and I had to wander round the camp while Chloe and Orla followed us, from a distance, taking photos as we reached five different locations. We had to try and spot them to win. In reality, had we been bad guys, 007 and his lady friend would end up dead. We'd shoot them the minute we realised they were on our trail, and there'd be no second round to be had.

The game, coupled with the fact it was November and the sun had now sunk well beneath the clouds, allowed us to dash into our tents and get warm clothes on, clothes which would keep us camouflaged as we made our way around the camp. Black coat over my hoodie, and wellies, thick, green wellies I'd owned since I was twelve or so. They had a teensy hole in the bottom now, but it wasn't wet enough outside for me to be concerned. It would rain later, Chloe kept saying. The clouds were getting darker.

As bad guys, Kayleigh and I had a minute's head start. Chloe and Orla had to cover their eyes and count to sixty as we ran off into the trees, in the opposite direction to the cliffs, where the paths leading into the countryside were laid. We weren't allowed to leave the campsite itself, we'd been told. If we were spotted outside of the forest which surrounded the field, we automatically lost.

The forest was still lush, losing more and more leaves by the second, falling from the canopy and settling in the mud. Wellies had been a mistake. They were loud and thrashed through the undergrowth, snapping twigs and causing noise to ricochet through the trunks. Kayleigh couldn't help but giggle as I tried to step lightly, and a shout emerged out of the site itself – "We're coming to find you!"

"Shit!" she hissed, grabbing my hand. "We've barely even left the field!"

It was a mad rush, crashing through the trees like that, trying to get as far away from the camp as possible. Kayleigh had a plan, she explained. Find somewhere to hide, then wait until we had Chloe and Orla in our sights before setting off again. If we were following them, we could shout "Found you!" before they had a chance to snap us.

"That's against the rules," I told her, rolling my eyes. "We're supposed to keep moving so that that can't happen."

"The rules are flawed," Kayleigh insisted. "Like Sharon said, her niece came up with this game. It's not exactly foolproof."

We kept going, leaving a silent trail behind us. Kayleigh was out of breath before we knew it, and we had to stop against a tree trunk so she could catch her breath. I passed her an inhaler, one I never knew she needed. She took several swift pumps before handing it back, to where it nestled in my backpack.

Around us, the forest was silent. It was dense, much more dense than the one which had stolen Lexie, and the ground got slippery and slick with brown leaves the further we went. I'd expected us to reach the other side by now, but all we'd found was trees, trees and more trees, which went on and on and on, the distance dark and shaded.

"Where now?" Kayleigh asked, frowning as she got her breath back. "I don't want us to get lost, but we're so exposed here – there's nowhere for us to hide, and if we keep going, they'll approach us from behind. They'll have a clear line of sight to snap pictures."

"Then let's go left," I suggested. "At least then we'll be close to the site still, and can loop round and run back towards the tents."

Kayleigh nodded, grabbing my hand again as we set off, my wellies still making a racket. Hers was soft and clammy, and her breath was coming out in rasps. Mine was cold, going numb as we walked further into the cold of the forest. I felt her rub her thumb against my palm as though she could tell how freezing I was, and we continued faster, further and further through the forest. There was still no sign of Chloe or Orla.

The trees were thinning now, as we looped back to the edge of the site. We could just make out the field, our tents in the distance, but no Chloe or Orla, just a harassed Sharon trying to tidy up the mess from breakfast. She appeared to be talking, her mouth opening and closing as she soaked pans and plates in the pump by her tent, but I concluded she must have been singing. Some crappy oldie from the terrible radio station she insisted on always playing, perhaps; that must've been it.

"Stay within the trees?" Kayleigh suggested.

I nodded.

There wasn't anywhere to hide, it looked like. The banks of the nearby stream were too short, and if we tried to lurk in the water, Kayleigh's trainers would get soaked. I was shivering like mad now, despite the coat, and Kayleigh needed her inhaler again after all that walking. Why had this game ever seemed fun?

That was when we spotted it.

Some wooden planks, almost completely disguised from view, blending into the trunks. It was the red door which gave it away. Painted crimson and hung with a pretty welcome sign, a few measly leaves painted over the wooden exterior to act like climbers.

A treehouse.

It was built high into the trees, the door on its front presumably just for show. As we approached, we noticed a ladder built onto the trunk itself, the centre of the treehouse holding a little trapdoor.

"That's sick," Kayleigh whispered, letting go of my hand and pulling out her phone to take a photo. "It's a *proper treehouse*."

But her phone had died. She quickly plugged it into her portable charger, but there was no way to record the little house, to add it to our weekend's timeline. My own was still in the tent. There was no one else here to snap a pic of the treehouse, to render it permanent in the history of the forest.

The treehouse was suspended against the trunk, of course, brackets holding one side into place, the four corners held up by wooden pillars. Kayleigh went first, climbing up the rungs and fiddling with the latch to get into the house. The trapdoor opened upwards, and the inside of the house looked dark and uninviting, like the kind of place feral cats and spiders would lurk, waiting for their prey. I waited a second before glancing around, in case Chloe and Orla were watching, snapping photos of us.

"It's the perfect hiding place!" Kayleigh breathed above me.

Five rungs and I was in, pulling myself up by the edges of

the trapdoor, emerging into the space. Kayleigh was fiddling with something in the wall, so I passed her my torch in the dark; just as a pair of shutters swung open, and light flooded through the treehouse.

It really was perfect.

A cosy wooden space, just four walls, the red door at the front nailed shut and shutters on either side, the second of which Kayleigh opened, grinning. There were a few cobwebs lurking in corners, but someone, probably some little rainbows or brownies, had left cushions and blankets up here, along with an aged bottle of cream soda which looked well past its sell-by date. I nestled into one of the cushions as it squeaked, and a mouse shot out, disappearing down the trapdoor and into the forest.

"Oh my God," I mumbled, shuddering, as Kayleigh snorted. She was smiling. Properly smiling. Like this treehouse was the coolest thing ever, and finding it was the best thing to have ever happened to us.

There was another squeak from below then, followed by an outraged, "Shhh!"

"Chloe! Be quiet, you idiot!" Orla's tone was unrecognisable.

I half expected Kayleigh to shut the trapdoor and insist we hid, aware that the aim of the game meant Chloe and Orla wouldn't want to be spotted, either, that they'd probably wait somewhere to take photos of us as we emerged from the treehouse. But she didn't. The treehouse was much cooler than Sharon's weird little game of spies, and so she stuck her head out of one of the shuttered windows and yelled, "Chloe, Orla! Get up the ladder and come join us!"

Chloe went first, rolling her eyes as she stuck her head up and caught my eye. "I guess this means you win."

Orla was on her tail, crawling into the space and beaming as she looked around. "This is so cute!" she exclaimed. "Hopefully there are no spiders…"

Glancing at Kayleigh, I could tell we were both deciding not to tell her about the mouse.

"It's pretty sick," Chloe said, trying to sound aloof. "Hey – sound idea, right, guys? We bring up all the alcohol later and have a midnight feast here, string up some fairy lights, you know. Sharon will never hear us drinking if we do it here."

Chloe was right. It *was* a sound idea – better than sound, in fact. We each nodded our approval as she grinned, pleased that, once again, she was taking over, elevating the camp from s'cool to *seriously* cool.

"Plan," she confirmed, holding up a hand to high-five us, any of us. "Now that that's sorted… how about we just take some random photos, and tell Sharon we won? Anything to end this dumb game."

We couldn't not agree.

29

Lunch was those BLTs, with soup made from the remaining butternut squashes. We were all pretty butternut squashed-out by now. Sharon thought it was hilarious how out of practice we were with healthy eating; all of us, even Chloe, were craving a McDonald's, a juicy burger or some sumptuous fries.

"I'll go get us all pizza tonight – how about that?"

It had been suggested on the planning sheet, but hearing her confirm a takeaway rose our spirits.

"Sick, Sharon!" Chloe said, grinning and nodding. "I mean – thanks!"

We went on a hike that afternoon, the five of us, through the luscious countryside between North and East Yorkshire. Rolling fields, dotted with dying heather and rich, winter-struck grasses, and tumbling fences, hedgerows near completely bare. A few trees remained, wilting with bare branches and a few orange leaves hanging on for dear life. It was still autumn, but the countryside felt bleak as we waded in our best hiking shoes and snapped pictures of the scenery, which was just as depressing as the season.

Even the clouds were grey and miserable, growing ever darker. They were blowing overhead so fast it was hard to keep up with them. Snippets of blue sky shone through now and again, a horrid shade of azure which seemed out of place in November. The sun was nowhere to be seen.

It felt a world away from the morning's sunrise, hiking away from the coast as a procession of five... but it wasn't all bad. We were happy, laughing and joking and posing for selfies, trying to find landmarks on the map Sharon had marked out. An old church; the site of a Norman castle; a weird tree which had been struck by lightning five years ago and had burst into flames. Only the trunk remained, too saturated to have burnt completely, though it was blackened and falling apart in great chunks.

Yet despite this, there was no sense of foreboding, no foreshadowing the fact that everything was about to go wrong. I know that's what Officer Joy and Pudrow are hoping to hear, but it's true – everything felt normal. Better than normal, in fact. Like we were all friends again, on a hike through the countryside. Just four ordinary teenage girls.

We got back around five, mud-splattered and exhausted, and collapsed into our tents to change into something warmer. It was chilly now and the sky was darkening fast, both as the sun set and clouds swam together in all shades of black. I don't fully remember what I wore, which is a laugh; they were the last clothes I wore that weekend, before changing on Monday morning, ready for the police to arrive. Leggings, I think. Maybe a hoodie. I'd gone clothes shopping with Nora the week before, and everything was new... I can't even recall what I packed for the camp.

Sharon insisted she'd be fine going for pizzas by herself, as long as we sat tight and didn't leave the camp while she was gone. She clearly still had no idea about the festival. One margherita, two meat feast, two Hawaiian and a garlic bread. Two sides of chips with chip spice, of course. Four diet cokes.

She didn't lock the gates behind her, but we felt safe as we sat around the campfire and waited, chatting amicably about the hike, the sunrise, our plans for later. Chloe still had all that alcohol stored in our tent, and now we had the treehouse, too. We'd bring a blanket or two each, and two strings of fairy lights. Our camp mugs would have to suffice.

"We can play truth or dare!" Kayleigh suggested. None of us had the heart to point out what happened last time we played truth or dare... or maybe they didn't remember. Daring Lexie to try out that tyre swing, late at night, without Sharon's supervision. Not having a clue she'd go back later to try it out for herself.

Sharon returned after forty minutes or so, with a huge bag packed full of takeaway boxes and some fruity cider, a "treat". She clearly felt cool for bringing us alcohol, so we smiled and thanked her and tried to act appreciative, though we'd all drunk enough strawberry and lime over the last three or four years to last us a lifetime. We cracked open the cans as she passed round the pizza, Sharon herself taking a few slices and a handful of chips, retreating to her tent to leave us in peace.

That was the last we saw of her that night.

The pizza was good, if a little cold. I always played it safe with a Hawaiian, but the pineapple was still hard and juice-filled, like it hadn't been properly cooked, the ham too chunky and ladened with gristle. Orla was sorted with her margherita, and Chloe tucked into a meat feast, spilling barbecue chicken all down her front. Kayleigh went for Hawaiian, too. She had excellent taste.

The campfire continued to burn. It was about seven now, maybe eight. Or maybe it was later. It hadn't started to rain yet, but we could smell it in the air. Moisture, waiting to burst.

"Shall we go put our PJs on soon?" Chloe asked, wrinkling her nose. "We need to be in warm, comfy clothes for... later."

Later. The treehouse was waiting beneath the trees for us, in all its wooden glory. We all nodded our agreement as we polished off the pizza, Kayleigh reaching for the last few chips, Orla drinking up her coke in one long swoop.

She hadn't checked her phone all day, not since we'd wandered to the cliffs this morning, watching the sunrise and snapping photos. She clearly felt awful after last night, guilty for what happened and yet all mixed up after confessing what a bad boyfriend Aaron was. She seemed absent as we gathered around the fire, tidying things up and ditching the takeaway rubbish in the binbag Sharon had provided. There was no movement coming from Sharon's tent, and there didn't seem to be a light on inside it. We still tried to talk quietly, however. We were naïve enough to assume she'd care if we disappeared into the forest that night, leaving her to make as much noise as possible.

Chloe and I went to our tent, Kayleigh and Orla to their own. Chloe needed me to take some photos for her Instagram. She'd been gifted a bikini top by some small boutique, and they were paying her a hundred quid to pose with it in our tent. It was more like a bra than a bikini, totally see-through, but Chloe was Chloe, and what Chloe says goes.

They were the photos Officer Joy was talking about. The "racy" ones, whatever that means. They weren't that racy, anyway. Top a bit revealing, bottom half fully covered. Chloe was makeup-less and pouting, holding her perfect hands up to her chest to model the garment, throwing her head back and laughing, blonde hair mussed up. I took them with the flash on, capturing every detail of her perfect body. Looking back, it's a wonder I didn't feel jealous. I was so secure in the fact Ethan liked me that I didn't need to worry about not looking like a model, didn't envy my friend at all.

We took five in the end, which she edited using one of those proper editing apps she paid for. She tried to explain the ins and outs of influencing to me as I nodded and smiled politely.

We got the stuff ready next. The bag of alcohol, waiting to be tugged to the treehouse; our many blankets and cushions, stuffed into my duffel; a spare string of cherry fairy lights. Chloe insisted on dressing up for more photos, pulling out a fancy pink top and joggers which looked to have cost a fortune, grinning as she saw my face.

"Get yourself a cute outfit, Luce, and I'll take some for you too."

"I'm fine as I am," I objected, glancing down at my outfit. "I don't need to take *more* photos, Chloe."

"Think about Ethan!"

I thought about Ethan, and still didn't change.

We were stood at the entrance to the tent, listening for Kayleigh and Orla. All was silent. They must still be in their tent, getting ready, though God knows what was taking them so long. I glanced at Chloe and said, "Shall we go get them?"

This is where the story changes.

I tell Officer Joy and Officer Pudrow that we went to get our friends from their tent. That they were occupied by a game on Orla's phone, and that was why they were taking so long. I tell them we then walked through the forest and climbed up the ladder to the treehouse. That we opened the trapdoor and spilled inside with all our blankets and cushions, scattering them around then collapsing against them with our bottles and mixers, pouring drinks and snaffling popcorn from the big bag we had between us.

I tell them we heard nothing from Sharon that night. That I can't say any more, not today, not when it's still so fresh, traumatic. I've told them what they need to know about the first and second day; can I have a break? I'm tired, so *tired*. There are tears in my eyes. I've done what I came here to do, and now they feel sorry for me. Officer Joy even looks *sorry*, handing me a tissue for me to blot my eyes. She nods her sympathy as I explain how hard it was for me to recount the events, to explain what happened leading up to Kayleigh's death.

They have what they wanted. They have a story, a story they think will help towards their investigation. They have times and places and a beginning, the beginning of something terrible. They think they can work with it. They have a version of events, events they can use to pinpoint three deaths, three gruesome deaths, like they're playing Cluedo with our lives.

Only… that version of events isn't *strictly* true.

"Thank you for your cooperation, Lucy," Joy says, patting my hand. She's not supposed to touch me – right? – but she's on *my* side now. I'm being good, assisting their little investigation. If they really were playing Cluedo, I'd be one of the playing cards, the answers spelled in bright red letters. Weapon? Location?

Who did it?

"Can I go home now?"

"Of course, of course."

The shuffling of papers, then a cough.

I take a sip of tea, but it's gone cold.

"We have more to work off now, so we won't have to see you again until next week. Thank you again, Lucy. We understand how hard this is for you, but the fact you're assisting us is really, really great. You're doing great. I know this must be highly traumatic for you, but you're handling everything so maturely. You know, at the end of all this, you could be in line to get an award… for services to your community, that sort of thing."

I smile. Show all my teeth. Take another sip of tea.

"But yes, thank you, Lucy. We'll see you in a week, yes?"

I nod. Stand from the chair. Push it back, so far back that it hits the door behind us.

A week.

I have another week.

PART TWO

Dear diary,

It's funny how this very notebook is turning into a confession.

I bet Officer Joy would love to read this. To flick through the pages with a little smile on her face, pulling the dots together with her painted fingernails on her night off, toddler on the chair beside her and dog at her feet. Her husband watches football alone in the kitchen while she works, picking at Kayleigh's murder like a scabbed wound.

The other girls would love to read this too, right? Chloe, unveiling how perfect and pretty I think she is, the star of the show as always, making the camp so much more interesting than it had to be. And Orla, misunderstood, trapped in her relationship. Finally set free.

And Kayleigh.

Kayleigh.

I never quite realised how much I liked her until that weekend. In another life, I think we might've become good friends. Over the years, years of bullying and name calling and horrible messages sent straight to her inbox, humiliation and hurt, she'd grown humble, kind, gentle. She was understanding and funny and enthusiastic, and I could tell she was a good girlfriend. That she loved Dan a lot.

Maybe she wouldn't have gotten on so well with Nora and Alicia – she was different to them, after all – but I think she could've fitted into my life well. She was real, raw, genuine. I never knew she was the kind of person I was missing.

I guess I'll never know what Kayleigh and I could've become. I guess I'll never find out whether she and I had it in us to survive in the real world.

And who can I blame except myself?

30

I sleep for at least thirteen hours, waking to find light peeping through the windows, my bedroom cold. I don't go to school. I don't do work. I'm too drained from the questioning to even move from my bed, lying with all the blinds closed and curtains drawn as my phone buzzes with unread messages and my head reels.

I've been running out of time, and I didn't even realise until now.

Whose idea was it to tell Officer Joy and stupid Officer Pudrow what happened those first few days of camp? Did we not consider the fact we'd have to eventually admit the truth about the next few days, that it would only put a stopper on the investigation short-term? I'm all out of ideas and inspiration, out of excuses. We're stuck. When they realise they won't get any more answers from us, they'll assume we were involved, and ramp up the investigation. Even if they never find out the truth about that weekend, they'll accuse us of something even worse.

I feel sick just thinking about it.

Mum and Dad don't press me once I say I'm not going back to school yet, though they're adamant I need to revise – and send off my university applications. I show them the flashcards I've been making on Thursday night, over tea, and by Friday, I have my personal statement all polished up. It's pretty bland, but better than nothing. Mum and Dad both tear up as they read it, fish and chips wrappers splayed across the table before us. They get up in turn to hug me.

"It's brilliant, Luce," Mum says, squeezing my shoulder. "All the stuff about your Duke of Edinburgh award, your hockey achievements, the volunteering you did last year at Brownies… I'm so proud of you. You've written it so well, in such a humble voice. They'll have to offer you a place, they can't not!"

I smile, but it doesn't quite reach my eyes.

"I second that," Dad says, reaching over to hug me from the other side. His breath reeks of vinegar and I fall into his soft stomach, heart pounding. He shouldn't be proud of me. Neither of them should be. But something deep inside me still wants them to be, so I keep my mouth shut.

"Where are you applying?" Mum asks, recoiling and resting her chin on her hands. I'm still in Dad's arms but they're both watching me, smiling, waiting for my answer.

UCAS allows you to apply to five universities. You only pick your top two once each uni has responded to your application. Most people pick four decent choices and one lower ranked, just in case of a disaster on results day; I've always had it in mind to pick five top unis, ignoring the safety net. I never thought there'd be any chance of me fluffing my exams.

But as I look at my parents' hopeful faces, I feel a trickle of guilt.

"I… I decided to look further afield," I say, making sure to keep my voice light. "After everything that's happened, I'm not sure I can stomach staying in this area, with all the same people. I want to push myself."

"Go on," Mum says, though her smile has dropped.

"Well." I try to remember the five universities I picked, on a slight whim. "There was the University of Exeter, which has a great English and history course. Then the University of Bath, and the University of Warwick. The University of Liverpool, because it's on the water. And… and the University of Glasgow."

Dad blinks, pulling back from me. "Glasgow? That's… in Scotland."

"It looked like a nice campus."

"What happened to York?" Mum adds. "It's only a forty minute drive. It's beautiful, and highly ranked in English…"

"Or Durham!" Dad says. "It's one of the best in the country, and such a lovely city. It's not too close…"

Orla.

Orla is thinking of going to Durham, since she didn't get into Cambridge.

"It just didn't appeal to me," I say, though my cheeks are flushed bright pink. "It was too… upper class. Like, that's where all the posh kids go, you know? I wanted somewhere normal, and… with more to do at the weekend, more shops, cinemas, that sort of thing."

"So you picked Warwick?" Dad blinks. "You do realise where the University of Warwick is?"

"And most of those universities are down south!" Mum continues, shaking her head at me. "They're so *far*, you'd have to get multiple trains there and back, and we wouldn't be able to come and pick you up regularly, even on weekends. I just…"

"I can't stay close to home just because you'll miss me too much –"

"It's not about that!"

"Alicia's going to London, and Nora's literally going abroad for a term –"

"But you're not like that."

I pause, instantly hurt. "What do you mean?"

Mum and Dad exchange glances, which only makes things worse.

"What do you mean? That I'm not going to cope well with uni? That you want me to stay close to home so you can *keep an eye* on me?"

"Lucy, don't be daft," Dad says, his cheeks pink. "We just mean that you've been through a lot, and moving away from home is a huge, huge upheaval. We're not sure whether moving further away would be difficult for you, that's all. At least if you're close to home, we can come and see you at any time, as can your friends! What about that lad Ethan, the one who's staying in Hull? Don't you want him to be able to see you, too? And your other friends, when they're not at uni?"

"And Grandma and Granddad?" Mum adds. "And Aunty Jo, when she's back from Mauritius?"

"Well, yes, but I can't just stay around here for them, not if the best university for me is… I don't know, down south, or in Scotland, or even overseas! You can't hold me back just because you –"

"We're not trying to hold you back, love." Dad pats my hand, and furious tears come to my eyes. "We're being sensible, because we love you and want you to be happy."

I know that. I want to stay round here too, stay close to my family, stay in the north.

But if by any chance I don't get arrested within the next week – if by any chance I even make it to uni – I want to be far away. I want to be a hundred miles across the country in a city where no one knows me, and no one can find out about what happened. I want a fresh start.

I especially don't want to be near Ethan.

"Just think about it, okay?" Mum says gently. "Maybe swap Glasgow for Durham, so you at least have the *option* to pick it as your top choice, yes?"

"Fine." I smile through gritted teeth, and Mum and Dad beam triumphantly. "I'll switch Glasgow for Durham, but that's not to say I'll *pick* Durham, even if I do get offered a place."

They continue to beam as we polish off the rest of the chips, and guilt steams inside me. I've pleased them. They're even more proud of me, now.

Which is all the more reason not to confess.

31

We're waiting in the car, come out quick or your dad will pounce on us and try to feed us his carrot cake. Lish says she's dieting again so that's a no-no.

Wait, Lish says she isn't actually dieting, she just doesn't want a food baby this afternoon in case she wants to try on any clothes.

THIS IS ALICIA ON NORAS PHONE, HURRY UP I DO NOT WANT YOUR DADS CARROT CAKE OK

I smile into my phone, my two best friends blowing it up with messages and silly selfies. They're waiting in the car for me, so I put the finishing touches to my makeup and pull on the leather jacket hung behind my door. I look good. White flares, black cropped shirt, brown leather jacket, my Doc Martens. Getting ready this morning gave me something to do, to take my mind off everything.

I submitted my university application last night, Mum and Dad watching over my shoulder. They clapped and cheered and we all opened a bottle of Prosecco, then paid for a film on Amazon Prime and watched it with toffee popcorn and homemade cocktails. The three of us went to bed a little tipsy, smiling and laughing and taking our time in the bathroom, but it felt weirdly nice, like old times. A few weeks ago, I was closer to my parents than anybody else in the world. Things have drastically changed since then.

I didn't realise, but we only have two weeks left of school now. Mocks begin on Tuesday. I have to go in for them, or risk not receiving grades at all. It wouldn't make a difference, but Mr Roberts is funny about that sort of thing. I received a sharp email from him this morning, insisting I make sure I'm there first thing on Tuesday morning for the English mock… or I'll be in "serious trouble", whatever that means.

I think I can do it. I don't have to worry about my next interview until Wednesday night, though I've planned in my head a little speech to tell the officers, something about me needing to focus on my mocks and revise in the evenings, building up to them postponing any interviews until after the exams. I know Orla has mocks just a day after me, and Chloe's super busy right now with her Mum's salon, on the run-up to Christmas. It could work, moving our next set of questions at least another week into the future.

But I don't need to think about that yet. Alicia and Nora are waiting outside, and we're going into town to sift through the charity shops, trying to find an outfit for Oli's party next Saturday. I don't think about the fact Ethan will be there. Or about the message his ex-girlfriend Lauren sent him just days ago, asking to meet up this weekend for a coffee. I mean, I *do* think about it, but I try hard not to. Very, very hard.

I put the finishing touches to my eyeliner and smile into the mirror. I look fine. Happy, chilled. Fine.

The car is hidden by bushes as I make my way out of the house and down the path. Dad was in the living room watching morning TV when I said goodbye, and did in fact offer us each some carrot cake, but I politely declined, dropping a kiss on his forehead before I left. He told me to have fun, and not to get pregnant. I told him not to eat too much cake.

"Why hello, girls," I say as I slip onto the backseat, trying on my biggest grin. "Guess who submitted their UCAS application at last?"

There are twin squeals from the front as my best friends turn round to grab my hands and squeeze my cheeks, jumping so much that the car rocks. I tell them about my choice to go further away, how I picked Durham to keep Mum and Dad happy, and they nod their support. If it crosses their minds that I might not "cope" so far away from home, they don't say so.

"That's great!" Nora says, then turns to Alicia to pull a face. "I mean, I guess Ethan won't be seeing much of you. But... I don't know how to say this. Do you want us to say this?"

"Say what?" I feign innocence, though I'm pretty sure I know what's coming.

"Your little display at Maguires really did the trick," Alicia says, squeezing my hand. "He's out today with Lauren, getting coffee or whatever. Because you pretty much broke his heart, and according to Kev and Oli, he thought he had nothing to lose."

"By getting coffee with his ex?" I ask, then realise how I sound. "I'm not jealous –"

"Oh, you're *totally* jealous." Nora grins at me, then takes my other hand. "But it's okay, because we're going to fix this, yeah?"

"How?" I continue, suspicion rising. "If Ethan wants to see Lauren –"

"Then we're going to interrupt." Alicia beams back. "I never did like Lauren anyway. She was too perfect, too *nice*, like Barbie. You can never trust Barbie."

And even though it's a terrible idea – a terrible idea that

will never, ever work – I bloody love my friends.

***

Town is heaving. It's a Saturday in Vibbington, so all the mums and toddlers are out in force, trundling to the many coffee shops and playparks in their winter woollies. Christmas shopping has begun, and my friends and I walk together in a line as we battle the shoppers, the middle-aged mothers and thirteen-year-olds in sparkly crop-tops, elbowing our peers as we make it to the first charity shop.

"Oli says they're meeting at one," Alicia mutters to me as we make our way inside, out of the cold. "At the new coffee shop on New Street, I think – is it called the Nude Lion? So we'll make our way there for about quarter past, as if we're just off for a nice coffee and a catch-up, then pretend to notice them and ambush!"

"I don't think that's going to work," I say slowly. "Are you sure they won't notice what we're doing?"

Alicia isn't exactly known for being subtle.

"It's *Ethan*," she replies, rolling her eyes. "And Lauren hasn't seen us in months, so she'll probably want to catch up. Besides, she has no idea you and Ethan have a thing for each other, and –"

"We do not have a thing for –"

"Luce," Nora cuts in, "you totally do."

"So anyway, we'll ambush them, then pull up chairs around their table and ruin their cosy little date. It'll be perfect. That's where our plan comes in…"

"What plan?"

"You'll see."

"I'm not sure about this." I skip from foot to foot as we

wander towards the back of the shop, where they keep a rack full of old designer pieces and random pairs of trainers. Alicia and Nora are a wonder at DIYing clothes to make them look brand-new, and Alicia cuts and sews all her shirts into crops, her skinny jeans into flares. She has all these embroidered patches in a basket in her room, which she covers her tops and bags in. "I don't think it's right, anyway. If Ethan wants to meet Lauren for a coffee, why should we…"

"Because you like him," Nora says, squeezing my hand. "I know you're trying to protect yourself, but you like him, and you need to show him that. Lauren's great, but she broke up with him because she wasn't getting enough sex, for God's sake. If they get back together it won't last five minutes."

I try to smile and nod, but she's wrong, so wrong. I'm not trying to protect myself. I'm trying to protect *him* from someone like *me*. But some stupid part of me wants to believe my friends when they say this will work. The same stupid part almost *wants* to split up the rekindling of Ethan and perfect Lauren. And that *same stupid part* will take any opportunity to distract my brain from thinking about Kayleigh and the case, worrying about what the hell we're going to do.

Nora and Alicia find matching skirts at the back of the shop, which they insist they can jazz up with gems and sequins. I nod, keep nodding when Nora picks out a mesh top she can pair with a plain black bikini, holding it up with a frown. They try on the clothes in the changing room as I watch, smiling, clapping as they parade out in their new outfits. They look incredible, of course. Slender and confident, Nora's tanned complexion against Alicia's milky white.

We have to go to a few more charity shops to find Alicia a top and me a whole outfit, talking all the while about shoes we'll lend one another, accessories we have in the big box we share at Nora's house, deciding we'll go there before the party and order Chinese food. I'll definitely have to phone Officer Joy and postpone the interview, I decide, and get Chloe and Orla to do the same. They shouldn't mind; it's not as if the police don't have enough evidence to be working off after our latest revelations. Hopefully, they'll be as confused as we conspired.

We eventually find Alicia a tiny crop-top in bright pink, a totally Alicia piece, and a matching pair of disco-ball earrings, at which she squeals so loud the woman behind the counter tuts.

"I know, I know!" she gushes, holding it up to her chest. "Christmas puddings on my chest, and red boots – with those red Rudolph ears we bought from the school fair last year! And I'll lend you my Mrs Claus scarf, Nora… and those Uggs I got for my birthday."

They both look at me, frowning.

"Still haven't found you anything, have we?" Nora says. "I think we're looking at the wrong section. How about a dress? After today, you'll have to knock Ethan's socks off, cement the final part of our plan…"

But I'm not listening. I'm gazing across the road, heart beating, hands curling into fists by my sides.

My friends don't notice. They're too busy looking at dresses, holding them up to the light and commenting on cut, shape, material.

Orla is stood by Greggs, hand in hand with Aaron. She's wearing his fleece again. I watch as she reaches up to kiss him and he kisses her back, before pulling away stiffly, mindful that they're in public.

I don't understand why she's still with him. After

everything that happened that weekend, everything that changed, how can she wander hand in hand and kiss her jerk of a boyfriend as though nothing's wrong?

How much has she told him? They used to share everything, back when they were close. *Everything.* Surely not now. Not now she's participated in a murder, shagged another guy in the back of an ice cream van. Surely, surely not.

I feel sick. I'm fine. But I feel sick.

"How about this one?" Alicia's holding up a red dress. It's red and skimpy and dips in the chest area, and she's grinning as she twists it round. "It definitely has the wow factor."

"Sure," I say, smiling as I twist back round.

Sure.

Surely *not*.

32

When it gets to one, Alicia and Nora exchange excited glances and rush to take my hand.

"Are you ready?" they echo, and I roll my eyes as I nod.

We make our way to the Nude Lion, which is a newish café-slash-coffee shop on New Street, one of the road leading from Vibbington's centre. The town only really consists of coffee shops, charity shops and takeaways, surrounded by countryside and forestry, including the scrubby patch of forest Macey was found in all those years ago. Aside from its purpose as a suicide bridge, it's usually littered in condom wrappers and crisp packets, crumpled cans of Red Bull.

I've been there twice since, to pay my respects and lay flowers. I've been to her headstone, too, which is usually neglected, though her friends and family leave fresh flowers when they can. Out of all the headstones in the cemetery belonging to dead children, Macey's is the least looked after. Lexie's is still there, of course, her ashes scattered somewhere or other, name etched into the stone. Kayleigh's sits towards the front. They're running out of room, the council keeps saying. If people *keep dying*, they'll have to build a new cemetery on the outskirts of town, closer to the crematorium.

Nora and Alicia natter on about dresses and makeup and jewellery as we make our way to the café, presumably to take my mind off things. It doesn't help. I can't stop thinking about Orla, about her hand in Aaron's and lips against his, secrets held between them for the first time. Or not held, if she's told him. And if she's told him…

"You ready?" Nora asks as we get to the door.

I grimace. "As I'll ever be."

The stairs up to the café are tall and narrow, and Alicia leads the way. My heart is in my mouth, fists clenched. It's warm, that familiar coffee smell drifting towards as the sliding door opens and we flood into the room.

We spot them straight away; it's almost empty. Only one member of staff stands behind the counter – Kara from sixth form, a typical mean girl with patchy fake tan and dyed hair, and a best friend of Lauren's, predictably.

Ethan and Lauren are sat across the table from one another, engrossed in an argument. They don't even look up as we walk in. Lauren's voice is raised and Ethan is shaking his head, looking guilty, trying to calm her down as she says, "I'm just asking you to listen to me, Eth! It's not difficult. It'll only be ten more months and then I'm here, full time, in Hull, and we –"

"It's not just distance, Loz," he responds. I wince at the use of her nickname. Loz sounds an awful lot like Luce. "I don't feel the same way as you do, like I've said a hundred times. You can tell me long-distance will work all you want, but I can't change the way I feel. It's been too long, too much has changed. I've changed."

There are tears in her eyes as she stares back at him. The three of us are frozen in the doorway, too awkward to interject.

We shouldn't be here, listening to this. We shouldn't.

From the sound of it, we didn't need to break up their meet-up for them to not get back together. Or is that just wishful thinking?

"How have you changed? You used to love me, and you can't just *lose* those feelings, not really. They say you always love your first love. It's a thing. I don't get how you can… can *not* feel that still."

"Haven't you met anybody new?" Ethan cuts in. My heart soars, which it definitely shouldn't, as my friends exchange glances. "Haven't you been seeing other people, Lauren? Don't lie to me."

"I mean… I have, but just casually, and…"

"Have you slept with anyone since?"

Silence.

"I mean… yes. Just twice. This guy from college. We were talking for a while, and…"

"Exactly. It's ruined, Loz. You dumped me. Even if I still had feelings for you, there's too much hurt there, too many memories. I've changed too much, and I'm over you now. If breaking up with me was a mistake, you wouldn't have slept with someone else, would you?"

"It was all a mistake!" Lauren continues, and she's crying now, openly crying. I shouldn't feel glad that she's an ugly crier, but of course I am, trying my best to feel sorry for her as she wails at him with her mouth wide open and nose running, face bright red.

"I'm sorry," Ethan says, like there's no other words left. "Honestly, I am."

Alicia glances at me then, and I can tell from her face that she's going to step in. Before I can stop her, she's striding towards the broken couple, leaving Nora and I staring after her in despair.

They look up as she approaches, not spotting us at first. Ethan's expression contorts into one of confusion as he goes to greet her, before his eyes meet mine and it drops. We hold gazes for a moment, those brown eyes glued onto mine. It only takes a second for my stomach to turn to mush, and then he's gone, glancing back down into his hot chocolate with pink cheeks.

"Come on," Nora says, and we follow Alicia towards them.

"Nora!" Lauren exclaims, eyes wide as she looks between us all. "I'm so sorry, I never cry, let me…" She busies herself trying to find a tissue while we dawdle awkwardly, before Ethan springs up and offers to pull over some chairs.

"It's okay, we can stand, or –" I try to stop him, but he's already pulling three from a nearby table, positioning them around his and Lauren's. I make sure to sit as far from him as possible, though we're both blushing and it's clear our choice was obvious.

"It's so good to see you again," Lauren says, wiping her face with a tissue and smiling at Nora. Her eyeliner's all smudged, but now's probably not the best time to bring it up. "Honestly, it's been too long. I kept meaning to message you, but I've been too busy in Nottingham, you know how it is…"

"Oh, same," Nora replies, and I don't know how she keeps her smile from looking fake. "I kept wanting to catch up, but never found the time. You know, seeing friends and stuff, revision…"

"Yes, yes, of course." Lauren nods, then looks at Alicia and I for the first time, visibly confused. "Were you all just here to get coffee, or…"

"We were," Alicia says. "Mocks start on Tuesday, you know, so we thought we'd take a break from revision to come get drinks, do some shopping."

"Shopping? In Vibbington?"

What a *snob*.

"So…" I cut in. My cheeks are still pink but I try my best to sound normal. She clearly has no idea Ethan and I are even close friends, let alone anything more. "How *is* Nottingham?"

"Oh, you know, you know…" I nod, but we don't know, obviously. "It's nice, really nice, but I've missed all my mates and stuff back here. I was just saying to Ethan, school was so fun, you know? And living in a small community, all that. It's cute, quaint. All my friends in Notts say it sounds really humbling, living somewhere so out of the way… and with so few amenities."

"Yeah," Alicia replies. "*So* humbling."

Lauren doesn't spot the sarcasm.

"Anyway," Alicia continues, smiling with all her teeth. I spot Ethan narrow his eyes at her, as though he knows exactly what she's doing – and why we're here. I glance away as he meets my eyes, cheeks once again flushing red. Lauren is oblivious. She really doesn't have a clue that he likes me, or *liked* me, whatever he feels. She's so much prettier and smarter than me that she probably assumes he's out of my league… and knows it.

"Anyway. How's your love life back in Notts, Loz? Met anyone new?"

Ethan cringes at Alicia's question, an act which reverberates around the table.

Lauren opens and closes her mouth, eyes wide, before saying, "It's… I mean, I'm still single. But obviously I've been talking to boys, you know, here and there. Nothing serious, just… you know."

"Oh yes," Alicia continues, "we know."

Stop with the teeth, I want to tell her, but my own lips are clamped shut, hands held tight between my knees.

"Speaking of single…" Nora picks up from Alicia, turning

to me with a too-big grin. "You're going to be blown away by the dress we've got for Lucy, Ethan. She'll look absolutely stunning –"

"Nora!"

"Agreed, agreed," Alicia adds, beaming. "You won't be able to resist her!"

My cheeks are on fire, whole body burning. Ethan is equally red, staring at the table as though he wants to look anywhere but at Lauren and me. I don't want to look, either, but I apparently have no control.

She's staring at me. Properly staring. As if she's only just realised I'm in the room.

"Am I missing something here?" she asks slowly. "Because I wasn't under the impression…"

"That Ethan might have met someone new, too?" Alicia's expression is so unkind I almost don't recognise it. Then I blink, and she's just my ridiculous best friend, trying her best to defend me and to win back Ethan. It's stupid and it's embarrassing, but I'm so grateful for it that I almost throw my arms around her right there and then.

Lauren's own cheeks are pink, eyeliner still smudged and fake freckles all rubbed off. She sniffs, hand going to her bag's handle, and pulls up the neckline of her top uncomfortably.

"I'm sorry, I think I got things wrong," she says, standing to leave. "I'll… I'll see you girls around, yeah? And… I'm sorry for what I said earlier, Ethan. I was wrong, and I wish you and Lucy all the best."

She's out of the door before any of us even have the chance to say goodbye.

There's a silence as Nora and Alicia share triumphant glances, while Ethan stares at the table, simmering. Then he tilts his head up and looks me right in the eye, gaze not shifting as he stands up and pushes in his chair.

"Can I speak to you outside, please?"

Oh.

I follow him out of the café, down the stairs and through the ground floor door, out onto the street. Lauren is stood a little way off, waiting to cross the road. She starts moving when the little man turns green, and we watch her retreating figure without saying a word. She clearly dressed up for today. You can see her tiny waist and pretty, tear-stained face as she makes her way down the street without a single glance back.

Ethan's looking at me. I can feel his eyes on me as people walk by, still engrossed in their Saturday of shopping, kids tugging on their hands to make them go faster. It's painfully awkward. I only suggest we go to the park so that we're out of the way, so that we don't have to have this conversation in the middle of Vibbington.

It's only a short walk through the backstreets, and everything still looks pretty and autumnal, the beginning of December settling all around us. Miniature Santa Claus figures dot garden paths and Christmas trees are lit up in front windows, covered in tinsel. Ethan stares at the floor as we walk, expression unreadable. Is he mad? Is he mad at *me*?

The park isn't packed, but all the benches are full. I unwind my chequered scarf and drape it across the wet grass, gesturing for us to take a seat.

Ethan doesn't say anything for a moment, continuing to stare at the ground.

Then he glances up again, and his gaze is so piercing my stomach does a flip.

"Did you orchestrate that?" he asks. "Did you know we were going to be there, and interrupt us just so Lauren would leave?"

I hesitate, unsure of what to say. I don't want to lie to Ethan, but telling the truth doesn't sound so appealing, either.

Instead, I nod.

"Okay." Ethan breathes out, nodding with me. "Okay. But… why?"

"I just…" I falter as his eyes meet mine again, heartrate speeding right up. God, what *is* it about him? He's just a boy, like any other. Why can't I form audible sentences around him. "Alicia and Nora knew you were going to be there, and when they suggested it, it seemed like a good idea. I haven't seen Lauren in a while, so…"

"Don't lie to me, Lucy."

I flush again.

"Why did Alicia and Nora make it sound like we were getting together? You know that's why Lauren left, right? She wanted us to get back together, that's why she was crying, but obviously I said no –"

"Why?" I can't stop myself. "Why did you say no?"

Ethan blinks at me, shaking his head. "Why? *Why* did I say no? Why do you *think* I said no, Lucy?"

"I don't know –"

"Because I like you, that's why!" He pauses. "I really, *really* like you. I thought that was obvious?"

And even though it really shouldn't – even though it's wrong, wrong, wrong, and I know I'm no good for him, that it's only going to end in disaster – I can't help the shot of euphoria which goes fizzing through me.

"What?" My voice is breathy, short. Ethan's eyes crinkle. "Do you really mean that?"

"I think I've made it pretty clear. But it's fine, you don't like me, I get that, I just couldn't get back with Lauren while I still have feelings for –"

"I never said I didn't like you."

Another pause. Ethan is still staring at me, like he's scared that if he makes another noise I'll stop speaking altogether, and he'll never find out what I was going to say.

"I do. I do really like you. But… I'm damaged. I'm sad and stressed and worried all the time, and this case is driving me mad. All the interviews, the blame… it's too much. It'll be too much for you too, and I don't want you to have to deal with that."

"I don't mind," he says. It's automatic, just like that. *I don't mind.* "Luce, I really don't care. I want to help through it, take your mind off things. You don't even have to talk about it if you don't want, if a distraction is all you want –"

"I can't put you through that," I repeat, though I sound less convincing now, and I can't keep my eyes away from his. "It's not fair on –"

"Hey!" He takes my hands from where they were flapping in mid-air. Holds them still, safe. Warm. "Hey. That's my decision to make, okay?"

"But –"

"No buts." He smiles at me, shuffling closer. Too close. "I want you. I want you *so* bad, Lucy, I have done for ages. I don't care if you think I shouldn't, because I do, okay? And I'm here for you. I want to make things better."

I don't want to nod. I really, really don't. It goes against all my better judgement as a human, all the rules I've made for myself over the last few weeks. But I can't help it anymore.

"We're okay?" he checks, voice low, raspy.

"We're okay."

33

"Hi! It's Lucy."

There's a pause down the line as I jump from foot to foot, floorboards slippery beneath my socks. It's Sunday evening and I'm all dressed to go to Ethan's, but there are three last calls I need to make before I can properly let go.

"Hi?" Chloe's voice is hesitant. "What do you want? You know you shouldn't be calling, right?"

"I know. That's why I'm calling on Nora's landline."

"Sneaky."

"Very."

Another pause. I suck in a breath, suddenly unsure of what to say.

"I wanted to ask you something," I say. "Something which will buy us more time in the long run."

"Hit me."

"Cancel the interview this week."

I hear her thinking, before she says, "Continue."

"I have mocks, and so does Orla. They'll still have a load of information to chew over from what we told them on Wednesday, and if we ask them tonight, they're likely to agree."

"Cancel it until *when?*" Chloe asks. "Indefinitely? Forever?"

"Just until next Monday," I tell her. "To give us time to properly think of our next plan, to get our story into shape. We'll have to meet, you know. All three of us. To talk about what to do next."

"Agreed." She goes silent for a moment, before adding, "Can we merge the call with Orla, please? I'll do it from my phone, wait a sec…"

I wait as I hear a few harsh beeps, then the long, ding-dong, ding-dong of Chloe's phone ringing. I play with the wire on Nora's family landline, heart thudding. I came round this afternoon for some last minute revision, and she said she didn't mind me using the phone, as long as I was quick. I got Chloe to call me back so that she's paying for the minutes, and both Nora's parents are out. There's no need to worry about being overheard.

Nora herself is tucked up in her bedroom, headphones in, concentrating on crocheting the bralette to go under her mesh top for Saturday's Christmas party. Even though she always denies liking Kev, she got weirdly excited when he invited us all round for pre-drinks before the party, reaching for her crochet hooks and disappearing into a hole filled with Taylor Swift and pink wool.

There's a loud beep as Orla connects, her suspicion filling the line.

"Hello? What do you want? And who's the other number?"

"It's Lucy," I say, trying not to mind the harsh greeting. "I'm using Nora's landline –"

"What do you want?" she repeats. "I'm at Aaron's, revising for this week…"

"So you haven't broken up with him yet, then?"

There's a whole lot of defence in Orla's voice as she says, "No? Why would I do that?"

"Because some ginger stoner shagged you at the festival?" Chloe says this in a baby voice, clearly mocking her, but I can practically hear Orla's blush as she adds, "Taking your precious-weshus –"

"Okay, okay!" Orla cuts in. "Unnecessary, Chloe. It was a mistake. Anyway, what did you actually want? I still need three As if I want to go to Durham, preferably more, you know. I'm super busy with revision, up to my ears in flashcards, and –"

"You won't be going to Durham if you don't shut up for a second," Chloe snaps, and Orla falls silent.

"Well," I say, dropping the wire. "We've agreed to ask Joy to postpone the interviews, at least for another week while our mocks are on."

"Okay…"

"It'll give us time to work on our stories and come up with a reason for what happened that night. We can say we need to focus on our mocks this week, and that Chloe's busy with Christmas stuff at the salon, though it would be unfair for her to do it separately to us anyway, especially when we're all supposed to be traumatised."

"*Supposed* to be?"

I ignore Chloe's sarcasm.

"Anyway, I thought it would make the most sense." I wait for a response, adding, "Do you two want to ring Joy, or shall I do it?"

"I will," Chloe says. "I'll tell her I saw you two in Vibbington today, madly revising, and that we need the week off. It'll definitely work, I'm pretty sure she has a little crush on me…"

"Isn't she married?"

"So?"

We hang up at the exact same time, leaving Chloe to ring Joy. I stand there for a moment, by the phone, heart still beating ten times its normal rate. I can hear Nora's Taylor

Swift playlist even from downstairs, despite her wearing headphones.

Easy. That was easy.

Too easy.

I want to say that everything's sorted now, that everything's fixed, but there's an awful feeling of unease in my stomach. I'll have to see Orla and Chloe again, that's for sure. We haven't spoken in real life since the funeral, and the thought of seeing them in person is enough to put me off my food.

My best friend is still buried in her crochet when I knock, and beams as I enter. She pulls off her headphones and holds up the bikini top she's been making, which is tiny and baby pink, edged with white.

"Like it?" she asks. "I've done the stitches super close, so you can't see through it…"

"It looks great," I say, going to sit on the bed. "*You're* great."

"Thank you, bestie!" She grins, throwing it down. "I don't know why I'm even getting in a flap about it. It's not as if I like Kev, I don't think. I mean, we've known him our whole lives, and realistically, he'd never want anything to happen…"

I smile. Kev's had a crush on Nora since we were in year seven, and the only person who seems oblivious to it is Nora herself. He's never told anyone, and we've never discussed it, but it's painfully obvious when they're together. He can't keep her eyes off her, only looking up from his revision long enough to catch her eye. They'd be sweet together, but they're not even going to the same university, and Nora isn't one to try long distance.

"Why don't you think you like him?" I ask, scrunching up my nose. "He's different to your last exes, and they were all *disastrous.*"

Nora's had two boyfriends before, both losers. One was a freak called Simon who told all his mates all kinds of lies about her, and the next was his mate Callum, who only got with her for that reason. She slept with a boy in our geography class on a school trip to Calais, but he moved to Turkey three weeks later and never kept in touch.

Both my best friends have a body count of three and a kiss count much higher, but they're still completely clueless when it comes to boys. I smile at her now, poking her cheek as she blushes.

"I know, I know," she says, shaking her head. "He's kind and sweet, and now that you and Ethan are basically together, it'd be *perfect*…"

"We're not," I insist, but we both fall about giggling as soon as it's said.

"And Alicia and Oli are always flirting…"

"Alicia flirts with everyone."

"I know, but still." She sighs, shrugging. "We'll see. If he makes a move on Saturday, I'll take the chance, but I'm not just going to… I don't know, make it obvious."

"Nora, Kev's never had a girlfriend before! He probably wants you to make the first move."

"Oh, *God*."

"Just try it. Kev's lovely, you never know."

"I said we'll see!" She puts down the bikini top and turns to me, frowning. "Anyway, more important matters are at hand here. Why did you need to use the phone just now? I know it was to call your old friends, but… I don't get why you couldn't just use *your* phone."

I hesitate, pretending to open my phone and check my messages, though I'm surprised by how direct Nora's question is. I've always been closer to her than Alicia, but it still surprises me, especially given my reaction last week after hockey. She doesn't like Chloe or Orla, she never did. While she was sad to hear that Kayleigh passed that weekend, she hadn't seen her since year eight. She only felt touched by the news as it was so surreal to hear Kayleigh had been the same age as us, had her whole life ahead of her.

"We're not allowed to speak to each other," I say, trying to keep my voice light. "Because of the investigation, in case we're conspiring to lie to the police or whatever. It's stupid, but we have to comply."

Nora nods slowly, a frown spreading across her face. "So, the investigation's still going on, then?"

"As far as I know."

"When are you next being interviewed?"

"Probably after our mocks. They're being really cooperative in terms of our education, you know."

"That's good." Nora smiles, but it's like she's trying to read between the lines, like she knows I'm not telling the whole truth. I don't blame her. But I also don't want to tell her more.

"Anyway," I say, standing from the bed. "I better be going to Ethan's now. We're going to run through our history notes together, compare sources, make sure we're fully prepared. I'll see you at school, yeah?"

"It'll be good to have you back." She gives me a quick hug, then winks at me as she opens the door, shooing me out. "Don't do anything I wouldn't do at Ethan's, yeah?"

"That gives me quite a wide scope!"

Nora laughs, but her expression is empty as I disappear down the stairs.

34

I stay at Ethan's until gone nine. We play Minecraft and snaffle sour cream Pringles from the tube under his bed until the sun goes down and he stands to switch on his LEDs, which flash all colours of the rainbow as we play. Ethan makes a village he calls his haven, and I make a grand hotel, filling it with swimming pools and televisions and all the luxuries a person could ask for.

We kiss, too. We kiss far more than we revise, my history flashcards untouched on the floor between us. We kiss until Ethan's mum knocks and breaks the atmosphere, Daisy hurtling through the door and settling her stinky body on my outstretched legs.

All the while, I try to not feel guilty. Guilty for how little I've told him, and for how maturely he's handling this whole situation. Guilty for the way he views me, for the way he keeps looking at me, like he can't quite believe I'm real.

Any other week, this would make me uncomfortable for entirely different reasons. A month ago, I was just Lucy. Mousy, quiet, kind of ordinary. What did Ethan see in me? I was so *different* to Lauren. He was my first, and I was his second. Why me? Why not Nora, Alicia?

Now, I'm Lucy on steroids. The paranoid, suppressed version of the girl who existed all those weeks ago, the girl whose only worries involved exams and university and what clothes I'd wear to that weekend's sixth form party. That girl didn't *need* to worry about much else. Certainly not hiding from the police, keeping secrets from her family, her new boyfriend. She didn't need to worry about whether Sharon Jones would wake up from her coma, blowing my entire life to smithereens.

Chloe messages me around nine, neglecting to use Snapchat this time.

All good, we don't have to go in again until next Monday. Good luck with your mocks.

My heart stings then. She said good luck. *Chloe* said good luck. Chloe, who pretends she cares so little about other people, who's usually so wrapped up in her own existence that she has no time to fuss about anything other than her Instagram or Tobes.

I'm smiling into my phone when Ethan jabs me in the ribs, his breath hot on my neck.

"Who was that?"

"Just… a friend." I turn to look at him, an idea sparking in my mind. What was it that Oli said last week, when he first invited me to the party on Saturday? That I could invite my other friends, the ones involved in the case? That it might help to take my mind off everything, distract us from the case?

"So…" I continue now, averting my gaze. "I was wondering. You know Oli said I could invite a few friends to the party? Do you… I mean, would you mind if I asked Chloe and Orla to come with me?"

Ethan cocks his head to one side, frowning. "I thought you guys weren't that close?"

"We're not, but just for old time's sake, you know. And

because we've all been so bogged down with the case, and with… with remembering what happened that weekend. To Kayleigh."

That's right, Lucy. Play the trauma card. *We lost one of our oldest friends. We need the party to let loose, to cheer us up after everything that's happened.*

"That's understandable," he replies, a smile creeping over his face. "I always got on with Chloe, she was a laugh back in school. I don't think I've spoken to Orla much, but her boyfriend was okay. What was his name again?"

"Aaron. They're still together."

"Aaron, that's it!" He pulls a slight face then. "He won't be coming too, will he? I'm not sure if Oli meant for you to invite the entirety of our old school year…"

"No, no. Just Chloe and Orla."

"I *certainly* don't have a problem with that."

I'm grinning as I kiss him again, and he turns back to Minecraft. I unlock my phone again, click onto Snapchat. Go to The Very Best Group Chat. Start to type.

Okay, I have an idea. Do you two want to come to Oli's party on Saturday night? It starts at ten, I'll send you the address. If we go to a party together, we'll have an excuse to talk properly before we do the next interview. It's gonna be pretty chill, just a load of people from sixth form and a few others. He says you're both welcome.

It takes a few minutes before I get my responses.

Sounds good, I'll be there. Orla, I'll walk to yours to collect you around half nine, yeah? Meet you at the party, Luce.

Orla sounds sceptical, but her agreement gives me hope.

Fine, but I can't stay too late, I sleep at Aaron's on Saturdays.

I'm smiling into my phone again, but Ethan doesn't notice, focused on adding a field of pigs to his Minecraft village, next to his funny little allotment. My face hurts from grinning so much.

Everything's going to be okay. Things are getting better.

I just know it.

***

Mocks begin on Tuesday, but going back to sixth form doesn't feel as strange as I expected it to. Very few people stare as I walk into the common room on Monday morning, and I have my friends to back me up as I take a seat on our usual table. Although the three dead bodies have been on the news pretty consistently over the last few weeks (not that I've actually seen the news), people don't seem to care that much that I was there that weekend, or that I used to be friends with Kayleigh. Our school has had enough tragedy for it to seem that important. Ben Margate's sister gives me a sympathetic smile as I'm walking to English, but that's it. No one else seems bothered by my reappearance.

Mr Roberts calls me into his office before our history exam starts on Tuesday morning, closing the door behind me, and insists I take a seat on the sofa in the corner of his room. He talks at me for ten minutes straight about the unnecessary pressures of exams and how I need to focus more on myself and recovering after all the trauma, and I can't look him in the eye because it all seems such *bullshit*.

"Are you okay, Lucy?" he asks, frowning. "Are you listening?"

"Of course!"

The exam starts at ten on the dot, in the sports hall a little way off the main site. It's been crammed full of seats and desks to make space for the immense number of students wishing to take their mocks today, the papers laid out on the table ready for us to turn over. The questions are on Henry VII, and we've been given four sheets of A4 lined paper to answer fully. I cover three, considering that a mission well done.

Ethan meets me outside after, Nora and Alicia trundling over with dour expressions. We all found question one weirdly specific, but question three wasn't specific *enough*. It helps to discuss the exams, like everything's back to normal and they actually matter. We buy chocolate milk from the canteen to celebrate and drink them with Oli and Kev on the picnic benches outside, despite the December chill.

There's another mock in the afternoon, politics this time, and I'm pretty sure I flop it. It's the subject I care about least and zero effort goes into filling out the question and answer boxes, matching up the terms and definitions, scribbling over my terrible first attempts at guessing. Ethan's sitting a few rows in front of me and turns around when it's over to smile in reassurance. My stomach flips right over, and I wonder, for a second, whether the rest of my existence can be as innocent and exciting as this.

We go back to the park after school, just the two of us. His parents have family round and mine are a little too keen to know what's going on between Ethan and I, so we sneak between the trees for privacy, kissing and talking and flicking through silly Snapchat memories as it gets dark. My heart is so happy it could burst right now and I'd have no objections, and Ethan keeps running his hands through my hair, up and down my back. I feel so unashamedly good that I want to cry out in joy.

Everything will be fine. It has to be. For my mum and dad's sake, and for Ethan's.

And for *mine*.

I want the rest of my life to look like this. Exams which take up most of my conscience, boys who taste of chocolate milk and sour cream Pringles, a floppy-eared dog that loves me even more than its master. Evenings in the park in December, huddled under my wide scarf and staring into Ethan's soft brown eyes as the sun sets and a chill descends through the trees.

No more interviews, no more scandal, no more news reports or lies or stories. Chloe, Orla and I, surging through it all to carry Kayleigh's memory the way her family would've wanted. I've sent off my university applications now, and it doesn't matter *where* I end up, because Ethan and I care about each other enough to make it work. I'm convinced that I have it all sorted. That the rest of my life will follow in this pattern.

I try not to think about the timer on our lives, the clock tick-tick-ticking as we run closer and closer to the next interview. Officer Joy and Officer Pudrow are still listening to our recordings, going over the evidence. They've been challenged with getting to the bottom of this case, and they're making progress – at least, they think they are.

There's only one thing which could still put an end to the investigation once and for all, placing the three of us behind bars, or whatever happens to seventeen-year-old offenders nowadays.

We just have to hope Sharon never wakes up.

35

The rest of the week follows a similar pattern. I do all of my mocks, drink three more cartons of chocolate milk, and consume a whole lot of Pringles on Ethan's bedroom floor. The week acts as a holiday from everything else that's been going on, giving me time to relax and look back on the events of the past month. I try to push any stress and worry from my mind, but it continues to peer round the corners at me as I sleep, read, revise, watch TV.

Even as I'm kissing Ethan against the beanbag in his room, I feel those bloody hands continue to leave imprints across his body, tainting him in the blood I carry. It's not just Kayleigh's blood this time. It's Carl Hall's, deep red and stinging. It's the blood of his poor children, now without a father, a guardian. There was a piece about them in the paper last week, showing them sat against the bent knees of their grandparents, who offered to take them in until they find a foster family. The little girl is seven, and the boy is five. They were staying with their grandparents the two nights Carl visited Sharon at the camp.

The girl reminds me of Lexie, in a way. Wide grey eyes, wispy brown hair. Her mouth is puckered into a pout, though one of misery rather than contempt. Another life, ruined, even younger than the last. Her five-year-old brother has red cheeks and bleary eyes, like he hasn't stopped crying since he found out his daddy was never coming home.

Lexie had a brother. A boy called Daniel, who was a few years younger than us in school, I think. They took him out of Vibbington Secondary a year after Lexie passed, placing him in a private school they in no way could've afforded before. Lexie's death brought in tens of thousands of pounds in donations to the family, the story getting worldwide attention after Macey killed herself. I see Daniel around sometimes, in his fancy new uniform. He's so serious, silent. He smiles at me occasionally, but mostly walks with his head down, eyes focused on the pavement. And every time I see him, I can't help but think, *I caused that. We* caused that. We caused the silence, the tears. We caused his life to change forever.

Even though Carl's death wasn't our fault, I feel an awful drop of guilt curdle in my stomach every time I see those two little faces staring back at me through the paper. The faces of children whose lives will never be the same again.

There's a feature about Steve Jones, too. I read it as I sit in bed on Saturday morning, hours before I'm due at Nora's to get ready for the party. Mum left this week's paper outside my bedroom door for me, and I haven't put it down. It's not exactly riveting, just… *disgusting*. The photos are mostly ones found on Facebook, meaning I've already seen them. I can barely bring myself to look at Steve's face now, at that bald head, tiny pig eyes.

WEEKEND OF HORROR STOLE THE LIVES OF THREE EAST YORKSHIRE RESIDENTS.

Of the three found dead, Steve Jones was Vibbington born and bred, wife of Sharon Jones, who remains in a coma. Steve, pictured above, was a man well-loved by his community and peers. He was a dedicated husband to Sharon, and has been buried in the grave

prepared for them in a cemetery near the village they grew up in.

Steve and Sharon met when they were five years old, though they didn't get together until much later in life. At primary school, Steve would send Sharon Valentine's cards year after year, which stopped as the pair grew older, and he lost hope. Those who knew him say he never stopped loving Sharon, eventually finding the courage to ask her on a date when her first husband died more than twenty years ago. The pair have been devoted to one another since.

I skim the details of their wedding, feeling slightly sick. The paper has really tried to push the narrative of Steve being this kind, gentle man who loved his wife more than life itself, which in some ways is true, I guess. The photos show them travelling the world together, arms round one another, in hot tubs and swimming pool and volcano craters, running across beaches at sunset and watching the fireworks at Disney.

Steve Jones ran a charity in Vibbington making sculptures from old, forgotten toys, which were sold at auction to raise money for kids with life-threatening diseases. His peers describe him as selfless, the most giving man, and told us of how he quit his job five years ago in order to raise money full-time. He was a huge help to Sharon as she ran camps and events for girl guides across the county and will be sorely missed by all.

There's no evidence as to how the three victims ended up dead that night, but speculation is yet to fall on Steve. Those who knew him say there's just no chance he was involved, which makes his death even more of a tragedy. A kind, honest man who would never so much as hurt a fly, Steve was an innocent bystander that weekend, and his legacy will live on in our town as someone who deserves to be remembered with respect and dignity. May he rest in

peace.

I read the rest of the article in stunned silence. Then I start back at the beginning, tears creeping round the corners of my eyes.

How could they get it all so wrong; so dreadfully, awfully *wrong*?

Mum and Dad are making pancakes downstairs. I eat mine without saying a word, piling on golden syrup and lemon juice and sugar, mind anywhere but on the plate.

It makes no sense. There's no evidence that Steve was involved with the deaths, but there's no evidence he *wasn't*, either. I tip on more sugar, making the dish as sweet as possible so that I can actually taste it. I can't swallow. My saliva is thick, syrupy.

"Are you excited for the party?" Mum asks, beaming at me. I look up and nod, though it's half-hearted. "We're going to go out for tea on Monday night, after your interview, in celebration of you finishing your mocks. How does that sound?"

"Great, thank you," I reply, trying to smile. "Yeah, great."

"You could invite that friend of yours," Dad suggests, winking. "*Ethan*."

"Yeah," I say, hardly taking it in. "I could."

"Will he be at the party tonight?" Mum adds. "He always did seem like a nice lad, you know. I'm glad you're close with him, Lucy. He seems like someone you can really trust."

"Okay?"

I stand up, pushing away my plate. The images of Steve are still rushing through my mind, his tiny blue eyes on mine, bald head glinting.

Am I okay?

"Are you okay?" Mum echoes. There's a frown on her face. "You're acting odd, Luce. Did you get enough sleep last night?"

"Yeah, I'm fine. Just excited for the party, you know?"

I let them hug me as I go upstairs to get ready. I pull on a tracksuit and trainers, pushing the red dress into my bag along with my makeup bag and straighteners, phone charger and accessories. I have a pair of black heels left over from my year eleven prom which I drop in beside everything, glancing round my room for one last time before I close the door.

The paper is still open on my bed, Steve staring out of it. I go to close it, leaving my bag by the door. But as I reach my bed, my phone buzzes from beneath my dress and shoes and everything else. Closing the paper, I dig deep inside my bag for my phone. Switching it on, I note a notification from Officer Joy, and my stomach drops.

It's a voicemail message.

I click onto it, breath held. Dial. Wait as the instructions reel through my mind, loud and clear.

Joy's voice fills my ears.

"Hi, Lucy! It's Officer Joy here, calling from the station. I tried to ring you earlier, but you must've been eating breakfast. We just wanted to call to update you on some really, really good news regarding the case and Sharon Jones' state. We heard from the hospital earlier. She was transferred to the smaller Vibbington hospital this afternoon, due to be taken off life support very soon. Her position is stable. They're hoping she'll wake up over the next day or two."

My body is still. My heart is hardly beating.

I listen to the message again. And again.

It stays the same.

Sharon is due to wake up in a day or two. Sharon, who

knows the truth about what happened that weekend. Who has the power to ruin all our lives just by speaking a few words, telling the police exactly what they need to hear.

She might have suffered brain damage, memory loss. I don't know how much the hospital know about her condition. But if not, it's all over. Everything. Our lives are ruined.

Oh God.

I'm clutching my phone so tight I swear it's going to snap. I delete the voicemail message.

Chloe and Orla will have gotten the same message. They'll be listening to it now, as I am, stressing out, overthinking, hyperventilating. But there's nothing we can do now. Sharon won't be awake for another day or two anyway, and until then, we can't do anything. I need to wait until tonight, where I can talk to them both properly.

They messaged me this morning, confirming they're both still down for the party. Which is good, of course.

I have no idea what's going to happen tonight. The six of us – Nora, Alicia, Ethan, Kev, Oli and I – are meeting at seven for pre-drinks, before we make our way to Oli's for the party at ten. Ethan wants us to sneak off to kiss some more once we're there and have the whole night to ourselves, but I need to speak to Chloe and Orla as a matter of urgency. Our whole lives depend on it.

I swallow. I was being far too optimistic when I assumed everything would be fine, that my life could continue in a mismatch of kissing and schoolwork and unimportant, pointless acts, ones which assume the attention of ordinary teenagers leading ordinary, ordinary lives.

We're too far gone for that.

36

It's over. It has to be. Sharon knows exactly what happened that night. Why would she keep quiet? Why should she? Even though she passed out well before the real drama occurred, I have no idea how much she was conscious for, how much she remembers. What if her information is enough to put a whole new slant on the case, eliminate our chances of escaping from this unscathed?

I try to breathe, to calm myself, but I can't, I *can't*. Fingers fumbling so much I almost drop the phone, I tap onto Snapchat, navigating my way to The Very Best Group Chat.

Did you get the voicemail message? I'll talk to you at the party.

Because there's nothing else I can do about it now, is there? We've screwed up well and truly, and there's nothing we can do but sit tight and pray to God Sharon doesn't wake up over the next few days.

I shout goodbye to Mum and Dad before heading down the drive, making my way to Nora's. I practically run there, walking so fast you'd never know I was stuck in thought, lost in worry. It's cold, but I barely feel the chill, and my phone is switched to silent. Nora's house looks warm and inviting, but I have to swallow back a lump as I make my way up the path. I'm fine, I really am. I'm going to get ready for the party, then talk to Chloe and Orla, sort this once and for all. That's the sensible solution, right?

I don't knock, smiling briefly at Nora's bewildered mum as I go straight upstairs. I don't even knock as I enter Nora's bedroom, and she looks up in surprise from where she's trying on that crocheted top in the mirror.

"Luce!" she says, spinning to face me. "You okay? You look like you've run a marathon!"

"I'm great!" I say, pulling on my biggest grin. I drop my bag by her door and pull off my hoodie, then tug the dress out of it and continue to smile, showing every tooth in my mouth. "I'm just so excited for this party, obviously!"

"Okay…?" She smiles back, clearly bewildered. "Lish is in the shower, shaving her legs."

"Wonderful!"

My best friend watches me as I dig further into my bag, pulling out my sheer tights, heels, my makeup bag. Her eyes are wide as she says, "Luce, are you *sure* you're all right?"

"I'm fine," I throw her back my most dazzling smile, even though it almost splits my face in half. "Who's ready to glam me up, then?"

***

We spend the next few hours getting ready in Nora's room, all dressed and waiting in our new outfits, Alicia helping with the makeup and Nora strictly on hair duty. We're blasting cheesy Christmas songs on Nora's speakers, and I'm ashamed to say that this is the most festive I've felt since last year, despite the fact we're a week into December. Alicia starts out with Christmas music, socks and earrings at the start of November. It's clear I'm letting the team down.

"That dress is perfect," she says now, shaking her head. "Wasn't it just the perfect find, Nora?"

It *is* perfect. Just the right level of fitted and flowy, dipping where it's supposed to and clinging to my miniscule curves. I twirl around with a grin, fluttering Nora's freshly applied false eyelashes and grinning back at my besties. They look fab too, of course, half a bottle of vodka on the floor between us and another of cherry Tangyz propped against the door.

"Ready?" Alicia asks, holding up her hand for me to grab. Tugging her to stand, we twirl around on the spot, almost colliding with the alcohol as Nora lets out a squeak and goes to move the filled shot glasses out of harm's way.

The three of us make our way to Kev's, just a street away from Nora's, on slightly tipsy Bambi-legs. We've already drunk ourselves silly and the night is young, an evening of music and flirting stretching out ahead of us. This is why we have parties. So we can let loose, forget about everything, do daft things until the crack of dawn. Half the sixth form will be there. Chloe and Orla will be there.

Kev opens the door to us with an easy smile, eyes falling on Nora first. She throws herself at him, all screeching voice and long brown arms and tiny crochet top, and he leans back in alarm as we tumble in behind her.

"Hi, Kev!" Alicia squeals, squeezing his cheek. "You look *adorable*."

Kev's kind of short, all tanned face and freckles and dark hair, but I can make out his blush as I follow my friends into the house. The door closes behind us.

We're in.

Oli and Ethan are waiting for us in the living room, sat on sofas and beanbags around Kev's mum's polished coffee table. His parents are having drinks in the hot tub outside and won't disturb us until we're well on our way to Oli's party, which the boys spent all of today setting up across Oli's downstairs and back garden. I sit on the sofa beside Ethan, leaving a suggestive gap. Alicia drops next to Oli, who curls an arm round her shoulders, and Kev can't believe his luck when Nora ends up on his lap.

"Hey, you," Ethan says, smiling softly and slipping a hand into mine. "You look beautiful."

Beautiful.

Not pretty, not hot or fit or gorgeous.

Beautiful.

My tipsy brain clearly can't compute this because tears spring to my eyes and I sink into hugging him with a choked-up sob. I can hear Nora and Alicia laughing, joking about how I'm a lightweight and the drink has already gone to my head.

All I can think is how Ethan won't be calling me beautiful once Sharon confesses to the police, but I can't worry about that now.

We play a simple drinking game first, though I can't grasp my cards properly so Ethan is forced to play for me. He takes half my shots for me like the champ he is, though when it lands on me to chug the rest of the WKD bottle Kev passes my way, I hold my hand up to drink. It tastes of sweat and sugar as I chug, alcohol dripping down my chin and onto my chest, Ethan's finger lapping it up.

I'm unaware of most of the game, mind spinning, stress building, eyes focused on the table between us as if it'll somehow ground me. I'm not worried – *I'm not* – because there's nothing I can do to fix things yet. Orla and Chloe will be here later, and I can't do anything until then.

I focus on Ethan again, but his face is fuzzy this time. He

doesn't seem to notice how far gone I am and starts telling me about Daisy and his dad on their walk this morning, something involving a golf ball and a hole, and I nod along with him, pretending to take it all in, but I lose it halfway through. Have I really drunk that much? Did I eat enough this morning to soak up all this alcohol?

I dash to the bathroom as the game ends and the next one starts, splashing water on my face and downing a whole glass of it from the cup on the windowsill. Said window is open a crack, looking out onto the side of the house, where the hot tub is. Kev's parents are still there, arms wrapped around each other, properly snogging. Should old people snog? Is that allowed? Why am I not snogging Ethan?

I collapse down onto the toilet seat. Swallow some more water. Swill it round my mouth to get rid of the sour taste there, lingering on the back of my tongue.

I check my phone.

Me and Orla should be right on time, and I need to talk to you as soon as possible, Luce.

I read Chloe's message several times before swallowing again and nodding to the empty bathroom.

"Chloe needs to speak to me," I say out loud. "She's going to speak to me and Orla about Sharon."

No one hears me, of course, not even Kev's parents, too busy trying not to make love in time with the radio to pay attention to the likes of me. I push my phone back in my pocket, filling the plastic cup again and going for a final drink. I feel better now. More sober. I can do this. I can have fun. I'm not going to think about Chloe and Orla. Why should I? I'm not seeing them until we arrive at the party later. I have ages.

Back in the living room, my friends are chatting amiably. They've given up with the games and are sat around the table drinking from assorted bottles and cans. There are a good five or six still left by the door ready to combine with the terrible concoction of fruit juices and lemonade, waiting in the paddling pool on Oli's kitchen floor. I take my seat next to Ethan again and he wraps an arm around me, kissing the side of my face. It's warm and sloppy, and I turn my face to the side so he can kiss my lips, hard. No one else seems to notice.

Someone's talking to me. I hear my name and open my eyes again, meeting Ethan's brown ones with a pang. God, he's beautiful. He's so, so beautiful…

"Lucy?"

I swivel round. Nora is looking at me with a frown, waving a hand.

"Earth to Lucy! God, how drunk are you?"

"Not at all." I'm surprised by how stable my voice sounds.

There's a pause, then Nora says, "I was just telling the boys who I saw today."

"Who you saw?"

"Yeah." Another pause, Nora scanning my face with her eyebrows furrowed, as though trying to work out whether she'll regret telling me this. "Emilia Kettering."

I freeze. Try my absolute best to not let the shock on my face show, the horror and pain.

Emilia Kettering.

Kayleigh's younger sister.

The girl who stood at the funeral in silence, completely composed, hands crossed over her lap. Just a year younger than us, I barely knew her. She'd been given a scholarship to this brilliant private school the year before Lexie died when we all started year eight, never getting to Vibbington Secondary, completely out of the way when Kayleigh had her scandal. She was smart and serious and dressed in this ridiculously preppy funeral outfit, all blue chequered tie and black skirt and LGBTQ+ flag pin on her breast. She'd even brought a friend, who stood in a short black dress and frowned at everyone who couldn't wrap their head around the trans colours of her scrunchie.

I don't follow Emilia on social media. I always just assumed she wasn't close to her sister. She wouldn't look at Chloe, Orla and me the whole time we were at the wake, supping squash and trying to avoid crossing our paths. Even if she wasn't close to Kayleigh, they were still *sisters*, and that made me feel all kinds of uncomfortable.

"She was in town with her mum, and that friend of hers – Roderick? Only she's called Rosa now, I think. Lovely girl. She was in my form, just started sixth form. Anyway, she gave me the dirtiest look – Emilia, that is. I mean, what did *I* ever do to *her*?"

I shrug and shake my head, though I'm zoning out, tripping over my thoughts.

Emilia Kettering gave Nora, my best friend, a funny look, a *dirty* look.

Of course she did. Can Nora really not figure out why?

It seems Alicia can.

She's looking right at me, noting the panic on my face, in my eyes. Realising what Nora's saying, how ignorant it sounds. That Emilia Kettering lost her sister and still hasn't received any answers as to how that happened, as to *why*. That Emilia Kettering probably blames me. Probably blames all three of us, and anyone else who still chooses to associate with innocent little Lucy.

"Anyway, I smiled at her, you know, still being polite and all, but God, what a –"

"Shall we play another game?"

I've never been so grateful for a sixth round of shots.

37

I'm more than just tipsy by the time we leave Kev's, just over an hour before the party's due to start. An hour before I have to see Chloe and Orla, face up to everything at last. An hour before my life changes forever, in every way but for the better. I'm not going to waste a second of that.

Ethan and I are holding hands as we walk to Oli's. The streets are silent and we've all coupled off. Nora and Kev, shy but electric every time they glance at one another, wandering slightly behind; Alicia and Oli, bounding on ahead and set alight by the alcohol, who are very clearly going to end up together in Oli's bed at the end of the night.

Every time Ethan turns to look at me, I feel another part of me go up in flames. Is this what it feels like to be in love? I don't deserve it, but I think I feel it anyway. His hand, warm and tentative as it pulls on mine. The soft outline of his tubby stomach, soft nipples, through the fabric of his t-shirt. That gooey smile, those brown eyes, like melted chocolate. Ethan is cookie dough, salted caramel ice cream. Ethan is bliss.

We arrive at Oli's to find the house in darkness. Most teens have a chronic fear of being early, so no one's here yet, the kitchen silent and paddling pool of punch ready to be addled with. We're all giggling as we start pouring the alcohol into the shallow piece of plastic, Oli opening a bag of tinned pineapple and mango and throwing both in for some pizazz. It's not very festive, but I feel far from festive anyway, even in my red dress, a Christmas tree on the counter. We all grab a glass of punch each, and it tastes of summer and smiles and happiness as we take the first sip.

Alicia makes herself busy setting up the party, taking care of everything Oli forgot, while he pushes his family's prized ornaments into drawers and cupboards to avoid disaster. Nora and Kev are chatting to one side of the room, lost in each other, oblivious to everybody else.

I take another glass of punch, drinking it fast, before I can think too much about it. I check my phone again. It's Chloe, and, despite everything, my heart soars reading it.

We're going to be an hour or so late because there's a mini crisis at home, and Mum needs me to drop my cousin at her dance class. Who the hell does dance this late on a Saturday? Orla, don't you dare go without me, I'm not walking into the party looking like a right loner.

An hour or so late. Meaning they won't arrive at the party until eleven at the earliest.

It's only just gone nine, and the guests aren't due to arrive for another hour or so. I smile into my empty cup of punch, chewing on a piece of frozen pineapple.

Perfect.

Ethan is looking at me. Noticing the smirk on my face, he says, eyes bright, "What's up?"

"I…" I glance back at our friends, who are all still busy setting up the party, chatting and laughing. Alicia is busy pouring alcohol into the shot glasses she has lined up on the table, vodka and cider and beer, peach Schnapps and some lurid orange liqueur. "There's still an hour until the party starts. The bedrooms upstairs are empty, right?"

Ethan frowns.

"Are you thinking what I think you're thinking?"

I nod. Nobody else has even noticed we're speaking, too wrapped up in their own lives to notice silly little Lucy make a move on her crush – boyfriend? My head is fuzzy with drink but I'm somehow speaking clearly, eyes focused on Ethan, on his beautiful face and beautiful body and anxious, caring expression, staring right back at me.

"Lucy…" He holds out a hand to me, like he's unsure whether I'm real, or whether I'm about to break the bubble around us. "Are you sure? You've had a lot to drink."

"I haven't really," I say, and he raises an eyebrow at my obstinance. "I'm sure, Ethan. You don't have to baby me."

"Lucy," he says, voice lower this time, face close to mine. "Lucy, I'm not taking your virginity in Oli's bedroom, okay? You've had a lot to drink. You're not thinking straight."

But I am. I so, *so* am. I have two hours until my life changes forever and Ethan drifts out of reach, and I want to spend them doing exactly what I've been waiting for these last few months. I want to do it. Does he *not*?

"Lucy," he repeats, but I shake my head at him.

"I'm not too drunk," I say, and the voice I hear is confident, proud, so not the one I'm used to, the one I've heard inside me these last few months. "I know what I want, Ethan."

The room is noisy, Oli's speakers now pumping out old Stormzy songs and random early 2000s pop, but between us the air is silent, still.

"I want you."

***

Ethan doesn't object as I lead him upstairs, by the hand. He keeps his eyes on me and breath short, though I can feel his apprehension floating away in waves. Oli's house is small and cramped, and the landing above the stairs is just a short strip of beige carpet. I swallow, still clutching his hand. Oli's room, or Oli's parents' room? Which is less weird? I don't know. I'm the girl at house parties who hides in the kitchen with a can of cider and cleans up sick from the brick exterior. I don't do… *this*.

"Oli's is that one," Ethan says, nudging the door open with his toe. "There's a lock, too."

Of course Ethan knows which room to use. He's probably done this heaps of times before, with *Loz*.

We push inside, shutting the door behind us and locking it tight. Ethan slides the bolt a few times just to be sure, then looks around the room, cheeks pink. There's a single bed in the centre – *Oli* has a single bed? – and a few posters of Marvel characters and Star Wars memes. Oli's not a nerd, not by a longshot. I wonder where his lady friends sleep when they stay over.

I wonder where Alicia will spend the night.

Whether she ever has.

Ethan looks anxious, nervous, like he doesn't know what he's doing. His soft hair is mussed up and his brown eyes catch mine as though for reassurance.

And in that moment, I swear I love Ethan Morgan.

I love him. I love his kind smile and cookie dough stomach, his warm skin and gentle hugs.

I love him.

There's no time to lose. I have an hour and a half left.

I throw my arms around his neck, pressing my lips against his. He leans back, visibly startled, and lets out an awkward chuckle before kissing me back. He's gentle and warm, lacking my urgency, so I press my body up against his to try and spark some sort of desire.

We continue to stand like that for a moment longer before I pull him onto the bed. It really is tiny, rickety too, no doubt a forty quid Argos bargain Oli's cheapskate mum thought was good value. I'm almost scared to break one of the slats as Ethan lands on top of me, arms and legs on either side, and whispers, "Are we turning down the lights, or…"

But there's no time for that.

With Ethan guarding me, I wriggle to tug off my knickers beneath my dress. It's hard to do so without dislodging Ethan's cage, but I manage to fling them away, where they wrap around the wardrobe's hand and stare back in embarrassing baby pink. Ethan tries to land another kiss on my neck, my jaw, but I'm wrestling with the dress, the dress which is ridiculously tight and why did I buy a dress this tight –

"Lucy, are you really sure this is a good idea –"

And then it's off, over my head and laid beside us like a guilty promise.

I'm naked, completely naked, lying beneath my boyfriend and gazing up at him with the most beseeching gaze I can muster.

I'm sure Ethan's about to do the same. I reach down, touching his belt buckle and letting my fingers trail it, tug it open. When he doesn't react, still staring at me as though he can't quite believe I'm real, I yank it right out of its holders and go to his zip, tugging it down, trying to pull his trousers down.

That's when he jumps.

As though only just realising that I'm not wearing any

clothes, that the lights are still on and I'm lying on Oli's bed waiting for him like this, Ethan Morgan leaps backwards and hurriedly starts pulling up his trousers. I sit up indignantly as he tries his best not to look at my body, which I don't understand, shieling his gaze and saying, "Luce…"

"Ethan?" I sit up properly, staring at him, trying to catch his eye beneath his hand. "Ethan, what are you doing?"

"Luce… Lucy, put your dress back on, please. You're drunk, you're never usually like this. Please, I don't want to look at you while you're –"

"While I'm what? Do you not want me? Ethan, what's going *on*?"

I think I know exactly what he means.

"Lucy, I want you to be ready and *sober*, okay? Not… this. Not in Oli's room, when you've clearly got a lot going on and aren't thinking straight."

My hands are shaking as I reach for my dress.

"I really like you – who am I kidding, I… I *love* you, Lucy. But… I don't want it to happen like this, okay? That's all."

He loves me.

He loves me.

I don't say anything as I pull it over my head and back down over my stomach. I don't say anything as Ethan finally drops his hand, and looks back at me with an almost… guilty expression.

"I should never have come up here in the first place," he says, shaking his head. "God, I feel like I took advantage of you, I –"

But before he has time to continue, I start to cry.

I don't know where they come from, the tears. From somewhere deep inside me I've tried to press down, evidently, some hollow inside me packed full of suppressed emotions.

Ethan doesn't speak as he clambers back onto the bed. Warm, pillowy arms, wrapping around me, holding tight, safe. My boyfriend smells of fruit punch and Daisy the dog as I sink into him, the tears flowing out like they've been there all along, body wracked with it all.

This, with Ethan, was never going to fix everything. It could help, but I was the one taking advantage of him by using my fear as an excuse to have sex.

Even my drink-addled brain can see that.

An hour and a quarter. I can feel the clock tick-tick-ticking beneath my skin as I cling to him, a gulp resting on my tongue.

Tick, tick, tick.

"Lucy," he says, pulling back. "Lucy, talk to me. Tell me what's going on."

I can still feel the truth nestled under my skin, leering at me, taunting me.

"Lucy," he repeats, trying to look me in the eye. "I know it's about that weekend, Luce. You completely froze over when Nora mentioned Emilia Kettering. I know we said we wouldn't talk about it, that you'd process it in your own time, but it's driving you insane, babe, anyone can see that."

I flinch at the use of "babe".

Babe. Someone sweet, endearing, sexy. The perfect girlfriend, a charming individual. Trustworthy, the keeper of no secrets. *I love you, babe. I trust you.*

"I'm a bad person," I whisper, shaking my head at him. "You have no idea how shitty of a person I am, Eth."

"Then tell me," he murmurs, pressing his forehead against mine. His breath is warm and sticky and smells of cherry Tangyz, and I want to kiss him again, want to kiss him so, *so* bad, but I'm terrified that it's ruined.

"I love you," I say instead.

It's the first time I've said it out loud. As soon as it's out there it feels too sudden, not the right timing. Ethan leans back in surprise and swallows as his dark eyes meet mine. I smile, cautiously, testing the waters.

"And I love you too, Lucy," he says. "But you need to tell me. Tell me about that weekend. I won't love you any less, you must know that."

That's not a guarantee he can make.

"Fine," I say, "I... I'll tell you about that weekend."

Ethan reaches out to place his hands on my back, holding me safe, firm.

This is okay. I can tell him the story. I can explain what happened that weekend.

I mean...

I can tell him at least *half* of it.

38

I told Officer Joy that on Saturday night, Chloe and I ventured out of the tent to find Kayleigh and Orla glued to some smartphone game, Sharon tucked safely into her tent. That we collected them and ran off to the treehouse with all our alcohol, giggling and waving the Tangyz bottle like it was our lime green flag. It was apple, of course. *Perfect* with lemonade.

That's a lie, of course.

It had already started to drizzle a bit as Chloe and I made our way out of the tent. We had the carrier bag between us, as well as all our cushions and blankets, our supplies. Chloe was shivering, but tried to act like she wasn't cold as we hurried over to Kayleigh and Orla's tent and unzipped the flap.

They weren't on their phones, playing some app. They were stood, ears pricked and expressions tensed, listening to… something.

"What's going on?" Chloe asked, frowning, but the other two shushed her and held insistent fingers up to their lips. "What? I can't hear –"

Then she stopped.

We all stopped.

I'll spare you the details. Sharon was in her tent still, the one pitched next to Kayleigh and Orla's, with another individual. From her gasps and the various male mutterings, it was clear what was going on in there.

Wide eyed, Chloe turned back to us. Her expression was probably mirrored on my own face.

"Sharon? At a… camp?"

Apparently so.

"Clearly Steve couldn't wait until she came home," Kayleigh said, shivering. "It feels so weird, but I guess old people still… you know."

"So it's definitely Steve she snuck in?" I checked. "You actually saw him arrive?"

Kayleigh and Orla exchanged glances, as though the possibility was only just dawning on them.

"I mean, no, but…"

"So big Shazza could be having an affair?" Chloe's eyes were glinting in a way I found horribly familiar. "Oh my God, this just keeps getting better…"

"*Better?*" Orla insisted. "But poor Steve! She could be cheating on him…"

"We *hate* Steve," Kayleigh cut in.

She had a good point. None of us had ever liked Steve, not even a little bit. He freaked us out, made us feel… uncomfortable. No guy married for this many years should be so ridiculously obsessed and in love with his wife, unless he was a control freak or… about to murder her. Call us presumptive, but Steve had always seemed like the former. We heavily disliked him for that.

"It *has* to be an affair," Chloe insisted. "It's Steve Jones, for God's sake. He definitely hasn't snuck into our camp just to *spend the night* with Sharon. They've been married years and years, it's cold and miserable here, and he's the most boring man on the planet. *That* must be why she's having the affair…"

"You're speculating a bit there, Chlo," I said, as a chill

darted up my spine.

It didn't feel right.

None of it did.

We didn't hang around to hear more, of course; we weren't that sick in the head. Grabbing Kayleigh and Orla's blankets and snacks, we hurried from the site, confident now that Sharon wouldn't notice our absence, following Chloe across the field to the forest. The treehouse wasn't embedded too deeply into the trees, and we found it quickly, giggling as we pulled down the hatch. My hands were shaking with excitement as we disappeared up the ladder one by one, two by two.

The treehouse was much more eery in the dark. Even the addition of fairy lights did nothing to mask the sound of rustling trees and rain, pitter-pattering on the roof of the little house. It felt relatively warm and dry as we threw the cushions out of the trapdoor, filling it with our own furnishings. Chloe set the alcohol up to one side, where it rested along the wood in a mismatch of coloured glass and half-drunk bottles.

"This is cosy!" she said, grinning with pride. "Selfie?"

Orla chose that moment to open the WKD, starting light, and any mention of photos dissolved into an excited mash of teenagers filling their camp mugs with weak alcohol and pop, cheering to each other, to happiness, to this moment, right now, in the treehouse.

Everything felt so... good. Happy.

But not for long.

***

It started properly raining later, though I'm not sure of the exact time. We were playing a game of truth or dare, careful with our questions and cautious not to veer outside of the tent. It was absolutely chucking it down now, and none of us were properly dressed for the weather. The fire would have long blown out, and no doubt the tents were sagging beneath the weight of all that water.

There weren't exactly many truths left to ask. We knew all about Orla and Aaron, Chloe and Tobes, Kayleigh and Dan. I'd kissed Ethan *once*; it wasn't exactly hot gossip. Chloe tried delving deeper into Kayleigh's sex life, but she wasn't having any of it. Dan was a lucky guy, I remember thinking. Kayleigh had an awful lot of respect for his privacy.

"Fine," Chloe said, after the third unsuccessful round of truths. "It's time for the real deal."

We watched as she took the vodka bottle, a horrid smirk on her face. She proceeded to fill four shot glasses with the stuff, passing one to each of us. Then she smiled, necking hers in one.

"Just to get me started."

She poured herself another as I lifted it up to sniff. We usually stuck to lighter stuff at parties, too poor and anxious to fill our bodies with such a substance. I swallowed a breath and it almost tasted as bad as the shot itself, still waiting in my glass.

"Okay," Chloe said, leaning back. "We each go and stand outside in the rain for sixty seconds… *or* we do the shot."

Orla and I immediately scoffed, placing down the shot glasses and moving towards the hole, but Kayleigh seemed apprehensive, frowning at Chloe.

"But it's pitch black!" she objected. "And *freezing cold*."

"Then do the shot," Chloe said with a wink. "It's just a vodka shot, Kayls. You're not a baby."

You're not a baby. She said the exact same thing to Lexie all those years ago, or some variation of it, when she refused to use the tyre swing. The tyre swing she went back and used late that night, with Macey, and fell to her death from, plummeting through the trees and landing with a smack on the river's glassy surface.

We all watched Kayleigh, trying to guess what she'd do, how far she'd go to impress Chloe this time. In the end, she rolled her eyes, placing down the shot glass and saying, "Fine."

It was only a minute, standing in the pouring rain and gazing up at the black sky, a much kinder prospect than downing a whole shot of vodka this early in the night. But Chloe knew the forest was far creepier than we'd ever admit, than we even wanted to *think*.

I went first, climbing down the slippery ladder and standing, breath held, as the others chanted to sixty above. It was freezing, rain lashing through the canopy and dotting me in ice, but the sound of their voices was comforting, grounding. The thick downpour created a haze of mist, meaning you couldn't see more than a metre before you in the dark, the forest completely masked from view.

"Well done, Lucy," Chloe said, grinning at me as I made my way back upstairs. "You've proved yourself worthy."

Worthy? Worthy of *what*? Worthy of Chloe, of these girls? I rolled my eyes, sinking back beneath the blanket and going to squeeze the rain from my ponytail.

Orla went next. She didn't seem fazed, climbing back up and grinning her victory. Chloe reacted similarly patronising, clapping her on the back and announcing her success to us all.

Then it was Kayleigh's turn.

She was visibly nervous as she disappeared down the trapdoor, leaving her phone up there with us. That was when it buzzed. We all turned to it with wide eyes.

"Kayls!" Chloe hissed, grabbing her arm to tug her back up. "You have signal up here, in the treehouse! The rest of us don't! How did *that* happen?"

"I must be on a different plan," Kayleigh said, frowning. Her head was just above surface level while the rest of her was submerged, and she crawled up a little so as to look at her phone. "Who's the text from, Orla?"

Orla checked, tapping on Kayleigh's screen with a frown.

"Um... Dan, I think. Is that who 'Loverboi' is on your phone?"

"Obviously!"

"Reply later," Chloe said, flapping her hands in Kayleigh's direction. "Go on, Kayls, do your sixty seconds before it stops raining, otherwise it's not fair!"

So Kayleigh disappeared back down through the hole, while the rest of us clamoured to read the text. Kayleigh was still just as daft as she had been all those years ago, apparently, because she still didn't have a password on her phone, and we were able to swipe through onto the messaging app with ease.

I counted out loud, so she could hear at least one of us, while Orla and Chloe giggled and whispered. I craned my neck to see what the message said, smiling as I read Loverboi's Loverboi-ish text to Kayleigh.

Missing you so much, my bed's so cold without you. Hope you're having an amazing time at the camp, message me as soon as you get signal! I love you! We'll have a huge Shrek marathon when you're back, Christmas special and all. I'm watching Strictly Come Dancing now without you, so I've propped up your

photo to pretend we're watching it together.

"He's actually the soppiest man on the planet," Chloe whispered, rolling her eyes. "It's disgusting. If Tobes sent me this, I think I'd break up with him there and then."

I wanted to retaliate, but I daren't stop counting. I was at thirty now, halfway through Kayleigh's time outside, and watched as Chloe started tapping out a response.

I miss you so much too, my juicy, juicy boi. You better rock my world so hard when we're back. I'm hungry. Don't think I can wait till Monday, becos I'm famished.

Followed by some rather crude and unnecessary emojis.

"Chloe, you *can't* send that!" I hissed as I stopped counting and Kayleigh's hands appeared on the top rung of the ladder, already making her way back up to us. But Chloe was already switching the phone off and placing it back on Kayleigh's cushion with an innocent expression on her face, smiling at our friend as she clambered up.

"Kayls! I tried to google something using your phone, but it just died…"

Kayleigh frowned, tapping her screen as she nestled below the blankets again. "Odd. It had twenty percent left…"

"Must have been the cold," Orla retorted, trying to hide her peals. "Shame, though."

Spoiler incoming.

That was the last text Dan ever received from his girlfriend. I don't know what he thought of it. Whether he guessed it was us playing a prank, or thought Kayleigh had been body snatched the night she died. I don't know what he replied, or what the police thought about the message. Was it considered suspicious? Is it something they discussed with

Dan, causing memories and regret and guilt to flood back through his mind? Did it even register in their peripheral vision?

Kayleigh wasn't bothered by her "dead" phone. She hadn't spoken to Dan all weekend anyway, and seemed secure enough in their relationship that they didn't need to talk 24/7 to know they were thinking of one another. Must be nice, I remember thinking. Very nice.

I look at Ethan now as I tell the story, holding his hand tight beneath mine. It's cold, like he knows what's coming. I let my thumb circumnavigate the skin of his palm, his fleshy wrists. He doesn't react as I lean forwards to plant a kiss on his lips.

That night, that Saturday, is as much a blur for me as it might seem to you. I'm filling in the blanks with the specific dares and anecdotes, that dreaded last message, but the evening itself won't form in my mind, just a blob of laughter and alcohol and sleazy jokes. We continued drinking as the rain poured all around us, cocooned inside our treehouse high up in the forest, taking shots and downing mugs of Tangyz mixed with lemonade as our stomachs swashed with liquid. We crept down the ladder in pairs to squat in the undergrowth and do our business, shaking off and clambering back into the warmth.

It was about midnight when we heard the scream.

39

The scream, the infamous scream.

The scream which changed everything.

It was short, piercing. It shot through the trees in a matter of seconds, electrifying our little treehouse and sending sparks ricocheting through us. We all paused, shot glasses held at our lips.

Chloe downed hers first, staring round with her black eyes wide.

"What was *that*?"

It was still chucking it down outside, the only comprehensible sound coming from the rain and swallowed atmosphere. The closed windows of the treehouse gave nothing away. Yet something had changed. We were all shaken, visibly so. The jokey terror of earlier was replaced with something far more sinister. When we'd hurried down the ladder to spend that minute stood in the pouring rain, we'd done so in order to prove that there was nothing scary about the dark woods, the fact it was past twelve and the night was fast encroaching. We hadn't really felt scared. There was nothing to be scared *of*.

Not now.

There was something *real* to fear, some unknown force lurking nearby. Kayleigh was the most sceptical, staring round at us in wonder and biting her lip.

"It… it could have just been Sharon," she said, trying to

make sense of things. "Maybe she saw a spider, or thought she heard someone wandering past her tent…"

"She wouldn't scream like that," Chloe countered. She still seemed to almost be enjoying the drama, basking in Kayleigh's terror. She filled another shot for herself, counted down from five, then watched as we all tipped the lurid green liquid back. "She wouldn't want to alert us to the fact she has her fancy man tucked inside the tent with her. She's not stupid."

"What, then?" Orla queried. "What do *you* think the scream was about?"

We fell silent.

I spoke first. "Maybe… I don't know. Maybe something's wrong."

All three turned to look at me. It was silent in the treehouse, but every sound coming from outside felt dangerous, like a threat, a source of trouble. The rustle of deadened leaves scraping against the wooden roof; the insistent *splat* of raindrops on the walls; the *hiss* and *squeak* of animals nearby. We were tense, clutching our shot glasses and trying to stay orientated as the alcohol swilled around our minds and stomachs.

Across the circle, I caught Chloe's eye. She was thinking, turning something over in my mind. I hated that face of hers. It was dangerous, not for repurpose. I swallowed, trying to stay calm, placing down my glass and saying, "You want us to go and investigate, don't you?"

I was met with a mischievous glint, a cackle. Chloe was nodding. She kept nodding as we stayed put, no one moving a muscle.

"Sharon might be in danger," she said simply. "It would be *so* irresponsible to not go and help…"

"Wouldn't it be *more* irresponsible to *wander into the danger?*" I retorted, and Orla and Kayleigh tittered nervously in agreement.

"Not at all." Chloe smiled. "We'll stay in the trees, watch the camp from a distance. And then... I know, I know. We're still playing truth or dare, right?"

We exchanged uneasy glances.

"Yes," Orla replied, "but..."

"And it's my turn to dare you guys."

"Chloe..."

"And I dare Kayleigh," she continued, eyes fixed on Kayleigh's pale face, her wide eyes. "I dare Kayleigh to investigate."

"Chloe," I said, more firmly now. "Kayleigh isn't doing anything. Do you have any idea how reckless that would be?"

"We'll all be there with her!" Chloe insisted. "If she doesn't do it, you have to. Or Orla does. And if you don't... I'll give you a forfeit. A *truth* forfeit."

Orla and I exchanged glances. We knew how awful Chloe's forfeits could be. Terribly personal, deep truths, ones you'd never, ever want to admit. And if you couldn't answer, she'd give you another. And another.

Kayleigh was trying to stop her bottom lip from trembling, though she wasn't doing a very good job. I didn't know what to do, in that moment. As delusional as Chloe was, I didn't want to do the dare myself... and if the three of us went with Kayleigh to investigate, what was the worst that could happen? Besides, I was almost certain Sharon's scream hadn't been fatal. Right?

Orla answered for me. She nodded at Chloe, saying, "Fine. Just do it, Kayleigh. It's not as if it's a hard dare."

Kayleigh's eyes were wide, frightened. I don't tell Ethan

this, of course. I dumb down how nervous she was, play it as though she was excited to go and investigate, prove her worth to us. In truth, she had no other option, though the fear on her face was evident.

"I…" Kayleigh paused, still chewing on her lip. "I can't."

"You know what'll happen if you don't," Chloe said, smiling sweetly. "You'll have to answer one of my truths. A very… personal truth. About Dan."

That sealed the deal. Kayleigh loved Dan; she respected his privacy, the fact that he was a very quiet, intimate person. Her mouth opened and closed as she tried to figure out what to do next, before sighing.

"Fine," she said, though the resignation in her voice was clear. "I'll do it. But you guys are coming with me, right? And if nothing seems untoward, I'm not creeping into Sharon's tent to peep on her like some perv, okay?"

Chloe smiled again, holding Kayleigh's gaze. "Would I ever ask you to do that, Kayls?"

Wouldn't she?

We pushed our shot glasses into one corner of the treehouse, crawling towards the exit. One by one, we retreated through the hole. It was still absolutely bucketing it down, but Chloe's eyes were wide and cold as she went first. She always looked so scary in the dark. I think it was Macey who once made a joke about how her eyes looked like bullet holes, as we played hide and seek among the pews in the chapel. They really did look like bullet holes now. Like someone had shot right into her eye sockets and left a gaping expanse of black.

Soaked to the skin and shivering, the four of us made our way through the dark forest. Chloe led the way, despite it being Kayleigh's dare. We kept inside the trees, of course, both because of the rain and because we half expected some mythical beast to pounce on us the minute we entered the field, the cause of Sharon's terror. Every now and then Chloe made some crude joke, or turned around suddenly to make us jump. Kayleigh was on edge, hands shaking as she followed behind.

"Sorry," I whispered, reaching out to grab her hand. "Sorry I didn't agree to do it instead."

"It's okay," she hissed back. "I wouldn't have been brave enough, either."

We exchanged weak smiles in the dark.

There was still a shred of moonlight shining through the rain, and that was the only way we were guided back to camp. Another trickle of light was clear through the trees now, coming from the fairy lights strung inside mine and Chloe's tent. Sharon had a lamp hung in the centre of hers, though I thought it had been switched off when we left earlier. Eyes wide, Chloe continued forward, running now, fast on her feet as we made our way through the undergrowth.

The camp was closer, though we still couldn't hear anything. No screaming, no commotion. Just that lamp, swinging from the roof of Sharon's tent, flickering golden light into the raindrops around. I swallowed, letting go of Kayleigh's hand. My clothes were so wet now I could've filled a whole milk bottle with collected water, heavy against me as I moved. The four of us came to a stop inside the trees by the camp, staring at the now drenched firepit, the three tents, drooping under the weight of the rain.

We'd remembered to zip them up, of course, even doing up the outer tent, just in case.

Sharon's, however, hung wide open.

"It was zipped up when we left, right?" Chloe hissed. "This

is *Sharon*. She'd never leave it open for even a second, especially when it's raining…"

It was true. Sharon was the one who'd drilled into us the importance of never leaving a tent flap open, even a little bit, letting in all kinds of bugs and mozzies, spiders. If rain got into the tent, there'd be no way to get it dry again until the camp was over. We'd been girl guides of some sort since we were all five years old. We knew better than to leave a tent flap gaping.

"It's perfect," Chloe continued. "You can go and investigate, Kayls, by just peering in. And if Sharon is in there, you can just say you got lost or something, or… I don't know, that you need a paracetamol."

"That I *got lost?*" Kayleigh repeated, incredulous. "My tent is right next to hers."

"All right, all right! The paracetamol thing."

Orla's eyes were narrowed, taking in the scene. I held my breath, waiting to hear what she had to say.

"Nothing seems out of place," she concluded, turning to us all. "Like, completely normal. So I think you'll be fine, Kayleigh. Go see if Sharon's okay, then run back to us, okay? You'll be *fine*."

I nodded, giving Kayleigh's hand a squeeze, finding it in the darkness. She looked back, visibly terrified.

"I *can't*."

"You can." I shouldn't have said that, of course. But I did.

"What if…"

"What if *what?*" Chloe scorned. "Don't be such a baby, Kayleigh. Just go and have a look, okay?"

Breaths held and eyes focused on Kayleigh, we watched as she broke free of the group. Swallowed, eyed the tents nervously. Left the shelter of the trees, the protection of our waiting group, stood between the trunks, shrouded in darkness. The light coming from the tents caught her wet hair, her glistening skin. She'd been caught, spotted. The light wouldn't let her go, now. It followed her as she made her way to Sharon's tent…

The second scream of the night was even more shrill than the first.

40

Kayleigh's scream ripped through the trees, shattering the dark blue sky above and sending it falling all around us like fragments of glass. Or maybe that was due to the fact it had started hail-stoning; Kayleigh's body was dragged inside the tent before any of us could do or say anything, staring at the shadows reflected through the canvas with wide eyes.

A figure, holding Kayleigh. I can only describe what I saw through the tent wall, the light behind them displaying the action in HD quality. Something – maybe a scarf, the sleeve of a hoodie – was wrapped around her neck, tugging, tight. The sound of tiny balls of ice smacking the ground around us drowned out any other noise, but I can still picture her gagging, trying to breathe, those stubby fingers grappling with the noose, trying to rip free. We heard the last strangled sob erupt from her mouth as she broke away, her silhouette falling back against the floor of Sharon's tent. Her attacker wasted no time. We watched, unable to do anything to help, as they grabbed an object and used it to hit her head, once, twice, three times.

Then came the knife.

It was like a scene from a horror movie. That black figure, only just visible through the tent's wet fabric, grabbing a long-bladed knife – God knows where they'd gotten it from – and proceeded to stab our friend, right in the heart.

Officer Joy said it missed any vital cords, that stab wound.

Kayleigh was already gone by the time the knife sunk in.

Silence. The three of us didn't move, didn't even flinch. We were frozen, still hidden within the trees, unable to do anything but hold our breaths steady and stare.

She was dead.

None of us wanted to say it – to even *think* it – but the truth was undeniable.

Kayleigh was *dead*.

We were all too shocked to process it at first. I glanced at Chloe, then at Orla, but both had the same blank, horrified expressions, unsure of what the hell just happened, of how on earth we were supposed to get away from this, of how Kayleigh could even be *dead*.

We didn't have much time to think before the figure emerged from within the tent, knife in hand, stood by the now depleted fire and staring around wildly, at the other tents, the site, the trees.

Right at us.

Steve Jones had a face of fury as he locked eyes with Chloe first, then Orla, then me. His gaze didn't move from mine as we stared at one another, trying to take this all in, figure out what was going on. The knife pointed down, at the ground. It was dripping with red, the rain intermingling with Kayleigh's blood and falling to the ground in great pink splodges.

"Guys," Chloe said, wasting no time. "I think we need to run."

We didn't need to be told twice.

A few minutes ago, we were disorientated with alcohol and delirium, rushing through the trees to the campsite like we were making a good decision.

I still felt drunk now.

What the hell just *happened*? There was no way Kayleigh

could be dead, no way at all.

But the truth was hard to deny when it happened right in front of our eyes.

We ran fast, hard, feet pounding on the forest floor as we raced. I didn't dare turn around and spot Steve, and I couldn't hear his footsteps over the sound of our own. It was still raining, which no doubt gave us the advantage; you could hardly see more than a few metres in front before the haze overtook all vision, the sound drowning out our frenzied gasps and shouts.

If we could just make it back to the treehouse…

Chloe and Orla were faster than me, though Orla grabbed my hand through the darkness and we began to run together, gasping for breath. Chloe was speedy and reached the ladder first, coming to a stop and pausing at the bottom, glancing around. There was no Steve to be seen, no flash of a torch or heavy footsteps, knife glinting with blood. We must have lost him.

"Should we keep running?" Orla asked, through wheezy gasps. "Surely if we go into the treehouse, we'll be trapped!"

"It's chucking it down," Chloe said, shaking her head. "We don't have any torches with us, and Kayleigh took the phone with her. Using mine will run down the battery in no time. We… we need to stay together, stay dry, wait it out. He's just *killed* someone, guys. He's not going to hang around."

I felt Orla swallow, too.

Chloe didn't waste time in hoisting herself up, two rungs at a time. We followed, fast now, determined to get off the forest floor and close the trapdoor behind us. Chloe did so once we were all tucked up with the blankets and cushions, then switched off the fairy lights, plunging us into darkness.

Silence. The rain was still pitter-pattering against the treehouse, the room inside shrouded in quiet. I could feel every breath, every shred of hesitation, regret. Tension, rising all around us. The tip-tapping of Chloe's fingers as she tried to figure out what just happened, how it *could* have happened.

"We killed her," Orla said, after a moment. "We... killed Kayleigh."

"We didn't," Chloe retorted. "*Steve* did. Steve bloody Jones, husband of the century."

"But we led her into the camp," Orla responded. I couldn't see her eyes through the gloom, but I imagined they were dark and angry, glaring into Chloe's own. "We dared her to go and investigate, even though we thought it would be dangerous!"

"*Steve Jones* killed her," Chloe said, and her voice was hard now, cold. "It's not our fault, Orla. I thought something bad was happening, but I didn't think it would be... that."

Another pause, tension building. I didn't know what to say, what to do. There was a lump in my throat and I couldn't seem to process it. Was that a dream? Was it *all* just a dream?

"She's dead," Orla said suddenly. "She's... dead."

"No shit, Sherlock."

"Steve Jones..."

We were all thinking the same thing. Wondering how we'd been so blind, so naïve, assuming Steve was harmless, just a bald goon obsessed with his ageing wife. Still trying to understand how that had actually happened, how Kayleigh had been so brutally murdered right in front of our eyes. How it was *real*, not a movie scene or production. She'd been strangled, bludgeoned, stabbed. How she was *dead*.

There was nothing else to say. The three of us were silent

as we continued to sup on the drinks, too stunned to do anything else, the storm waging on outside. The thunder and lightning was a shock, but we welcomed the distraction. Steve Jones wouldn't patrol the forest in this weather, surely?

"I'll set an alarm for tomorrow," Chloe said eventually. I heard her pull out her phone and turn it on with a buzz, adding, "Still no signal."

"We'll get back to the camp tomorrow," Orla replied. "We'll sneak back, two of us on watch. There's that landline one, plugged into the office space, the one we could use in emergencies. The line should be back working by now, right?"

I nodded, though they couldn't see my head move. Chloe's face was illuminated as she set the alarm, early, so we could get out and away while Steve was hopefully still asleep. There was a tear slipping out of one eye, down the side of her nose.

She switched the phone off again before I could say a thing.

41

I don't know how any of us got to sleep that night. All I know is we must've been pretty exhausted… both from getting up at sunrise earlier the previous day and from watching one of our best friends, our sister, get *murdered* in the forest in the middle of the night. Light poured through the slats of the treehouse and Chloe's alarm beep, beep, beeped as the three of us came to, rubbing our eyes and yawning.

"Please tell me last night was just a bad dream," Orla said, sitting up from where she was nestled in the blankets. She pulled a horrific face. "Oh, God. Where's Kayleigh?"

It all came flooding back, then. Our friend's body, tugged into that tent by Steve Jones, strangled until she fell back in a lifeless lump. His tubby hand beating her head with that object, then plunging the knife straight into her chest as we watched, unable to do *anything*. Steve, storming out of the tent. Staring at us with that blank expression, Kayleigh's blood dripping to the ground beside him.

Ethan hasn't said a word as I relay this part of the story to him. His mouth is open wide, not quite understanding how a murder just north of Vibbington could be quite so… brutal.

"It gets worse," I tell him, to which his brown eyes practically bulge out of his head.

The three of us couldn't get dressed that morning. We couldn't eat breakfast, the leftover pizza from last night or the rest of the eggs Sharon had saved for eggy bread. We couldn't clean our teeth or brush our hair. But what was the point in all that anyway? Kayleigh was dead. She'd been murdered, and we were stuck on a campsite with the man who'd done it, the man who'd killed Kayleigh Kettering and done God knows what to Sharon.

Chloe spoke first, sitting up and eyeing us both.

"We need to move," she said firmly. "I bet Steve is still on the site somewhere, sleeping. It's seven in the morning. We need to be quick, get to the phoneline and call for help, for the police, anyone."

I watched as Orla frowned, replying, "What if Sharon's still on site, too? Shouldn't we alert her to… everything that's happened?"

But Chloe just looked at Orla like that was the most stupid thing she'd heard all week.

"Orla, if Steve Jones was lurking in Sharon's tent with a knife, don't you think the new Yorkshire Ripper would have slashed her too?"

I frowned. "I don't really think you should compare the cases…"

But Orla was flushing, hanging onto something else Chloe had said. "You… think Sharon's *dead*?"

She sounded clueless, but I knew exactly how she felt. None of us wanted to actually believe that anything bad could have happened to Sharon, that another person was *dead*. Kayleigh was bad enough. But Sharon… Sharon was predictable, reliable. She'd been there for us our whole lives, since we were little rainbows, aged five. We were now great teenagers, huddled in the treehouse with the remnants of last night's alcohol and that familiar Tangyz waft drifting all around us.

It was the first time in many a month I hadn't woken up

with a hangover after consuming that much drink.

"Do we have a plan?" Chloe continued, whacking her hand against the floor for emphasis. "We're going onto the site, calling for help, then running back here to wait for reinforcements. Me and Orla will stay in the trees, and you can go get the phone, Luce. We'll keep a lookout for Steve…"

"Why should I go by myself?" I objected, taken aback. "That's exactly how Kayleigh got herself killed."

Chloe rolled her eyes, though the reality of the situation was clearly dawning on her, and she added, "Fine. I'll come with you. Orla, you stay under cover in the trees, watch out for Steve. Don't move a muscle until we're back, okay?"

"What if he spots me too?" Orla said, eyes wide. "I can't stay there all alone! I won't stand a chance."

"Fine, fine! We'll all go together."

And so it was decided.

The forest was silent as we lowered ourselves back down the ladder. That fresh, early morning smell had returned all around us, and I breathed in deeply, trying to calm down. Although it wasn't raining, dark clouds rumbled ahead, and we could all smell another storm brewing. The forest was calm, silent, a mist settling across the floor. Leaves of red and orange and brown were scattered all around. The place would have looked romantic, ethereal, if we weren't so tense.

"Okay. I'll go first." Chloe started walking, moving ahead of us, breath held. I could tell she was nervous because her shoulders were clenched and she walked on tiptoes, Orla and I walking behind, all of us trying to be quiet. The trees around us watched.

We arrived back at the camp in a matter of minutes, surprisingly quicker by daylight. The three of us stood there, watching the three tents, unmoving. Despite the mist, you could see right through our site and to the building beyond, where there was a shower block and phone chargers and that landline we so needed. The fire was still burnt out, of course, the rain subduing any chance of it springing back to life.

"Okay," Chloe said. "We'll go round the back of the tents, crouch down, and run to the block. Once we're inside, we can look around, check Steve isn't in there, raid the fridge for breakfast stuff. There'll be some bread, cheese…"

She went first again, hurrying forwards, running and crouching at the same time so that she looked like a little turtle. Orla followed, me behind, the three of us disappearing past the tents and towards the block. The campsite was silent, eery. I tried not to think about Kayleigh's blood-soaked body lying in that tent.

The block was equally quiet, dim. There weren't any lights on and the door didn't even squeak as we pushed through it, into the main hall. It was empty. There was no sign of Steve Jones.

"Come on!" Chloe hissed.

Through to the kitchen, where there was a fridge and several cupboards, space for food and drinks. Chloe dug through them quickly, pulling out bagels and a whole block of mild cheddar, passing the bags to us before finding a cucumber and two pots of Greek-style yoghurt. Orla and I clung onto them as we hurried out of the kitchen, checking all the time behind doors and in the corridor, arriving in the back office space to dial 999…

Chloe let out a gasp from up ahead, and we stopped moving.

"What?" I whispered. "What's wrong?"

"The lines have been cut."

Her voice was flat as she held up the phone and its holder.

The spiral wire was split, as though sliced open with a knife.

My heart dropped.

"It's like... a warning," Orla murmured, staring at it. "It's like he's telling us we're trapped, that we can't call for help because there's no signal here and the phoneline has been spliced..."

"But he doesn't know Kayleigh's phone gets signal in the treehouse."

We turned to look at Chloe, unease filling my gut.

"Chloe, you know the phone is in Kayleigh's pocket."

"I know."

"We couldn't." We couldn't... or we wouldn't.

More like we wouldn't.

"We have to." Chloe's face was straight, but I could sense the fear in her eyes, the way she was hardly breathing, staring at us with such intensity. "We need to get help, guys. Steve Jones has *murdered* people. He's left us trapped here, so guess what that means? Oh, hmmm, let me see... It means he's going to kill us too, dopey! And if we don't get Kayleigh's phone, we have no way of getting help!"

"We could run to the coast, try and get signal there..."

"Even at the festival we couldn't send a message, it was too weak."

She was right, of course. But the thought of combing over Kayleigh's body to get her phone just felt... wrong.

"I'll do it," Chloe continued. "I'll go in the tent and get Kayleigh's phone, if you guys keep watch."

If we *kept watch*.

I swallowed, nodding.

"Okay." Chloe nodded back, like she was trying to psyche herself up. "Okay. You guys keep hold of the food, then we'll all go back to the site, okay? Steve must have left, or... I don't know. But we haven't seen any sign of him, so we should be careful, and…"

"Just go," Orla replied. We all joined hands in the middle as we agreed.

The site felt even more eery now, so still, masked in despair. My heart was in my mouth as the three of us treaded lightly over to the spot where Kayleigh was killed, where Sharon's tent was pitched. Orla and I couldn't bear to look as Chloe disappeared inside the tent flaps, but we caught a glimpse anyway. Kayleigh's signature nondescript brown hair was stark against the green grass. Her head protruded from the tent's entrance; she was lying face down, mouth against the muddy ground. One hand lay above her head, the other lost beneath the blood pooling from somewhere inside. Her fingers were blue, nails black.

We kept a lookout for Steve as Chloe rummaged through the tent, pulling out the phone with a triumphant gasp. There was a horrid smell reeling from the tent, one of salty blood and sweat, the early stages of decomposition.

"Come on," she said, emerging from the tent with a grimace, face slightly green. "I've got it. Let's just get back to the treehouse, and –"

I spun around, the edge of the tent now in sight.

The third scream was by far the loudest of the weekend as it left my mouth.

42

"Lucy, shut up!" Chloe's eyes were wide as she stared at me. "What is it? Do you want Steve to come and find us, or..."

Her voice trailed away as she noticed what I was staring at.

Another body, that of a man, lying butt-naked on his front with his legs outstretched and arms held high above his head. He was spindly and pale, covered in dark black hairs, and from the blood-soaked grass around him, it was pretty clear to see that he was dead.

Another body. A second – or third?

I couldn't tear my eyes from him, from those splayed out limbs and blood-splattered skin, from the ground turned dark red with blood and sweat and a dead man's fluids.

"What the..."

"We need to run," came Orla's voice from behind, as we spun around to face her. "I think I heard a movement from inside one of the other tents..."

For the second time that day, we didn't need to be told twice.

We tore across the site, Chloe lingering for a second by the camp table to grab one of the knives we'd left there the previous day. It was the big heavy one, which we'd used for chopping vegetables. There'd been two – one with a blue handle, one with a red – but the blue was nowhere to be seen.

"Come on," Orla urged as we picked up our pace again, hurrying into the trees. It was starting to rain again, just a little, but not enough to disguise us as we tore through the forest, not daring to look behind and check if Steve was on our tail. We weren't brave enough, too shaken by the series of events to do the sensible thing and look. We made it back to the treehouse in the nick of time, where we hurried up the ladder, two at a time, shutting the trapdoor hard behind us.

Once we were safe again, none of us said anything for a moment or two. We were all too stunned to speak. Chloe had the knife clutched on her lap. Orla, eyes wide behind her glasses and nostrils flared, shuffled across the floor of the treehouse to take her seat above the trapdoor and stop anyone from pushing it open, from reaching us up there.

"Okay," Chloe said, after a pause. "This is good. We have the phone now."

She pressed the side button, hard, willing it to power up.

The phone did nothing.

No vibration, no colour to its screen. We watched as though it would burst into song at any moment, but it stayed silent, dead, beneath her fingers.

"No," Chloe whispered, shaking her head. *"No."*

She tried one more time, pressing down so hard that her nailbeds turned white, but the phone wouldn't budge.

It was completely and utterly deceased.

"What do we do now?" Orla asked, immediately panicking. "We're trapped up here in a treehouse, with no way to escape –"

"Who was that man?" Chloe ignored Orla, probably to stop us all from freaking out, and focused on me, eyes glassy. She blinked, trying to bat the tears away like I hadn't already noticed. "That man, the one next to the tent. Why did Steve kill him too?"

"Maybe he was the guy Sharon was sleeping with," I said,

the pieces all falling together in my mind. "That would make sense. He had no clothes on, and…"

"That must be why Steve turned up at the camp…" Orla nodded.

"Of course!" Chloe continued, joining up the dots. "He suspected Sharon was having an affair, and so he turned up here to see for himself. That must have been what the scream was about. Shazza and her lover found Steve leering above them with the knife, and…"

I blinked at the unnecessary use of *Shazza*.

"So Sharon and Steve fought, and the other guy tried to leave, but Steve stabbed him to death, which is why his body was outside the tent and not inside –"

"What about Sharon?" I didn't want to ask the question, but I had to. I *had* to know.

"She… seemed dead, but I can't be sure." Chloe's face was more serious than I'd ever seen it, eyes still glassy, a tear forming at the rim. "There was no blood around her, just marks on her neck from where she was strangled, but she wasn't moving, and… her pants and trousers were off, she was just wearing a bra."

I didn't know what to say to that. My heart was pounding, phlegm thick in my throat.

Not Sharon, our Sharon. She was alive, thriving, bringing us pizza and planning new adventures to compensate for the loss of Lexie and Macey. She was our leader, our confidante.

She couldn't be *dead*.

"So Steve killed three people," Orla concluded. "*How?*"

"The kitchen knife, the one which was missing. He must've taken it."

"I… I don't get it. I know none of us ever liked him, but he was just some pathetic middle-aged bald guy, not a *murderer*. How could he have stabbed people to death like that, strangled Kayleigh? He was so... mild. I don't understand."

"It's always the quiet ones," Chloe muttered, to which Orla raised an eyebrow.

"What's that supposed to mean?"

"I didn't mean you, I just meant –"

"Guys." I held up my hand, silencing them. Chloe and Orla stopped bickering, staring at me with as much apprehension as is necessary for what they were about to witness, what I'd just heard.

Footsteps, crunching on the undergrowth below. The sound of a wheezing, gasping man, right underneath us. A voice, clearly one we'd heard before, calling up through the wooden slats.

"Shit," Chloe hissed, staring at me, shaking her head. "Shit!"

"Girls!" The voice was high-pitched, feminine, two scratchy blue eyes staring up at us through the floor of the treehouse. "I've found you!"

We all just sat there, tense, eyes bulging, as Steve Jones began to climb the ladder.

43

None of us dared move. Steve Jones was still making his way up the ladder, puffing and panting, those tiny blue piggy eyes focused on the treehouse above as we stared through the slats at his bald head.

"He can't get in," Orla hissed, though her eyes were huge behind her glasses. She was shaking, properly shaking. "He... I'm sat over the trapdoor, he can't push it open."

Slowly, Chloe and I shuffled towards Orla. All three of us now held our weight over the little wooden door, which was latched shut and safe. My heart was pounding in my chest, moving fast up to my mouth. I could feel it there, pulsing away against my tongue, throat so full I could barely swallow.

Was this a nightmare? It didn't quite feel *real*.

"Don't move," Chloe whispered back. The sound of the rain masked the sound of Steve Jones pressing against the trapdoor, but we could feel the weight beneath us, his hands trying to budge the wooden slats. He wasn't a strong man, and three teenage girls were an easy match in the ring.

"Girls!" he called in that familiar sing-song voice, the one Sharon had adopted her whole entire guiding career. It was a voice of campfire songs and delusion, too cheerful to be genuine. "Come on down, girls!"

Chloe's face was a picture; that I can remember. She was holding the knife still and frowning down through the slats. I didn't want to follow her gaze, but I couldn't help it... Steve was staring up at us, and I caught his eye through the gap. Vivid, sharp blue, gazing at me out of nowhere. I gulped cold air, backing up. He continued to stare, smiling now, that bald head glistening with raindrops and dew.

"Come on, Lucy! It's Lucy, isn't it? Just open up the trapdoor so we can talk. There was a misunderstanding last night, I think…"

The phlegm in my mouth was thick, sticky, as I pressed down hard on the trapdoor. Orla's bottom lip trembled as she nestled closer to me. Chloe was still guarding the knife as though her life depended on it. It did.

"It's Chloe and Orla, isn't it? You remember me, don't you? I'm Steve. *Steve Jones*, Sharon's husband."

I looked at Chloe then, who was frowning, shaking her head, like she couldn't believe the audacity of his manners. She ran her finger along the edge of the knife, not wincing as it speared the end of her finger.

"Come on, girls! Don't you want to talk to me?"

"No!"

I blinked at Orla's outburst. She was staring at the wall ahead with glassy eyes and a furious expression, hands shaking by her sides. I put mine out to clasp hers and it was cold, so cold, as rain pitter-pattered all around us and Steve let out a hollow laugh from below.

"We don't want to talk to you," Orla continued. "You killed *Kayleigh*. She did nothing wrong, and you killed her!"

"Like I said, it was a misunderstanding," Steve replied. "I thought she was… a bad guy, another one, like that man my wife was with. You saw him, didn't you? The man she's been sleeping with."

I hated the way he said this. So matter-of-fact, so cold. Like he wasn't *bothered* by the fact Sharon was sleeping around, more concerned with the fact she hadn't done her duty as his wife, hadn't remained *loyal*. There was no emotion there, no... anything. He didn't seem to care that he wasn't loved, that she'd betrayed him so easy. All those Facebook posts, the cringey messages, the fact he'd been in love with her since he was a kid...

I tried to swallow again, mouth still thick and slimy. Something didn't taste right. Something didn't *feel* right.

"She and I have been married for many years now," he added. "She was my everything, but apparently that didn't matter much to her..."

"So you killed her?" Chloe. Her voice was cool, disdainful. She caught my eye and held it for a second or two, and something inside me settled. The nerves, the fear. *We've got this.* "Why didn't you just divorce her? Or... I mean, you killed that other guy. Why kill Sharon too?"

"Because she was disloyal." A pause. "Twice."

"Twice?" Orla squeezed my hand, tight, shaking her head. "What... what happened the first time?"

"Never you mind," Steve retorted, but we could hear the change in his voice, the shift from confident to emotional, remembering back, thinking again. "She was my everything, and I was *nothing* to her."

Was that true? I couldn't tell you, even now. Steve had always seemed more into Sharon than she was to him, of course, but they seemed... happy. Content. They had their little life mapped out from day one, and Steve had a lifetime of love to give. Sharon was sensible, smart, pragmatic. Steve was erratic and disjointed, her perfect balance.

"She *deserved* to die," Steve added, though his voice wavered. I could hear the unease, the overthinking. Wondering whether we were right, and he had been wrong to do what he did. "Any wife who isn't loyal to their husband should be taken down, taught a lesson."

"Is that what you turned up here to do?" Chloe asked. "Teach her a lesson?"

I echoed her words in my mind, too scared to speak. Somewhere across the forest, a flock of birds went racing from the canopy, screeching and flapping their wings right into the sky.

"I... I... no, I didn't."

"Then what?"

We heard Steve inhale, and Chloe took a firmer grip of the knife.

"I came to spend the night with her. She's... been having a difficult time recently. As you know, she's getting on a bit, and we never had children. We went to see a specialist a few months ago about having IVF, and they said the risks were too great this close to the menopause. Sharon took it hard. She's been spending more and more time away from home recently, with her friends, at work. At least... I thought that was where she was."

I couldn't quite believe what I was hearing. Aside from everything he was telling us about their personal life, the fact that Steve Jones was even here, confessing all of this to us as Sharon, Kayleigh and some strange man lay dead less than a hundred metres away felt so *bizarre*.

"I never suspected an affair, exactly, not after twenty years of giving my life to that woman. I've loved her since I first laid eyes on her. We were only five, you know, when we met. It took me more than fifteen years to get what I wanted, but..."

Fifteen years. I hated the way he said it, like he'd been biding his time, waiting to pounce. Sharon had married young, I remember seeing somewhere online, but it clearly hadn't worked out.

Steve was her second. Sharon was his first.

It was just like me and Ethan.

"I brought champagne, pickled onions, tiger bread. The gates had been left unlocked, which was… surprising, but I didn't think anything of it. And then when I arrived at the tent… I couldn't take it."

Chloe was still listening, hanging onto his every word, clutching the knife tighter and tighter. She caught my eye again and nodded.

"You just snapped, Steve," she said, keeping her voice light, sympathetic. "You loved her so, so much, put so much thought into what would make her happy, and she was betraying you."

A choked cough, a subdued sob. Steve Jones snuffled, releasing his pressure on the trapdoor and sagging backwards.

"It's understandable, Steve," Chloe continued. "You were angry. Anyone could see why you'd do what you did. You could even claim that… that that man, whoever he is, tried to attack you first, that it was self-defence. You must've grabbed the cooking knife once you heard what was going on, right? You couldn't take it anymore."

"That's right," Steve murmured, the tears on his face clear, though I didn't dare look through the slats at him. "I… I heard them in there, and I couldn't take it. I just ran and grabbed the knife from the table, and…"

"You strangled Sharon," Chloe added. "What with?"

"The leg of her trousers," Steve admitted. "Surprisingly convenient."

It was almost too fitting to sound real. Sharon Jones, strangled to death using her iconic waterproof trousers. The thought was so comical I almost choked on my laughter.

There was a short silence, as Steve composed himself below and Chloe gave us both a triumphant look, one which said we were making progress, that we were finally *getting somewhere*, wearing him down.

Then Orla spoke.

"Why Kayleigh?" she asked. "Why did you have to kill her?"

That was a mistake. Chloe and I both knew so as we caught each other's eyes, hearts thudding.

Why?

Just... why?

I held my breath as Steve straightened up again. We all flinched as he applied pressure to the trapdoor, trying his very hardest to push it open, to get inside. We could hear him huffing and puffing, using all his strength, heart pounding so loud you could hear it in every breath –

"Because she saw what happened," he said, all composure returned, collected once again, calm. "She saw that I killed Sharon, and I couldn't let her get away. Just like I can't let you three get away."

Orla closed her eyes, and we all collectively winced.

Chloe clutched the knife so tight I swear it could've sliced right through her palm.

No one was breathing.

"And so," Steve continued, "I'll be waiting right here for you. Good luck getting away from me, girls."

We heard him retreat down the ladder, hands slippery on the rungs. His feet hit the forest floor and he turned, grin glinting through the rain.

Steve Jones took a seat on the bottom rung of the ladder, right below us, guarding the treehouse.

His own knife sat next to him in the mud.

44

I tell Ethan the shortened version, of course. How we waited most of the day, missing lunch, with only the bread and cheese to snack on. Steve didn't speak again, didn't leave to get food, to check on the bodies of his victims. Chloe had the knife. It's not so unbelievable that she could have been the one to stab him, to break our freedom, is it?

"So what happened?" he asks, eyes wide. "Chloe hurried down the ladder when he wasn't looking, and just... stabbed him?"

"We threw Kayleigh's phone down first," I say. My heart's thudding, hands locked between Ethan's. Can he tell I'm lying? "We... threw it really hard, so he was surprised and in pain, clutching the back of his head."

I can still picture Steve now, clutching the back of his bald head, blood creeping through his fingers. Blue eyes angry, hurt. Looking so innocent I almost felt... guilty. His knife had been left a metre or so away as he stood up and staggered.

"And then Chloe went down the ladder with the knife, and stabbed him... where?"

"In his lower abdomen, groin area. Several times. Like, three or four, I think. I don't know which bit killed him."

Ethan's eyes are wide, shocked. "You saw all of that? You saw a man *die*?"

I nod.

Liar, liar.

"All of it?"

I nod again.

Liar, liar, pants on fire.

***

I was the one who suggested throwing the phone at him. It was the only hard object we had, apart from the bottles, which we thought would be too... obvious. And so Chloe took it from Orla, angling it so that it sliced through the air like a boomerang towards Steve's bald head, which was waiting for us at the bottom of the ladder.

He let out a yelp, of course, staggering and stumbling forward.

The next bit was my idea, too, though it was Orla who insisted I go along with it.

"Go!" Chloe shouted, as I stumbled away from the trapdoor, pulling it open. Chloe dropped out first, falling to the ground and quickly pulling herself up, reaching for Steve's knife. She grabbed it before he even knew what was happening, staring round in shock and clutching the back of his head, which had a severe cut and was bleeding through his fingers.

I fell out next, only briefly using the ladder for assistance. Once my feet had hit the forest floor, I didn't think twice about what I had to do. The knife was in my hands. It wasn't raining anymore. We'd waited hours in silence, Steve Jones sat there on the ladder below, biding his time, trusting that we'd give up and go tumbling out to his waiting jaws.

It was already going dark, but that didn't matter.

I'd never seen more clearly.

One swift jab was all it took. A bone-crunching crush of

flesh and sinew and skin beneath the blade of the knife... I watched as my hand, detached from my body, shot out and into Steve's t-shirt, to the skin below, the lower flesh of his stomach. That second yelp, a sound of pain and surprise, horror. Blue eyes wide, filled with the knowledge that he didn't have a chance.

Blood squirted up and out, over my hoodie, face, hair, hands, trainers. It clung to my fingers, drip dripping as I plunged the knife in for a second time, higher up this time. Watched his eyes roll back into his head, nostrils flare, body go flying back into the autumn leaves behind him.

Chloe did the third and fourth stabs. I couldn't breathe, staring at his blood-soaked body, hands trembling. She let the knife sink right into his fleshy stomach, blood drip over his eyes, nose as she retracted the knife. His blood was so much darker than expected, like chocolate sauce. I was still struggling for breath.

"We did it," Chloe whispered, taking a step back and breathing out, a long and shallow sound. "Fuck, Luce, I..."

"Is he definitely dead?" Orla asked, appearing beside us with a shaky voice. "Is he..."

Slowly, I knelt to the ground beside Steve Jones. His eyelids were fluttering, mouth muscles spasming. Pressed two fingers into his neck, where his pulse should be. Held them steady over the next minute as they slowed, stuttered to an eventual stop. Rolled back onto my hunches and said, "He's dead."

The forest was silent, sky above starting to turn black. Chloe and Orla were staring at me, Chloe still clutching the knife. She wasn't so splattered as me, but it was still clear she'd had something to do with his death. We stood there for a few moments longer, the body of Steve lying heavy below us.

"What now?"

45

Steve's death probably didn't really look so collected as I remember. I don't know how my stabs looked to the others. Weak, pathetic, so much so that Chloe had to finish the job for me. We don't know which stab was fatal, of course. All we do know is that Steve's death was undeniable, unavoidable. Once it was over, everything just... stopped.

And we were left with four dead bodies.

We kept Steve where he was, at first. There was no point moving him; he wasn't exactly *going* anywhere. Chloe and Orla were tense, but I felt this weird sense of closure. It was over. The last twenty-four hours, I'd barely felt anything, too terrified to process what was happening. But now Steve was dead, gone. No one else could get hurt.

"We need to burn our clothes," is what Chloe said first, as we hurried back to camp. "That's a must, okay?"

The showers were by the main block, through a side entrance. There were only two, built into one cubicle at the bottom of a long row. Chloe went first, Orla and I perched on the sinks and staring at our bloody hands as she peeled off her reddened clothes, teased the blood from her blonde hair. She left the door open and pink water trickled from the shower all the way to the sinks, where it fell through the drainage holes, releasing our crime to the pipes below.

She came out stark naked and shivering, lips blue. Orla volunteered to go back to the tent for towels. We didn't speak as we waited, Chloe's clothes in a pile in the shower, the blood soaking out of them like cranberry juice.

I showered next. Stood under the jet of cold water as the red left my hair, my nails, fell through the gaps in my fingers, my eyelashes. Splatters etched onto my skin so I scrubbed hard to get them off, using the cheap shower gel Sharon had left there the day before. It was mango, like Nora and Alicia love so much. I can no longer distinguish between the scent of tropical fruit and blood.

It was freezing in the shower block, but soon Chloe and I were bundled in towels and waiting for Orla, who was by far the cleanest of the three. If I understood anything, however, it was how desperately we all wanted to scrub the scent of Steve's murder from our skin, even if the blood was long gone. It's why I can hardly look at my body now, convinced my skin is covered in splatters of red, that I'm leaving bloody hand and footprints everywhere I go.

"They need to work on heating the water here," Orla said as she emerged, but none of us laughed.

We dressed in the tent, as the sun continued to set and the camp was submerged in black. Chloe had the bright idea of hurrying into the forest to rummage around for dry sticks and logs and leaves to get the fire going again, so Orla and I traipsed round to the back of the block to see if there were any logs left in the store. Chloe took charge lighting it, using a few matches from Sharon's pack and a healthy glug of firelighter.

"Use the hand dryers in the bathroom to get the water out of the clothes," she instructed. She couldn't look us in the eye as she said this, prodding the fire and frowning. "If we put them on while they're sopping wet, it'll just go out."

Orla and I took our time drying everything, unspeaking.

We wrung out the clothes first, holding each item beneath the hand dryers until it was as light and airy as possible, careful to not let the old clothes touch our new ones. We had no idea how much else we were going to have to dispose of, but it was best to stay as uncontaminated as possible, now.

Back at the camp, Chloe used a long stick to lower each piece of clothing into the fire. We watched as the flames took their hold, hearts in our mouths.

It felt so… wrong. So strange. Here we were, disposing of our murder outfits in the forest, Kayleigh's dead body just metres away from us, along with Sharon and her lover. Steve was still deep into the trees, out of sight, but we could feel his presence as the scent of his blood shot into the air, burning flesh and human remains and one fateful sleeping bag slept in by Steve Jones, our very own murder disappearing into the sky away from us in tiny particles.

"We'll keep the fire burning for as long as possible," Chloe said, nodding to herself. "That way we can burn anything of significance, get rid of all the other rubbish, wrappers and stuff… and also mask the fact we were burning clothes here."

It didn't surprise me that she was taking charge. Orla and I might have been the ones to suggest the attack on Steve Jones, but Chloe was the calm one, the only one who could stomach the third and fourth stabs, who knew how to stay composed in a crisis. I couldn't help thinking that she had more to lose, too, as she prodded the flames and sent sparks flying up into the sky. Her reputation, her Instagram, her mum's business… Tobes, her rich, beautiful boyfriend. Orla and I had uni and our educations, of course, but Chloe was going places. She wouldn't be going *anywhere* if anyone ever found out about this.

The clothes burnt to a crisp, of course. The pizza boxes,

sweet and doughnut wrappers, the bags we'd used to transport food and drink. There were still all of those bottles trapped up in the treehouse, but Chloe said we could dispose of them later, figure out what to do. We just had to make the camp as clean and tidy as possible, in case anyone arrived to check things out, wondering where Steve or Sharon or any of us had got to, why they couldn't get hold of even the campsite's phone.

Which meant moving Kayleigh's body so that it wasn't hanging out of the tent, and covering the naked man.

We used a blanket from one of the other tents, keeping the fire burning so that we could dispose of it later. Orla draped the man in it, all of us repulsed by the smell, the sight of him sprawled like that across the ground. It was green, the blanket, and the site was almost black; if anyone arrived before morning, you'd never know there was a body there.

Kayleigh was next. We were careful not to look at Sharon's body as we moved our friend's head to the inside of the tent, mouths closed, trying not to breathe out loud. Orla was red-faced and Chloe's lips trembled, but we remained composed. Two brief zips and the tent was all closed up, the campsite back to its pristine condition.

"Now it's time for Steve."

Chloe had properly examined the forecast before coming away that weekend. She knew we were meant to have heavy rain again, that any other traces of our scandal would be washed away before morning rose. We could drag him through the trees, no problem. The traces of his blood would be lost forever within the forest floor.

We knew the way to the treehouse off by heart by now. Steve's body looked the same as when we left it. Bald and pale, clad in a t-shirt, plaid overshirt and chinos, which were bloodstained, discoloured. We'd nabbed a torch from the tent and Chloe flashed it about as we tried to figure out the best way to do this.

"You two grab his legs," she said, shuddering. "I'll... I'll grab his neck."

We knew it would be clear his body had been moved somewhere, but the location of his murder couldn't possibly be calculated, surely? We took the two knives back to camp as we lugged him through the trees, to the clearing beside the other man's remains. We left Steve just close enough that the blanket would cover them both. He was heavy, probably due to too much of Sharon's infamous lentil dahl and squash soup. Our arms and legs ached as we staggered back. There was no time for relaxation now.

Chloe knew what to do next, of course. She led us back through the trees towards the treehouse after scrubbing our hands thoroughly with soap and water, using some of the hand sanitizer she kept in her washbag. We took the cushions and blankets from the treehouse and stuffed them in a binbag – they weren't contaminated, and were unlikely to be tested, right? – then pushed all of the bottles and cans into a second bag, along with the knives, covered in our fingerprints. Back at the site, we scattered our belongings around our own two tents as though they'd been there the whole time.

"You know what we need to do with this alcohol, right?" Chloe said. "And the ashes from the fire?"

"What?" we echoed, as she placed the blanket onto the fire with a final hiss.

"We'll wait for this to burn, then check we've covered our tracks, made this whole thing a mystery." Her voice was level, confident, but I knew Chloe better than that. She was just as terrified as we were, doing her best to stay calm. "We need to clean the shower out – properly, I mean – with all the disinfectant and bleach stuff they keep in the storeroom. Sharon has a key. We make sure every speck of blood is gone from our own bodies and from the site, and we bring Kayleigh's head out again, make this look more… accidental."

"What's our story?" Orla asked, but I could see what Chloe was getting at, now.

"We don't have one," I said slowly. "We're traumatised. We don't want to say what happened that weekend, but four people are now dead, and we can't talk about it because it was so… difficult."

Orla's mouth opened and closed as Chloe nodded.

"Exactly. It's the only way. Foolproof, I say."

Foolproof, maybe.

Smart, it certainly was *not*.

Cleaning was the easiest part. No bodies, no pools of blood. Invisible specks to flake away, to scrub at with the sponges and disinfectant, which we then burnt, too. Chloe stayed behind to inspect the crime scene, to sort out Kayleigh's body and make sure Steve wasn't too close to that other guy. She had the strongest stomach. There was a bloody stain on her t-shirt as she came to find us in the shower block, so she went through the rigmarole of changing it, throwing the previous onto the fire.

We scooped the ashes into the binbag with the bottles, checking for one final time that the camp was clean, neat, a weekend accident gone horribly wrong. Looking back, we could've just dragged the other man – now known as Carl Hall – to the cliffs with us, thrown him over the edge. If his drowned body was ever found, there'd be little to link him to our camp, just the stab wounds, which could've happened anywhere… and the blood in the grass, maybe. But we didn't, of course. We weren't thinking straight.

It was three or four in the morning by the time we had everything sorted. Chloe carried the binbag as we scurried after her through the trees, all three of us clutching our phones tight. Kayleigh's had been scrubbed with hand sanitizer and pushed back into her pocket, and we were all shivering as the rain began once again.

We reached the cliffs in no time. It wasn't so scary, this time, getting close to the edge. Standing over the ocean and throwing those bottles into the sea, one by one, lids on and filled with the hope that they'd be carried far, far away. The cans were kept behind, to push into random bins as we walked. The knives, thrown into the waves like boomerangs, shooting away from us.

Chloe disposed of the ashes.

We watched as they soared through the air, tiny particles of grey, fluttering into the sky. Our clothes; the blanket; the pizza boxes; Steve's blood. Intermingling with the splotchy rain, which was only getting heavier.

"It's done." Chloe put down the bag, which was now only housing cans and clutter, the evidence long gone. "I don't know what else we could've done."

"We've been safe," I reassured her. "We covered our tracks, and the rain will help now –"

"No." She paused. "I mean, I don't know what else we could've done about *Steve*."

We were silent as we stood there, staring into the abyss, tossing things over in our mind. It was done now, no going back, but we were going to rethink it over and over, of course. That's just what happens when you do something stupid, reckless. When you risk everything simply because you don't know what else to do.

"I think we did the right thing," Orla said after a while. "We couldn't have got down from the treehouse without him… hurting us. Even if we managed to run away through the trees, find the nearest village, get phone signal on some hill somewhere… I don't know, it would have been such a risk. And he deserved it anyway, didn't he?"

"He deserved to rot in jail, get abused to death by his inmates," Chloe replied, and I heard her jaw clenching as she said this. "That wasn't the answer. It *wasn't*."

She blamed us. Orla and me. We'd come up with the idea to kill Steve – not Chloe. She'd gone along with it, though. And I knew Chloe. She never did anything she didn't want to.

Right?

"It was the only option," I said, reaching to take her hand. "We'll never know whether we would've gotten out alive, otherwise."

"Yeah." Chloe squeezed my hand back. "I guess we'll never know."

46

Ethan has stopped moving, breathing, speaking. He's listened to me explain how I covered up a murder – technically three, though we thought it was four – and I don't think he'll ever look at me in the same way again.

"You…"

"We killed Steve, yes."

He still thinks it was Chloe who threw those three, four stabs, who punctured his t-shirt with blood.

It wasn't, of course. It was a combination of meek little Lucy's courage and Orla's ingenuity…

Chloe just finished off the job.

"My God." He pauses, still circling my palm with his thumb, and says, "I mean, I can see why you did it. Why you felt you had to hide what you'd done from… everyone. Even when it should be self-defence, if you're not actually in danger, they can sometimes view the attack as… unprovoked. I think. I'm not an expert, though."

Music started up downstairs about half an hour ago, and from the sound of the front door banging over and over, the party has probably already begun. I check my phone. There's still an hour to wait until Chloe and Orla get here. I have time.

"The fact you didn't tell the truth straight away could be seen as a problem, too," Ethan continues. "Again, I can see why you did that, but… I don't know, Luce. I don't know what you should do next. I wish I could help, but…"

"It's okay." I press a finger to his lips, leaning forwards into his warmth. "You listened. That was enough."

His arms go around me, breath hot on my cheek. "I'm glad you told me. You shouldn't have been bottling it in, you know. I feel privileged that you trust me, Luce. It means a lot."

"I love you," I repeat, if only to cover my lies.

We stay like that for a minute, before Ethan pulls back and says, "When did you realise Sharon wasn't dead? You told me Chloe assumed she was gone the minute she saw she was unconscious, that she'd been strangled…"

"That morning, when the police arrived."

It had taken us a good three hour walk to get signal. By that time, it was seven in the morning, and we were standing at the edge of a village in North Yorkshire, a five minute walk from the main road. The police picked us up there, followed by an ambulance and a car filled with paramedics. They found Sharon's pulse the moment they arrived on the scene, moving her into a stretcher and carrying her away, into the ambulance and off to hospital in a matter of minutes. The other three bodies were covered and carried away by police, who had grim expressions and wouldn't look us in the eye.

We weren't questioned straight away, of course. There was no need. Twenty-four hours went by, then forty-eight, before we were reintroduced to Officer Joy and Pudrow, who had been working on a separate case during the initial recovery of the camp.

"It must have been so traumatic for you…" Ethan whispers now, stroking my hair.

It was, in a way. But I was also just in shock. Ethan helped, of course, messaging me to check up on me, the case, the funeral. And the funeral itself. Saying goodbye to Kayleigh, apologising for letting her go into Sharon's tent alone. Seeing her family, Emilia Kettering and co., offering our condolences. Eating so many mini choux buns we thought we'd overdose on the sugar.

They announced Sharon was in a coma when the first article came out about the accident. Before that, all we knew was that it was touch and go. I'm no doctor, but I'm pretty sure the whole thing meant that Sharon was being kept in a coma, because her condition meant she wasn't strong enough to keep herself alive – something like that. The injuries were too great, or whatever. I don't know. All we were told was that they had no idea when she would wake up, and wouldn't be able to tell us that for weeks, maybe even months.

Until now.

Ethan is shaking his head as he listens to me speak. The sympathy on his face is too much to bear.

"Do you think we should go down and enjoy the party?" I ask, moving away from him and going to stand. I blush when I notice my pants still slung across the handle from earlier, and wrestle to pull them on under my dress. "The others will be wondering where we got to…"

He nods, standing to straighten his t-shirt, sort out his hair. We stand for a moment, staring at one another, as someone turns the music up downstairs and the beat starts pulsing through the floorboards.

"I really do love you, Lucy," Ethan says suddenly. "I didn't just say that because… of what was going on. I genuinely do love you. I have done for months."

I can feel myself blushing as I nod back, hands behind my back.

"Even after what I just told you?"

Ethan smiles. "*Especially* after you told me that."

I assume he means after I proved that I trust him, not that he loves me even more after finding out I'm a murderer, but guilt writhes in my stomach once again as I stand on my tiptoes to kiss him.

I'm a bad person.

I'm a very, very bad person.

Ethan doesn't know that though. He takes my hand, grinning all the while, as he opens the door and says, "How about we go and enjoy this party, then?"

***

The celebrations are in full swing when we get downstairs. The punch is already discoloured and the sound of music dances through the doors into each room, covering us in sweat and euphoria.

"I'll get us a drink!" Ethan shouts. I smile and nod back.

Nora and Alicia are in the living room, by the buffet table Alicia has generously set up. Oli is ordering pizza by the door, and Kev has been ambushed by a girl in his extra-curricular debates class who is stroking his cheek and whispering into his ear, much to his bemusement.

"Who does she think she is?" Nora whispers, pulling a face. "She's such a tart!"

Alicia looks up as I snag a sausage roll from under their noses, face breaking into a beam. "Oh my God, Luce, we thought you'd disappeared into Ethan's luscious arms forever!"

I pull a face, but seeing them already makes me feel so much lighter, more confident about the night ahead.

"I managed to pull myself *out* of his luscious arms, thank

you, Lish."

Alicia grins, wiggling her eyebrows and murmuring, "We saw you two go upstairs…"

"To have a deep chat, yes!" I roll my eyes as they exchange knowing glances, adding, "Trust me, you guys would know if anything else happened."

"We'd sense it," Nora replies.

"We'd *smell* it," Alicia corrects.

Our song comes on then – Alicia's favourite Christmas tune, and mine and Nora's least favourite, ever. It's a running joke between the three of us that whenever this particular song comes on, we have to get up and dance, no matter where we are (cinemas and supermarkets included).

I let them pull me into the centre of the living room, where debates-class-Caroline has Kev by the arm and is trying to dance with him, but he's so far restraining. Alicia starts prancing about straight away, not bothered who else is watching, but Nora looks nervous, self-conscious, trying to catch Kev's eye. I smile as he breaks free of Caroline and goes spinning away from her, collapsing beside us with a relieved gasp.

"She kept saying she wanted to put my debating skills to the test," he says as he joins the circle, bobbing up and down, immediately more comfortable. "With a dance contest, would you believe!"

Alicia and I laugh as Nora takes his hand, the two of them moving away across the dancefloor (Oli's stained carpet), grooving in time to the music, faces a little too close. I take my best friend's hands as we continue to dance, the room pulsing all around us, kids from sixth form still spilling round the doors and into the room. Oli's pizzas have arrived, and he carries them in balanced on one hand, receiving a cheer from the rest of the party. Alicia rolls her eyes, but I can see the secret smile on her face as we go to help lay them out.

I feel pretty sober now, and the pizza definitely helps. I scoff slices by the dozen as we stand around and make small talk with these ditsy girls who sit on the table next to us in the common room, try to laugh when they laugh, nod along to their mindless chatter. Ethan returns with a lemonade for me and a beer for him, planting a kiss on my hairline as he slides it into my hand, smiling. Something passes between us, then. A secret smile, a look which indicates we share something special now, that the truths revealed earlier brought us closer together.

We dance as a four for a while, moving right into the centre of the room and taking over the floor. Kev and Nora join us, smug smiles on their faces, and Nora catches my eye and nods when Kev isn't looking.

"I kissed him!" she hisses, and I laugh, squeezing her pink cheeks and grabbing her hands to pump them up and down.

I must lose track of time, somewhere down the line. The night drifts away in a mash of dancing and laughter and pizza breath, my friends and me moving in time to the music, Christmas song after Christmas song playing over the speakers. The clock hand must edge closer to eleven, but I'm having such a good time that Chloe and Orla disappear from my mind. I'm so focused on just having fun that when Ethan turns to me with a blank expression and screws up his nose, I look back in confusion.

"They're here," he says, right in my ear.

They're here.

I turn around slowly, towards the living room door, the one leading in from the corridor. There are people blocking my view, but as the ditsy girls from sixth form move out of my way, I get a clear line of sight.

Chloe and Orla are stood in the doorway, completely out of place at such a party. Neither of them are dressed for the occasion… but then what *is* the occasion? It's clearly not what I was expecting.

But the expressions on their face are clear.

It's over.

47

I lead them outside, into Oli's front garden. A menagerie of teens are clustered in the back garden by Oli's now infamous paddling pool, sucking punch through a straw. Things are only going to get more wild as the night drags on and all of the kids we *definitely* didn't invite start to arrive.

Chloe stares round with raised eyebrows as we make our way down the corridor and out the front door, like the whole party is beyond her comprehension.

"Is this what sixth form parties are like nowadays?" she asks, scoffing at the tame level of alcohol, the sign on the door welcoming everyone in. "They never used to be this lame…"

That might have something to do with the fact that Chloe was only fourteen or fifteen when she started hijacking parties and swallowing gallons of alcohol with her older boyfriends, and probably thought *anything* the upper sixth did ridiculously cool. But I don't say that, knowing I'd prefer Oli's bash any day of the week to one involving Chloe and those horrific vodka shots again.

"Out here," I say, gesturing for them to follow. The street is silent, empty, the final few partygoers trailing in from the opposite direction, already pumped full of sugary pitchers from the Maguires in town. "We don't want to be overheard…"

Outside Oli's house is a snicket filled with broken leaves and mud, leading back into the centre of Vibbington via the more industrial side of town. The hospital, school and petrol stations are planted there, amongst beds of grass which are supposed to make the area look soft, lived in.

The snicket is dark, veering into nothing, so Chloe flicks on her flash, muttering something about her battery dying. It's all too familiar. Only then do I take them in properly, analyse their expressions, the fear in their eyes and on their mouths. Orla bites her lip as Chloe starts pacing up and down, up and down, shaking her head to herself as I try to breathe normally.

"Okay," I start. "What did you guys think to the voicemail message?"

Orla looks up first, face indignant. "What did we think? It's… it's horrible, that's what it is. Sharon was there, knows that she was having an affair with Carl, probably even saw Steve stabbing Carl. She'll know that Steve then strangled her, even if she can't remember it, and they'll assume the rest. Surely that's obvious, Lucy?"

I flush, though they can't see my pink cheeks in the darkness. "Yes, I know, I know. I meant… I… I don't know what I meant."

"We don't stand a chance," Chloe cuts in. "Sharon's going to tell them the truth, we all know that. They'll figure out what happened, arrest us, and we won't get off lightly because we lied to the police for so long. God, look at me. A right blooming genius."

"She might have memory loss?" I suggest. "She might… I mean, it must have been a traumatic injury for her to have been in a coma for so long. What if the trauma of the event has led her to black out what happened that night, before we all arrived and found her? What if she can only briefly remember sleeping with Carl Hall, and then…"

"Oh yes, she can only briefly remember shagging a guy for months and months behind her husband's back. Memory loss is a real lifesaver, am I right?"

I scowl at Chloe, who glares back as though she knows I'm losing.

"Come on, Lucy. Think clearly for a second. Sharon's going to wake up from her coma to find out that everything in her perfect little life has gone tits up, that her boyfriend is dead and her husband has also popped his clogs. She'll never be respected by her family again because she had an affair, and the guiding community will kick her out after she lets *another* girl die under her watch…"

"What are you saying, Chloe?" Orla asks, suddenly nervous, voice wavering.

I know what she's saying.

I know *exactly* what she's saying.

"You're saying we should kill her," I say, staring at Chloe. "You're saying we should kill Sharon."

Beside us, Orla lapses into silence.

"I'm saying it's an *option*," Chloe replies, though her voice is stronger now, more convincing. "Sharon will be heartbroken when she wakes up, will lose everything, might even be physically altered by the injuries. She's lost Steve, her family, guiding, the man she probably loved. And… and so have we."

"What do you mean?" Orla repeats, though her voice is little more than a whisper now.

"We'll lose everything," Chloe says. "Respect, status, boyfriends, friends. The chance to go to university and start a new life without this hanging over us. I just turned eighteen, had a low-key party last Saturday. Orla's birthday is in a month or so. They'll have no obligation to protect our names in the press or online. We might even have to serve prison time, Orla. Think how that'll look if we ever want to get a job, start anew."

"And killing Sharon?" Orla counters, eyes wide. "What will that do for our precious respect?"

Chloe pauses again, and I know what she's going to say next. Although these ideas are all Chloe's, we have a lot more in common than I think even she knows.

"We run away," she says. "Start new lives, somewhere above the border. Scotland... or we could travel down to Wales. I've been using fake IDs since I was fifteen to get into bars and shit. I know a guy in Hull who charges a hundred quid for a proper passport and provisional licence, and these blue cards you get online to prove you're an adult. He does them for people smuggled in from the port, but I know he'll give us a few if we pay properly, with real cash. I still have heaps from my birthday, ages ago, and from influencing jobs. I've transferred a ton into a second account, a temporary one, so we can take out the cash. You guys can pay me back."

"Chloe," I say, shaking my head. "We're not running away. That would be..."

"Stupid?" she finishes with a snort. "Beyond daft? But what about *staying*, Lucy? How silly would that be? If we kill Sharon or not, we're in huge trouble. We'll lose everything either way."

She's right, I know she is, but I don't want to believe it. I can't believe it. Running away to Scotland with a fake ID, two murders hanging over us... I know in my heart that we'd never get away with it.

Right?

"What about Aaron?" Orla echoes my doubts, but I can tell from her voice that she's seriously considering it, that her doubts are almost quenched. "And my place at Durham, my family?"

"You cheated on Aaron, and would've broken up once you got to Durham anyway." Chloe rolls her eyes. "And university is overrated. As for family... do you think I want to do this? To leave my mum, my new little half-sister, my cousins? But it's not forever. We'll come back one day, when it's safer, when we can trust they won't tell on us. It's just for a while, till we get sorted."

"And how will we *live*?" I ask, still not fully believing that she's thought this through, that it will ever work. "Where will we live? How will people not realise it's us?"

"Like I said, I have a ton of cash saved from my influencing jobs and ads, from working for Mum while you two read textbooks and sit on your arses! Tobes will lend us some, too, I guess, if I contact him... and we'll cut our hair short. If we get an apartment in Edinburgh, Glasgow, we can start afresh, use our ID to get good jobs there, even if they don't pay much. Then we'll be able to move round a bit, never stay in one place long enough to rouse suspicion."

"Our faces will be everywhere," I say, though my doubts are easing, much as I hate to admit it. "And our identifying features..."

"Makeup," Chloe suggests. "Hair dye, clothes, piercings. I know how to do all that shit from working at the salon. I can give you nose rings, lip studs, semi-permanent brow tattoos... Or I know this woman in Hull who does it behind the authorities, you know. She can make us all look like whole different people."

I can't tell if Chloe's trying to sound hard, or whether this plan – this crazy, ludicrous plan – will actually work.

"And if this *does* work," I say, heart thudding, "how do

you propose we kill Sharon?"

Chloe grins. I hate that grin.

It always means trouble.

"That's where you come in, Orla."

48

We're running, running, away from Oli's dark street and down the snicket. It's freezing out and my red dress barely covers my thighs and chest, let alone anything else, but Chloe was clearly banking on us saying yes to her mad scheme. She has a bag full of spare coats and jeans and woollies with her, and throws them at us willy-nilly as we make our way to the hospital.

"Sharon was transferred there today, right?" Chloe checks as we stop for breath. I pull on a pair of her jeans, praying they won't be too tight, and tie the bottom of my dress into a knot by my belly button so that it sort of looks like a top. My shoes are wildly inappropriate for running and I'm out of breath, but we set off again anyway, Orla shouting over our shoulders.

"Yeah. My dad told me this afternoon, after the voicemail!"

Orla's parents are both doctors, but her dad works in the Vibbington branch. It used to be private and he made an absolute killing, but the company went bankrupt several years back and the NHS took it over. He still works there now, so Orla knows her way round it surprisingly well.

"The place is always half empty – most cases are taken to hospitals in Hull or York – so Aaron and I sneak in there all the time to have some quiet time in the empty rooms. The only reason they still have the room Sharon's in, all the machinery and stuff, is from when it was owned by this big company. The security cameras are hardly ever checked, only checked in the mornings as a precaution. The system itself is kept in a back room with all of the monitors, and the night staff aren't supposed to go in there anyway. Dad's always complaining about how slack they are; the good nurses are all given decent shifts, daytime and that, while their kids are at school."

It's crazy. All of this is crazy.

Orla is crazy.

"So what's the plan?" I ask, though I almost daren't say it, still unable to digest that we're actually about to do this. "We sneak in, and then…"

"We turn off Sharon's life support," Chloe says, slowing almost to a stop. "And then we have this."

She pulls something from her bag, almost in slow motion.

A serrated kitchen knife.

"To make sure we do the job properly."

The job.

The job being to *end Sharon's life*.

"We have black tape, so I'm going to tape over as many cameras as I can before we get to Sharon's room." Orla's voice almost breaks then, but she speeds up, beckoning for us to follow. "It's just down this street…"

I'm trying not to think, to not fully register what's happening. To not think about the fact I'm never going to see Ethan again, or Nora and Alicia, or Mum and Dad.

What other choice do we have?

"It's better this way," Chloe says, as though she can sense my thoughts. "It's kinder for Sharon, too. She's lost everything, Lucy. *Everything*. She never would have wanted to wake up in a world where her husband is a murderer, her lover has been slashed and she's lost pretty much everything else that mattered to her. Come on, Lucy. You can see that, can't you?"

"I know," I say. Because I do know. It makes sense, but...

The hospital is small and white, just one storey high and built from solid wooden panels. Orla knows what's she's doing, clearly. She tears off a small piece of tape and hurries over to the side of the building, slinking along the walls until she can reach up and slap the tape across the camera without it noticing her – or us.

"I forgot to mention," she says, rushing back with a grin, "I did my EPQ on breaking and entering. Guess which building I used as a case study?"

"You're a legend!" Chloe claims, and I try to agree, squeezing Orla's hand.

"It's how Aaron and I knew about the accessible rooms..."

The side door is apparently the staff entrance. You can tell if the corridor is empty by whether the lights are on, we're told. They're automatic, but the sensor is in the middle of the room, not on the door. If we do another Orla and make our way down the corridor stuck to the wall, we'll never be detected, and the lights won't turn on. The cameras there don't like the dark.

"This is when I become thankful that Dad didn't use my EPQ report as a reason to update the security system..." Orla says absently, shaking her head. "I guess this is the last time Aaron and I will be doing this, won't it?"

I see Chloe roll her eyes in the dim, but she opens the door before Orla can second guess herself.

The corridor is quiet, but our feet squeak on the polished floor as we dash down the edge to the double doors at the end, pushing through them one by one. The main reception area is silent, the chairs turned upside down so that the cleaner can push a mop beneath them early tomorrow morning – or this morning, should I say, as my phone announces it's already past twelve. There's a text from Ethan asking where I am, but I don't have time to reply, not now.

"Won't the police be able to track our phones?" I ask suddenly, frowning. "Our locations and that?"

It's clear this is the first Chloe has thought of such a thing, as she pulls a face and reaches to grab mine off me. I don't even know if that's true, or just something I've seen on TV, but the panic is setting in now, so heavy it hurts.

"Solid point, Lucy." Gesturing for us to follow, she dips into the nearest bathroom. I glance around reception, paranoid, but Orla was right. The staff are all in their positions, and the waiting room is dead.

"Okay," Chloe instructs once we're inside. "Do a factory reset first, then hand me your SIMs and any SD cards or batteries, if your phone's old."

I exchange glances with Orla, who's biting her lip.

"But… all my messages from Aaron, phones, memories. They're all on this phone, Chlo."

Chloe simply rolls her eyes again. "Then you should've backed them up, shouldn't you?"

I can't overthink this. I can't. Ignoring Orla's objections, I click onto my settings, onto the little reset button.

Are you sure you want to do a factory reset? Any data you haven't backed up will be lost forever.

I agree before the message has chance to register.

My SIM card is tiny, my SD pathetic and ancient. Chloe has scissors in her bag – I don't want to know why – and snips both up with a click-clack. She does the same with her own, then snatches Orla's because she's too nervous to do the decent, mature thing. Once our data is lost, she pulls off our cases and pop sockets and stuffs them in her bag, then drops all three in the sink.

"Just in case," she explains.

We watch as she fills the sink with hot, soapy water. Then she takes each one and throws them into the sanitary bin, just like that.

"The police will never fish through manky pads and used tampons to get them out."

Back in the reception area, it's still silent. Orla says the front doors are locked overnight, the staff entrance utilised until three or four am when the cleaners unlock everything else. There should be three nurses on duty tonight, outside the three main wards. Sharon isn't being kept in any of them. She has her own room, one of two rooms in the hospital with proper life support – whatever that even is. The nurses usually check on the patients every ten to fifteen minutes, so we need to stake out the room, wait until they leave.

Orla continues to tape the cameras according to the plan as Chloe and I follow, breaths getting shorter and closer together, heart pounding. The camera in reception only faces the main doors and so there's no point going near it, but all the main corridors are missing them; the only other cameras inside are those on the landings leading to the three wards. Sharon's room has none.

It's almost like the hospital wants us to kill Sharon. Like it knows it's for the best, and is encouraging us on our journey.

Orla leads us up the final corridor, into a small square room which acts as a sort of waiting area. She puts a finger to her lips and indicates for us to glance through the nearest door, which has glass windows and a little peephole.

"You check Sharon's alone, I'll keep watch."

My heart's still racing, climbing so high I can barely breathe. Sweaty palmed, I press my face up to the glass.

Sharon is laid on a bed of green plastic. She's wearing a hospital gown – white – and is linked up to all these wires, a machine to one side of her and a tray full of equipment and containers to her other. Her roots have grown out since the camp, and her face is pale, lined. She looks ten years older than when we last saw her, never mind a month.

"Quick!" Orla hisses suddenly, and we leap back from the door. Grabbing both our hands, she tugs us backwards, into a corner. There's a sofa there, and a potted plant. Gesturing wildly, she makes us climb behind the sofa and duck down, so that it conceals us from view.

Squeaking on the linoleum; a sigh as someone pushes open Sharon's door. We can't see anything from behind the plant, but I can only imagine the nurse disappearing behind the door to do her business, get Sharon sorted.

"Right," Orla whispers. "She might be in there one minute, she might be in there five, depending how Sharon's doing and which check this is. Either way, we need to be ready to dash out as soon as she's gone, yeah?"

"Then we'll only have ten minutes to get out and away, right?"

Orla nods, though I can see her bottom lip is trembling as she glances over the top of the sofa. "She's still in there. She must be… I don't know, doing whatever nurses do to coma patients.

"Changing her nappy?" Chloe suggests, but it's not funny. It's horrible. The joke alone makes me feel sick.

Four or so minutes pass. We hear the door handle

clanking, those bulbous feet squeaking as she disappears off down the corridor again.

I swallow for the six hundredth time tonight, trying to remove that sour taste from my mouth. Everything feels so tense, so raw. But it has to be done.

"Go!"

Chloe hurries out from behind the sofa, Orla and I on her tail. We hurry to the door, clustering inside, minds on fire, hands nervous, itchy. Chloe finds the sockets along the wall in no time, swearing when she realises the machines are hardwired into the plasterboard, that you can't just switch off Sharon's life like you see in the movies.

"Now what?" I ask, half hoping they'll go back on the plan, admit that it was all a terrible idea and we've lost, we've completely lost.

But Chloe and Orla are giving each other the same knowing looks, and I hate the expression which passes between them.

This doesn't feel like such a good idea anymore.

"We use the knife, then we run." Chloe's dark eyes are gleaming as she pulls it from her deep jacket pocket, where it glints in the LEDs. I can't bear to look at Sharon's body, lying on the bed like that, aware that it might change my mind. "Come on, Luce, lighten up. It's only a knife."

Then she runs it along her fingers as though to prove how safe it is, how little harm such an evil object can do.

It doesn't even draw blood.

"You need to use force," she says, reading my mind once again. "Obviously, Lucy."

Time is running out. We all know that. Chloe even knows that, which is why she's drawing things out, creating a scene.

"I'll count you down," Orla says. "Three, two, one…"

Three, two, one.

Silence.

Then Chloe plunges the knife into Sharon's chest, watching it sear through the hospital gown and into her flesh with a horrible, sinking crunch. The yelp we all hear comes from my mouth as Chloe moves the serrated knife around, creating as much damage as she can before the beeping starts. It's loud, so unbelievably loud, ricocheting through the air around us as we run.

And oh boy do we run. We run, run, run, past the taped cameras, the bathroom, reception. Those squeaking nurses chasing after us, half-asleep and full of too many biscuits and cups of tea, losing us the minute we hit the door. We run until our legs ache and our chests whistle, until we're out of the hospital and out of the car park onto Vibbington's streets.

It doesn't happen like it would in a movie. The sirens don't start until we're at the taxi place, paying ten quid each for a ride to Hull, no return. Vibbington is sleeping, but the sirens bring it to life, cause windows to flicker with light and kids to awake from their dreams, alive at the call of something much more sinister.

It doesn't matter how many people see us. The plan failed. We ran out of the hospital so fast we tripped the light censors in the final stretch of corridor, the cameras catching the three remaining Guides as we raced away from our second ever murder. We just need to get away.

"To Hull," Chloe says, handing over the money in cash. "How long will it take, roughly?"

"Twenty minutes, tops."

"*Perfect.*"

49

We arrive in Hull before I even know what's happening. The taxi passed more police cars and an ambulance on the way, making small talk about how awful the situation must be, maybe another killing, surely *not*. We laughed and nodded and reciprocated his friendliness, but we were all shaken, faces pale and brains unable to process what just happened.

We killed her. We... killed *Sharon*.

There's no going back now.

We're dropped into Hull's centre, where the three of us thank the driver and slink out into the cold. Chloe passes us more woollies and a thick coat each, then insists we follow her; she knows where we need to go next. To sort our disguises, she says, winking. Then to get our fake IDs.

None of this feels real. I don't even understand how Chloe *knows* these things as we follow her out of the centre and down a side street, hearts thumping in time with one another's. It's freezing cold, the night dark, and Hull is all but empty apart from street vendors feeding kebabs and cheesy chips to the drunk of East Yorkshire, university students tumbling down the street in tiny dresses, making their way home from the clubs.

"First," Chloe whispers, jerking her head sidewards, "we go see Mo."

"Who's Mo?" Orla hisses back, as Chloe stops partway down the street. She knocks on a door, ears pricked, head cocked. It looks like an ordinary terrace, tidy and tucked out of sight amongst the other properties, but when a woman answers the door, Orla and I both flinch.

"Hey," Mo says, curling her lip but seemingly unfazed at the three of us turning up at such an odd hour on a Saturday night. "What do you want?"

"We want fixing up," Chloe says, pulling on the familiar mean girl expression we're both so accustomed to by now. "Piercings, the odd tattoo, a haircut, dye. We'll pay cash – two hundred quid between us."

Mo is a huge woman, all bulging arms and legs and tattoos laced across her skin, and her eyes protrude from her head as Chloe says this. "Prove it."

We watch as Chloe pulls a wad of notes from her pocket, flicking them across her skin. Mo's eyes open even wider.

"Don't ask questions, and we won't tell anyone you're running an illegal body modification service, without a licence," Chloe says. "Can we come in?"

Orla and I glance at each other, shocked, as we step inside the house.

It's shabby, dark, LED strip lights stuck to the skirting boards and dank paintings hung here and there. They're good, the paintings, if a little creepy, but there's no time to stare as Mo leads us down the corridor and into what I assume is her workshop. My hands are shaking and I'm so, so tired, but I try to stand up straight, determined not to flounder yet.

When Chloe said tattoos, she didn't mean *all* of us, did she?

"This is Carmel," Mo says with a grunt. "She helps me out with the tatts, does a bit of hair washing."

Carmel doesn't look up from where she's tracing designs

onto some sort of special paper, frowning. She's pretty, mixed-race, and I feel like I've seen her somewhere before.

"She does temporary tatts, too," Mo continues, gesturing to the wall. "They're good if you girls are looking for something less permanent, a disguise to get you through... whatever it is you need. No offence, but you don't exactly look like inky types."

"Orla and Lucy will take temporary," Chloe says with a sniff. "I'll take a real one, if that's okay."

"It'll be extra."

"I have the money, don't you worry."

Carmel looks up then, bemused. Both she and Mo are around twenty-one or twenty-two, about the age Macey would have been by now. She has chocolaty brown curls and even, pristine skin, and is dressed a bit like the quirky girls at school, the ones who refuse to listen to modern music and buy clothes from anywhere other than Depop. I smile at her, irrationally worried that getting on her bad side might end in having a temporary penis printed on my arm, and she raises her eyebrows back.

We get started on hair first. Chloe is just having a cut, whereas Orla and I are getting trimmed and dyed – which feels a little mean to me, but I'm too nervous and exhausted to say anything but follow Chloe's plan. They push us into our seats and wrap the familiar black capes across our fronts, Mo on my head and Carmel on Orla's. They'll set the dye in first, apparently, then leave it to work its magic as they give Chloe a cut and get her tattoo done.

Mo starts by collecting a bottle of bleach from her cabinet, fetching some red dye for Carmel. I must look nervous, because she snorts and waves the bottle of bleach in my face, saying, "I'll only do the front bits and some other highlights, don't worry. I don't think you're cut out to go full peroxide."

Carmel does Orla's whole head in the ginger, working away as alternative music booms in the background and the room pulses with colour. We're left with hair wrapped in tinfoil and temporary tattoos sinking into the skin of our arms, our hands, as they move onto Chloe. She wants a proper cut, she claims, to go all out. Think Ellen DeGeneres, her blonde hair trimmed and shaped against her skull. It'll grow back anyway.

This isn't the same Chloe we're seeing, the girl who loves fake nails and fake tan and fake boyfriends, the girl who was always too pretty for her own good, too popular to have any sense. It's a new Chloe, a scary Chloe. A Chloe who's spent her whole life being "cool" that she no longer cares about the consequences.

The hair looks great, of course. Short and choppy and dipping over one eye, her trademark blonde now ice-cold and smooth, contrasted against her black eyes. She grins the whole way through her tattoo, which is a dolphin, an electric blue colour across one arm. It's huge and bold and daring, but she justifies it by claiming that dolphins are her spirit animal, that she's always wanted it done. When the clingfilm goes on, she bounces from her chair and claims it never even hurt.

Our foil is removed next. They use those proper sink things to wash the dye and bleach out, with a little shower attachment and headrest, and Orla emerges first with her usual mousy colour now a plunging red. She looks weirdly... striking. Like she was meant to be ginger all along.

"It suits you," Carmel says with a shrug. "You look... *eclectic*."

Mo focuses on washing the bleach from my own head as I

lie there, staring up at the ceiling, at the brightly coloured LEDs and the pounding room. Chloe and Orla are laughing, debating how much of Orla's new ginger hair to chop off, as I try to block it all out, to forget where I am and to focus on why we're here, why we're doing this. There was no other option, and we were doing what was best for Sharon. This is my only choice. I can't back out now.

When Mo has finished, she steps back and prods me to sit up. She towels my hair a bit before I'm allowed to look in the mirror, but when I do, I can't help but gasp.

I look… good. Weirdly like myself, even though the blonde makes my green eyes stand out even more than usual and the brown around it is softer, warmer.

"I like it," I say, surprising myself, to which Mo grunts again.

Orla goes for a bob in the end, just below her chin, while I stick to longer hair, alarmed enough by the change in colour. Chloe's tattoo actually looks quite cool up close, the dolphin a beautiful shape and shade, surrounded by bubbles and waves, very detailed for something which only took an hour or two to complete. It's one of Carmel's original designs, she explains. It's pretty… well, *sick*, as she would say.

"Did you guys want piercings too?" Mo asks, sipping from her can of Venom. It's four in the morning already, somehow, and all three of us are exhausted, drooping, our modifiers working off energy drinks and delusion. I glance at Orla, who's almost falling asleep, then back at Chloe, whose eyes are twinkling.

"Yes, actually," I say, to Mo's evident surprise. "I want my nose pierced."

"And I want my eyebrow doing," Chloe says, pointing to the stud she already has in her nose. "And Orla… I mean, you as a ginge is already weird enough. I think you'll be fine waiting it out."

The piercing hurts way more than I was expecting. I squeeze Chloe's hand so tight as the needle goes in that I think she almost screams out in pain, but then it's over, the stud sliding into place and connecting with the soft flesh of my nostril. It's edged with a tiny silver star, a nod to how late it is and how dark the sky is outside, pinpricked with white. I love it.

Chloe almost loses her shit when her eyebrow piercing is done, letting out a yowl as Mo draws blood. Carmel is sketching us from the back of the room, a small smile on her face, and even Orla looks amused, though her eyes are nearly closed and she's clearly exhausted.

When we hand all two hundred pounds over to Mo, plus the extra for Chloe's tattoo, we're not the same girls we were when we arrived. Covered in temporary tatts and sporting new hairstyles, makeup smudged and in need of retouching, we look edgy, lived, like we have the experience needed to start our new lives.

"Thanks," Chloe says, nodding to Mo and Carmel, who's lurking in the dark of the corridor, clutching her sketchbook. "You have no idea how much you've just done for us."

***

Chloe leaves us outside as she ducks through the door to check that Big Paul, whoever he is, is still in business. We flinch as she appears again, grinning and beckoning. It's too late for this. It's almost five in the morning and we're tired, so, so tired, but we're catching the train to Edinburgh at half six, and everything needs to be sorted by then.

"He just needs to take photos for us," Chloe says as we follow her up the stairs, leading to an office room where Big Paul apparently works nights providing a service to the people of Hull. Paying prostitutes and selling drugs, alongside flogging fake IDs and reinventing the identities of murderers like us. It's a world away from Vibbington, and I've never felt so naïve.

There's a pot-bellied man sat behind the desk, wearing nothing but a pink robe and scowling at us. His weedy assistant instructs us to lean against the wall so that he can take our pictures properly, and we stand, one by one, unsmiling and with our hands flat against the plaster as he snap, snap, snaps away.

"Three passports," Big Paul says, grunting, "and three provisional driving licences. Just don't get into any trouble, if you can help it. You'll just be using them for clubs and that, yeah?"

Chloe nods, taking them from him and flicking through them with a frown.

They're good, of course – for the money. Big Paul has all the correct equipment and printing services, and the passports especially are professional, clean cut. I don't really understand how it all works, but he lists off all the things we can and can't do with them, and in my exhaustion most of the chatter goes over my head.

Elizabeth Gherkin. I frown at the name on my passport, turning it over in my hands. Elizabeth Gherkin. Lizzie Gherkin. I like Lizzie, because it sounds more like Lucy.

"I'm Olive Payton," Orla whispers to me. "So... I guess that's a bit like Orla?"

I smile, catching Chloe's eye as she continues to butter up Big Paul. She winks back at me.

For all her faults, the girl certainly has our back.

50

The train to Edinburgh only has one change, but it's absolutely packed as we crowd onto it at half six on Sunday morning. Chloe's clutching our meal deals and frowning – or should I say Claudia, now – and bustles past an angry group of hikers in order to get us four seats with a table.

"Here we are!" she announces, beaming and placing down the sandwiches. Prawn for Chloe, cheese and pickle for Orla, tuna for me. Lizzie, Olive and Claudia certainly have good taste.

We bought the tickets on the platform, as we no longer have phones or apps or internet. Chloe's going to get us cheap pay-as-you-go mobiles once we arrive in Edinburgh, where we'll stay the first few nights before travelling to Glasgow, rent a small flat, maybe, and get jobs. Chloe wants to start up social media again, under the new guise of Claudia, editing her face as much as possible to not draw similarities between her new identity and Chloe Alize. As long as she can make some money online, we'll be okay.

Orla says she wants to waitress, but I'd rather work behind the till somewhere, in a Poundland or Lidl or some sort of Scottish newsagents. Chloe wants to try different avenues... Stripping, pole dancing, selling photos online. All the things she would've tried back home if she wasn't too ashamed, too worried of what people would think.

They're just pipe dreams, of course. Theoreticals. None of

us know whether we'll even get to Edinburgh, let alone Glasgow, or whether we'll be ratted out the minute we arrive. We haven't been able to access the internet in almost twelve hours, so we don't know how much information the police have, whether they really suspect us. There's no way to get in touch with our families, our friends. Even if we wanted to, I can't remember their numbers, and my parents don't have Facebook, Instagram.

I try to push the thought from my mind as we slide onto the seats.

The sandwich is nice, if a little dry. I got a Babybel and coconut smoothie with mine, while Orla and Chloe both went for diet cokes, carrot sticks and hummus. It's a nice distraction, eating our sandwiches and playing make-belief, pretending we're not eating lunch at seven in the morning or travelling across the country to a whole new city the night after planning and committing a murder. On this train, we're just Lizzie, Olive and Claudia, three beautiful, edgy teens with their whole lives ahead of them. There's no need to worry.

I take a final sip of my smoothie, leaning back in my seat. The countryside whirs past in a mess of green and brown, purple and yellow, brown and orange. I pick at the fake tattoos on my arms, the symbols on my fingers. Chloe's dolphin is trapped under its clingfilm wrap, sweltering and suffocating, while the angry fox on my wrist prances across my skin. I wonder who hurt him?

Orla's cheese and pickle stinks, and the man across the aisle frowns at us in disgust. It's cold on the train, that wintry draft finding its way into our carriage. It feels like years since we were at Oli's party, dancing to Christmas music, eyes closed and bodies writhing in time to the music –

Ethan, kissing me, my neck, my cheeks, my mouth. His soft t-shirt and the outline of his tummy, that beautiful smile, warm brown eyes. My chest aches just thinking about him. How long will it take for him to forget about silly little Lucy and move back to Loz, his one and only, his first and last? Probably not too long.

What about Aaron? He'll never find love again, that's undeniable. Aside from his little problem in the bedroom, he was a weedy, drab guy, no personality, all pale skin and nothing else.

But Orla loved him.

I look at her properly again, her new ginger hair and brighter green eyes, matching mine. She catches them and smiles. She looks different. So much older, more mature.

We all do.

Maybe this was necessary. This change in our appearances, our personalities. Maybe it was the nod we needed to change our lives, to step away from Vibbington, from our social roles and cliques and friendships, toxic or not. And from Lexie. From the reminder of what we did to her, how we ruined her life as well as our own.

Chloe notices my expression and flicks a carrot stick towards me, trying to make me smile. "Cheer up, Luce. We did it. We got away from Vibbington, the accusations…"

I nod, but my mouth just won't carve upwards. Orla's face is equally forlorn as she shivers beside me, taking another sip of her diet coke.

"What's up with you two?" Chloe asks, frowning. "Come on, cheer up! This is exciting. It's sad, yes, but…"

"But what? Kayleigh's dead. Sharon's dead. This is all so…"

"Huge?" Orla suggests. "Terrifying?"

"I mean, I agree," Chloe says, but her eyes are still glinting, bright. "But... it's a fresh start, guys. This is exactly what I – what *we* wanted, what we needed."

She's right, isn't she? This is what we wanted, what we needed. To get away from Vibbington and its secrets and lies, the trauma and memories and constant reminders of what we did, what we've done...

But as the train continues on to Edinburgh, I can't ignore the icky, sticky feeling of regret inside my stomach, swirling around, making a mess.

The feeling that although things feel fine now, we've a whole lot of trouble coming our way.

Dear diary,

Is this really it? Is this really... the end?

We just arrived in Edinburgh, on the train. I no longer have a phone to record any of this, to take photos etc, so I'm going to have to write things here for now, in my diary. At least if I ever lose it, no one will know our next move.

Chloe is sorting everything. Maybe it's bad that she's the responsible one, that Orla and I would be lost without her. She's been looking at trains to Glasgow, but it seems we'll have to stay here for a little while, because moving on looks expensive – and risky. We saw the front page of a newspaper just an hour ago, and Sharon was already on the front page. GUIDE LEADER INVOLVED IN MURDER CASE STABBED WHILE IN COMA, or something equally dramatic. Everyone picking it up had a sort of awed expression on their face, like what we did was horrifying, scary. It still feels like a dream.

I'm trying not to think about Mum and Dad. I know they'll be devastated. I'm their only child, and I've ruined everything. They had such high hopes for me, but they also loved me, and would've been happy to see me doing anything with my life. Uni, an apprenticeship, working at the local shop... they wouldn't have cared. But ending up in prison at eighteen, or running away to

Scotland after stabbing a woman in her sleep? I don't think that was in their life plan for me.

We're in a hotel room now, under the guise of Lizzie, Claudia and Olive. There's a double bed and a cot-thing under the window, with an impressive view of an overflowing skip and a den of teenage boys smoking weed and passing around last week's maths homework to snort something not so healthy. It was cheap, fairly close to the city centre, and doesn't smell too badly of damp, so I guess that's something.

Maybe later on we can go and explore.

None of this feels real. Right now, it feels like a dream I don't want to wake up from. It's an adventure, a holiday, Christmas in a new city full of pretty streets and stalls selling roasted chestnuts and <u>love</u>, love everywhere.

But if I'm really, truly honest with myself… I'm still waiting for the nightmare to kick in.

acknowledgements

I decided to write 'Wasted' because Macey's story never quite felt finished. I knew that Lucy, Chloe, Kayleigh and Orla would be traumatised by the events in the first book, that their lives would be changed forever by what happened that fateful night in August... so I thought it would be so fun to catch up with them five years later, on a second devastating camp.

So firstly, thank you to everyone who read and enjoyed 'Guided'. The first book I ever self-published, releasing it into the world felt like such a huge risk, but it definitely paid off. I met so many incredible writers and readers alike through the world of books, and its reception really gave me the boost of confidence I didn't know I needed. Thank you to every single person who has followed me, read or bought 'Guided', left a positive review, sent me a lovely message or comment, entered one of my giveaways, encouraged me to write more, and showed me so much excitement in anticipating this book's release.

Thank you to the girl guides who reached out to tell me how much 'Guided' meant to you, or that you were reading chapters to your own guides at bedtime... and that seeing girl guiding represented through fiction made you feel seen, in some way. Being a guide (and then a ranger, just like Lucy!) made me so happy, and inspired me so much. It's lovely to know that other girls feel the same.

Thank you to all of the small businesses, Instagram and TikTok accounts, reviewers, book boxes and more who supported 'Guided' in any way. To name a few... Chloe from @writersandroses, Aimee from @bookbabesuk, Willow from @willowxreadz, Alyn from @alynsbookshelf and Emma from @teens.love.reading... I appreciate your support so much. Thank you to all of the other self-published authors out there, whose inspiration and advice proved invaluable. Ashlea Stannard, to name just one, as your debut novel inspired me so much and showed just how talented our generation is.

Thank you, as always, to my writer friends in real life and online, and to Sana, my saving grace always, for our absolutely crucial chats about the *Gilmore Girls* boys and every story idea ever. Thank you to all of the other writers who supported 'Wasted' when I first wrote it and who I know will support it now... Bridget, Martha-May, Ada, Isobel, Christina, Nadiyah and Hannah.

Thank you to everyone else who makes writing feel worthwhile. The UKYA community, led by some incredible writers who inspire me daily, and our little corner of the internet. The young adult mystery lovers across the world. My favourite authors, favourite creators, favourite artists of all media.

Thank *you*, for following the gang on their journey, all those years later. I hope you spotted little references to Carmel, Nima and Loz. I hope 'Wasted' felt like a satisfactory end to 'Guided'...

And I very much hope you enjoy what's to come.

NOBODY KNOWS...

GUIDED

BOOK ONE

EMMA SMITH

NOBODY KNOWS WHAT HAPPENED
THAT NIGHT... NOBODY BUT MACEY.

"I'M FINE..."

DEAD FINE

EMMA SMITH

BECAUSE WHEN LOYALTIES ARE
TESTED, IS LOVE EVER ENOUGH?

EMMA SMITH

is a young adult author from Yorkshire, England. She wrote and illustrated her first "book" when she was seven years old and hasn't stopped writing since. When she's not walking on the beach or drinking an iced coffee with a crumpet and some chocolate, you'll probably find her reading something dark and mysterious… and most certainly YA.

@themmasmith on Instagram

emmasmithbooks.com

Printed in Great Britain
by Amazon